MISS EMILY
THE YELLOW ROSE OF TEXAS

MISS EMILY
THE YELLOW ROSE OF TEXAS

A Novel
by
Ben Durr
with
Anne Corwin

First Fiction Series

SUNSTONE PRESS
SANTA FE

Sunstone books may be purchased for educational, business, or sales promotional use. For information please write: Special Markets Department, Sunstone Press, P.O. Box 2321, Santa Fe, New Mexico 87504-2321.

FIRST EDITION

10 9 8 7 6 5 4 3 2 1

Library of Congress Cataloging-in-Publication Data:

Durr, Ben, 1933–

Miss Emily, the Yellow Rose of Texas: a novel / by Ben Durr with Anne Corwin. —1st ed.

p. cm.

ISBN: 0-86534-322-5

1. Texas—History—Revolution, 1835–1836—Fiction. 2. San Jacinto, Battle of, 1836—Fiction. 3. Racially mixed people—Fiction. 4. Women—Texas—Fiction. I. Corwin, Anne, 1944– II. Title.

PS3554. U693 M57 2001
813'.6—dc21 00-066145

Published by SUNSTONE PRESS
Post Office Box 2321
Santa Fe, NM 87504-2321 / USA
(505) 988-4418 / *orders only* (800) 243-5644
FAX (505) 988-1025
www.sunstonepress.com

"Miss Emily, The Yellow Rose of Texas"
is dedicated to my beautiful wife, lover and best friend of 38 years,
Carolyn, who has been my constant source of encouragement.
Her pallet knife yellow rose paintings were my inspiration
in the development, completion and publishing of this book.

Foreword

This is the story of a legend. Set in the days of slavery and rebellion and rapid changes in the lines that marked the boundaries of our nation, Miss Emily has remained the unsung heroine of the expansion of those borderlines. As rumor and myth would have it, she played a crucial role in the Battle of San Jacinto, where the Mexican Generalissimo Santa Anna de Lopez surrendered to General Sam Houston his sword, his army and Mexico's claim to the frontier land of Texas.

Celebrated only in the romantic ballad, "The Yellow Rose of Texas," our heroine's existence may or may not be factual. But there are persistent reports of a "high yellow" woman in Santa Anna's tent on the day Sam Houston romped across the battlefield with a few hundred ill-disciplined troops and took Mexico's finest by total surprise.

We believe in that woman. We have given her a history, traced back to the first landings on American soil. We have given her a family, such as it is, as well as a mentor, a lover, a child and a job that is almost a career. And then, we have cut her loose to come to the war in Texas and, in the end, to being no longer at war with herself.

This is a woman's story. Our heroine, like most women, is a paradox, even in name: Rose and Miss Emily. Slave and not-slave. Black and not-black. White and not-white. Free and not-free. Frightened and unafraid. Self-centered and unselfish. This is the story of her reconciliation to that paradox and her emergence into integrity.

This is also a man's story. Rose/Miss Emily's reconciliation with herself takes place as a very real piece of history—the Battle of San Jacinto—which crashes around her in a shower of blood and guts. It was the first and last time that Sam Houston, commander of the rebel army of Texians, faced Santa Anna, commander of all of Mexico. The independence of Texas awaited the outcome.

And the outcome, according to legend, rested on the Yellow Rose. Her ambition had carried her to the pinnacle of women's power over men. Her loyalty would determine the future of nations.

The cruel irony is that her most loyal act would never be known. She must have been aware, or feared at least, that whatever choice she made as she lay captured in Santa Anna's silken tent, she would be remembered—if at all—as no more than a prostitute: a pretty, light-skinned servant-girl who was used by both Santa Anna and Sam Houston.

Because she took the risk, we want to set the record straight.

This is the story of the surrender of ambition to love. Because a man wrote it, the love encompasses a nation—because a woman also wrote it, you may better understand the cost.

This story, like Miss Emily Rose herself, is both true and untrue. Where you recognize a name, be assured that the historical facts about that place or person have been researched. We do not contradict history, though we elaborate on it. So where the story shifts to fancy, relax and enjoy it.

—Ben Durr with Anne Corwin
November, 2000

ACKNOWLEDGEMENTS

Numerous people have encouraged and helped me research, collect, develop, edit, refine and finalize the writing and development of this book.

I am particularly grateful to Anne Corwin, Charla Carter, Benca Hronas, Victoria Wallenburger-Durr, Phyllis LeBlanc, Dr. Stephen Kerbow, Juanita Smith, Elmerita Ware, Bonnie Latino, Leilani McClure, Bill Sanford, Dr. Ernest Green, Jan Burnight, Judy Stern, my Friday lunchbunch, the editorial staff at Sunstone Press and all the friends who have encouraged me along the way.

1

Sam Houston was not among the mourners at the gravesite. Pausing to look on her way up from the dock, Rose swallowed the disappointment at not seeming him before her eyes found Emily bowed over her husband's coffin. For the first time in memory Rose felt no envy for her. She suddenly considered the pain her cousin must feel and wondered whether they might find a meeting place in this new loneliness they had in common. Sharing a family, a home and even a name with her cousin had never been enough.

She could not help feeling her sense of separation. It was tragic, that Emily should lose her husband at such a time as this. But, there had been so many losses already for Rose and so few she could share with anyone at all. Even her name had been given up when she came to Texas, accepting her white cousin's name as her own passport to what she once imagined to be freedom. And though Sam Houston had called her Rose, she was known as Miss Emily now to almost everyone but herself.

The real Emily had no such secrets. Warm sunlight, open as the air, she had breezed through their childhood with never a care beyond the worry she sometimes expressed over Rose's youthful moodiness. "Never you mind," she would say, soothing her cousin the best she could. "Never you mind, Rosie. It'll all work out right. It really will."

Remembering, Rose swallowed a brief smile of grim satisfaction. Now you'll see, too, Emily. It doesn't always work out right. It really doesn't.

She'd heard that General Sam Houston had returned from New Orleans where extensive surgeries had saved the foot he almost lost on the battlefield. She was glad he still had his foot. It would be hard to imagine a man so big reduced by so much. Not that his size or shape or future had anything to do with her. Not anymore. She had played her part in the drama he dictated and the play was over now. She did not regret the role though the ending was not one she would have chosen. She'd had no wish to disappear. She'd never imagined herself so misunderstood, though the General must have known from the beginning.

She had forgotten the man who brought her there until he touched her arm. "We had better go down," he said quietly. "They'll be finishing the service soon."

Shrugging off his hand Rose moved forward, her head high and her eyes steady behind the black veil. She marveled that she had dared to hope some miracle might bring them face to face again. But Sam Houston had left her life as abruptly as he had come into it, as dead to her now as Lorenzo de Zavala was dead to his wife.

The funeral was as small as the day was bleak. Just beyond the cemetery, a cold November wind whipped the waters of Buffalo Bayou, frothing into muddy brown peaks. Dust swirled from the open grave and pushed against the heavy black skirts of the woman who stood there, her veiled head bowed, hands clutching at three small children who stood silent and wide-eyed beside her.

The voice of the priest droned on. She had no tears left and she found no comfort in his pronouncements. She found no comfort anywhere in this godforsaken land. She could not look at the casket already lowered to the bottom of the six-foot hole.

Lorenzo de Zavala was a good man. So much honor and so many honors in his life and to what end? Three children who must grow up without him. A few books that might be read again some day. A paragraph in history. Gold and silver medals on a dead chest. A well-made coffin and a score of men to bid him farewell forever.

There was no comfort in those thoughts either.

The horrible irony of it all. To have gained and to have lost the ideals of two republics. To have helped produce a responsible government first for Mexico free of Spain and then for Texas free of Mexico, then to feel them both corrupted. To have survived the battles for Texas independence and then to die in mourning for both the victor and the vanquished. To give up his own nation for a better, and somehow lose them both within the space of half a year. He could not take it lightly. He had become too ill to keep on working.

She had been sure he would recover from the disappointment of plans gone wrong. With Antonio Lopez de Santa Anna, *El Presidente* and Generalissimo of Mexico, vanquished on the field of San Jacinto, the future stretched limitless for the victors. Having won Texas, General Sam Houston, like Lorenzo de Zavala, sought no revenge. But Houston's sense of honor was not equaled by many of his countrymen and when the Generalissimo was incarcerated, despite all the promises of amnesty, it had been a crushing blow to Lorenzo. Five months past victory, he had resigned his place as vice-president of the new republic and refused further involvement. "How can we unite in honor behind a broken promise?" he had said, staring out the window and pacing the floor, day after day. "Fools! I will not work for a nation of fools."

She had been sure the children whom he loved so much would bring him out of his sorrow. Sure, that for everyone's sake, he would find his way back into this new nation's heart and from there re-knit the diplomatic ties to Mexico. Sure he would reconcile himself to these rough men whom he had tried so hard to guide along the subtle paths of international diplomacy. Instead, a bare month after choosing private life, that stupid accident, crossing Buffalo Bayou in his rowboat with Augustine, their firstborn. And the blue norther blowing in, freakish for November, flipping the boat. He kept the little boy afloat but when they dragged them in to shore, he was chilled, almost to death. The boy recovered soon enough and she kept on believing the man would not be far behind. At forty-six, he was almost twice her age but there were so many more years left. She had a lifetime, still, to share with him, she whispered to him as he lay gasping, shaking and burning with fever. He had opened his eyes, finally, and looked at her. And then he was gone.

There was a stir behind her, as another man made his way to the graveside. Resplendent in his naval uniform, Colonel James Morgan firmly declared the homage due from Texas to the dead man. Only twelve years ago, he said, far south on the Yucatan Peninsula, Lorenzo de Zavala had helped to craft a government for Mexico that fairly represented the will and welfare of the people. He had served faithfully as a governor, a Cabinet member, an ambassador. However, when his country sank into dictatorship under Generalissimo Santa Anna, Mr. de Zavala had come north to the *Tejas* frontier, leading other self-reliant Mexicans to join the kindred spirits he had found among the immigrants from the United States. As a daring entrepreneur, a scholar, a philosopher and a faithful servant to the cause of freedom, he had joined wholeheartedly in the Texas campaign for independence and helped to write the Texas Constitution. Though his life was tragically shortened, his legacy was planted in the birth of this new nation.

It was, first and last, a political speech, and Emily West de Zavala could not listen. Her husband, as principled as Morgan was pragmatic, had disagreed with the Colonel on many things and had not lived long enough to resolve them. The Mexican Constitution of 1824, of which Lorenzo was the primary author, did not allow for slavery but his efforts to offer the same freedom in the new nation of Texas were overruled. Though few Texians were likely to proclaim that the right to own slaves was high on the list of rights for which they fought, the slaveholders settling in Texas had no intention of giving it up. Certainly not Morgan, who owned many.

For the first time in the weeks since Lorenzo had resigned from the government, Emily wondered what had happened to Rose, her cousin and her friend, the daughter of her grandmother's slave and her mother's brother. She had seen so little of her in Texas, busy as both women had been within their different circles. Since the escape from the mainland to Galveston that spring, fleeing Santa Anna's army, she had not seen her at all. The warehouses and hotel that Rose had managed in Morgan's Point had been burned to the ground. She could only hope she was still alive.

There was some mystery there she could not understand. Her husband had alluded to it once, not long after the Battle of San Jacinto. "You must take care of Rose," he had said. "She has performed a service for the country but it may not go well with her afterwards." But when she asked him to explain, he would not. He had not mentioned it again and Rose had never come.

The wind was picking up. The clouds lowered in from the north as the day darkened. She had never felt so cold. Had he felt so cold before he died? It seemed impossible that a man who felt so much could never feel again.

The waves of memory washed over her, driving her almost to her knees. The first time she had seen him, he had been a Mexican diplomat invited along with Morgan to her father's house in New York. The way they had danced, already falling in love while Rose—poor Rose who was celebrating her eighteenth birthday that night—passed the time with Morgan and waited in vain for her father to return for one more dance.

But Benjamin Sturn, Emily's uncle, had not come back and Emily could hardly share her own joy with her cousin. She alone knew how long Rose had waited for that first meeting with her father, how many dreams she had spun around the single scene. He meant more to her than any lover ever could—and he would have preferred she not exist. It was no wonder Rose was so determined to make something of herself. But Emily's home was the only one Rose had ever known, and when her husband called her to Texas, it was not difficult to persuade Rose to come, too, given Morgan's offer to let her manage his warehouses and hotel.

A shuffle of feet in the dirt announced the scene was changing. She lifted her head, held up her chin. "Be brave, *Querida*. The time has come. . . ." How many times had she heard him say that as they had faced yet another parting in their short five years together. But not like this. Never like this.

"*Descanza en paz*. . . . " The hollow sound of dirt on the coffin. She could not look. Surely she would not have to stand there while they filled the hole. She heard whispers. More shuffles. Eyes were on her, watching. For what? Dust whipped into her eyes through the veil. The children whimpered a moment and reality slipped as she waited for her husband to lead her away. But her husband would never leave here. Her husband was in that hole.

"Lorenzo," she murmured. "Oh Lorenzo. . . ."

The baby, barely two, standing like a soldier at her feet, tugged at her skirt, pointing. "Papa?" he said. "Where papa?" Oh God! She should never have brought the children! They told her not to bring the children. But there was no one else who loved her in this barren land. New York was as far away as the Yucatan and with Rose gone and Lorenzo, her husband's oldest son from the wife who died in Mexico, still down in Mexico City trying to bring about his father's peace terms, there was no one from either family present. So she would be brave. And the children would have to be brave. Something like a giggle, hysterical, touched her throat.

Deaf Smith touched her arm. "Ma'am. . . ."

His lean face was carved of granite but the eyes showed a rare concern, a rare question. "You'll be wanting to get the children out of this wind, ma'am? Getting fierce out here." Head down, she nodded as he lifted the baby and took hold of her elbow, guiding her toward the wagon as the group proceeded back toward the dock.

Behind her she heard the rustle of skirts, the light sound of a woman's approaching feet. There had been no women at the graveside, she was sure of it. She would not look. She needed no false sympathy at this late hour. Oh, they had all liked her husband well enough when they needed him. But with the war won, what was he to them? Just another Mexican, however well spoken. Except for General Houston and Steve Austin, they had not really trusted him when it came time to make the peace. And now Mr. Austin was ill—on his deathbed, some said—and the General was too occupied with the affairs of his new office as president of Texas to come to the funeral.

She had sent no messages, too stunned to get word to anyone, leaving all the arrangements in Colonel Morgan's hands. She wondered how Deaf Smith had known about the funeral. But of course, he was said to know everything that went on in Texas; the General had called him the best scout in all America. She liked Mr. Smith. There was an honesty in the stillness of his face, in the wide eyes that hardly seemed to blink. Deaf as he was, he seemed to listen deeper than anyone else.

"Ma'am," said Smith, hesitating as the footsteps paused in front of her. She kept her head down. She did not want to talk to anyone. No women had come while Lorenzo was ill except those she paid to help. But Mr. Smith had stopped and she could not go on alone. She could not.

"Emily. . . ." The voice was familiar though the hesitation was not. "Emily, I'm so sorry. So very sorry."

The woman in front of her was tall, almost as tall as Mr. Smith where Emily barely reached his shoulder. A heavy veil concealed her face; her black dress of coarse cotton showed the tops of well-worn shoes. The woman was surely not of her circle. And yet there was a rare grace about her and that slim figure had a familiar shape. She knew that shape, if she could only remember. But the memories were scrambled and she stood silent. The baby began to whimper in Mr. Smith's arms. The children tugged at her skirt.

The woman stared at her through the veils, sensing the blank eyes. She touched her shoulder. "Emily, it's me. Rose."

Something collapsed inside her. "Rose! Dear God! You came!" She felt the tears, then a rush that began in her chest and threatened to engulf her. "Rose! He's gone. He's gone and I thought I had lost you as well. Oh Rose, thank God you came!"

Above her head, Rose glanced at Smith. The deaf scout nodded slowly. "You'll go home with her, miss," he said in that odd, flat voice. His grimace might have been half a smile. "She'll be needing a woman friend."

"Of course," said Rose.

A man stepped up behind her. He was slim, elegant, of indeterminate middle age, in full uniform and wearing a sword, his face set carefully in solemn lines. Rose nodded at him, then turned back to Emily. "Major Isaac Moreland," she said briefly. "Mrs. Emily West de Zavala."

The man bowed. "At your service, ma'am," he said. "If I can be of assistance—"

Rose shook her head. "I'll be accompanying Mrs. de Zavala to her home," she told him. "You may call for me there on Sunday if you wish. There are many arrangements to be made."

An eyebrow flickered upward in the cool, almost sardonic face. "Very well, Miss Emily," he said. A moment of hesitation. "Rose."

Emily glanced from one to the other, confused. Rose shrugged. "They call me Miss Emily, here," she said. "It's easier." The full lips curved upward for an instant. "It goes with the passport. On which I had to take your name, remember?"

"Ah, the passport," said Moreland, turning toward Emily. "It was lost, you know. But I have written to the Secretary. Mr. Austin has promised–"

"Later," said Rose, cutting him off. "This is not the time to speak of such things."

Moreland's eyebrow rose again. "As you wish." He turned and bowed to Emily. "I am at your service, Mrs. de Zavala. She can tell you where to reach me." His high heeled boots kicked up the dust as he strode back toward the dock where a half-dozen rowboats waited to take the mourners back across the bayou.

Rose put her arm around Emily's shoulder, guiding her toward the wagon where the children were being gathered in by Katie, the Irish maid. "There, there, my lovies," the girl whispered to them. "'Tis over now. We'll go home, now. You'll have your supper soon enough."

Deaf Smith hesitated a moment at the step. "Would you be needing anything, Ma'am?"

Emily shook her head, placed a hand on his shoulder, mouthed the words carefully as she faced him. "Thank you so much, Mr. Smith. You have been a great help."

She does not know him well, thought Rose, watching. Deaf Smith could read lips at a hundred meters in a dust storm, some said. But the man merely nodded, touching his cap, before walking away. He moved fast and silently like an Indian. Before the wagon had lurched into motion, he was settled in a boat with Moreland and each was plying an oar.

Emily remembered suddenly that Mr. Smith had lost everything in the war when Gonzales was burned. Lorenzo had planned to help his family though she could not remember where they had moved. Perhaps, when everything was settled, she would find a way to carry out his wishes though she was not at all sure Mr. Smith would receive her help. She did not have Lorenzo's tact, though she did her best.

The grave was not far from the house that sat in the curve where Buffalo Bayou joined the San Jacinto River and the bay. In the best of times she had loved the wide sweeps of sky and water and the long-legged birds that were at home in either. The clouds told stories and the wind sang songs in Texas, her husband used to tell her, holding her close when no one else was about. But he would not tell her the stories, nor sing her the songs. She must hear them for herself, he explained.

On that day of mid-November, 1836, the wind was strong, chilling the women and children who huddled on blankets in the rough-made wagon. Beating down the tall grass and rattling through the live oak leaves, the wind that afternoon was sounding out a funeral dirge and the sun was hiding from the stories told by clouds that scudded greyly across the sky. No birds sang. Even the children were silent on the short ride home.

It was good to get out of the dust at last, to move through the familiar door into the house they had occupied together for less than a year. Adequate, but not grand, it had eight rooms, four up and four down, with a wide porch facing the waterways. Nothing fancy. Nothing like her father's house in New York but it was all they needed. There were more important uses for their money, Lorenzo had said, half-apologizing as he wrote her of the plans for their new home on the Texas frontier. She had not minded. The luxuries of New Orleans were only a few days' reach across the Gulf. And as for comfort, his presence was enough.

That was all gone now. She repressed a sob as she unpinned her hat and veil. "Be brave, *Querida*. . . ." She had to be brave. Hugging her children, she sent them off to supper. Thank God for Katie! Emily's grandmother was also named Kate and had also come from Ireland. Perhaps she should go to Maryland and visit her within the next year. It would divert the children. And it would be good for them to know more about their heritage. Particularly when half of it had died.

There was no way to escape her loss. Nowhere she could turn and not miss him. A hole had opened inside her and she was falling. Putting out a hand, she steadied herself for a moment against the wall before looking back at her cousin.

Still standing near the door, Rose also had removed her veil. Her face was an anchor in the storm of emotions. The wide sorrowful blue eyes, slightly tipped at the corners above high cheekbones gave it a slightly Indian cast. Lightly tan skin was smooth as silk against the thick black hair, drawn back so tightly barely a curl escaped. A smattering of freckles across a stubby nose marred what would otherwise have been a classic beauty. Rose had always hated those freckles. Memories of their childhood, peering together into the mirror, brought the trace of a smile.

"I'll ask Katie to make some tea," she said, straightening up to lead the way to the front parlor and setting a match to the logs laid in the fireplace. "And then you must tell me all the news. We were–"

"You need to rest," said Rose, giving orders. "Katie and I will look after the children. There will be time to talk later. You must go and lie down."

How like her! Emily thought. Though Rose was two years younger, she had always been the one to take charge. Getting them into mischief, like as not. It was good to see some things had not yet changed. But this was her house, after all. She must take charge herself. Lorenzo would want all courtesies maintained.

"Nonsense!" she said. "I'm quite all right." She seated herself on the velvet settee they had brought from New York and gestured to the place beside her. "Do, please sit down. We have so much to talk about."

Odd, that hesitation in Rose. Not like her at all. Brushing at her coarse black skirt, she settled finally, not on the couch, but on a straight-backed chair across the room. Neither woman spoke for a long moment.

"You've been well?" asked Emily, finally. "You look well."

"So do you," said Rose with the smile that Emily remembered, opening up her whole face and showing the dimple she had inherited from her father. "It only shows how little looks reveal, don't you agree?"

So they were finally on familiar ground. "Oh Rose." The tears were starting again. Like a river. Like the wretched water that took him under. She covered her face with her hands. "Oh Rose–"

And then her friend was beside her, holding her, smoothing the blonde hair back from the pale forehead, producing a kerchief to wipe the tears that flooded her blue eyes. "Oh my dear, I'll help you all I can. Our lives may be very different now but the love I have for you is the same."

"I just cannot imagine it," Emily whispered. "I cannot imagine how I shall go on alone."

Safe from the shrieks of the rising wind, she rested her head and wept. "Just talk to me, Rose," she said when she could find her voice again. "Tell me about your life so I can forget about mine. How have you managed all alone? What has happened to you since the battle of San Jacinto?"

But Rose remained silent, still holding her friend. Words could be lies. Misdirections. She had more than enough of subterfuge and as for relating what had happened on the field of San Jacinto–how could she ever explain that to Emily when Sam Houston himself denied knowledge? What did Emily, so well-bred and well-brought up, know of Negro exigencies? Rose herself had been barely aware. But close as the two girls once were, Texas had severed their womanly experiences as sharply as a sword. Everything had changed on the journey there aboard Colonel Morgan's ship and their infrequent visits afterwards were marked more by unspoken secrets than by the pleasantries exchanged before they went their separate ways.

Rose remembered that voyage all too well. Emily's excitement. Her eager anticipation of a new beginning. And Rose, too, embarking with such ambitious plans, the taste of adventure sweetening the bitterness over what she had to leave behind. So ignorant of the cost. She had always expected to work. Had always known that her place was not the same as Emily's. Emily was the daughter-heir and she was but a foundling. A cousin by blood, in fact, but still a foundling. What matter who her father was, when her mother was a slave?

But the subject rarely came up in the Clarence West Jr. household in New York City where she was raised. Her mother died there when she was six and though she remembered the stories the tall, frail woman told her, she had no pictures and barely remembered her face. It was Maxine West who had raised Rose, giving her almost all the advantages showered on her own daughter. She had eaten at the family table, sharing room and toys, books and governess with her cousin. And by the time she realized, and almost resented, that her clothes were always Emily's hand-me-downs, she had outgrown her, shooting up to five feet six by the time she was fourteen, while Emily remained a bare five feet tall. So Rose received her own clothes: rich velvets and satins for Sundays when she sat in the family pew at the beautiful Church of the Transfiguration and soft flowered cambrics and cottons for everyday. How incredibly peaceful and far away her childhood seemed to be.

Her fingers smoothed the rough textures of her skirt. It was the first time, she realized suddenly, that she had ever sat in her cousin's front parlor in Texas.

In New York, she had not really minded being left at home when the family made their formal calls, especially since Emily often insisted on staying there with her. It was never fully explained. Aunt Maxine would only look distressed as Emily pleaded. "My dear, it just is not done," she would say and then take extra time to find a special book or a little gift for Rose. "You spoil the child," Uncle Clarence would say. "How is she to know her place if you keep treating her like kin?"

"She is my kin," her aunt would reply, tightening her mouth in that stubborn way she'd passed along to Emily. "And her place is with us, Clarence." Not wanting to quarrel, the man would turn away. But Rose sensed his wanting her to grow up and go away. She had not imagined where she might go. In New York she rarely left the house except to visit Dr. Connie.

If it had not been for Dr. Connie Cassal, the Negro midwife who delivered her, she might have denied her African heritage altogether. Locked into the white world as she was, she thought more often of her father than her mother, though she knew him not at all. But Dr. Connie had insisted on remaining in her life, taking her home with her on many Sunday afternoons. Dr. Connie's little house in Harlem was a far cry from the mansions along Fifth Avenue where the Wests socialized, but it was cozy and calm. Curled on the couch with Luke, Dr. Connie's son, she would listen all afternoon as he talked of philosophy, of poetry, of religion or business opportunities. He was a very serious boy, reading all the time. Mountains of books. Just six years older than she, he had a sense of direction, of focus, from the time she could remember. Inherited, no doubt. Dr. Connie was as focused a woman as Rose had ever met, black or white.

But Rose, herself, was white, whatever her parentage. If her hair was a little too curly and her lips a bit too full, well, she could as easily be Italian, Emily would assure her as the two girls studied their faces in the mirror, growing up. With those blue eyes, no one would ever guess. So when Luke, turning twenty, began to talk about the Negro issue, about the wrongs of slavery and the rights of all men, Rose did not want to listen. She noted, instead, how dark Luke's skin was, how thick his lips, how kinky his hair. He was different. Not like her at all. She tried not to notice his height, the width of his shoulders, the lightly controlled looseness of his stride, the strength in his long brown hands, the glow of his amber eyes, unusual in so dark a face. He was not for her. Never for her. Her future lay in escape, not connection.

Dr. Connie usually busied herself elsewhere during those discussions but Rose remembered her once, standing in the kitchen door and smiling as Luke talked on and on about the "responsibility" and "challenges" that awaited him. Rose was feeling a little bored. "Responsibility" was such a heavy word. She'd rather think about the new dress she'd been promised. Red, she hoped. She looked quite well in red. Emily could not wear it at all with her pale hair and eyes. Whereas on herself. . . .

"You aren't listening, are you?" Luke had interrupted her daydreams. "You get that glassy look in your eyes and I might as well be talking to the stove. You had better listen to me, Rose, if you want your life to have meaning. Why do you think you were put on earth, anyway? To look pretty?"

She still remembered blushing. It was uncanny the way Luke read her mind. In confusion, she turned to Dr. Connie. "You tell us," she demanded. "Why are we put on earth?"

The woman never hesitated. "To do good," she said. "God made us to do good. Simple as that."

Rose was not at all sure she wanted to focus her life around simply doing good. She was going to be somebody. Somebody special. And someday she would meet the man who would give her the status, through marriage, that she could not claim by birth. She was certainly pretty enough to be chosen by someone worthwhile. It was not that she didn't care for Dr. Connie and Luke. In truth, outside of Emily and Aunt Maxine, they were her only friends. But they could not elevate her status and Rose fully intended to rise.

Luke went away the summer after she turned fifteen. She had answered once or twice when he wrote to her from Bowden College in Maine, the first college in the country to accept a Negro student. She was proud of him but why encourage what could never be between them? She liked him too well for that.

But though she denied him, he would not let her go entirely. She still carried the last letter he had written to her, sent in care of Colonel Morgan and brought to her by Deaf Smith a week before the battle of San Jacinto. She still wondered if General Houston, knowing her secrets, had timed that delivery as he timed everything in his plans for victory, hoping to sway her emotions if he could not sway her mind. Gentleman though he might be, the General would go to any length to have his way. Well, he had won and she had helped, though that was a secret only someone like Deaf Smith could understand. Luke's idealism was more straightforward.

"*I am determined, under God, to right what wrongs I can,*" he had written from Tennessee where he was starting an underground school for Negro children, slave or free. "*It could be my death if I'm caught, but those of us who are blessed with freedom and an education carry a heavy responsibility for our brothers and sisters.*"

That was the way it was with Luke. Always more responsibility. Always the call to arms. But this letter, unlike any other, had contained a poem—a song.

"*I'm trying my hand at dialect,*" he wrote, smiling, no doubt, in that ironic way he had. "*I need to practice if I'm going undercover further south, and I must, Rose. The need is enormous. Meanwhile, though you refuse to answer my letter, I can play my banjo and dream of seeing your pretty face when you read the song. I only wish I could sing it to you.*"

It was a simple song. She could almost hear the banjo twanging, feel the drums in her heels as she read the words. Texas, at least, had opened her ears to Negro music and the rhythms were more exciting than any she had heard before. The song seemed to sing itself, the music came to her so quickly. It was something to sing on a cold wet morning, or a long hot afternoon. Something to take the sting out of a misspent day or lonely night. It was something to remind her she was loved.

There's a yellow rose in Texas
That I'm a'going to see
No other darky knows her
Nobody, only me.
I cried so when she left me
It like to broke my heart. . . .

Rose sighed, shifting on the hard settee, coming back to the present and the blonde head that still rested on her shoulder, though the tears were slowed. Yes, she had a great deal to tell Emily. But whether or not her friend could hear it was another matter.

"The world is too much with us, late and soon," she murmured, remembering a fragment of the poem by Wordsworth that she and Emily once memorized together.

"What did you say?" asked Emily, raising her head and wiping her eyes. "What about the world?"

"Too much with us," said Rose. "And too much we don't know about each other's. But I'm sure you do not feel like talking now. You really need to rest, Emily. I'll be here in the morning, you know. It has been a wretched day for you. You need some sleep, dear. Katie can show me where to stay. I'm quite accustomed to taking care of myself."

Emily shook her head. "It will be too hard to lie down again in our–in my bed. There is too much I cannot bear to think about quite yet. You must entertain me, Rose. You must tell me about your life in Morgan's Point and where you have been since. We have hardly talked in the year we've been in Texas."

"You've hardly visited," said Rose, a touch of the old asperity creeping into her voice.

Emily flushed. "I've been so busy, Rose. There was so much to learn with Lorenzo being so involved with the government. So many people to entertain. And the children–" She looked down, plucking at her skirt. "Please say you understand. It is not that I did not care." She met Rose's eyes, reaching for a smile. "Tell me about Major Moreland. Is there something between you I should know about?"

Rose looked away. "He's been my protector, you might say. After General Santa Anna, after the battle I lost my passport." A touch of bitterness twisted her mouth. "People like me have to have papers or there can be trouble so I sent word to General Houston through Mr. Smith. I would not have presumed to do such a thing but Mr. Smith found me and asked how he could help. Then he sent Major Moreland." She shrugged. "Really, I had nowhere else to go."

Emily looked puzzled. "But what of Colonel Morgan? What of us? And if you know General Houston, you must have many influential friends. Could you not choose among them?"

"I did not trust Colonel Morgan and I would not intrude on you. My friends–what few I had–have no real power to help, being Negroes." She pressed on, voice roughening, ignoring the sudden pity in Emily's eyes. "And that's how they regard me here, of course. Everyone, black or white. They have a name for someone of my background. I'm 'high yellow.'" Her mouth twisted again with that bitterness Emily had never seen before. "By law in the United States, a drop of Negro blood makes one a Negro, though some of us cannot be told from white. We are quite expensive in the slave markets of New Orleans where Colonel Morgan trades. Upwards of a thousand dollars, I have heard. And someone with my education. Some gentlemen prefer to be entertained by a well-spoken woman. And I can even recite poetry." The bitterness had moved across her face, shadowing her eyes. "They say the women are even allowed to keep some of the money they earn for their masters."

She received small satisfaction from Emily's little gasp, the drain of all color from her face. "But surely you have not–"

"Before the battle, I simply did my job as manager and was paid and treated well, though Colonel Morgan insisted I sign papers making me an indentured servant for the year of my contract to work. The Mexican Constitution, you know, forbid slavery, but there are many who want no free blacks in Texas."

Emily was staring at her. "When did he do that?"

"On the ship. Just before we arrived in New Orleans."

"And now?" asked Emily. "What is your status now?"

"Since General Houston won the Battle of San Jacinto, we are no longer a part of Mexico. Texas is its own nation. A slave nation." Again the twisted smile. "And I helped, in however small a way, to bring that about. So now I may be considered a slave and the truth is, Emily, I have often felt like one since I came to Texas. I felt angry, resentful and full of self-pity. But there has been a divine providence that has kept me thinking free. I thank God for that."

"What do you mean?"

"I mean I still make my own choices, based on a principle, regardless of the outcome." Her dimple flashed. "One can force my actions but not my will. And in the end we all become what we will."

"But what did you will, Rose? Who did you help? And how?"

"It's a long story. I willed my freedom and in the end I found I was only free to choose whom I would serve. But there's a freedom in that, Emily, come what may."

The women fell silent, each occupied with her own thoughts. The windowpanes clattered in the wind as the evening shadows filled the room. The fire flickered, adding its own changing shadows as Katie appeared in the doorway, a lamp in her hand. The children, fresh-bathed and in their nightclothes were with her. "Ma'am, if you'd like to tuck the little ones in. . . . "

She set the lamp down on the table as Emily went to them, kneeling to gather them all in her arms before taking them off to bed. Rose walked to the window, staring out. A thin line of red between the bank of clouds and the low distant hills cast the occasional hackberry and wild persimmon tree into black relief above the black waters of Buffalo Bayou. It was beautiful country, seen this way in silence and space. But she would not be sorry to leave it behind.

The live oaks that rose in the marshes across the water were black now but she could almost see the place the war began and ended. Could almost smell the bodies, left there until they rotted. The refusal to bury them, she heard, was Houston's only revenge. They were Santa Anna's responsibility, he had insisted, though whether he informed *El Generalisimo*, no one knew. Ignored on either hand, over six hundred Mexican soldiers decayed where they fell until only bleached bones were left by the wolves, the coyotes and the carrion birds.

The dark had fully enveloped the land by the time Emily returned, coming to stand quietly beside her. "It would help," she said after a while, "if I knew what you are speaking of. What role you have played in this war and what needs you have. You must know that what I have is yours. Lorenzo taught me that: *Mi casa es su casa.* My house is your house."

Rose could not speak, still seeing the battle and the bodies cut down around her. She had never imagined so much blood. Such final realities of pain.

Emily waited and went on. "Tell me about Major Moreland. You said he was your protector? He seemed an elegant gentleman. Do you not like him? Was he not kind?"

Rose would not look at her. "Major Moreland is an ass," she said. "I do not mean he is a bad man, or even a foolish one. I understand he is brave in battle and quite honest as a lawyer. No doubt he will be a judge someday. But he is a Southerner. Negroes are not quite people as far as he can see. He may call me Miss Emily and refrain from molesting me against my will but he will never respect me as he does you."

"He said something about a passport," said Emily, deciding she would have to ignore some things. She could only take in so much tonight though she found herself deeply grateful for the distraction. "He is helping you get a passport? You lost yours in the battle?"

"I lost everything in that battle, Emily. Everything I had not lost already. Except my life. I find myself very grateful for that, especially seeing the loss you are suffering now."

Emily returned to the settee. Rose remained at the window. "As for the passport, the Major has written to Secretary Austin and assures me a new one will be prepared within the month. I must have it soon, Emily. I am afraid to stay in Texas." There was wistfulness in the shadow that crossed her eyes. "And I am equally afraid to leave."

"But surely we can protect you!" Emily exclaimed, then realized, with a catch in her throat, that she had spoken as if her husband were still alive. "Forgive me for not understanding but you were free before you came and your year of indenture here is almost over. What is it that you fear in either place?"

Rose sat on the straight chair, holding her hands carefully, a child almost, reciting verses. The lamp across the room reflected pinpoints of light in the darkness of her eyes. "It's very hard to explain," she began. "I hardly understand it myself, though it has everything to do with who I am and want to be. I was raised free but almost always there was slavery behind it. I was always running from it somehow. Always trying to get past the condition. Denying I was one of them. But on my way to Texas it was made plain to me and for all I was getting paid for my work, there was no denying it. The discounting was always there, all around me, and I was one of the discounted. It became an inescapable fact of nature. I thought I had no choices. And then, with Santa Anna. With Santa Anna and Sam Houston, I tasted the freedom to choose and I find I cannot let it go." Bitterness twisted her mouth. "Nor do I see where I can express it as I choose."

Emily waited, wondering.

Rose stood and walked back to the darkened window, staring at nothing. "Can you not see? I have always wanted to be someone special, Emily. I have always needed to prove myself. Lowborn is not the same as highborn and I yearned to rise to your level from the time I realized mine was different. But I know now that whether I return to New York or remain here, I can never be a lady to anyone who knows me. To remain is to acknowledge myself among the slaves whether I be free or no. And to return--" She stopped. Her mind was full of Luke. His blackness. And his strength. "To return is to acknowledge myself a Negro whether I be white or no. It is not a choice I would have willed. I wanted only to escape the issue."

"Escape what issue, Miss Rose?"

Luther Collins stood in the doorway, his hat in his hand as the wind whipped his black cloak about him. "Forgive me, Mrs. de Zavala," he hurried on. "I knocked and knocked but this wretched wind drowns out all human sounds and I could not leave again without expressing my sorrow over our loss of your dear husband. If my mule had not stepped in a hole and broken his leg, I would have arrived in more timely fashion."

"You are always most welcome!" said Emily, taking his cloak and ushering him in. "You see, Rose is distracting me with history and philosophy from her own life. But I fear we have both reached the point of helplessness about our futures. Who better than you, dear Quaker Friend, to help us see the light when all looks dark."

The Quaker turned to Rose, refusing the seat he was offered, warming his hands at the fire. "I'll ask again, then, Miss Emily Rose. What issues do you wish to escape?"

Rose managed a smile, approaching to touch the man's hand. "The issue of my own history, I suppose. I must decide what I will do next and no one can help me. It is my own past and future I must take into account." She moved back to her chair, sighing, as Collins took a seat. "I thought I'd forgotten my mother's stories. God knows I wanted to forget. But I've remembered them all lately, lying awake at night. My father is a free man. My grandfather is a free man. My great-grandfather was a free man. And my great-great grandfather was a chief in Africa." There were tears in the beautiful blue eyes; she brushed them angrily away. "That's all I want, is freedom. Though I'm a woman with Negro blood, it's not so much to want, is it? To be free? Just to be free."

She has seen too much, thought Emily. Too much to keep it all inside.

She crossed the room, reaching out to her friend. “It’s everything,” she said.

But Collins, sitting still, shook his head. “Whatever we may think or plan, there’s only one real freedom we can claim,” he said. And then, to their surprise, he quoted Rose’s words. “In the end, we’re only free to choose who we will serve.”

2

Rose's great-grandmother was herded into Virginia from the deep hold of a slave ship. Among that shambling mass of bodies the child was quite alone. Her mother had died in route from freedom. Her father, the chief, was away from the giant river visiting a neighboring tribe some leagues into the bush and had escaped the pre-dawn assault on their village. He should have been back long before then but the god had kept him gone. How, she would never know. Her mother had worried, imagining death in the jungle. Some distant disaster. The girl had listened to her fears, uneasy, stalked by shadows without a name.

The shadows had names now though she would not call them out. "Be brave, my daughter," her mother had said day after day, slipping away from her down in the black bowels of the ship. "You have his blood and he is free. Be silent and stay alive." Her mother would not eat, passing her portion to the child, keeping her still. "Be strong," she whispered. "The god will listen to your silence." Then she, too, became silent. And then she died.

The child was twelve years old, small but sturdy, when she stepped onto American shores in 1764. Strengthened by her double portions, she held her head up and her mouth steady. Eyes wide and nostrils dilated, she gulped the salt air, breathing in the sky, reaching for land. She would not die. It was past time for that. Through the despair surrounding her she marched, remembering her father who was free.

The child caught the eye of John Paul Thames who had come to the docks to watch the unloading, pre-selecting hands for his plantation in upstate Virginia, close to the bay. He prided himself on his blacks, picking the best of the lot, never minding the price. He treated them well, or at least as well as could be expected and, once broken, they worked well for him, fearing more cruel masters. His wife, a Quaker he had met and married in Pennsylvania, did not approve of slavery but he had silenced her, finally, with his refusal to leave the land and his insistence that only slaves could keep the land producing. Tobacco here, cotton further south. Where would the colonies be without those crops coming in?

And where would she be? he would ask her. If she used the money their tobacco brought into the bank, how could she protest the way he had to grow it? She had settled down at last and made it up to her conscience with a program of caretaking that upset the other owners.

"An infirmary!" they would sniff. "Letting those slaves lie around like that! Get to thinking they're white folks and where will you be then, John Paul?" John Paul would spread his hands, mild-mannered. "Healthy niggers work better," he would say. "I'm telling you, just look at my production rate." It was true enough. The Thames's estate was possibly the richest plantation in the Virginia lowlands. It took a hundred slaves to work it. And John Paul could afford to buy the best.

He certainly had no need for a child, he thought, his attention still held by the pride in the young girl's chin. And certainly no need for a girl. But there was something there, a fearlessness that captured him. His wife would like her, he told himself. Priscilla needed a child around to pet now that her own were grown and gone. It would give her a rescue mission. Bring her out of the doldrums she'd been afflicted with lately. He pointed her out to the thick-set man beside him. "That one," he said. "Looks to be ten or twelve years old. Shouldn't cost anything much." The man looked surprised, then grinned. "Well now, Mr. Thames. Gonna be a good-looking bitch, that one." He faced away from John Paul's frown. "Course now, you're taking twenty at four hundred a head. Reckon I can throw her in for a hundred or so. Worth it, I'd think. She's forming up nice."

"She's for my wife," he said curtly. "Good training age, I'd think." He turned his back on the slow shuffle across the gangplanks. "That'll do it. You have them ready for me in the morning. I'll bring the men in to pick them up. But mind you, no money until I've checked them over."

"They'll be ready," said the broker.

The girl did not respond to Priscilla's petting but she obeyed instinctively and without fear. Priscilla started her in the kitchen under the eye of the cook who had been with them for a generation and knew the ways of white women as well as anyone could. The child learned to wear a dress, to scrub the floor and the dishes, to eat at a table and use a fork, to speak English and say "Yes'm," when she was spoken to. She learned the names of strange new vegetables and fruits and of the white people who swirled beyond the kitchen doors. She learned about Jesus and the great white god in the little chapel built for the slaves to gather every Sunday, clapping hands and dancing as if they weren't in hell. A day off every week was good for business. John Paul insisted to the naysayers who surrounded him. "Keeps them strong."

"You'll be building them pews next," they snorted. But still no one could argue with his production rates.

The child, daughter of a chieftain after all, kept herself aloof, curled on her blanket at night in a corner of the large shed that accommodated the new-bought slaves. A white man, steely-eyed and lean, slept in another shed just past the single, padlocked gate, accompanied by a bloodhound, a pistol, and long black bullwhip. He could use all three and did sometimes, but not too often. Things were worse in other places, the black men whispered to each other, coming back from the fields, or squatting around the fire inside the fence, dipping their hoe cakes into the molasses bowl. At least there was plenty of corn and fatback. Salt, too. At the mistress's insistence, it was said, the slaves were always let off work before the sun went down. Saturdays, they stopped mid-afternoon, though they didn't eat 'til then, either. They were driven hard enough but if you kept up and you didn't make trouble, you didn't get beat. And the master never sold off any but the real trouble-makers.

The women, grouped together, studied the men and made their picks. Once mated, they could build their own little sheds, working on Saturday evenings and Sundays with wood the master provided. There would be children. If they were healthy, they would live. The infirmary did not accommodate children nor could their mothers stay at home to tend them. Children who got sick, died usually. There were a lot of little crosses in the graveyard just behind the chapel.

The child, "Betty," they'd named her, resolved that she would never be among them. Never, at least, until she was an old, old woman. And by then, maybe she would figure out a way to be free. Her father, she thought to herself almost every night as she watched the men by the fire making light of their bondage, her father was free.

There were always many more men than women in the big shed and as Betty grew, she felt them watching her. Coming back from the big house every night, already fed, she huddled in her corner and ignored them all. She'd be no slave's wife. As for the women, settling for the best they could find behind the fence, she wanted no part of them, either. She stayed in the kitchen until the cook shooed her out long after dark; before dawn, she was back there, waiting by the closed doors.

The mistress took note of her. "Dedication," Priscilla called it to her husband. "She's a loyal one. And smart." The master shrugged and smiled, glad she was interested in something. The mistress hadn't been interested in much since their last daughter married.

Priscilla started taking the child along when she went to visit the infirmary to hand out teas and poultices, bandages and bitter herbs. The girl caught on quickly. The mistress was delighted by the aptness of her pupil. "Sixteen now, and still a virgin, I declare," Priscilla told her husband. "She won't even look back at them. Just holds that chin up and does her job. I wish our daughters had some of that kind of sense."

The master frowned. He'd never gotten used to the kind of comparisons she made between whites and blacks, almost as if they had the same kind of souls. Nor did he intend to get used to it. Seditious, that's what it was. But he knew better than to argue with his wife. It only set her up against him and his bed got very lonely when she turned her back. Mildly he said, "You just be careful about talking that way, now. Don't let anybody hear you but me. You know how folks are around here."

She sighed, knowing all too well. But it pleased her that he didn't argue. Not anymore. And the child was a wonder. If only—But no. John Paul would never let her teach the girl how to read. She contented herself with teaching all the medicine she knew. Her own mother, a settler in Indian lands, had learned a lot from the natives and passed it on to her eldest daughter. Not one of Priscilla's own four daughters had cared a fig for medicine. But Betty did.

Betty was in the infirmary the day they brought the Indian in. He'd been shot, a glancing blow through the shoulder, by someone, doubtless hunting deer. John Paul out riding his perimeters when he found the man, couldn't imagine what an Indian was doing around there anyway. Most of them had run for the mountains as the white men took over their lands. Staying out of sight, the Indians would barter only with the trappers who took the same steep routes back up and away into the forests.

But whatever the cause that brought the bronze skinned man to the lowlands, he was definitely an Indian and definitely alive and, if John Paul left him there in the piney woods at the edge of the plantation, the Indian was definitely going to die from that festering wound in his shoulder and then there'd be buzzards and a big stink that could only hurt morale when the niggers found him. Besides, he thought, tightening his lips into a small smile as he spurred off to find a man to bring him in, Priscilla will approve.

But it wasn't Priscilla, it was Betty who met them at the door, who spread a quilt on the floor for the man and put water on to boil, who searched through her sack of roots and leaves, and finding the right one for the job, dropped it into boiling water, then moved the iron pot off the stones to cool. She cleaned out the wound with a clean wet cloth while the leaves simmered into mush and the Indian watched her, stoic, unmoving. Neither did the girl make a sound. From the doorway, despite himself, John Paul watched them both. She knew her stuff, that nigger girl. Might be some use after all.

The wound took weeks to heal and there was no getting around his wife's insistence that the Indian stay 'til he was well. Stopping by daily, justifying his curiosity with the thought of who knows what that savage might do, John Paul watched Betty and the Indian fall in love. They never said a word he heard but he watched their eyes and knew. A slave holder learns to watch the eyes. That's where rebellion is born. And Betty, bless her heart, had never learned to look away and down. "She's never been scared but once," John Paul thought, looking straight back at her as she slid past him at the door and hurried to the ever present pot of herbs and water. "I reckon that was when they took her in Africa. But now, look at her. You'd think she thinks she's free."

But freedom is an independent state and Betty, once captured by the Indian's eyes and the strong brown hands that touched her own more often as he grew stronger, was less free than she had ever been. The Native and the African learned to talk together, a little in the English he had learned from trappers, a little in his and her own languages. They gestured extravagantly. She heard herself giggle for the first time in many years and he, returning from death to her gentle hands, smiled broadly and laid his hand on her breast questioning.

And one hot day when everyone was in the fields and the infirmary, for a change, was empty, she slipped away from the kitchen to look in on him. He stood up as if he had been waiting and when she went to him, he unbuttoned her dress and let it drop to the ground. Laying her down on his quilt, he took her. There was pain, yes, but something more and it was enough, or almost enough, to be worth whatever it might cost.

But she couldn't go with him she explained the best she could, pointing to the bloodhound tied in the yard outside the sleeping shed. She pantomimed the gun, the bullwhip. She pantomimed that runaways were beaten, then sold. Always sold. The Indian argued with his hands. She shook her head. There'd been a dozen or more attempts in the four years she'd been there. Everyone was caught. Caught and beaten. Then sold. She knew no other master as good as theirs. No other mistress who cared half so much. She'd met a lot by then, watching from behind the doors, talking to other slaves in the marketplace, hearing from the new ones who came in. She didn't fear the faraway where he wanted to take her. She'd come from faraway. But she feared beyond courage the road to get there and she wouldn't go. Couldn't go, she said again and again. "No go."

She couldn't meet the master's eyes the next day, seeing him watching as she hurried to the infirmary after lunch with food for the patient. He followed her. The Indian was sitting in the sun outside the sickroom. His eyes met and held the master's.

"You well. You go." John Paul said, signaling with his hands.

The Indian stood and reached out to Betty, took her hand. She kept her head down. "I stay," he said. "With her."

"You stay. You work," said John Paul. "Like everybody else. You hear? Understand?"

The bronze man turned his steady gaze on the girl. She raised her dark head to meet it, eye to eye. "I stay," he repeated. "With her."

"You go with the men then, in the morning," John Paul said, turning on his heel. "I'll send Pete over for you." He went to tell the overseer about their new hand. Pete didn't like it.

"Indians ain't no damn good in the fields, Mr. Thames. Nothing but trouble. Can't stand the heat. Can't stand the work. Rebellious as hell. I'm telling you. I've worked on them a time or two. Sneaky as the devil. And pretty soon everybody's slacking and thinking about running off."

"Well," John Paul thought about Priscilla, wondered what her reaction would be. She'd know soon enough that her pet had married the Indian and he was working there, same as everybody else. It was true Indians didn't make good slaves. Just gave up and died if they couldn't run away. But what the hell, if the man was willing.

"Just try it a few days," John Paul told his overseer. "A week or two. But don't be too hard on him. He's not used to it, of course. And he's probably still weak. Put him with the women and see if he works out. Then put him with the men. If he wants her bad enough, reckon he'll learn to carry the load." He grinned, man to man. "He's stuck on Betty, that gal that looks after the infirmary when she's not in the kitchen."

Pete snorted and turned away, figuring it wasn't worth the argument and wondering what anyone would see in that gal. There were plenty of gals around and Pete had his pick whether they were married or not, but he never had liked

Betty. She was too—too African. Sullen and silent and dark, he thought. And uppity. If she hadn't been Mrs. Thames's pet project, he'd have taught her a thing or two. Well, maybe it wouldn't be such a bad thing to have a go at the Indian. Show him a thing a two.

But the Indian stayed. Only God knew what he went through day after day in the fields so far from home, marching to orders he had never heard before, lowering his eyelids over his private revolution, finding small comfort in the tribe that was so unlike his own, the tribe betrayed and beaten into deep submission. But the arms of his wife, the succor late at night in the small shed they'd built together before the first snow fell, ah, that was reason enough for a while. He had always been a loner, even among his people. But with this one other, this dark and silent woman who smiled straight out from inside herself, with her he was not alone.

It was not enough. He left her in the springtime, unable to bear the beauty of bird flights and dancing butterflies, of new green leaves and flowers and the soft sighing of the winds. His very bones ached for home, for his mountaintops and ridges and the wind rising up past the deep green valleys between. For the tall trees and the mosses and the water sparkling over the rocks. For freedom. He could walk on fire, leap from cliffs, face arrows, teeth, claws, or bullets for his wife. But he could not face slavery. His heart was rotting. He could feel it. He found no comfort in Sunday meetings. The dancing was not his dance; his rhythms belonged to the wind, not the river. And the white god was far too small, confined to a cross, to suffering and death. What did that have to do with the Great Spirit who blew as free as the wind, as close as breath and as far away as the space beyond the stars? Who spoke through lightning bolts as well as lizards. Who lived in every creature he'd encountered in the forest. Who gave itself, again and again, in sacrifice so he could eat and be thankful. Who could be thankful for this white man's food, passed out as if to children, meant only to keep bellies and mouths from growling?

Betty was pregnant when he left her. Cupping his hand on her belly as she lay sleeping beside him, he almost faltered. Two more moons. Or maybe three. He knew a little about such things, his mother having helped bring many babies into birth. The belly under his hand moved a little, a tiny kick. He shuddered and took his arm away. If he saw it, then he'd never go. Not walking. Not alive. It was better this way. Silently, he lifted himself from the quilt on the floor, disturbing not even the corn husks beneath it. The girl sighed in her sleep, dreaming of him perhaps. Dreaming of his leaving.

He turned once at the door, watching moonlight illuminate the dark face, and then he stepped sideways into the shadows and slipped away. He did not think they would send the dog. He had not cost them anything, after all, and they had gotten work enough out of him. He took nothing except the cotton pants he wore, not nearly so fine as the buckskin he had left behind at the infirmary. But there were deer waiting, he knew. Deer that would sacrifice themselves to dress him, to feed him, to shelter him. He thanked the waiting deer as he ran swiftly towards the pines at the perimeter, hardly bothering to disguise his trail, trusting the stars to guide him westward. Running free.

Betty stifled her cry when she woke to find him gone. The overseer would know soon enough but if she cried out, the way her people did when one was lost, she would cost him precious moments of escape. She could not wish him back, enslaved. Thinking fast, she hurried to the house, asked trembling for the master. Told him he was gone. "Don't send the dogs," she begged him falling, for once, to her knees. "He come free. Let him go free. You got me. I have baby. One for one. Please, Master, Please."

John Paul was not surprised but he was angry. "Eat through the winter and run away when the work starts," he grumbled. "Might have to bring him back. Teach him a lesson."

"Please, Master. Please," said Betty, heart beating so loud she was sure he could hear it. But her eyes were dry. "Please, Master," she said again. "He come free. Let him go free."

John Paul looked down at her. It would be an ugly scene, sure enough. Priscilla would be sure to hear of it. She'd turn her back on him for weeks if he had to discipline the Indian. And then what? Who'd want to buy him? "I'll go talk to Pete," he said, turning away. "You get on to work."

The baby was born in May of 1769, a pretty thing. A girl with skin more bronze than black and hair that curled in tiny ringlets on the perfect little round head. Her eyes were narrow, like her father's, and her fingers long and thin, like his. Holding her for the first time, Betty cried. There were only women in the room, African women like her. They keened together for the child who had come to the father who had left. "He free," she whispered to the child, offering her breast, watching the tiny mouth grope and grab a'hold. "Your father free, child. Your father free man. Like mine. You remember that." She called her Winona, remembering a name the Indian used once, and kept the child beside her as she grew, teaching her silence and self-restraint—the first rules of getting along.

Rose's great-grandmother, Betty, married again, though "mated" might be a better word, to a man selected by the master. The black man, an underboss in the fields, loved her but it was never the same. Betty stayed in the big house from dawn 'til after dark, doing her work with so much will that, little by little, she became the keeper of the master's grandchildren.

Priscilla's second daughter had come back home, widowed by a gambler's bullet and left with a quiet and thin-faced boy of four and a pudgy little girl of two. Betty slipped them cookies in the kitchen, pitying their loneliness in the big house where their mother slept all morning and visited her friends all afternoon. They liked her baby, tickling and teasing her 'til the little thin feet waved wildly and the gurgling giggles started. The children called her Winnie and it stuck.

Betty had three more children, born one right after another, but she did not worry so much with them. They stayed at home, playing in the dusty alleys between the tiny shacks and lying on the quilts she had pieced together and laid down on the corn husks that covered the dirt floor. She fed them morning, noon and night, but they were loved mostly by their daddy, a big man who tempered fierceness with resignation. Faintly superior and still in love with her Indian, Betty kept her distance and bided her time.

When Winnie was turning five, Betty asked for a place for herself and her daughter in the back of the master's house. She talked to the mistress first, but Miz Priscilla said she'd have to go to Mr. John, herself. "You'll stand a better chance than I have of getting him to agree," Miz Priscilla said, smiling as if they had a private joke. Betty didn't smile back but she marched off bravely enough, praying to Jesus that the master would listen. She could take care of everything better from inside the house, she explained to him, her eyes more bold than was her wont as she searched her master's face, willing the kindness to spill through, the flickering sense of mutual humanity.

"All right," he said at last. "You've been good with the children, real good." His eyes raked her body briefly but found little there to interest him. She was dark, thick-lipped and very African. She raised her chin a little, proud of it. He laughed. "Go on with you," he said. "There's room enough. I'll get a bed for you and her," jerking a thumb at the wide-eyed child who hovered at her knees. "And I reckon you'll want some blankets. Rather you didn't bring nothing up from the quarters. The mistress will fix you up with what you need." He gestured towards the child again. "You and her."

He called her back as she turned to go. He was still smiling, but barely. "Mind you don't take advantage of me, now. I don't want y'all around unless you're working. And I better not see that kid running around here getting in the way of people. Fact is, I don't want to see her at all unless she's right with you."

Rose's great-grandmother had nodded. She had won the first round. "No suh. I thank you, suh. I keep an eye on her. We won't be no trouble to you, suh. No trouble at all."

She kept her word. Her child grew up beside her and beside the master's grandchildren. Betty fed them all in the kitchen except on those special occasions when the white children got all dressed up and joined their grandparents at the dinner table, spied from around the corner of the kitchen door by the brown child who took careful note of manners. She was a curious little girl. "Liable to get into trouble," Betty would mutter over and over, belying the pride in her eyes. The child was a pretty thing. Her hair, thick and kinky, twisted into two fat braids that stayed put. Her lips and nose were thinner than she would have liked but the little face reminded Betty of the Indian. She liked being reminded.

In the schoolroom, looking over the white children's shoulders and listening to the governess while her own mother dusted very slowly in the distant corners, Winnie learned to read a word or two, then more, until the books made sense and she could read them to her mother late at night, smuggling them from the bookshelves to the bed they shared. No one must know, her mother warned her. "Slaves ain't sposed to read. It scares 'em," she explained to the inevitable "Why?" "Pretty soon they get worried that we think we good as them. Then what? Then how come they own us? Don't you say nothing about it, you hear? Nothing to nobody. Just keep working at it. Keep looking and listening. And keep quiet."

Little Winnie had nodded, serene in the comfort of the hard-soft body that curled around her every night. "Yes'm. I won't tell. I'll be careful."

So Rose's grandmother grew up, a favorite of the family. Thanks to her mother's pride she had a sense of who she was, a special gift. It conveyed in the set of her head, the rare smile, the easy grace of her own giving. And she was pretty, even to a white man, finer featured than her mother from the Indian in her. Lighter, too. The master watched her as she trotted along behind her mother to the infirmary, following her as Betty had followed Priscilla. "She's a fine one," he thought. "Bright, too." And his pride was a little more than the pride of ownership. He sloughed it off, turning away. "Not that it'll do her much good."

And then, the summer that Winnie turned fourteen, the master's second daughter married again. And the master's wife died. A winter flu deepened and filled her chest, rattling her breath as the fever took her. Sweating and shivering for a few days, she grew weaker and weaker for all the doctor could do. Her pale face glistened on the pillow. "You take care of everybody, John Paul," she whispered. "You take good care, now, you understand?" He had nodded, mutely, holding her hand through the long and silent night that followed. And then she was gone.

The marriage and the death came so very close together that there was no time for wedding parties. Not that the master would have wanted any celebration. He didn't like his daughter's second husband much better than he'd liked the first one. Will Miller was a handsome man sure enough, but weak. And probably a gambler, too. He had no proof but there were rumors. Not enough so he could refuse his blessing but he tried to warn her. Did no good. No good at all.

He had bowed to the inevitable but when Priscilla died he couldn't bear it. To see that man and his daughter every night right there at the dinner table, acting like they owned the place. To have no one to go to afterwards. To see a shadow, turn a corner, half-expecting his wife and meet instead those insolent pale blue eyes, that barely mocking smile. He put up with it for almost three years, imagining a man could get used to almost anything. But he couldn't. He found himself thinking of death, more and more often but at sixty-seven his health was still robust.

Perhaps it wasn't over for him yet. The world was settling down after the Revolutionary War. Ships were regularly plying the seas again. He found himself wondering why he'd never taken one. Of course, there had always been so much to do at home. And Priscilla had hated the sea. The trip down the Chesapeake from Baltimore when they first married had left her green and gasping. "Never again, Mr. Thames. You will never get me on a ship again!"

"I'm thinking of doing some traveling," he said carefully, one night at dinner. "Thinking about getting back to England for a visit before it's too late." He essayed a chuckle. "Might be too late already but I'm going to try it. Got family over there I've never seen and I've seen about all there is to see around here. Captain James Doyle is taking his ship back to London end of the month. I've booked passage."

His daughter stared. His new son-in-law tried not to smile.

"You can't mean it, Daddy!" said his daughter. "Whatever will we do without you! First mother and now this."

" Well now, sir," said the young man.

They deserved each other, the old man thought to himself. As for what he'd done to deserve either of them. Well, that was neither here nor there.

London! He'd never been to London. And with the Revolution there'd been little chance. Not that he'd participated much in the war. Hell, he loved America but he was too old to fight. Didn't really believe in fighting anyway. Priscilla didn't hold with war. Killing. He was glad it was over. New opportunities were fine enough, but it was high time he investigated the old civilization. His smile was a little grim. His son-in-law's face was poker calm.

"There'll be papers and such we'll have to arrange," he said. "Times being what they are. Well, you never know. Best to have everything in order." He looked straight into the pale blue eyes, challenging, not caring anymore. "Reckon you can handle the place?"

His son-in-law spread his thin hands. "Well now, sir," he said.

The old man nodded. "Reckon you'll have to," he said. "I'll ask Mr. Southerly to come around tomorrow. He's been handling my business for just about as long as I've had any. You'll need to get acquainted. He pushed back his chair, almost happy for the first time since Priscilla had died. "Mind you, I don't want you changing the way I run things. Don't want you selling off any land, or any slaves."

'Well no, sir. Of course not, sir. You'll be back of course."

The old man nodded again. Best to leave it so. No telling what trouble they'd get into if they thought he was gone for good. And he wanted to leave an inheritance for all his daughters, not just for the one who'd landed back on the doorstep and stayed. He sighed, getting up from the table, moving off towards his bedroom. He'd see Captain Doyle tomorrow. Make that pretended passage a reality. Funny, he'd never even imagined leaving his land. But without Priscilla. He'd never imagined his house could feel so empty.

London, then. That might not be so bad. At least he wouldn't be expecting her around every corner over there. Might not be bad at all. See his cousins before he died. Sleep in a castle. Maybe go on over to France. Italy. Had cousins all over the place from what the letters said. Certainly he'd had invitations enough. And, thanks to tobacco, money was no problem. He could even leave a stake for his son-in-law. Not much. Just enough to get going and hold on if the boy was careful. And if he weren't–

"You'd like England, Priscilla," he mumbled into his covers, almost smiling. "No slaves there." And then the emptiness filled him again and for the first time in more than sixty years, he turned his head into his pillow and wept.

Will Miller did not do well with the master's land. No estate can run itself however solid its foundation, and Will was not much given to studying the ways and means of making money. He preferred the gambler's dreams to late nights poring over lists of assets and liabilities. Within a year, production had dropped. It was all because of the revolution, he explained to his wife. "Market's dropping off. Got shipping problems, too. And half those slaves aren't earning their keep."

His wife, deprived of her new spring wardrobe by the market, the shipping and the slaves, pouted. "You could get rid of some of them, couldn't you?" she said, then smiled into her husband's face. "I mean, I know you promised Daddy that we'd keep them all but he's been gone a year and his last letter doesn't much sound like he's coming back." Will still looked reluctant. He had, after all, given his word, and a man's word was his honor. "Things might pick up," he mumbled, turning away.

She followed him, coaxing. "You could sell them together. Families. Or a couple of couples. To somebody around here. It's not like selling them down the river. Just a few. Please, Will. How am I going to hold my head up around here in the same old rags I've been wearing all year? And just to keep feeding some do-nothing slaves! It's not fair, Willie! It's just not fair!" She grabbed his arm. "I know you want to be proud of me, Willie. I know you want me to look good."

"Yes ma'am," he said, ice-blue eyes sliding down the length of her. "I sure do want you to look good." He laughed. "I'll look into it. See what we can do."

It did not take long to find a buyer though Will Miller had no intention of selling his father-in-law's slaves to anyone local. It could create a scandal if the old man actually came home and protested. But Miller knew a lot of people. Though the local landowners tended to shun the cool young man, he was quite at home in Jamestown's better taverns where the landowners' sons were prone to gather for talk of politics and games of chance, joined by an occasional outsider. Will kept his ears open, waiting. And when Jared Stone, an inveterate gambler who traveled the coast from Charleston to New York, stopped in one day to brag that he'd just won a couple sections of land in Maryland and wasn't sure exactly what to do with it, Will was ready.

"Got a house on it?" he inquired.

"House? Yes, indeed. Needs a little fixing, but it's sound enough. Got a well. Garden. Fields been cleared and plowed at least once, I reckon. Don't know what they were growing, though." He grinned broadly, flashing a gold tooth. "Never did much growing, myself. But maybe it's time to settle down. Find a wife. Plenty of women around, of course, but I'm not about to marry one who'd take up with a gambling man. A real lady would want someone, umm, more substantial, don't you think?"

Will sipped his ale and thought about it. Stone, calling for drinks all around, was flashing quite a load of silver. Sure would be nice to relieve him of some of that weight. His own lady sure wanted some new clothes.

"Got anybody to run the place for you?" he asked.

" Run it? No, not a soul. It's just sitting there, waiting. Don't know what I'm going to do with it yet. Might sell it."

"Ought to get yourself a few good slaves. They'll hold it together for you. Experienced niggers, I mean. Niggers who know what they're doing. No trouble to you, that way. Get the place in shape. Keep it going," he smiled broadly. "All you'll have to do is entertain your wife."

"Never had slaves," said Stone. "Never could quite see it. Owning somebody, I mean. But then, I never needed to before. Not a bad idea, Mr. Miller. Have another drink?'

"Wouldn't need many," Will went on, raising his glass again. "Get yourself two or three couples. They'll have babies soon enough. They like to breed, them niggers. Reckon it's about all the entertainment they got." Laughter echoed along the bar. Stone looked interested. Will leaned forward, not wanting to be overheard. "I tell you the truth, I got a few too many of them over at my place. Good, healthy niggers, well-trained, but I can't use them all. Might could let a few go if you're interested. Get yourself a few field hands and a cook. Maybe a lady's maid for later."

He waited. Stone gulped his drink. Set the glass back on the bar. "I'll come by," he said. "Tomorrow be all right? Might as well get settled while I'm of the mind for it."

Betty knew there was something wrong when the stranger drove that wagon into the yard. It was heavily loaded, a canvas covering the front half of the long wagon bed. A thick coil of rope lay in the empty back section and a pistol rested on the seat beside the driver. There'd been strangers enough visiting lately but despite this one's fine clothes, he was no gentleman. And the way he looked at the servants, eyeing them like so many pieces of meat, but furtive, not looking anyone in the face. A sense of foreboding seized her as Master Will pushed back his chair from the dinner table, telling her they'd have dessert later; he wanted to show Mr. Stone around the place. The men rode off, headed for the field where the slaves were picking tobacco that afternoon.

"You stay out of sight," she told her daughter when Winnie came out on the porch to watch them coming back right about sunset. Five slaves walked well behind them: two women and three men. They were all young and one of the women was obviously pregnant. They all looked scared. "Lordy, lordy. Mistress would turn over in her grave. Looks like Master Will done sold some niggers."

"What you mean, sold them, Ma? Master John Paul said he don't sell nobody less they try running away. Ain't nobody tried to run away!"

"Master John been gone a long time," said Betty. "Master Will is mighty different from Master John. And I reckon he figure he ain't coming back. You just get on back to the bedroom. Quick now."

But the girl, fourteen and pretty as she'd ever been, caught Stone's eye before she disappeared. Betty's heart sank, seeing the finger pointed in the direction the girl had taken. She followed Will, prepared to beg for the second time in her life.

"She be too young, Master Will," she murmured, coming up behind him. "You can't sell her off so young. She be good around the house, suh. The mistress couldn't hardly do without her."

"You mind your own business and get to the kitchen, Betty. Mr. Stone and I will be wanting supper in half an hour."

"But Master Will."

"Don't you talk back to me, nigger." He raised his hand as if to slap her. She stood her ground.

"He could take me, Master Will. She, she don't know nothing about men yet. She belong here, Master Will. Mr. John Paul promised."

The slap echoed down the wide hallway as it knocked her to the floor. She wiped the blood from her nose as she pushed herself back up. Will's voice was a husky whisper. He didn't wish to be heard upstairs. "You do as I say, nigger, and you do it when I say or you'll see something worse than selling off that wench to a gentleman who wants her for a lady's maid. Now get on back to the kitchen."

They let her say goodbye, but not for long. Will appeared at the kitchen door to announce that Mr. Stone would not be staying for supper. And she was to get to her room and help Winnie get her things together. She'd be going with Mr. Stone straightaway.

Hugging her daughter, not weeping, she put the best light on it that she could. "Gonna be a lady's maid," she whispered. "It won't be so bad, honey. You do as you're told and don't forget none of what you've learned. She pulled the tearful child to her feet. "Might not be so bad, now. Might be he not so hard a man. Might be we see each other again. Not now, then sweet by and by. Jesus be with you, girl. He love every color. Don't you cry, now. They be more cruel when you cry. You just hold your head up, baby. Your granddaddy was a chief, you recollect. And your daddy was free Indian. Maybe you be free, someday, too." She pulled a smile out of hell, put it on for her daughter. "Then you come back and get me, you hear?"

Snuffling back her tears, Winnie went out to the wagon where the other slaves were waiting, bound about the ankles. Her new master gestured to the seat beside him, moving the pistol to the other side. "You get up here," he said. "And I don't want no trouble. You treat me good, I'll treat you good."

He cracked the whip over the horses' backs, a grin suddenly splitting his face as they picked up to a gallop. "Yahoo," he yelled, as they passed the gate. "We're going to Maryland!"

Not daring to wave, Winnie watched the dark figure on the porch grow smaller and smaller. She never saw her mother again.

Jared Stone was not cut out to be a farmer. He tried tobacco. He tried corn. He even tried cotton, though he was told it wouldn't grow there. The slaves worked hard at first, knowing their business and not wanting worse luck than a master who rarely beat them. But the land was not right for growing. The tobacco curled in the field and turned bitter; worms ate most of the corn, and the cotton plants were so sickly they picked hardly enough to spin for their own clothes. The pigs that rooted through the dying fields provided most of the food.

Stone stayed on the farm, lacking the wherewithal to hire an overseer, but his heart was not in it. The slaves slowed down their labors as Stone spent more and more time with the bottle. A few half-hearted courtships had not brought him a wife and he was not at all sure he wanted to bring a woman to that ramshackley house. About the best that could be said for the old place was that the rain didn't come in through the roof and the rats couldn't get in through the floor. But the unpainted walls and the broken steps remained unpainted and broken as four years went by. Even the garden didn't produce that last year though Winnie did the best she could with the few tomatoes and squash they managed to grow. A person got mighty tired of hoecakes and pork.

Winnie might have been a comfort to the man but the girl was untouchable as a porcupine. She would not have a thing to do with Jimmy, the black man he had procured especially for her, so she remained virgin as far as Stone knew. Somehow, he couldn't see his way clear to force himself on her. He reckoned he was queer that way but for all the church might disagree, it sure looked to him like the niggers had feelings same as anybody else. Having them work for free was enough. He didn't have to get all that personal with them though you couldn't keep them in line at all if you didn't whip somebody now and then.

But Winnie, he only hit one time. The look she gave him—he'd have died on the spot if looks could kill. Still, she never raised her voice to him again and he never raised his hand. As far as he had family, she was it, though she rarely answered when he talked to her. She ate in the kitchen after feeding the slaves outside and he ate alone at the big table in the hall. Visitors were rare and by the end, there were none at all.

She was the one he first told when he decided to sell out. She listened, her face motionless as he stumbled through the words, half-drunk, apologizing as he'd never meant to do. No wonder the neighbors shunned him, treating his slaves like they were white people. But then, he wasn't used to this. Didn't know how to be some kind of gentleman farmer. He was a gambler and he'd been away from it too long. Let somebody else teach those lazy bastards how to be proper niggers.

"You be going to sell us, Master?" He saw fear in her slighted, tilted eyes, masked quickly.

"Gonna sell the whole thing," he muttered. "Sell you all with the land." He grimaced, downing the glass of gin he held. "Hell, Winnie, it won't be so bad. You'll still be all together."

No one ran away when he left the next day for the Jamestown port. There was nowhere to run to. Giving up work altogether, the men squatted on their haunches in the sun, talking of what was to come while the women tended their babies and said their prayers. Winnie fed everyone, never lingering to talk. Inside the house, she fingered the old Bible Stone kept but never opened.

"Someday she whispered to herself," refusing to let hope die. "Someday."

3

Rose's and Emily's grandfather stood alone at the edge of the crowded docks of Jamestown. The wind off the ocean was cold for May but he had no desire for the heat of the crowds. He scanned the deck of the on-coming ship where skirts, lined hip to hip against the rail, flared in the wind. So many women! Eldon Sturn had not seen so many women in a long, long time. Most likely, never. The faces were not yet clear to him, twice-removed as he was: once by the water and once by the throngs. He did not mind. He could wait. The papers in his pocket would secure his bride, whoever she turned out to be. With thirty-two years behind him, the last ten spent here in America and quite alone, he had waited a long time already.

His family had sent him from Germany in 1777, staking the profits of a year's trade at his father's inn on the voyage and praying for a change in family fortunes. He was the youngest son of a youngest son and, though well educated, his inheritance had dwindled to a few leather-bound books and a mahogany sea chest. Accepted as an officer in the company of General von Steuben who was en route to become inspector general of the American revolutionary forces, young Eldon spent the war time mostly behind a desk, earning barely enough to keep himself sheltered and in uniform. The war's end, two years later, left him jobless, but he was disciplined, intelligent, and had learned to speak English with a gentleman's phrasing, albeit a guttural accent. Though hardly prepared for the hustle of the newly independent colonies, he was accustomed to strangers. Tall, blond and sturdily built, with an air of innocence that belied his ambition, he made friends easily and often.

He learned the brokerage business along the docks, becoming known as an honest and hard-working young man with an eye for a bargain and a head for trade, able to locate buyers and sellers for everything from candlewax to cotton. Though he avoided dealing in flesh, he had been known to find a slave or two for a special customer. Within eight years he had acquired, by careful saving, upwards of $10,000 in gold and silver coins. He did not trust the new country's paper currency and trafficked with banks no more than he must.

It was along the docks that Eldon learned that brides were also a business proposition. Most of the immigrants were single men, coming as he had to seek their fortunes. With money in their pockets and a piece of land beneath them, they found themselves thinking of heirs and a woman to make the place comfortable. And in Europe, currently racked by wars and famines, there were more than a few women willing to risk their futures on the chance of gaining anything at all. Nothing was guaranteed to them, of course. Some men spent everything they had to buy their brides, saving nothing for their life together afterwards. Others, like Eldon, came prepared for setting up a home, seeing the price of passage and the $250 brokerage fee as being but the initial cost of their investment.

Kathleen McCleary, her name was; sixteen years old, out of Ireland, "lively and well-featured, willing and able to learn whatever her husband requires." Her father had died in an accident and the latest famine had starved out the mother and seven of her ten children according to the letter Eldon had in his pocket. He had read it carefully. The dire straits that had brought him his bride, indebted her to him, of course, but Eldon was resolved to provide for her without stint for so long as she kept his house in order and bore his children. A bargain was a bargain.

The men in front of him pressed forward against the ropes as the bridge was lowered and the women queued up to approach the agent on the pier. The girls approached shyly, one at a time, or holding the hand of a friend. The agent would bend an ear, glance at the slip of paper each showed him, and announce her name. To much laughter and shoving, a man would make his way out of the crowd, red faced, likely as not, making a clumsy bow and mumbling his own name before the lady took his arm and walked beside him toward the taverns or the waiting line of horses and wagons. Eldon found himself moving closer to the ropes, studying each woman as she stepped up.

Now that one had an Irish look. Red-gold hair with curls escaping from an old-fashioned net, framed freckles splashed across a sun-burned face. The slight figure looked very young. No more than fifteen, surely. There was fear in the wide blue eyes but something else, too. Excitement, perhaps. And a bit of nerve. There was a stubborn set to her jaw, held almost in defiance. That might be a hard one to tame. He wondered.

"Kathleen McCleary," shouted the agent. "Kathleen McCleary! Who's here for Kathleen McCleary?"

He found himself bowing before her, awkward as a boy.

Papers were exchanged. He offered his arm. He was not accustomed to a woman on his arm. There was a tightness in his loins. He almost stumbled. Caught himself. Spoke the lines he had practiced.

"Welcome to our country, Miss McCleary. Perhaps you would like supper?"

The girl nodded, speechless. Staring at him with those huge, dark-blue eyes, she could hardly be called modest. But she was young. She would learn.

He led them a few streets back from the wharf into a more genteel quarter. The Dove's Rest was as packed as any of the taverns nearby but the crowd was less noisy. Searching for a quiet corner in which to complete arrangements with his bride-to-be, he noted the couples sitting at almost every table. Most of them were silent, shyly watching or not watching each other, though here and there an animated conversation was taking place.

"Afternoon, Mr. Sturn. Ma'am," said the serving girl, recognizing him as she made her way back toward the kitchen. "There's a table just empty over there by the window." They turned in that direction.

Seated, the girl still didn't speak. Still stared. For once, Eldon's tongue felt paralyzed. And he was supposed to marry this stranger? This–this child?

"You'll be wanting supper, Sir?" The serving girl was at his elbow. "Nice beef stew tonight with roasting ears and rice or potatoes."

"Rice," the girl whispered.

"Is nice," Eldon agreed, his tongue loosened by her unexpected smile. If anything, it made her look even younger. God help him, he felt like a kindly father! "Had about enough potatoes, have you?"

"Tis all we was eating on the boat, Mr. Sturn. That and a few oranges to keep away the scurvies."

He ordered for both of them, hesitated, then asked for a glass of beer. She showed no shock. That was good. Eldon had met several Calvinists lately. He did not wish to be married to one.

Do you like America?" he asked her, finding nothing else–there being too much else–to say. "You are from Ireland, are you not?'

"Near to Belfast," she said, nodding quickly. "Beautiful there, it is." She smiled again, dimples flashing. "E'en the poor can enjoy the view."

"I am not a rich man," Eldon said carefully, wondering what she thought of his new coat and breeches, the best he had ever bought. He had been more anxious to impress his bride than he would have admitted. "I have, however, saved some money." He mentioned the sum and saw her eyes widen. So she was easily impressed, then. Well, it was easier to meet low expectations than high ones. Not that $10,000 was a piddling amount.

"It is my intention to buy land and build a house," he said, more didactically than he intended. "That is, if—" He cleared his throat. "I mean to say, I have not yet selected the land. If you—" He was not sure quite how to go on. He had never proposed before and somehow, in making all the necessary arrangements, he had not considered the need to actually talk to the woman he intended to marry.

"I thought perhaps you might have some preference," he said.

"I preferred to come, Mr. Sturn," she said simply. "I don't rightly know anything but that. And your name." Her tongue teased the "r's" into rolling. Quite charming, really. Even the freckles were attractive. But so young! Her face might be sixteen but her body looked to be several years younger than that. Was that what starvation did to one? He had not seen much starvation on this side of the Atlantic.

"I came from Germany, near Frankfurt, ten years ago," he told her. "I have found this to be a good land. There are many opportunities." He smiled, showing even white teeth. "I have taken advantage of some. I hope to take advantage of more. I hope to share those advantages with my children. And with my wife."

"Then I am to be your wife." It was a statement, not a question, and her dancing blue eyes held a sparkle of—was it mischief? Indeed, she was not modest at all! But he rather liked her.

"If you wish," he said. "That is the plan."

"Tis grateful I am, Mr. Sturn."

"You must call me Eldon," he said.

The food arrived, steaming, and they ate in silence. He could feel her watching as he kept his eyes assiduously on his plate. The shadows lengthened outside the window as the sky reddened from the west. Couples were leaving the tavern as single men arrived, ordering rum and slamming chairs around. Finishing his beer, he stood. "We need to see the immigration officials," he told her. "They will have to sign and witness the application for marriage. Then we must find a minister." Nodding mutely, she rose and followed him down the cobblestone streets, back to the docks and the long line of applicants who waited by the door of the customs shed.

It was almost dark when they left the Anglican church at the top of the hill, joining the stream of couples in search of rooms for the night. Eldon cursed himself for not having arranged for a room. It had seemed too personal, somehow. He had been with women before but only rarely and only with prostitutes. He was not entirely sure how one should behave with a wife. He took comfort in the sure knowledge that the girl would know even less about marriage than he.

She kept her head down as they approached the doorway of a house with a sign declaring: Rooms To Let. She did not watch the coins change hands, did not look at him as they followed the landlord up the narrow stairs and into a small room down the hall. A double bed took up most of the space. On a stand near the window, a large pitcher of water stood in a white enameled basin with a towel folded beside it. She put her worn carpetbag down on the floor and stood still, facing him.

She looked so young! What was he thinking of, marrying this child! Well, it was done now. She would have to make the best of it. He hoped she would not cry.

Turning his back, he removed his coat, undid his collar and began unbuttoning his shirt. When he turned around she was still standing there. Silent. Wide-eyed. He finished taking off his shirt and sat down on the bed. "Come here," he said, desire roughening his voice.

She came to him as a woman would. Though she winced one time, she did not cry. Holding her afterwards, smelling the blood and feeling the frailty of her bones in his arms, he felt within himself an unimaginable gentleness.

He left her sleeping the next morning as he slid out of bed at first light and got into his clothes as quietly as possible. The sun was barely breaching the ocean as he walked into the Boar's Head near the wharf. It would be a long day. There was much to be done. He had already put out the word that he was looking for land—a couple of sections not far from the coast, if possible. Buying should not be difficult. The tavern was full that morning and the conversation buzzed with business deals.

It was Lamar Clancy, a fellow broker, who told him that Jared Stone had land for sale. The gambler had disappeared for a few years, Clancy said. He'd won himself a couple of sections up in Maryland and decided to settle it. Nice piece of land, he'd heard. Real nice. Right on the water. Couple creeks on it. Pastures. Planting fields. Pretty good tobacco country up there. And there were about half a dozen slaves to go with it.

"Slaves?" said Eldon. "Where did he get his slaves? I was not planning to buy slaves."

Clancy knew where Stone had gotten his slaves but he also knew enough to keep his mouth shut about it "Reckon they'll go with the land," he said. "Don't believe Stone has the stomach for selling them separate." He laughed. "Maybe that's why he's had no luck with farming." He noted the tightening of Eldon's lips. "Might get a good price on it," he added quickly. And you're going to need a few slaves to run the place. Help the wife out."

"You know Stone?" Eldon asked. "I mean, personally?"

"That's him right over there," said Clancy, pointing to a heavily bearded man who sat alone near the back of the room. "Known him for some twenty years. An honest gambler, if there's such a thing. You talk to him, he'll tell you what he's got. It'll be the truth, for sure. 'Course I reckon, before you put your money down, you'll want to have a look at the place. It's right up there in the mouth of the Potomac on the east of the peninsula."

Jared Stone would not go lower than seven thousand. "House isn't much," he said, "but it's big enough and water tight and the land is plumb beautiful. Right on the Bay. Easy shipping from there. Rich land. Man could grow anything on that land if he put his mind to it."

What had he grown?

"Well, I had some trouble keeping my mind on it," said Stone, smiling as he added brandy to his coffee. "But them niggers I got know what they're doing. Trouble was, I didn't. You got to give them some direction if you want them to produce for you and I tell you the truth, Mr. Sturn, the only direction I wanted to go was back into town. Never did like farming. Can't imagine why I thought I could make it work." He sighed, draining his cup. "But I stuck it out for close on five years. That's saying something, now."

"I will take a look at it," said Eldon. "When are you going back?"

"Soon as I find a buyer and not before," said Stone. "That's what I said I was going to do. And that's what I'm going to do." He peered into the empty cup, sloshed in a bit more brandy, raised the cup. "You a buyer, Mr. Sturn?"

"I will take a look at it," said Eldon again. "I hear the Flash is sailing up to Washington tomorrow. My wife and I will be ready then if you are." He noted the other's hesitation. "I can pay your passage, Mr. Stone, since I cannot assure that I want the land until I have seen it."

"Got more care of picking land, than of picking a wife, I reckon," said Stone and laughed long and hard. Eldon did not join in.

That night, he lay awake beside his wife until nearly dawn. They talked of many, many things.

Kathleen loved the land. It was, she thought, walking uphill from the dock, quite the most beautiful place she had seen since Ireland. Not that she'd seen much besides water since then, she remembered, stifling a giggle. She had to be serious. She was a wife now.

She watched her husband taking it all in. Beyond the border of tall maple, pine and oak trees, behind the square, unpainted building that crowned a low hill, stretching far back to the woods were flat, green fields, broken by animal pens and out-buildings. A barn. A stable. A couple small sheds. And in the distance, behind the house, three tiny cabins stood beside a creek. She wondered if the cabins were used for guests. As big as this country was, when people came to visit, they would surely stay a while.

The green was only grass, she noted. The only crops she saw were corn, tomatoes and squash, growing among the weeds in a rather scrawny-looking garden patch, an acre or so located between the house and the cabins. She'd never seen squash or corn growing before, but Mr. Stone was being kind enough to tell her the names of everything. He did not seem to mind her asking, though Eldon had glanced at her sternly a time or two.

She sighed. She had so much to learn if she was to become a lady and it looked like a lady was what Eldon wanted. A man rich enough to buy this much land! Land enough for a dozen families with dozens of children back where she came from. But here. Oh, this was a rich country all right! Even the ground looked rich. She could not imagine a famine striking here.

She thought of her younger brother and sister still in Ireland, living with an aunt since their mother had died, sharing what little food there was with six other children. Perhaps someday she could bring them over along with all the cousins. Sail back with Eldon and bring them all over to America. Why not? Eldon would need more hands to work the land. No wonder it lay fallow with only Mr. Stone to work it.

They had not yet arrived at the house. Eldon was circling, led by Stone who was in no hurry to show off the ugliest part of the bargain. The barn was in good condition, put together, it would appear, by an excellent carpenter. A milk cow stood patiently in one of the eight stalls. In the barnyard, a young heifer pulled at a pile of hay and nearby three scrawny pigs grunted and grubbed in a small sty while a few chickens scratched in the dirt behind a pole fence. Even the fence was well built, Kathleen thought. Too bad the place had not been kept up. But that would all change. She couldn't wait to get started.

The stables were empty, the horses at pasture, Stone explained. "Got a fenced in piece over there. Just got two horses but it's cheaper to let them graze when they can." He moved resolutely forward. "Reckon I'd best introduce you to the help."

He clapped his hands as they walked towards the cabins. "Get on out here," he called. "Line up, now." Figures appeared in the doorways. Eyes and teeth showed white in dark faces as the blacks moved slowly into a line in front of the owner. There were three couples and five children, ranging from a toddler to a seven or eight year-old. Finding their places, they stood silently. Not even the little ones moved.

"Jenny and Robert," said Stone, pointing at the adults. "He's a fine carpenter and has the makings of a blacksmith. She's real good with the garden when she doesn't have her mind on the pickaninnies. Then this is Lizzie and Joe. He's real good with the animals, horses especially, and does fine leather work when he wants to. Lizzie's good with the canning and churning up butter and such. Makes good cheese, too. This one's Jimmy. He's the main handyman. And this is Winnie who helps in the house with the cooking and cleaning and washing. All of them know how to do field work, too. Grew up picking tobacco on the Thames plantation near Richmond. All except Winnie." He smiled at the lighter-colored woman. "She grew up in the house. Wouldn't want to get her hands dirty."

The woman did not smile back.

"You've moved out here, Winnie? Moved in with Jimmy? Can't believe it! Hard as I tried for five years to get you married off and here I am, gone two weeks and you've finally moved in with Jimmy! Better make some babies quick now. Master Eldon and Miz Kathleen could use some more niggers around here, much work as they're planning to put into the place."

The woman regarded him, unblinking.

"Slaves they are?" said Kathleen wonderingly. "Slaves we'll be having, Eldon?"

Her husband did not look happy. "Apparently so," he said.

"But—and didn't you tell me there's a wrong in slavery, Eldon?" she said, not wanting to argue with her beautiful man; just wanting to understand.

The Negroes waited, still faces revealing nothing. Eldon kicked at the dirt, batted a fly on his arm.

"I need help, Kathleen, and we can't afford to hire it yet. Besides, they come with the land. You heard what Mr. Stone said. They've always lived here. This is their home."

"But–and didn't you tell me they came from the Thames plantation, Mr. Stone?" she said, turning towards the gambler. Bought them from there, you did?"

Her shoulder was seized by a hard hand. Breathless, she swung around to meet her husband's angry eyes. His voice was more a whisper than a shout, but every sentence struck a blow.

"You are to shut up immediately. You are nothing but a child and I will not have you questioning me. And in front of Mr. Stone! And them! You listen good, now. I am the master here. I will try to be good but you are not to question my decisions."

She did not avert her eyes. Neither did the Negroes. Stone waited a moment, then led them on toward the house.

While he was teaching his wife to read and write, Eldon figured he might as well teach the blacks. His neighbors would not have to know; they already looked a bit askance on the familiarity with which the Negroes addressed him. Not that they forgot to say "Suh" and "Ma'am." Even Winnie, though overly familiar, had shaped up well enough. Kate sure liked her and Eldon didn't believe that groveling improved anybody's working potential. He wanted people who could take care of business. And slaves who could read and write could take care of a lot more business than those who couldn't. It was a good investment.

Eldon had not thought much about religion since he left Germany to come to the New World but the Moravian influence of his childhood still lingered in his dreams of a hard-working and cooperative community. What was good for the community, he often told his wife, was also good for business. Same as with the blacks learning to read. Nothing really altruistic about it. Just good common sense.

Kate approved. The back parlor, square and bare except for two pine tables and some benches, was a regular schoolroom now. He had Kate in there all the time, except when she was doing the necessary things around the house. He hoped she could learn enough to take over the teaching for him soon. Though he had been tutored through his own childhood, he had never been much for study but she was enjoying learning her letters so much it was contagious. The slaves would come in, two at a time, the women bringing their children for a couple of hours a day. He would spend a half hour with each class, then leave them practicing their letters with Kate and each other while he went out to keep the rest of them working. There was a lot to be done.

He had no interest in producing tobacco; there was plenty of tobacco growing already. Eldon wanted to develop a broader base of trade. With the brokerage contacts he had already made from Charleston to New York and even Boston, he had every reason to encourage the local production of as many goods as possible. Except during planting and harvesting seasons. Most of the big growers around him always had a few slaves they were willing to hire out for a share of the goods they produced. Besides he would be training their blacks in a craft. Improving their value. No one could object to that.

He started work on a tanning shed where Joe could teach a few of the other blacks how to turn out leather goods. A furniture factory was next with Robert in charge. Kate insisted that the first thing they make was furniture for themselves. He complained that there was no money in that, only expense. She said no one on their property was going to live like animals, not while she had breath. Each cabin had to have a table, she said. And benches, at least. And beds. You would have thought she was playing with doll houses, the kind of interest she took in it.

It took little argument for Eldon to decide it was good practice for them, after all, and let her have her way. He did not mind seeing a person have a little pride even if it was only a slave. And it came to be said that Eldon's niggers, for all their uppity ways, worked harder than any slaves in the county.

By the second winter, he had put a small forge in the back of the furniture factory, adding horseshoes and ironworks to his productions. A long smokehouse was built that year to cure the meats he bartered or bought from his neighbors. A porch alongside it, fitted with shelves, tables and a big iron stove, accommodated Lizzie's jam and jelly-making genius. For a penny or two, buckets of berries, plums and apples could always be had from the neighbors' children. He would even pay his own slaves to go berry-picking if they would do it on Sunday.

The third year, he planted his acreage in fruit trees, along with corn, beans and the yams his wife liked so much better than the potatoes of her childhood. Winnie's sweet yam pies joined the list of items he could barter with his neighbors. The garden, well-tended since that first summer by Jenny and her two oldest children, produced enough to provide canned vegetables all winter. He even sold a few, complaining to his wife that he could have sold a lot more if she hadn't insisted on feeding them to the niggers.

"Knee-groes," she said, enunciating carefully as she stared him down. "A dark-skinned race of African origin. Now isn't that the proper word, Eldon? You'd not want to be putting down those that are earning your bread, would you,

Dearie?" He snorted back that he worked plenty hard himself but he argued no more about what she served to the blacks. They were, in a manner of speaking, family after all.

Jenny and Robert had another son in early fall that year and Lizzie was obviously pregnant. Winnie confessed to Kate that she was afraid she and Jimmy weren't going to have children. "Wait so long, might as well give up," she said. "Might be a mercy, at that. Being slave ain't no situation to give a young'un. But I do say, a baby's a nice thing."

"Hasn't been so long a time, Winnie," said Kate, not understanding why any woman would want to "give up" the baby-making action she enjoyed so much. Not to mention how a husband would feel about being denied! She was getting a little anxious herself, though. A baby was indeed a nice thing. And with so much already done, the timing would be good.

"You just like the intimacy," said Eldon, when she shared her thoughts with him in bed that night. But he laughed as she snuggled into his arms and that night they were better together than they had ever been.

Their daughter was born in late July of 1791. Kate wanted to call her Maxine. It was Latin for "greatest," she explained to her husband, seeking his approval as she showed off her new knowledge of books. "Greatest, she is, now, is she not?" She turned back the cotton swaddling blanket to study the tiny face with its red-gold wisps of hair, the blue eyes still squeezed shut. Eldon touched a cheek, marveling, and agreed to the name. He had, for some reason, thought only of boys, though any child at all was miracle enough. Around them, the slave women paused in their clean-up work to coo at the new heiress. Only Winnie looked a little less than happy. She is wanting one, too, thought Kate, as Winnie put the baby to her mistress's breast and watched as it nuzzled and then held on. Poor thing.

Kate didn't mention it when she first noticed a definite bulge beneath Winnie's apron, waiting for the woman to tell her own glad news. But weeks went by. Christmas came and went and still Winnie said not a word. Kate could take the silence no longer. "You'll be having a child then?" she said, whispering in the kitchen one cold day in January as they planned the evening's meal. "Well now, that's a fine thing!"

"Not so fine as that," said Winnie, frowning.

"What can you be meaning? It's a baby you were wanting; you said so yourself. And Jimmy will be proud."

"No Ma'am," said Winnie. "This ain't Jimmy's baby, no Ma'am. This baby come from that green-eyed wagon man, Mr. Ralph, and it wasn't my idea, no Ma'am. Man grabbed me one night, getting done with milking and take me up on the straw. Then he keep coming back. I can't tell Jimmy. Jimmy ain't like them other niggers, put up with whatever a white man do. Jimmy like to kill him; and then they hang Jimmy for sure. So Mr. Ralph, he just keep on coming back 'til he start to notice my belly. Ain't been around since Christmas, thank the Lord."

Her face reflected utter misery.

"Jimmy, he'll be thinking it's his child, then?"

"Yes'm. And, oh Miz Kate, he so proud and what he gonna do when he see that child? He gonna want to kill it and me, both. And then set out after Mr. Ralph, 'cause he'll sure figure out who it was, much as he seen him hanging around here. He done told me he seen him making eyes at me. I just said, 'Go along, now! Ain't nothing.' But it something all right. Going to be something mighty bad."

The woman sank into a chair, her apron over her eyes. " Miz Kate, ain't nobody believe this 'cept you, maybe, but Jimmy's the only man I ever had. Couldn't abide none of them, that way, and the Lord have mercy and keep the masters away afore this. Ain't never felt so bad as when that man grab me like that. Ain't never hated nobody like that." Her voice trailed into sobs.

Kate knelt beside her, cradling the dark head. "It's a baby, all the same," she said. "It's a baby of your own that will be needing you, Winnie. Hating won't be helping it, now, will it?"

She straightened and walked to the kitchen door, making sure Jimmy was nowhere in sight. "We'll have to be telling him ahead," she said. "Maybe if he gets used to the idea."

"He ain't never be used to it, Miz Kate. I knows that man."

"Eldon will be talking to him. You'll be seeing."

Eldon was not happy. Owning slaves might be a necessity, as he saw it, but mixing blood was a wrong thing. Went against the laws of nature, he told Kate, glowering. "You wouldn't think a white man would stoop so low!"

Kate soothed him. The baby that was coming could not help itself, after all. And from what she had heard, it happened often enough.

"Against nature," Eldon muttered. "Ought to take a whip to that nigger. Likely she teased him along."

Kate stared at him, her chin lifted high. "You do that, Eldon Sturn, and I will never be sharing this bed with you again for so long as I live. You want to beat a woman for being raped! I never imagined you to be so mean!"

Eldon was silent. "I'll talk to Jimmy," he said finally.

Neither Kate nor Winnie ever knew what Eldon told Jimmy but the black man wore a face as long as the river right up to the time the baby was born that winter. He started sleeping in the barn, up in the hayloft where he could keep an eye on his wife as she went about the milking every evening. But he did not speak to her and he did not come near their cabin. "I done lost him, Miz Kate," Winnie told her mistress, wringing her hands. "He ain't never coming back to me."

Kate soothed her the best she could, hoping the man would fall in love with the baby that would be his to raise if he wanted it, whether his by blood or not. But Jimmy was nowhere in sight when Kate was called to the cabin one night in the middle of March to help Winnie deliver herself of a little girl. The infant was not nearly so dark as her mother though she carried the same Indian look about her eyes. Watching Winnie hold the baby close, Kate saw the pain in her face replaced by wonder. " 'Tis a beauty, she is," said Kate. "What will you be naming her?"

"Catherine," said Winnie, a slow smile finally breaking. "Like that queen you tell us about in that country, Russia." She looked down at the child on her breast, forgetting her mistress for a moment. "Maybe she think like a queen. Think free and maybe she go free by and by." Her eyes were dreamy, looking into some private past. "My daddy free man, my momma told me. He an Indian. Got hurt on Master John's place and she cure him with herbs. He stay with her a while, then go back to the mountains. Not made to be slave."

There was nothing Kate could say that would make everything all right.

"You be taking good care of that child, Winnie," she managed, stroking the tiny head before turning to go. She would have to talk to Eldon again. Surely they were making enough now to give the slaves some wages. Give them their manumission papers. She'd had enough of this business of owning other people. It was not right. There was nothing in the world that would ever make it right.

Eldon called her a romantic fool. Told her anyone could see the slaves were perfectly happy, treated as well as they were. Better than a lot of white children. They were eating almost as well as the two of them were. Working at trades. Even learning to read and write, for God's sake! What more could anyone ask?

"Wages," she said shortly. "Freedom. All day they work, daybreak to sundown. It's more than food they are deserving."

Anger crossed his face as he seized her shoulders. "I have no control over your thoughts, wife," he said. "But if I hear of you saying that to anyone–anyone, mind–I will whip you and do not you forget it." He turned and went out the door, leaving her staring after him. He sounded like he meant it, sure enough. It was not the first time she had seen his temper though it was rarely directed towards her. She could not bear it. Though he had never struck her in anger, she would not risk his wrath.

Going to the nursery, she picked up her own baby, finding comfort in the small body nestling against her. "We'll be doing what we can," she whispered. "Have mercy on us, dear Lord Jesus. Have mercy."

It was Eldon who first called the new baby Cat, watching her glide across the nursery floor in pursuit of Maxine's best baby doll, her green-gold eyes aglow. She moved with a graceful abandon, feline in feeling, though when she pulled herself to her tiny feet and lifted the doll to examine it, she looked as serious as any young queen. But Cat was easy for Maxine to say, and only Winnie called her daughter Catherine after that.

Eldon and Kate's second child was a boy, born a year later in April of 1793. Blonde and sturdy, the baby's lusty yells soon filled the air around the nursery. Picked up, he was a charmer, wooing everyone with dimples and big baby blues. Even his father came in out of the fields sometimes just to chuckle him under the chin. His mother held him, mostly, on one arm, leaving the other free to attach to Maxine who clung to her now as closely as did the baby.

They named him Benjamin. "Son of my right hand," said Eldon, who still remembered Scripture from his youth. He had thought long and hard about the name. He loved his daughter but it was a son he wanted to carry on his name. Benjamin Sturn. It sounded–substantial.

Kate did her best to love the baby boy as much as she did her daughter but her daughter seemed to need her so much more. Bennie was happy with anyone. It was easy to turn the child over to Winnie, who didn't mind nursing two. It was Winnie who kept the babies entertained all day. Arriving at the big house by sunrise with Cat on her hip and not returning to her cabin until the kitchen was clean, long after dark, Winnie was a great relief to her mistress. And though Eldon paid little attention to the darker-skinned child, he did not seem to mind the two infants being tended together all day.

Busy as Kate was with keeping the books and minding that all the women did their jobs, she had all she could do to keep up with Maxine, now two and into everything. It crossed her mind to bring in another servant but she would not have another slave and Eldon would not hear of her hiring somebody. "That is not how they do things here, Kate. And my business—our money—depends on getting along with them. You know that as well as I do so I'll hear no more about it."

"We should have gone further north," muttered Kate, her chin stuck out. Her husband's furious eyes silenced further comment.

With only Winnie to help, Kate got along the best she could in the house but in the field Eldon started bringing in more slaves. She watched the new cabins go up but, except for a formal first visit to be sure the quarters were adequate, she did not visit much down there anymore. As more sickness came on the place, she asked Eldon to build an infirmary. Sick people should be kept apart so the sickness wouldn't spread, she told him. And Winnie knew a lot about herbs and such. She would be willing and able to look after the sick.

"Better to keep them healthy, I suppose," he said, agreeing.

At first, Kate stayed with all three children while Winnie did her sickbed rounds. But by the time Maxine was five, the little girl insisted on going along. Kate worried a little and then gave in. The child absorbed knowledge like a sponge. Fascinated by Winnie's herbal lore, Maxine explained everything to her mother as they waited together for Eldon to come home for dinner. Eldon was usually late.

There was a sizeable pier on the river by then, paid for by both local investors and shippers from New York. From the time he was old enough to walk, Eldon took Benjamin with him when he went there on business, offering his young son a feel for the sea and its ships as he talked with the captains, negotiated with agents and walked the decks of the giant clipper ships. If he had it to do over again he might have gone to sea himself. Land was awfully confining.

By the time his son was twelve, he'd decided he wanted to be a captain. Eldon could not help but approve though he wondered often what would become of the land. There had been no more children, much as he and Kate had wanted a houseful.

Despite her husband's offer of a mansion, Kate insisted on remaining in the house where they had started out together though Eldon had not spent much time improving on it after the necessary painting and fixing up was done. It was big enough, after all, and she was perfectly happy with what they had. The neighbors did not visit often and when they did, the front parlor looked nice enough. He entertained his buyers at the tavern built near the docks and drank with the captains in their cabins, not wanting to inflict so many strangers on his wife.

Though Winnie refused to move into the house with her daughter, all three children spent most of their time there, attended as often by Kate as by Winnie who was increasingly occupied with organizing the flow of food from the kitchen. It was almost, Kate thought hopefully, like one big happy family. The children all took lessons together in the nursery, taught for a few years by a pale young fellow from New York. He read Latin and spoke both French and German as well as English. Kate loved to hear her husband discourse with him in the tongue so foreign to her. The more languages one knew, the better, Eldon insisted. It gave one a broader base of operations. Kate had little interest in learning foreign tongues but the children were apt quickly enough, Maxine concentrating on Latin treatises about medicinal plants while Cat and Bennie whispered to each other in French across the kitchen table.

Winnie would roll her eyes and shake her head, watching Cat. She was growing into a beautiful girl, long-legged and shapely with a fine set to her head.

"Girl be getting above her station," she said to Kate with a touch of pride. It worried Kate a little. What was in store for the poor child if something should happen to her and Eldon?"

As it turned out, death was not to be her main concern.

The first time she caught Cat and Benjamin hugging and kissing on the old settee in the nursery, she did not tell her husband. Shocked into violence for the first time, she slapped Cat's face and sent Benjamin off to his room with the threat of a whipping. Eldon would surely have carried it out which is why she could not tell him.

But the second time, she had to.

Father and son spent a long time together in the boy's room. Tiptoeing down the hall, Katie could hear no sounds of conflict, just her husband's voice, going on and on and on. She could not quite hear the words but the voice frightened her. The very calmness of it chilled her blood.

"Benjamin will be going to school in Richmond next week," he said to her at dinner. Maxine stole a look at her brother who kept his eyes on his plate. Cat, who never joined the white people at the dining room table, had been nowhere in sight for hours.

Kate waited, holding her breath. "I'm sending him off to boarding school. Captain James Morgan is sailing in eight days if all goes well. He has a son in school there; says it's a fine place, well-tended and there'll be no problem. He'll see to him arriving safely."

She could not say anything. The boy was only fourteen, for heaven's sake! How could Eldon–"

"You'd best start getting his things ready tomorrow morning. Captain Morgan gave me a list of sorts. What the boys need."

"But why?" she asked.

"I won't have it," said Eldon, shutting off discussion. "I won't have him getting into trouble around here."

She pressed on. "But boys will get into trouble any where. You can't stop that."

She recognized the fury rising but it was too late to stop it. Eldon dropped his fork, pushed back from the table, voice rising. "I can damn well stop it here! I won't have it, I tell you. I won't have him and Cat–"

His face was contorted. "If that boy's going to have any little bastards, I sure as hell don't want to know the mother!" He slammed down his wine glass as he stood. "And I'll be dammed if I'll listen to you beg for him."

The glass stem snapped, splashing red across the linen cloth. The children froze in their places. Kate watched the stain spreading as her husband slammed the door. She had never heard him curse before.

One big happy family was not to be.

4

Maxine missed Benjamin, but not too much. His holiday visits home were not enjoyable; all exchanges between him and Cat were carefully watched. Cat would be exceedingly sullen at those times and Maxine felt she had lost her best friend. The feeling persisted.

Maxine started spending more time with her father, growing tired of the tension at home and explaining to him that she wanted to learn more of the business. With Benjamin gone, Eldon acquiesced. The girl was, after all, seventeen and well-educated. No doubt she would marry someone in the business—she had certainly not associated much with the local boys—and it would not hurt her to learn a little about trade. A woman could be a great help to her husband if she knew what he was about. He did not know what he would have done without Kate. Besides, he liked having Maxine about; it helped fill the void of Benjamin's absence.

If her brother had been at home Maxine would probably not have seen young Clarence West down at the docks that April day when her skirts blew about so much she could not help knowing he had seen her ankles. He smiled when their eyes met, with no apology, and she was glad, suddenly, that she had on her laciest petticoats. He was a fine looking young man.

She had met his father before, a distributor in New York who came down often to negotiate with Eldon. She had heard that his ancestors were among the earliest settlers in that great port and had made a great deal of money since the Revolution. She thought Clarence West, Sr. a nice enough gentleman though a bit stiff and she had not been looking forward to the day's meeting, surprised her father had asked her to accompany him. But when she caught an exchange of glances between the two fathers, she finally understood what was happening.

Mr. West bowed to her as they left, asking if they could call on them at home and Maxine, watching his son through lowered lashes, felt sure she was the reason. Perhaps it was time she had a beau. He was certainly good looking enough, tall and dark with a certain measuring interest in his eyes.

They were married at Christmas that year, not long after her eighteenth birthday. Kate cried a little, adjusting her daughter's veil before the ceremony in the big front parlor, full of flowers for the occasion. Only the family was present. Maxine insisted she would not have a big affair. If her father wanted to spend the money, she told him, he could make a gift of it to help them get started in New York. Not that the Wests were lacking in funds for their oldest son, but there was something about them that made Maxine wish to keep as much independence as possible. She could only pray that her almost-husband would not age into their considerably less gentle set of mind.

Benjamin's dimples showed, grinning at her as she moved to the front of the fireplace on her father's arm. It hardly seemed fair that he should be the one to inherit her mother's dimples, she thought for the thousandth time, then chided herself. What a thing to be thinking on her wedding day! She looked up at the man who stood beside the minister, waiting for her, smiling. He would make a good husband. He was almost everything her parents wanted for her.

The Wests sat stiffly on their velvet chairs as the vows were said. Kate wiped away more tears. Benjamin smiled. Eldon looked solemn. And standing at the back of the room, Winnie and Cat watched silently.

There was feasting outside for all the hands. While a violinist played inside and the cake was cut, a banjo struck up a jig near the canning porch where the long tables sagged with the weight of food and drink. Afterwards, her hand on her new husband's arm, Maxine and Clarence stood by the back door while the slaves stepped up to wish them well. Mrs. West looked most disapproving, Maxine noticed. And when Cat had hugged her, well! The old lady's eyebrows nearly disappeared up under her hat. Maxine looked out at her own mother moving through the yard, speaking to the slaves as if they were people, and she knew with a sudden wrench just how much she would miss her. How rare she was. Much as she loved her father, he cared more for what others thought than her mother ever seemed to. She could only hope to measure up to that courage, though her mother never seemed to regard it as anything unusual. "You must mind the feeling of the thing," she had often told her daughter. "You must listen to your heart because that is where God speaks. And then it will not matter at all what other people say." Her husband's people were very different from her own. Mrs West did not look as if she would even admit to having a heart but she must get along with them the best she could. Clarence was insisting they live in New York. His father was training him to take over the business, he said. There was really no question of doing anything else. So she did not cry when she kissed her parents goodbye though her blue eyes glittered with the water held back.

Her new husband moved her into a sizeable house on the Hudson, a wedding present from his parents. Not to be outdone, her parents filled it with furniture. Altogether, it was most comfortable. Large enough to have guests (and children), but not so large she couldn't keep it up herself with the help of a maid, a cook, a gardener and a groom. Clarence agreed they would never own slaves but at least in New York in 1808, there were freemen and women enough for hire.

On September 9 of the following year, their daughter Emily was born. Her husband, brought home by a messenger when Maxine insisted on seeing him, looked a trifle embarrassed as he sat in the parlor, making polite conversation with his mother who had arrived for the event. "The child needs someone," she said disapprovingly to her son. "I can't imagine why her mother didn't come." Clarence cocked his head politely. Anything he said would only start a tirade. His mother was not happy about mixing his old blue blood with the daughter of new immigrants. The German had done well enough but her mother was poor Irish, for heaven's sake. A bought bride, no doubt! Barely spoke proper English!

But young Clarence was fond of the Sturns, finding their informality a pleasant change from the proprieties bred into his own childhood. He knew, having been there, just why Kate could not come. The harvest was just in, the ships were due to load and Eldon, no doubt, was insisting he could not get along without her. She had sent a letter by courier, bemoaning the separation.

"I know you have a good doctor, but, oh, my Dear, I do so wish. . . . Tell Clarence he must take good care of you."

She had showed him the letter without comment. "Do I not take good care of you?" he had asked.

"Of course you do, Dear. You never raise your voice to me, though I have to you. You don't mind whatever I do as long as I behave like a lady. And you grant me whatever I ask. You are intelligent and well-read and quite witty. Your company is my pleasure." Her smile was wistful. "Only you're such a busy man."

"Like your father?"

"And yours."

There had not been much more to say. Clarence was indeed very busy though he had been almost scandalized when Maxine suggested she might help. It was a man's job, he said, flatly, and he had men to help him. Yet he came home later and later in the evening. His father had been ill and he was having to handle things much sooner than he had anticipated. His own child's birth felt almost like an intrusion on the work at hand.

Amid the bustle in the room after the birth, as she and the baby were cleaned up, Maxine felt quite alone. Her husband's appearance at her bedside did not alter the feeling. He bent to kiss her cheek. "You will be all right?" he asked her. "I'll have to return to work, I'm afraid.'" He paused a moment to study the rosy red face of the infant at her breast. "What shall we call her?"

She knew he had wanted a son. The only names he had ever mentioned were boys' names.

"Emily," she murmured. "Do you like the name, Emily?"

He considered it a moment, dark head cocked in the questioning way he had. "It'll do," he said. "Quite nice, really. Emily it is, then."

Mrs. West's visit was even more brief. She said she would stay a few days. Make sure that everything kept running smoothly. She said the maid could call her if she was needed. She told Maxine to rest and almost hurried from the room.

In the dark room behind closed draperies, Maxine held her baby and longed to share her joy. The baby was beautiful! Her parents would be so proud! And Bennie–he would be teasing her now, making her laugh instead of want to cry. And Cat–Cat would be curled up beside her, scratching her back with her fingertips, making her forget the pain.

But one must be strong. She was a mother now as well as a wife. She turned her attention back to her child. "Emily," she said softly, stroking a tiny cheek, marveling at the nose so like her own. "I love you, darling daughter," she whispered. "Forever and ever."

Benjamin's eighteenth birthday fell during Easter vacation of the following year and a family reunion was arranged. It would be the first time Eldon had seen the baby though Kate had managed a month's visit before Christmas. She would bring her maid and the voyage would be a pleasure, Maxine had assured her parents by courier. Emily was quite shipshape and it was high time for some salt air. She was anxious to see her brother–her whole family–again. And with Clarence so busy. . . .

The house would be full again and Kate sang old Irish melodies that Eldon had not heard in years as she bustled about, making room for the baby. Eldon made room in his schedule for his son and delegated what work he could.

As it turned out, the baby took his full attention. Eldon quite lost touch with business as he sat for hours by the cradle, baby-talking like a man gone foolish. As for Maxine, she had so much to tell her mother that the women could not leave each other alone.

Benjamin felt a bit left out. He liked the baby well enough but a little grown-up conversation would be appreciated. His mother was too wrapped up with Maxine and the baby to spend any time with him and his father had barely a word to spare as he hurried off to the cradle. He hardly knew what his father was doing now. Not that he needed to know anymore.

It was his last year in school. Eldon had arranged for him to ship out with Captain Morgan that summer in preparation for a Navy career and this would be his last visit home before he came to them in uniform, prepared to sail. He had a lot of dreams at the moment, and no one to share them with. He could whisper them to the baby, perhaps, but there sat his father, already. Really, one would think a man would get tired of baby talk. He wondered what he was going to do for two weeks.

Benjamin found Cat in the kitchen on his third long day of roaming the halls alone. She merely shrugged when he stopped short in the door, staring at her, not sure what to say. They had hardly spoken since he'd left for school. He sat down a bit awkwardly across from her at the kitchen table. It was hard to remember how easy it used to be with her. She regarded him unsmiling, a question in her golden green eyes.

"You've been well?" he assayed conversation. Lord, but she was beautiful! Those tilted eyes and high cheekbones. And that mouth like a rosebud. Even her color wasn't bad. Not quite a high yellow as the boys at school called some of the quadroons they visited in the brothels of Richmond, expanding their education on their free evenings in town. Still, Cat was a rather nice shade of bronze. And that body! All filled out at the top and with those long brown legs he still remembered. He looked her over without thinking, surprised, when he raised his eyes to find her smouldering.

"Well enough," she said shortly.

"Oh Cat!" He dimpled and reached for her hand. "It's been so long."

"Long enough," she said, not moving.

The chimes on the hallway clock sounded ten. He wondered where everyone was. The house had been silent when he got up late that morning.

"Have you had breakfast?" he asked.

"Long ago," she said, and paused. "Shall I fix you something, Master Benjamin."

He laughed out loud, leaning back in his chair. "Don't you dare do that, Cat. Don't you dare call me Master. I'm your playmate, remember?" He leaned forward again, teasing her. "Do you remember our games, Cat? Do you still like to play?"

She regarded him steadily. "I've never played that game with anyone but you, Master Benjamin. Lost my taste for it when you went away."

"I'm back now," he said, waiting. Her reserve was melting. He was sure of it. He was not about to force a woman, not even a slave, but if she were willing.

"I've missed you, Bennie," she said. "All these years, I've missed you."

"I'm back right now," he said, rising to circle the table. He bent over her, cupping his hands beneath her breasts, finding no resistance. He pulled at her gently and she rose. A long kiss. Oh yes, she was good. She was very, very good. All that practice when they were kids. He doubted her word that she had not played the game since then.

"I'd like to have you for breakfast," he murmured against her ear.

"Oh Bennie," she said, clinging, "Oh Bennie."

"I don't guess anybody ever goes in the nursery anymore," he whispered, kissing her again, thanking God that the baby was cradled in Maxine's room.

"I clean it every week or so. That's about it," she said.

He turned, his arm still around her. "Come on."

They met every morning in the nursery while he was there. They laughed and wrestled, sweated and moaned, re-acquainting each other with their bodies if not their minds, out of sight and sound of everyone. He explained to his parents that he had work to do, books to read before returning to school and they left him alone until he came down for lunch every day. But Winnie was frowning one morning when he came in the kitchen as Cat was going out the back door.

"You watch yourself, boy," she told him. "You ain't got so big you can do what you like in this house. Your daddy have a fit if he know what's going on."

"Nothing's going on, Winnie," he said, helping himself to a porkchop from the plate she was fixing for lunch. "Nothing at all. Cat and I are just getting reacquainted. It's been a long time."

"Gonna be a long time more when you gone again," said Winnie. "Don't want to see that child suffer."

"On account of me? Don't be silly, Winnie." He wiped the grease off his lips and left the kitchen. But he avoided Cat the next day. It was almost time to go and he didn't want any farewell scenes with the colored girl. Especially if there were tears involved. He had enough on his mind already.

He saw the tall dark figure watching from the dock when he sailed away but he didn't wave. There were too many people watching.

Winnie knew her nightmare had become reality when Cat started throwing up. "You gonna have Bennie's baby, ain't you now?" she said sharply, catching her out near the bushes one morning, handing her a wet rag and a glass of water. "Here, wipe your face, child, and rinse out your mouth. We gotta talk. Don't you know nothing! This is trouble for you, girl. Bad trouble."

"I couldn't help it," said the girl, sullenly. "Veni. Vedi. Vinci."

"Don't you go quoting your schoolbooks to me, girl. I don't read those fancy books but look like I got plenty more common sense."

Cat started to cry. Head down on her mother's shoulder, the ache inside her found a voice. "Will he come back, Mama? Will he ever come back to me? I know I can't have him, Mama. But just for a little while. You think he'll come back to me sometimes?"

"There, there, baby," said Winnie, not wanting to answer. "There, there."

But after a while the tears had to be dried and plans had to made. This was not just another slave baby—there'd been plenty of those over the years. This baby was made by the son of the master and this wasn't an ordinary master. He was righteous, this one. And he didn't cater to mixed blood. Especially not his. Winnie could almost understand the man: How could he claim a Negro grandchild, what with all the neighbors watching? And how could he not claim it, having a heart like he did? And if he claimed it, how could he let it be a slave? But how could he free it with the neighbors?

He would sell her! He would sell Catherine! Winnie knew it with a sickening certainty. Didn't matter that he'd never done it before. Nothing had involved his blood like this before.

"We tell Miz Katie first. She mad, maybe, but she helpful." She sniffed. "Likely think you been fooling around with one of the hands. What's the truth?"

"Only Bennie, Mama," the girl said softly, straightening up. "It's the truth. I had him when I was fourteen and he was just growing. And I never wanted anybody else since. That's the truth, Mama. And I don't believe I'll ever want anybody like that again."

She held her stomach. "You believe me, don't you, Mama?"

"I do, child. I felt that way about your, about Jimmy. Didn't have nobody before. Didn't have nobody since. Except that time—"

"When you had me?" Cat had heard, often enough, that she had a white father. But her mother closed up completely when she mentioned it. She had never found out who.

"Who was he, Ma? You ought to tell me. I'm a woman now."

Winnie sighed. Might as well tell the girl the truth about it. "Ralph Pritchard. He grab me one night. Lord but I hate him since." She softly touched her daughter's head. "But I sure do love you so I figure everything work out for good to them that love the Lord, like the Bible say."

"Ralph Pritchard," said Cat. "The wagon maker? That tall skinny man who always smiles at me like he knows something I don't?"

"That's him."

"Then Jimmy wouldn't have you? When he found out I was part white?"

"Before that, even. Mr. Eldon told him ahead. Figured it was better that way."

"Oh Lord, Mama, what are we going to tell Mr. Eldon about my baby? Bennie's baby."

"We do what we can, honey."

Cat barely heard her mutter as she walked away to the big house. "Miz Katie won't let him sell her. I just know she won't let him." There was desperation in her voice. Cat shivered.

Winnie waited, not knowing what to say. By the time she spoke to Kate, it was October and the pregnancy was unmistakable.

"I will sell that nigger bitch! I swear I will sell her!" Eldon shouted. "I won't have a nigger child around here of my own flesh and blood. I won't have it!"

Kate drew herself up. "You'll be doing no such thing, Eldon Sturn. You call yourself a Christian man! You'll do no such thing."

Eldon sank down on the bed, buried his face in his hands. "How could she do this to us. After all we've done for her. Raised her like flesh and blood and she stabs me in the back."

"You're talking about stabbing, I expect it was Bennie stabbed her," said Kate. "She's been in love with him since he was born, anyway. She wouldn't think to say no."

Eldon looked up, wary. "You don't think he–"

"No, of course not," said Katie. "He's your son, after all. There are a lot of things he might do but falling in love with the maid is not one of them."

"I never exactly thought of Cat as a maid."

"None of us did, Dear. Least of all herself. That's the problem, I suppose." They were both silent for several moments.

"I won't sell her if you get her out of here, Kate," he said at last, rising to remove his collar, unbutton his shirt. "I do not care where but it had better be fast or I will do it myself. Captain Morgan's due from London before Thanksgiving and I don't want Bennie to see that girl. He'll have to know about it but I don't want anybody talking. She's not to set eyes on him again. She's got to promise me that."

But Kate couldn't bring herself to put it all into words and in the end Catherine herself brought the solution, coming to Kate with her mother, begging for refuge. "Maxine," she said, shyly. "Will Maxine let me come, do you think, Miz Kate? I'll help her with everything. We always got along good."

But how were they to get her to New York? Cat was terrified of ships, refusing even to board the ones in the harbor, and the girl certainly couldn't go overland alone.

It was Eldon who found the answer.

Ralph Pritchard was taking a caravan of his wagons to New York that winter. Loaded up with Sturn jams and jellies, hams and blackberry wine, he made extra profit on his journey. There was a market for all of it in New York—foodstuff, wagons and horses. It was well worth the journey but it was also a long hard trip and he tried not to make it more than once a year.

Pritchard had big ideas. With the migration going westward, he could see the market for wagons growing. He had twice as many for sale this year as last, thanks to the little factory he'd gotten started with Eldon's help. Now Eldon decided it was time for Pritchard to return the favor.

He invited the wagon maker over to sample the latest batch of blackberry wine. "Particularly good," he pronounced. Tipped back on the porch, the men discussed the weather.

"Reckon I'll have to clear out of here soon," said Pritchard. "Snow'll be flying in about a month."

"Long trip, it is," said Eldon. "Reckon a man might get lonely on a long trip like that. Might want some company."

"Got plenty of company," Pritchard snorted. "Got eight drivers to keep in line."

"Pretty rough company," Eldon agreed.

"You getting at something, Eldon? Cause if you are, you might as well spit it out."

"Got a favor to ask of you, Ralph. We're going to send Cat up to Maxine in New York. Girl's scared to death of ships so she's got to go overland and there's nobody to go with her right now. Thought maybe you—We'd pay passage, of course."

"Be a long rough trip for a woman," said Ralph. "And she's pregnant, isn't she? Why don't you wait 'til spring? Sure to be somebody going then. Liable to get mighty cold this trip. And with a baby due–"

"Not due 'til January," said Eldon. "There'd be time."

Ralph looked at him for a while, chewed and spat out tobacco. "There's more to this than you're letting on, Eldon. That your baby she's carrying? Don't want Miz Kate to know?"

Eldon looked genuinely shocked. "She's a child, for heaven's sake. Well, eighteen now, but a child to me. Lord knows I raised her right along with my own. And now this!" He lowered his voice. "It's Bennie's baby, Ralph. And I don't want them seeing each other any more. He'll be home by Thanksgiving and I want her out of here."

Ralph shrugged. "You could sell her. Girl like that would go quick. Pretty."

Eldon's shock deepened. "Can't say I didn't think of that though Kate disabused me of the notion mighty fast. But I'm surprised to hear you say it. Thought I heard–" He paused, it was a delicate subject, but hell, he'd told him about Bennie.

"Thought I heard she was yours," he said.

Ralph shrugged again. "As to that, it's not like I ever claimed her, " he laughed. "Only her mama and I know for sure and it was pretty dark. Her mama might not be all that sure.

"But you know," said Eldon.

Ralph chewed and spit tobacco.

"I can take her I reckon, he said at last, unbending from the chair. "Cost you fifty dollars, though. She'll need special treatment, I reckon."

"I appreciate that," said Eldon, shaking the man's hand. "You'll be leaving early next month, then?"

"Just get her ready," said Ralph. "And tell her she better not whine or I'll have her hide." He grinned at Eldon's scandalized face. "Joking," he said. "I'll treat her right. She's my blood for all that."

They sent Maxine word by courier that Cat was on the way. Pregnant. She would tell them about it when she got there but it was essential she come immediately. Eldon did not wait for an answer. Let the women deal with it if they were so bound and determined to protect her. Let Clarence deal with it. Maxine was enough like Katie, he knew who would win that round. He did not expect Cat would be walking the streets. But he did not want to think about the child.

October passed quickly. Kate and Cat packed, side by side. The big day came. Cat's trunk was loaded along with sacks of food for the trip and a box of books Kate bought for little Emily. "You can hardly start teaching them too soon," she said, hugging the girl goodbye.

Eldon gave Cat a hand into the wagon bed. Under the canvas one could hardly feel the wind. She leaned against the boards, her arms around her stomach. "Take care, Cat." he said. "You take care of that baby."

Kate came running back, a book in one hand, a flower in the other. "Give this to the baby," she said, handing Cat a leather-bound Bible. "And this is for you, Dear, it's the last yellow rose from the bush by the kitchen door. A yellow rose for remembrance."

Cat put the rose carefully into the book and pressed it shut. "Forgetting's not the problem, Miz Kate. Remembering's the problem."

From the doorway, Winnie held up her hand in farewell, unwilling to share her tears.

Ralph Pritchard climbed up beside the driver. With a crack of whips the teams moved slowly out of the yard. Kate waved until she couldn't see them anymore. Watching her face, Eldon knew better than to try to comfort her. He left for the warehouses immediately.

He hoped Maxine would let them know when Cat arrived. Hoped the girl would not spill the brat along the way. Might be the only child his son would ever have. Things happened that way sometimes. Like a punishment.

The wagons made good time the first week but on the other side of Baltimore a freak blizzard blew down out of the mountains and practically froze the axles. The horses made it to a farmhouse where the owner let them huddle under blankets in the barnyard, there being no room in the stables for eight teams. The drivers went into the hayloft. Pritchard peered into the back of the wagon where Cat huddled in a corner, shaking. Oh hell, he couldn't leave her in there; the canvas was soaked already and the wind came through like a blade. And he couldn't put her in the hayloft with the drivers. Pregnant or not, they'd make short work of her.

Cat started coughing and couldn't seem to stop.

Pritchard trudged back through the snow to the farmhouse. "Ma'am," he began, "my girl's awful sick. Got a cough that won't stop and she's shaking fit to turn blue. Wouldn't worry you with it, but she's expecting. . . . "

"Well bring her on in," said the woman, then hesitated. "She's a white girl, I take it."

"No ma'am. She's colored."

"Oh." She started to close the door. Pritchard put his foot in it.

"Ma'am, if you just had something for her cough."

The woman sighed. "Come on in then," she said, and left him standing in the hall, reappearing with a bottle in a few minutes. "It's honey, lemon and whiskey. Been a lot of niggers coming through here, told me about it. Call it nigger tea. Works, though. Soothe her throat, fight the cold and help her sleep. About the best I can do." She opened the door for him to leave. "Be warm enough in the barn, I guess," she said, closing it behind him.

Unable to carry her into the loft, Pritchard made a bed for her in a corner of the stable. All night he sat beside her, awake and watching, offering her water when she moaned in her sleep. She was burning with fever the next morning when he carried her back into the wagon but the snow was melting in a warm wind and the blizzard had already delayed them for a day. They'd have to keep moving, he explained, patting her awkwardly on the arm. She smiled at him. She was a pretty thing, even big like that. If she weren't his blood—

Well, he supposed there were some things a man shouldn't even think about. "You'll be all right," he said. "We'll just get you up to Maxine's and you'll be all right."

She nodded, saying nothing.

Her face looked yellow under the bronze by the time they got to New York. Yellow and sickly and slick with sweat. The potion had kept the cough down but her chest heaved with ragged breaths. Not good at all. Maxine was going to have a burden or her hands. Two of them. He was glad he was about to lay it down. Women were such a nuisance for all they felt so good sometimes.

Maxine made much of her, calling the butler to carry her into the house after she'd asked Pritchard if he had time to drive her on to the doctor and he'd said no. Clarence watched, unsmiling, standing straight by the doorway as the bustle went by him. Really, Maxine was not being reasonable. Calling him home from work to see to a colored girl! Not that he couldn't respect their affiliation, but really. The fact that his brother-in-law was the father mattered little to him. As he understood it, that happened all the time among slaves. And he'd never heard of the offspring getting much special treatment.

"We've got to get her to a doctor, Clarence. She's dying! Can't you see?"

Clarence studied the woman lying on the bed. She did look decidedly unhealthy. And pregnant. "I'll have Jim get the horses," he said. "Dr. Jamison will see her, I suppose. But you won't need me there. Jim can take you and bring you back."

At the doctor's office, the nurse said, "Of course, bring her right in." But when Maxine reappeared with Jim holding Cat up between them, she pursed her lips and disappeared into the other room.

"Doctor's awfully busy," she said, returning. "You might want to try—" She named a name. "He's in Harlem, down that street and—"

"I know where Harlem is," Maxine cut in. "It's a long way away and my friend is almost dead. You tell Dr. Jamison that if he wants the Clarence Wests for patients, he's to see Catherine right now."

They waited an hour but the nurse finally beckoned them back.

"Pneumonia," the doctor said shortly, having finished his tapping about on Cat's chest and back. He suggested Delaudid and other poultices. "Doesn't help that she's pregnant. Slows recovery. She'll need treatment at home and even then there's no guarantee." He shrugged.

"Is there anyone you can suggest who would see her at home, Doctor? My home."

"There's a colored woman who might come. Excellent midwife, I hear. They call her Dr. Connie. Connie Cassals, I think it is. From the West Indies." He scribbled an address on a piece of paper, smiled briefly. "I expect she can help you."

Dr. Connie arrived that evening accompanied by a well-behaved six-year-old. "You'll have to excuse him," she said. "There was no one to leave him with and I understood it was an emergency." She smiled at the little boy. "He'll sit right where you tell him and be no bother. Isn't that right, Luke?" Solemn, the little boy nodded as Maxine hurried her into the room where Cat was gasping for breath.

"Dear me," the woman said, studying the bulge under the covers. "Complications, I see."

"In more ways than one," said Maxine. A letter from her mother, delivered the week before, had told the whole story. "All I know is, we have to save her and that baby, both." She looked up at the dark face, trusting the woman. "I was raised with her and that's my brother's baby she's carrying. She's almost like a sister."

"But not quite," said Dr. Connie, chuckling a little as she went to work. Maxine did not see anything funny but the midwife's presence was reassuring. She came every day, applying poultices and offering herbal teas. Little by little Cat's breathing was restored. As Christmas drew near, she helped a little with the decorations, though Maxine tried to insist she not lift a hand. The cough was persistent; the green eyes alternated dull and fever bright.

Dr. Connie kept coming to check on her. Maxine enjoyed her company. Clarence tolerated it well though he was not home enough to take note of all the comings and goings. As long as everything was peaceful he did not care who came or where they sat. But when he saw Dr. Connie leaving one evening by the front door, he spoke to his wife about it. "It won't do," he said. "It simply is not done."

"I will not ask that good woman to leave by the back door," said Maxine, lifting her chin. "I will not, Clarence. She's educated. She's intelligent. She speaks better English than some of your agents. And, she's been an absolute angel to Cat. I will not insult her with her race."

Clarence studied his wife's face. She was exceedingly pretty when she was angry, he decided. The passion raised the color in her cheeks and heightened the blue of her eyes. But he had better ways of raising the color. More peaceful, so to speak. He smiled at her, patted her shoulder.

"Have it your way, my Dear. Just please don't invite her to dinner. At least not when I—when we have company."

"Dr. Connie is company," she said stubbornly as he turned to go back to work. "But I'll abide by your wishes." Her face broke into a smile as he looked back at her. "Master."

Cat passed her time reading to little Emily. The child adored her. She loved her color, her sound, her shape. Sitting on what lap she had left, the two-year old patted her belly. "Baby?" she said, putting down her ear to listen as Dr. Connie had taught her. "Baby, there?"

Cat would nod dreamily, fingering the Bible she kept beside her, whether sitting or lying down. "You'll see it soon," she promised. "Real soon, now."

The baby was born on January 3, 1812. It was snowing that day but Dr. Connie came in a hurry when Maxine sent for her. Brushing snow from her cloak, she rushed to the girl's side. Cat's lips were blue. She panted hard for breath. Dr. Connie prepared a poultice, set water steaming in the fireplace, added eucalyptus leaves and settled down to wait. Six hours of moaning later, the water broke. The women gathered around.

In the back parlor, Luke waited patiently, obeying his mother by entertaining Emily the best he could. They looked at a picture book together, Luke making out some of the words and making up the rest.

"It's a girl, Emily," said Dr. Connie coming to the door. "You want to see the little girl now?"

Emily jumped up, clapping her hands as she ran. "Sister," she said. It was the word Luke had just taught her. She liked the sound of it. "Sister! Sister!"

Dr. Connie shook her head at her son. "Now you know, boy—"

He regarded her innocently, eyes open wide. "I didn't say it was her sister. I just showed her the word. It's in the book. See?" The picture showed two little girls holding hands. "My sister goes everywhere with me," read the caption.

Dr. Connie shook her head again. Not always by choice, she thought to herself as she returned to her patient.

Maxine was sitting beside the bed, looking down at the blanket wrapped bundle in Cat's arms. The child was peachy pale behind the flush of birth. The dark fuzz on the little round head was barely curled. The wide eyes had a bluish tint and a faint tilt; the mouth was a rosebud, like Cat's. But the tiny nose looked very much like Kate's. If the baby had dimples, why she was almost as cute as Emily!

"What will you name her, Cat?"

A slim bronze arm reached out to pick up the Bible by the bed. She opened it to the rose, pressed flat, the yellow color still showing.

"Rose," she said sleepily. Your mama gave me this to remember her by when I left there. It's from the bush by the back door, remember? Bloomed like crazy, spring and fall. We'll call her Rose. To remember. . . . "

"Do you want to write it down?"

"You do it please."

Maxine hesitated on the last name. Sturn would be logical; Cat had belonged to the Sturns, after all. But Benjamin would not like that, she knew. And neither would her father. *Rose West*, she wrote. *Born January 3, 1811. By the Grace of God.*

"Rose," said Emily, tiptoeing to the bed at a sign from her mother. She stretched up on tiptoe, peering into the tiny face.

"Pretty Rose," she whispered as Luke watched from the door.

That baby could pass, thought Dr. Connie, not surprised. That baby girl surely could pass.

5

Cat never really recovered from that winter's illness. She might have said that only her daughter kept her alive. The child was everything she had dreamed of her being; and with the opportunities Rose would receive, there was hope in her future, though not for herself.

Certainly, Maxine could not have treated the two of them better. She and Rose had their own room and it was a far cry from the dirt-floored cabin to which she was born. Though it was in the servant's quarters, to be sure, it was all part of the house and the room was large and well furnished with lace curtains on the tall windows and two big dressers for their clothes. The maid's and the cook's rooms on the other side of the wing behind the kitchen were half the size.

Though a friendship among the three women in the quarters might have been natural enough, Cat held herself aloof. From the time Rose was born, little Emily was constantly seeking her out. Glad for the help at home, Maxine began making herself useful at her husband's offices near the port and Cat spent most of her time with the two girls in the garden or the nursery. Winter afternoons were spent in the library curled up together on the rug in front of the fireplace while she read to them from every book she thought they could possibly understand.

But much as she enjoyed the children together, her favorite times were at night sitting in bed with Rose in her lap, telling the little girl stories of the past. She remembered her mother's story about her grandmother working her way into the Big House with Winnie. Only she wasn't named Winnie then. She was named Winona, for the Indian, her father. Her grandmother was named Betty by the white people and she came over from Africa with a different name altogether. Her father was a chief.

So she talked on and on knowing, life being the way it was, that there would never be anyone else to tell the child those stories. Her body was weakening, she felt it in the coughs that racked her every winter and her mind slipped down, sometimes, on the sorrow of losing her daughter too soon. She told Rose about Benjamin, her father, making her promise never to tell "At least not while I'm alive, Honey." And though she didn't mention her own father except to say, briefly, that he was a white man, she told her daughter about the Indian who had been Winona's father and how he loved Winona's mother enough to become a slave for a little while but how he couldn't stay because people were meant to be free.

She told Rose about her great-great-grandfather, a chief in Africa, who escaped the captivity that killed his wife and took his daughter to America. She told her all the stories that the women before her had remembered and passed along. And she told her she was not to think of herself as a slave because she was born to be free.

Rose, never having experienced slavery, was not sure what her mother meant though she could see she meant it terribly. She would hug her mother and remind her of whatever plans they had made for the next day. And sometimes she would ask about her father. Was he really Aunt Maxine's brother? Would he come to see them soon? Did that mean she and Emily were cousins? Wasn't that nice because that was family, wasn't it? They were all family.

Cat's silence would finally bring the child's questions to a stop. "Why are you sad, Mama?" the little girl would ask. "Are you sad my father isn't here? He'll come back, Mama. Can I ask Aunt Maxine when he'll come back? Maybe she'll know."

"You are never to mention him to your Aunt Maxine. You remember what I told you? It would make her very angry. She might even want us to leave."

When Rose was past five years old, that answer was not enough. "Why, Mama?" she asked. "Why would Aunt Maxine be mad? Why isn't my father here like Emily's father? Doesn't he like me?"

"White people don't mix with colored people, Honey. At least, when they do, they don't like to talk about it."

"But Aunt Maxine says you're her best friend. She's always saying that."

"We were raised almost that way," said Cat. I mean, it must have seemed that way to her. I spent most of my time with her in the house—like you do with Emily. But I always went back to the cabin at night with my own people and Maxine always went upstairs to her pretty room. She didn't come down to the cabin much."

"But we have a pretty room here, Mama. And we live in the house."

"It's not the same thing," said Cat firmly. "We're colored and she's white and I know she doesn't forget it any more than I do."

There was a long silence. Rose chewed on her pigtail. "Emily doesn't care about colors," the little girl said at last. "I know she doesn't."

"You wait 'till she's older," said Cat. Then, seeing the hurt on the small face, she tried to take the words back. "Well honey, you're hardly even colored. You're about as white as she is."

"Do you think my father would like me?" the child asked. But when her mother started coughing and then crying, she was sorry about the question. She wouldn't ask any more. It was a mystery, like in the books. Someday she would find out for herself.

Benjamin had been to visit already, Cat knew. She had suspected before she was told, hearing whispers and noting the worried looks Maxine flashed when she thought Cat wasn't watching. But Cat was always watching. In the end, Maxine sent her to Dr. Connie's house with Rose, where they stayed for a week.

Dr. Connie had been a frequent visitor at the Wests' and had often invited Cat and Rose to her own home but this was the first time she had gone. Sitting in front of the fire that first evening, a comfortable litter of books all around and Luke and Rose engrossed with a plate of cookies in the kitchen, Cat had regretted her caution.

"It's like being home," she sighed, stretching out her hands to the fire. "Except I never had a home like this."

"You have a nice library there where you live," said Dr. Connie, pouring tea.

"It's not home," said Cat. "I mean–it's not my home. It'll never be my home." A trace of bitterness edged her voice. "People like me aren't meant to have our own homes. I'm still a slave, Dr. Connie, for all I'm being treated like a free woman. Nobody's mentioned signing manumission papers and Lord knows I wouldn't dare to bring it up. If anyone was ever dependent on charity, it's me. And, Rose."

A cough racked her body again. Really, the girl was quite wasted, Dr. Connie thought, watching her carefully. She didn't like the sound of that cough. But all her herbs and poultices had not been able to get rid of it. She was afraid, suddenly. What would become of the child? She didn't think Maxine would turn her out but one never knew with white people. She might well turn her into a maid. She might keep her a slave. Rose might be happier that way. More secure.

Lord, Lord, if those people could only see what they were doing. But that would take a revolution, for sure. A bloody one, no doubt. And even after that–how many generations before the whites could imagine colored people as their equals? Not in their children's lifetimes, she was sure. Nor their grandchildren or great-grandchildren, either, probably. The lie that made slavery possible had permeated the very fabric of the new American society. The lie that God did not love all His children equally. She was not at all certain the country would ever be free of it.

Not that Dr. Connie wanted to leave the country. Though her parents came from the West Indies, escaping in the tail of a pirate ship where her father had made himself exceedingly useful, she had been born here, as much a part of the United States as anyone and more a part than the immigrants arriving daily from Europe and the British Isles. Among the freedmen in New York there was beginning to be a lot of talk about going back to Africa. White people were behind it, she was sure, though it was cloaked to look like a favor. Send the free blacks back to Africa where they belonged. Have them be missionaries, taking the virtues of Christian civilization and modern agriculture back to their own people. *Get rid of them*, that's what they meant. She didn't think many of her people would want to go back to Africa when it came right down to it. They'd heard enough stories of savagery there to believe them, whether or not the stories were true. Even among slaves, a known evil was less frightening than an unknown. Even the whip was not as bad as the thought of being eaten by a wild black man in the jungle.

Get rid of all the free men and women and then the only blacks in this country would be slaves and the agitation for freedom would end. Without freedmen there would be no education for the Negroes. No periodicals from a colored point of view. No artists or actors of color. Nothing to aim for in the land of their birth. No agitators in the churches and the courts, keeping alive the notion that God loved all His children just the same and that the Declaration of Independence meant what it said about "all men are created equal." Without freedmen, there could be little hope of ending slavery.

As it was, there in New York, the process of emancipation had already begun. In 1799, a law was passed declaring that everyone born in the state after July 4th of that year would be given freedom someday—males at the age of twenty-eight and females at the age of twenty-five. A few more years and slavery would be outlawed altogether in the state. It was worth waiting for. It was a base from which to fight for freedom for their brothers and sisters in the South. She knew Luke would be participating in that fight. She was raising him to be responsible.

"A person has to do what they can," she murmured, putting her arm around Cat, smoothing back the curls. "You've done what you can for Rose and if it's meant accepting charity, well girl, it's not as if you don't deserve it. That child of yours is Maxine's own brother's daughter, after all."

Cat sat very still. "How did you know?"

"Maxine told me, before she was born. And I could always see the family resemblance."

"But you never said anything?"

"Honey, I figured if you wanted to talk about it, you would. But it seems I have to be the one to bring it up. Is it really that big a secret?"

"I promised I'd never see him again. Not that he wants to see me, I guess. I don't know." She buried her head on the older woman's shoulder. Oh, Dr. Connie, it hurts so much. It still hurts so much."

"Most things a person gets over," said Dr. Connie, still stroking her hair. "But some things–"

She had a feeling Cat had not cried like that in a long, long time. Perhaps never.

The girl took to her bed not long after that. She was only twenty-six but the constant coughing had aged her, drawn her skin tight along her cheekbones and wasted her arms and legs to sticks. There was blood in her cough now, flecking her lips and reddening the cloths she kept by the bed. Her eyes glittered with fever most of the time and she moved with difficulty to the chamber pot Rose emptied for her. The maid brought in her meals, though after a few rebuffs, she didn't linger to talk. Woman thought entirely too much of herself, the maid muttered, as Cat turned her back on her once again. Acted like she thought she was white.

Connie Cassals came every day that summer of 1817, doing what she could, but feeling, as she sat by the sick woman's bed and listened to the raspy breathing, that the end was not far off. She suggested Rose sleep in another room. There might be infection, she explained to Maxine, who nodded and spoke to Clarence about it. The plans did not appeal to him but in the end Rose was moved into Emily's room behind the nursery.

"Dr. Connie, you'll look after Rose for me, won't you?" Cat asked her one day. She was finding it hard to talk. The older woman leaned forward, reassuring her. Cat pressed on, "I don't want her to forget where she comes from. She's liable to forget, growing up with Emily, and then where will she be when she's grown and finds out her–her limitations"

She paused, gasping for breath. "I want her to be proud, Dr. Connie. Proud of everything she is. She's not white but she's not black either and she's being raised to be free. She's going to be somebody special, Dr. Connie, but don't let her forget her mother's people."

"I'll see to it," said the midwife. "Luke and I will see to that part of her education, don't you worry, Honey. We love her like she was our own. Now you just rest."

Cat died in her sleep that night, blood running from her mouth in a dam-breaking stream. The maid, finding her, came stiffly into the nursery to inform Maxine who uttered a little cry and ran out of the room. The maid wouldn't let the children follow.

It was a small funeral. Only Dr. Connie and Luke stood with Clarence, Maxine, the servants, and the Anglican priest as the casket was lowered into the grave. The girls were not allowed to come. It was too much for them, Maxine insisted. It was almost too much for her. She felt vaguely responsible, though God knows she'd done all she could. And she'd take care of Rose, she promised the dead woman. She'd take care of Rose as if she were her own child.

Clarence did not disagree when she told him her plans later that evening. She was a bright little girl, after all. Not a bad companion for Emily and since it seemed there might not be any more children. . . .

He sighed and put an arm around his wife and kissed her. "It won't be the easiest thing in the world," he said. "She's not one of us when it comes down to it and she's got to find out sooner or later." He paused at the look on his wife's face. "But as long as it makes you happy, you can have her. Just don't fill her head with fanciful notions, Maxine. Sooner or later, she'll have to know her place."

"Her place is right here with us," said Maxine.

Clarence sighed again and said nothing. His mother was not going to like the arrangement. He wasn't sure his father-in-law would either. On the other hand, they could always stay away.

The next day Maxine gave Rose her mother's Bible. It was a present from her grandmother, she explained, though she didn't say which grandmother. She gave it to your mother before you were born. Along with that yellow rose that's pressed in there. You were named after that rose, you know."

Wordless, the little girl examined the Bible. It was very nice with gilt edges and gold print on the cover. She had seen it all her life but her mother did not allow her to touch it. She turned it over in her hands, opened it to the first page. There was a spidery handwriting on it. She couldn't make it out though she'd already learned her alphabet.

"Read it, please," she said, handing it to her aunt.

Maxine took the book. "With best wishes to Catherine and her child from Kathleen," she read.

It did not sound like a grandmother, thought Rose. But that must be part of the mystery. She was not to ask about it. She knew that already.

"I'm very sorry about your mother," said Emily, a little stiffly, reciting words she had painstakingly practiced. "We will miss her but now my mommy will be your mommy, too."

Rose was not sure how that would work–Aunt Maxine would certainly not curl up in bed with her at night and tell her stories–but she hugged her friend anyway. "We'll stay together," she promised.

And together they remained through their growing up years, sharing everything from clothes to tutors. Though Emily was two years older, Rose caught up and then outgrew her, both physically and intellectually. Aware of her parentage, however welcome Maxine made her feel, Rose developed a fiercely competitive spirit, needing always to prove herself. Emily, on the other hand, recognizing intuitively that Rose would never have the advantages with which she was blessed, would not compete at all. As she grew older, she seemed to enjoy losing to Rose.

"You've done it again!" she would say whether they were comparing test scores or memorization skills, Rose's checkmate in their most recent chess game or the reflections in the mirror, studying each other preening in new dresses. "I just don't know how you manage to know so much, play so well, look so nice."

Rose would laugh and give her a hug. Winning made generosity easy. "You just don't concentrate," she would tell her friend. And once, finding honesty easy with Emily, she added; "You just don't want to win as badly as I do. You don't have anything to make up for."

"What do you have to make up for?" asked Emily, genuinely puzzled. At fifteen she was a pretty girl though not strikingly beautiful, intelligent without being particularly thoughtful, outgoing with no concept of rejection. The world had been kind to her. She had an attractive and compassionate mother, a rich and protective father, a lovely home and a good education. As far as she was concerned, all of that belonged to Rose as well. Except that Rose was more beautiful, more intelligent, and as quick with a quip or an argument as anyone she'd ever heard speak at her parents' table.

"For being a bastard," said Rose, rather enjoying the look of shock on Emily's face.

"What's a bastard?" asked Emily, "I mean, I know it's a bad word but what does it mean, exactly?"

"It means your parents weren't married when you were born or that you don't know who your father is."

"Oh," said Emily in a small voice.

"Bastard" was a word Rose had learned from Luke who explained that many colored children belonged to that category, given the fact that, being possessions themselves, they were not allowed to own even their own husbands or wives. True to her word, Dr. Connie had stayed in touch with Rose, coming to get her almost every Sunday afternoon. She always invited Emily as well but after the West child turned twelve, her parents preferred she accompany them on their Sunday afternoon social visits.

Those visits were the single facet of Emily's life in which Rose could not participate. On that one point Clarence was adamant and Maxine finally gave up pleading. "It will only cause more talk," he tried to explain to her, still finding pleasure in her smiles and hating to be the cause of her gloom. "People will wonder about her origins, Maxine, and what are you going to tell them?"

"That she's my niece, of course."

"And who is her mother, my dear?" said Clarence, sighing as Maxine fell silent. "You see, dear, it's better not to have the subject brought up at all."

The question rarely came up any more in the Wests' own home. Rose joined the family at the table and was welcome to meet whatever guests arrived for dinner or tea as long as Emily was invited to put in an appearance. The slave's daughter was, to anyone impolite enough to ask Clarence, "an orphan from Maxine's side of the family. We couldn't abandon her, poor thing."

Maxine, hating the lie while her brother was alive and well and recently promoted to first mate on one of Captain Morgan's schooners, grew skilled at simply ignoring the question. Pressed, she would volunteer that the child's mother, "a dear friend," had died and "we're raising her like our own. A beautiful girl, don't you agree? And so intelligent."

The guest would agree. That fact, at least, was self-evident.

Luke was seeing it, too, thought Dr. Connie, watching her tall, dark son take notice as Rose's body filled out and her face lost its babyfat, showing off high cheekbones and a fine jaw that accentuated the wide, tilted eyes and rosebud mouth. Luke started checking his appearance, greasing down his hair and getting into his suit before those Sunday afternoons together. Dr. Connie, unseen, would shake her head sadly. She hoped Rose would continue to appreciate what a fine-looking young man her son had become but she doubted it. She was too much a part of the white world. Her standards were their standards. However much she liked Luke now, Dr. Connie's son would soon become a "colored man" to Rose and she knew the child well enough to know her sights would be set much higher than that.

Luke, his amber eyes full on Rose's face, never noticed the pain in his mother's. He would take up the conversation with Rose wherever they had left off the week before. He informed her on the state of the union or, more particularly, the state of the union's slaves. The abolitionist movement, in decline since the Revolutionary War, was gaining a voice again in the northernmost states by the early 1820s; new states were coming into the union and each one's slave status was being bitterly contested. With Pennsylvania, all New England, New Jersey, and, finally New York granting constitutional freedom to slaves born within state borders, the ideological split widened in Congress. Politicians thought it best to maintain a balance of slave and free territories.

Freedom was one thing; socializing and voting were quite another. The revolutionary ideals which had prompted the freeing of slaves in regions where they were, after all, not much needed, were fading a mere twenty years later as the growing numbers of black freedmen seemed to strengthen white racism. Dark-skinned men and women who had mixed freely for a little while, found themselves relegated to the back of the church or meeting hall and ostracized from Anglo gatherings. Schools, courtrooms and voting booths which had been open to them were suddenly closed. Slave catchers from the south were allowed free rein to track their quarry into "free" states; and, once accused of being runaways, Negroes had little recourse for proving their emancipation under special court procedures which allowed no witnesses to speak on their behalf.

All these things Luke explained to Rose with a passion she could not share. Even when Luke informed her, that on July 4th, 1827, six months after her sixteenth birthday, she would be free by a New York law which applied to all slaves born in the state, it meant nothing to her. Had she not always been free? All she knew of slavery were dim memories of stories her mother had told her and the masters her mother described seemed kind enough gentlemen, if a trifle misguided. Nothing at all like the stories of whips and chains, burnings, hangings, and mutilations that Luke would sometimes describe to her. Really, it all made her most uncomfortable.

So did the way Luke looked at her more and more often. He seemed to see not just her face and body but her very soul. It was almost a trespass it was so personal. His eyes even followed her home; alone in bed their amber light still haunted her.

Most uncomfortable, really. And yet compelling.

"You like him, don't you?" Emily asked as Rose fussed over her hair one Sunday after church, getting ready for Dr. Connie's imminent appearance.

"Who?" asked Rose though she knew precisely.

"Luke, of course. You can't fool me, Rose. I've seen the way you glow when you come home from Dr. Connie's. And I know it's not on account of Dr. Connie."

"That's ridiculous," said Rose, deciding to leave her hair alone. This wet weather made it curl so! Usually she pulled it back tightly but Luke liked the curls; he would even tease them loose from her bun sometimes, touching her head with a long, almost brotherly finger. Almost. "It won't work, you know," said Emily.

"I don't know what you're talking about," said Rose, deciding she should change her dress. Luke had commented on the blue poplin last time she had worn it. The lace at the bodice was a nice touch. Concealing and revealing at the same time.

Emily was nothing if not persistent. "Luke. I mean it won't work out for you and Luke. He's too black. And you're too white. It's fine when you're just friends but when you talk about getting married. . . ."

"Did I say a word about getting married? Have I even thought about getting married? Now you listen to me, Miss Priss. Just because you'll be eighteen this fall and can't think of anything besides getting married doesn't mean I feel the same way. I'm still fifteen, remember? And Luke is just a friend. That's all." She decided not to change clothes after all. No point in making a show of herself for Luke.

Emily nodded. "I'm sure he's a very good friend," she said. "And I know you learn a great deal from him. He's very intelligent and advanced, I'm sure." She paused, studying both their reflections in the large mirror they shared. "It's just—well, he's a colored man, of course, and you're—well, you can do better than that."

Rose felt rare anger rising. She controlled it with an effort. One did not yell in the West home. But her face was flushed and her fists clenched as she faced her friend. "I happen to be colored, remember? Do you think you can do better than me?"

"Oh Rose!" Tears glistened suddenly in the blue eyes that faced her. You know I'll never have a friend closer than you! Why, you're as white as I am. Your father is my own uncle, whether he comes to see you or not. And your mother, she was—she was like a member of Mother's family, wasn't she?"

The doorbell sounded. "That will be Dr. Connie," said Rose, turning to go. She did not invite Emily. Not that Emily would have come. She would be going out to visit her fancy friends in their fancy houses as usual. Going to places where Rose would not be welcome. Would never be welcome.

Even so, Rose was careful not to slam the door as she went out.

It was not a good day for Luke to share his wonderful news. He had been accepted at Bowden college in Maine, the first college to accept Negro students. Luke would be one of only two at the school. She tried to share his delight but it was difficult. He was going away! What would she do without him? Who could she talk to? Who else would ever understand?

No doubt it was better this way. "Sharp cut, soon healed." Where had she heard that before? Dr. Connie, probably. She was full of wise sayings. Well, she'd had enough of wisdom.

She was shocked to find tears rising in her eyes. Turning her head quickly, she tried to hide them. It was too late. A long brown finger lifted her chin, turned her face to face him. "I've never seen you cry, Rosie," Luke said gently, wonderingly. " Never. Not since your mama died."

Rose could only stare at him. "Feels like it's you who's dying now," she whispered. "Dying to me, anyway." The tears spilled over.

Dr. Connie, coming into the room, stopped when she saw the girl's head on her son's shoulder, his arms around her, her fingers pressing into his back as if she would hold him forever. She saw the tears shining below the closed eyes and turned to go. But she heard the whispers.

"I love you, Rose. I'll always love you."

"I'll wait for you, Luke. I'll always wait for you."

"I'm going to count on it, Rose. Whatever happens, I'm going to keep counting on that."

I wouldn't if I were you, Son, Dr. Connie thought to herself, sighing deeply as she poured a cup of coffee and sat down at the kitchen table with a book. Might as well let the boy dream while dreams were still real to him. She was long past the dreaming stage herself. And Rose would wake up soon enough to look for other options in the white world she inhabited. But she knew her only son. He was due for a broken heart, sure enough. That boy had no sense at all when it came to dreams. Twenty-one years old, a black man in a white-ruled country, and he still believed dreams could all come true!

Rose, lying sleepless all that night, held no such illusions about black men. To be born black was to be born second class. Her mother had given birth to her in the Big House. It was up to her to earn the right to stay there. And she could do it if she could manage to ignore these feelings Luke aroused in her. She could go on passing. And passing for white was something Luke could never, ever manage.

Moonlight filtered through the lace covered windows onto Emily's face, pillowed on the bed beside her. The pale skin seemed to absorb the light and reflect it, shining and so close to her own. Her cousin was right, thought Rose, swallowing a sigh of regret. She could do much better than Luke. Not that she could ever tell him so.

"She is very old for her age," Dr. Connie told Luke the same night, afraid of the glow in his amber eyes. "She is much too old and smart for her own good. Or yours."

But Luke only looked at her and smiled that dreamy smile. Dr. Connie sighed and went off to bed. That night for the first time in many years she thought about the man who had fathered her son before he was killed in a fight on the docks. He was a golden man, the son of a southern planter who had set him free for reasons of his own and she had loved him so much that it seemed pointless, after him, to even imagine another man in her bed. And she had vowed to the infant he left behind that she would never teach him fear. But perhaps, she thought as she stared out through her little window at the distant moon, she should have made him more aware of the differences.

Rose didn't come the next week, sending a messenger on Saturday to let Dr. Connie know she would be unable to visit the following afternoon. She didn't offer an excuse. She had been honest with Dr. Connie for so long she couldn't break the habit, even when she wanted to. On the other hand, she couldn't face Luke again so soon after feeling his arms around her. She might break down again. Her vow to wait for him had frightened her and what if he asked her again? It could never work. There had to be someone else for her. Someone just right. Someone white.

She was prepared when she returned to Dr. Connie's, two weeks later. She avoided Luke's eyes and concentrated on his lips, his hair, his skin tone. Too thick. Too kinky. Too dark. She sat stiffly in a chair across the room and spoke of the weather," so hot for this time of year," and the Wests, "so much company! Uncle Clarence says business is really booming and he keeps bringing people home to discuss new shipping routes. Aunt Maxine has been so busy entertaining. And Emily and I must help her, of course." She fanned herself, avoiding Dr. Connie's eyes as well.

Looking puzzled, Luke tried to turn the conversation. Rose stopped him immediately. "Oh, please, Luke, let's not discuss the Negro issue any more. It really doesn't affect me, you know, and with you going off to college with all the white boys—" She tried a smile. It felt as stiff as bricks. "Perhaps it won't concern you quite as much soon." She tried again, seeing confusion gather on his face. He had been her friend, after all. "I mean, you'll have to get along, won't you?"

Luke's voice was rough. "I have gotten along well enough with you for all these years. And I guess you're white enough."

"Now Luke," Dr. Connie began. That is hardly—"

Rose stood up, gathering her skirts about her. " I really have to go," she said, addressing the older woman. "Aunt Maxine expressly asked if I could be there tonight for dinner."

Luke looked quite stunned. Dr. Connie got to her feet. "You'll be back next week? I'll come for you. . . ."

"I'll send word if I can't," Rose said smoothly. "No, please don't trouble yourself to see me home. I asked Jim to pick me up at four and I do believe I see him coming."

"She had it all planned," Luke said thickly as the door closed behind her. "All those years together and she walks out, just like that." His laugh was coarse, cynical. "So much for true love."

Rose, lingering outside the door, hand still on the knob, fighting the urge to turn back, overheard. Her hand dropped to her side as the unaccustomed tears burned again in her eyes.

All those years. She mustn't think about all those years. She had her life ahead of her and she was not—absolutely not—going to live it as a colored woman.

That night, she started a letter to her father. The salutation alone took nearly an hour. *Dear Mr. Sturn?* No. *Benjamin?* No. No. *Lieutenant Benjamin Sturn?* No. *Dear Father.* Oh no!

In the end, she used no salutation at all, opting for simple honesty: "I have been told you are my father and, as you must know, your sister has raised me as her own child since my mother, Catherine, died ten years ago. Emily is my best friend and constant companion."

She would not mention that Emily was now her only friend.

"It is my earnest desire that we will meet soon. I am half-past fifteen years now, well grown and educated in a manner to please the most discriminating tastes. Although I understand a little of the complications of my—"

Birth? Parentage? Illegitimacy? No. No. No! "background, I trust you will not hold against me those things over which I have no control."

She hated that last part but it had to be said.

New paragraph: "Aunt Maxine tells me you are now first mate to Captain James Morgan. I trust that on your next docking in New York, I shall have the great pleasure of making your acquaintance.

"Affectionately,

"Your daughter, Rose."

Half satisfied, she sealed and addressed it, "Care of Captain James Morgan." Uncle Clarence had told her that the ship's captains kept mailboxes at the freight office by the docks. She would have Jim take it down. No one else needed to know.

It was the first secret she had ever kept from Emily but she had the feeling it would not be the last.

Emily came out that winter in a flurry of ball gowns and tail-coated escorts. Rose was not invited to the balls despite her cousin's pleas. The girl even wept for her but Rose's eyes remained dry as she resolutely buttoned Emily's gowns, touched rouge to her pale cheeks, and told her how beautiful she looked. Holding her own head high, Rose avoided Aunt Maxine's pitying looks and Uncle Clarence's measuring glances. She was not quite sixteen, after all. Her day would come. Her own father would come back to claim her. And then they'd see.

But Benjamin Sturn did not respond. Two more years went by. Emily rejected all her suitors. Rose saw no one outside the house except Dr. Connie and her no more than once or twice a month. She had not seen Luke since the day she'd left him so abruptly. He had gone to Maine that week, explaining to his mother that he would need to find work before school started so he could meet his own expenses and not be a burden to her. His letters arrived faithfully every two weeks, one to his mother and one to Rose. Rose rarely answered. Thoughts of Luke enhanced her sense of alienation.

There would be no debut for Rose. Approaching her eighteenth birthday, she understood that well enough though she found it hard to accept. So she was pleasantly surprised when Emily burst into their room one afternoon, interrupting her reading to snatch her right out of the chair and waltz her around the room.

"We're having a ball!" Emily exclaimed. "Right here! For your birthday! Oh darling, it will be so fine. Mother is getting caterers and flowers and everything! All for you! Isn't it wonderful!" She pretended to pout. "The very first ball in our house and she's doing it for you, not me." The smile that replaced the pout nearly split her face in two as she led Rose, dancing, round and round the room. They were both breathless when they stopped.

"A dance? On my birthday? Here!"

"Oh, yes. We'll have to get a dress made for you. White of course. And we'll have to practice dancing. Did you and Luke ever? . . . "

"Dancing was hardly Luke's style," said Rose, interrupting her. "He was, if you remember, a very serious person."

"And so are you, Rose, but you must stop immediately. At least for a while, until some nice young man has been smitten by your beauty and made you his bride. Then you can let your brains show, but not before, mind you. Men are easily intimidated, my mother says."

Rose would not have known. Uncle Clarence was certainly not intimidated by her nor were any of the men who occasionally spoke to her at church. Luke had not been intimidated by her either. In fact, he loved it when she "let her brains show." But she was not going to think about Luke anymore.

Preparations for the party took most of the Christmas season though the guest list was actually quite short, as Maxine explained to both young women. They couldn't really invite their New York social set since—well, since Rose was not known to them. But there would be special guests arriving from out of town, very nice people, diplomats and officers. No. She would not say who. It was all to be a surprise, and besides, the girls hadn't met any of them before.

Rose's dress, made up in satin and velvet, was a dream come true. The neckline showed the beginning of her curves, enhanced by lace. Her waist, buttoned with pearls above the bustle and bows of her skirt, looked barely a handspan around. She practiced curtsies in front of the mirror, whirled prettily on Emily's arm and even, once, on Clarence's when Maxine talked him into giving his foster child the experience of dancing with a real man in preparation for the big day.

It was nothing to get worked up over, Rose told herself firmly, as Emily pulled her stays in so tightly she could hardly breathe, then slipped the dress over her head and began the lengthy buttoning process. Her hair was brushed high by Maxine's hairdresser, then teased into rolls, with curls pulled out to fall beautifully around her face and down her slender neck. A touch of color on her cheeks. Really, she looked quite pale.

"You're absolutely beautiful!" said Emily, standing back to beam at her before running downstairs to join her mother who was greeting the arriving guests. Rose stood still, staring in the mirror. The unaccustomed color made her eyes look bluer.

"She walks in beauty as the night. . . . " said Clarence, finding poetry unexpectedly on his lips as he came to the door. He had not thought of that poem since college. It must have been written for someone like this girl, suddenly a stranger, that he had promised his wife he would escort down the stairs. "Poor child," Maxine had said, "she doesn't know a soul around here besides us and she must have an arm to lean on, Clarence. You won't mind, will you Dear?"

Not at all. Not at all. Bowing to the girl in white, he offered her his arm. He had never seen Rose looking shy before. Well, well! Modesty became her. Not that her dress was exactly modest. Nothing like the clothes Maxine wore though Emily had flaunted herself a bit at her debutante balls. It was a woman's way, he supposed. He smiled, remembering that first sight of Maxine's ankles more than twenty years ago. And he still loved the woman. He hoped his daughter, and Rose as well, would find as much happiness in marriage as he had. Not that he had great expectations for Rose. But one never knew. Perhaps the Mexicans would not mind her parentage so much. And they were quite respectable, some of them. At least the ones he had invited.

In the knot of faces looking up as she descended the stairs, Rose saw only Captain Morgan, the one face she recognized from earlier visits. He was a tall man, silver-haired with a narrow face and a ruddy, wind-touched complexion. The man beside him, broad-shouldered, blond and dimpled, looked vaguely familiar, though she couldn't place him. She was pleased by the awe in both pairs of eyes watching her. Reassured, she looked around. There were over a dozen men, she noted, and the only women present were Maxine, Emily and herself. At least there would be no lack of dancing partners. She wished the thought of Dr. Connie had not crossed her mind. And Luke. If he could see her now! No, she was not going to think of Luke any more. Her husband might be waiting down there. She shot a questioning glance at Clarence. Who were those strangers, anyway?

"Texians," Clarence murmured in her ear. "And a few from further south in Mexico City. Fine people. We've been doing a lot of business with them." He smiled at her. "I'll introduce you to everyone."

It occurred to Clarence suddenly that he had no last name to place with Rose. None had ever been given, as far as he knew, though he supposed there must be one written somewhere. What was it? Not Sturn, surely. He couldn't say Sturn with Benjamin standing right there beside Captain Morgan. West, then? His mother would be furious but of course she wasn't here.

Captain Morgan had stepped up to the bottom of the stairway. Clarence turned her toward him. "Captain James Morgan. You remember Rose, perhaps, from your earlier visits?"

Morgan bowed deeply. "With great pleasure. And even greater–" his eyes lingered briefly on her bosom–" to see you now."

Clarence guided her away and around the room, performing a blur of introductions, including several in Spanish. She would curtsy. They would bow. Clarence would move her along. They paused a moment longer in front of a tall gentleman with a small moustache and an exceedingly kind, round face. "Mr. Lorenzo de Zavala," said Clarence. "Formerly a governor of Mexico, among many other honors, and currently an entrepreneur seeking settlers for an enormous tract of land between the Nueces and the Rio Grande." He smiled conspiratorially at the Mexican. "Land that may someday be part of these United States."

Rose noted that the man did not look pleased though he bowed gracefully enough. "By God's will," he murmured, "stranger things have occurred." He raised Rose's hand to his lips. "My pleasure, Miss West." He looked at Clarence. "Your daughter, Sir?"

"Ah, no. A relative of my wife. That is my daughter over there." He gestured towards Emily who was circulating with her mother among the guests. The string ensemble had struck up a waltz. Rose hoped the introductions were almost done. She wanted to dance.

"Another lovely lady," said de Zavala, studying Emily for a thoughtful moment. "You are blessed, Mr. West."

"Indeed," Clarence said, drawing a deep breath for the moment he had dreaded. There was one more person Rose must meet. The blond, broad-shouldered man was standing a little apart, arms folded, watching them.

"May I present Rose West," said Clarence. "Mr. Benjamin Sturn."

Rose gasped, her gloved hand fluttering to her mouth. Unperturbed, Benjamin bowed. "My pleasure," he said.

"You are–" She caught herself in time. Curtsied. "Delighted I'm sure, Mr. Sturn."

Well, well, thought Clarence. She handled that better than I expected. "I understand congratulations are in order, Mr. Sturn. Captain Morgan tells me you have your own ship now. *The Glacier*, is it?"

"I'll be sailing her out this week," said Benjamin, a note of pride in his voice. "She's a lovely schooner, I must say. If I have a crew to match we'll be in Galveston by the end of the month."

"Galveston?" said Rose, trying not to stare at this stranger. Her father.

"Off the coast of Texas," the man explained. "Your, ah, Mr. West has been negotiating a great deal of trade with the Mexican government. There are a number of Americans moving into the northern part of the country. What they call Texas. They are being encouraged by sizeable land grants. The Spanish are anxious to find settlers. Good for the economy, you know." He smiled at her suddenly, flashing dimples. He looked a little like Maxine's mother, she realized. That was why she thought she recognized him at first glimpse. "Shall we dance?" he asked, taking her hand.

What dreams she allowed herself as they floated off together! What a superb dancer he was! She could hardly feel her own feet as they moved in step around the room. Surely they were meant to be together now. Her own father at last! What an incredible birthday present! Perhaps he would take her with him when he left later on in the week. Texas. Why not Texas? She could make friends there, surely. Or, perhaps she could simply sail with him for a while. Perhaps there was a job for her on board. She was willing to earn her way. She would not take advantage.

"You've grown into a lovely lady, Rose," the man said then, teasing. "Or must I call you Miss West?"

"You may call me anything you like," she responded quickly. "And may I call you fa–"

She stumbled as his feet stopped, dead on the dance floor. "No!" he said shortly. "No, you may not." He remembered his manners then, and bowed. "You dance beautifully, my dear. You must indulge me again at a later date."

Before she realized what was happening, he was gone, leaving her standing alone in the middle of the room. Conversations eddied and swirled around her. She noticed Emily dancing with Mr. de Zavala, looking flushed and happy. And there was Maxine smiling up into her husband's eyes as he led her through intricate steps. But her father was nowhere in sight. How could he disappear so quickly! Her world, so full and free but a moment before, lay empty and leaden around her. It would have been better never to have met him at all than to have him desert her so quickly. She felt more alone after meeting him than before. At least in her dreams he had loved her like a father.

"May I have this dance, Miss Rose," said Captain Morgan, reaching for her hand.

Numbly, she followed him through the steps.

6

Rose visited Dr. Connie the next day, unable to bear the company at home. Benjamin had not reappeared and a certain set of Maxine's lips warned her not to ask about him. Emily, careful to say nothing offensive, cast sad, sidelong glances in her direction when she thought Rose did not see. And Clarence, who had smiled at her so fondly the night before was stiff and silent the next morning. Folding the beautiful white dress, Rose laid it away with a barely bitter smile. So much for dreams coming true.

So much for reunions.

So much for thinking of herself as white.

It was her first visit to Dr. Connie in several months but the pleasure on the black woman's face held no hint of reproof. "I was just thinking of you, child! Do get in out of the cold. Got a nice fire going. You just give me your wrap, now, and sit down. I'll get us some tea."

Silent, Rose stretched out her hands to the fire and relaxed slowly. The small sounds of kitchen comforts—the crackle of wood in the big iron stove, the tin lid popping on the tea can, the splash of water, the tinkle of china—eased the knotted places in her skull and leveled the upheavals on her internal landscape. If anyone could make everything all right, surely Dr. Connie was that anyone.

"Face looks like you lost your best friend," the woman said, reappearing with a tray of tea and cookies. Now you just take your time and sip your tea, but you'd best get ready to tell the doctor what your trouble is because trouble sure is showing in your face."

"I met my father last night." Rose wanted to say more but the words were stuck in her throat. Dr. Connie raised an eyebrow. She looked so like Luke when she did that, thought Rose, feeling a sudden clutch in her middle. Luke! How long since she'd even thought about Luke. Been so busy thinking about how white she was. And where had that gotten her?

Dr. Connie remained neutral. "And how was it?"

Rose's mouth twisted. "Everything I dreamed of for the first half hour," she said. "We danced and he said I'd grown into a lovely lady. He told me about

Texas and, oh, it was lovely! Then. Well, that was all there was to it. Then he left."

The women sat in silence for a while. Rose watched the fire. Dr. Connie watched Rose.

"Any idea why?"

"I made a big mistake, Dr. Connie. I started to ask if I could call him Father. Didn't even get the word out of my mouth before he was bowing and backing away. The party went on until midnight and he never came back. It was a little celebration the Wests had planned for my eighteenth birthday. Perhaps Aunt Maxine felt badly that I couldn't join any of the coming-out do's for Emily. Anyway, they invited that Colonel Morgan, a business associate of Uncle Clarence. He's a shipowner, doing a lot of trade with Mexico, and he brought some Texians and a few Mexican diplomats—people who wouldn't know New York society very well, if you know what I mean. People who wouldn't be insulted by an introduction to the daughter of a slave. People who wouldn't know any better than to come to my party."

"Reckon your father would have known better than to come if he'd wanted to stay away. Must have had considerable curiosity to show up."

"Curiosity! Yes, that's the word, all right. Curiosity. Like you'd have about some peculiar animal or a dog who could do tricks."

A blast of air rattled the windows. It looked like snow, outside. Rose did not ever want to go outside again. If she could only hide away in Dr. Connie's living room. Wait for Luke to come home.

No, that would not work either. She had already decided not to take her life in that direction. But so much of what she'd decided for herself was not, she was discovering, within her control at all. One could firmly determine to be somebody special but if one had already been classified and labeled as a lower level person, well then, what difference did it make what decisions one made?

"So you feel cheated of your birthright?" Dr. Connie was watching her closely. "You had these dreams—recognition, reunion, restoration to your place as your father's only child—and all those dreams were shattered in one evening?"

The lump in her throat was expanding. Rose nodded mutely. "That's about it," she finally whispered.

Dr. Connie put an arm around her and the lump melted into a flood of tears. Huddled against that shoulder, Rose cried for a long, long time. The fire crackled as drops of sleet made their way down the chimney. The panes rattled against the steady wind outside. Sleet turned to snow, white lashing the windows and piling up against the door. The sounds of horses, wagons and people on the street faded into the white fury of the storm. Rose raised her head from the motherly breast and wiped her eyes. Dr. Connie moved, put more wood on the fire, poured another cup of tea.

"We go on, dear. We just go on."

It would be impossible for her to get home, Dr. Connie pointed out. Two miles in such a blizzard, she could easily lose her way. And those thin slippers Rose had put on so hurriedly when she almost ran from the house that morning would never do for the walk home. "Not going to have the child dying of the pneumonia that took her mother in the end, no Ma'am,' she said firmly. You might as well make yourself comfortable because you're going to stay right here until this is over." She hesitated. "You told Emily you were coming here?"

Rose nodded. "They won't worry. Not that they would anyway."

"That's hardly fair, Dear. You know Emily loves you. And Maxine, too. I would even say Mr. West regards you fondly."

Rose sniffed.

The sky grew darker. Dr. Connie lit the parlor lamps, put more wood on the fire, and bestirred herself with dinner. The two women ate vegetable soup and cornbread at the round oak table in the kitchen, avoiding painful subjects. How many times Rose had sat at that table with Luke, poring through his books and talking. Always talking! How rich those days seemed suddenly. How did she come to feel so utterly impoverished? Nothing had really changed.

"It's the danger in knowledge," said Dr. Connie as if she'd read her mind. "When you find out something you didn't know before, it completely changes your picture of life. Sometimes it even changes your picture of yourself."

How strange it was, Rose thought. All the things Luke had told her about–the heritage of African-Americans, the injustices to black people, the issues of slavery and freedom–it had all been so academic. A play she watched without participation. And now, in one evening of music, dancing and handsome strangers, she had been thrown on stage, linked with her mother's line in a way she could never deny.

"I've always thought of myself as white," she began, hesitantly, more aware than she had ever been of Dr. Connie's blackness. It filled her vision, overshadowed her world. Odd that she should find it so comforting. She sought the older woman's eyes. Dr. Connie nodded. "I know."

"I mean, no one ever tried to hide what I am, who I come from. I still remember my mother well. But, well, growing up with Emily, sharing everything with her it was easy to forget. To think I would have the same chances. You understand?"

"Not really." Dr. Connie's laugh was dry, "but I do know what you mean."

"I was so blind. I patterned my dreams after Emily's. Marriage to—oh, not the cream of society, perhaps, but some well-enough-to-do young man. White, of course. And then children and a life as a lady. Given my circumstances up to now, what else could I expect?"

If Dr. Connie remembered a whisper from the couch, two years before when a dark face pressed cheek to cheek against the pale one across from her now, she did not mention it. But Rose remembered suddenly and with shame. "I'll wait for you," she had told Luke.

"What should I do?" she whispered. "I have to get away, Dr. Connie."

"Maxine would probably send you off to school if you asked. There are several fine female academies in Boston as well as in New York. Or, even Philadelphia. It would give you time to decide. To work out what you want to be."

"I won't ask for anything more!" Rose's voice was fierce. "I just want to be me. I won't get that sitting around with a lot of pampered white girls practicing to be a lady. And what school would take me as a colored woman? No, that's not the answer. I have to find work, Dr. Connie. I have to learn to make my own way. I can't stay hidden away with people who don't—who know I'm not socially acceptable."

Dr. Connie was practical. "What kind of work can you do?"

"I can sew and embroider. I know a little about herbs—what you've taught me. I can converse about poetry, current events, and artistic endeavors, thanks to Luke. I can play the piano. But there's not much call for paid help in those areas. Perhaps a housekeeper. I know how it's done though I haven't actually worked at it." A smile broke through. "I could practice. I could follow the maid around."

Dr. Connie stood abruptly and rummaged through a stack of letters on a corner table. "I know just the place," she said, pulling out a sheet of parchment and spreading it in front of Rose. "One of my former patients is now the headmistress of Wyman Female Academy in Boston. She wrote me a month ago asking if I knew—" She read from the paper in front of them: "A Christian woman of good bearing and comely appearance with a strong sense of integrity who could manage our boarding house. The job involves overseeing the cleaning and table preparation and making sure our young ladies commit no infractions of the rules." No doubt she has someone older in mind but I'm sure you could do it, Rose." She read on silently, pointed to another line. "The pay is three dollars a week plus room and board and uniforms. That would give you a start, Dear. And you would have time to decide what you want to do next."

Boston! It was far enough. And a job! She had never had a job before. But if Dr. Connie thought she could. . . .

Rose sat up straight. "I'll do it," she said. And she would not rest that night until Dr. Connie had written to Miss Ellen Goodwin, assuring her she had found someone, "imminently suitable, though only eighteen," for the job. Rose added her own note at the bottom of the page, expressing her eagerness to begin and mentioning her long friendship with Dr. Connie. Of her background, she said not a word except for the comment that she was "well accustomed to the proper behavior of young ladies in society," and trusted "that my experience will be of some benefit to your academy which Dr. Connie assures me is a fine one."

"I shall send it this week," Dr. Connie said, as they reviewed their letter one more time. "We should know within the month. Miss Ellen moves quickly and I do believe she has confidence in my judgment on some things. By Easter you may be on your way. It seems she needs someone as soon as possible."

She slept in Luke's bed that night, in the room she could still remember sharing with him on occasional long-ago nights when she was small and she and her mother took over the boy's bed while he slept on a pallet in the corner. Those must have been the times when Benjamin was visiting Maxine, she thought, staring into the dark. Of course! Emily had told her once that Cat had to promise never to see Benjamin again. She'd forgotten all that. Forgotten in her romantic illusion of a father-daughter reunion.

She turned her face to the window where the snow still beat against the panes, pulling the quilts up over her nose in the chilly room. She was over her illusions now. As she snuggled into the pillow, slipping into oblivion, her last thoughts were of Luke. Did he still remember? Was he still waiting? Was she?

"So what about Texas?" Dr. Connie asked her the next morning, frying eggs and bacon while Rose nursed a cup of coffee at the kitchen table. "Did you like the sound of it? Mexico's constitution forbids slavery, I understand. Have you thought of going there someday?"

"Next year, if all goes well, I will be at the Wyman Female Academy," Rose said. "Honestly, Dr. Connie, that's about as far ahead as I can think."

The snow had stopped in the night, the sun came out in the morning, and the white drifts were crystal brilliant as Rose made her way back to the West mansion, double-wrapped in one of Dr. Connie's cloaks and knee-deep in the older woman's rubber boots. She found herself singing that morning, old songs that her mother had sung; songs she thought she had long forgotten. The cold brought color to her cheeks and the brisk air seemed to wash her mind. For the first time in months, or perhaps even years, she felt utterly clean as she pressed the bell and waited for the maid to unlock the door.

"Darling! Where have you been! We were all so worried!" It was Emily, of course, running downstairs to seize her in a tight embrace before she'd even managed to remove the heavy boots. Emily rushed on, not waiting for an answer. "You were going to Dr. Connie's, you told us, but with the snow—oh, I was so afraid you had started for home and gotten lost."

"I feel more as if I've been found," said Rose, loosening her cousin's grip enough to get out of her outdoor garb. "Dr. Connie's been helping plan my future."

"Plan your future?" The blue eyes looked a little frightened. "But what do you need to plan, Rose? Mother and Father—"

"Are not my mother and father, after all. I really must see to myself, Emily. You've all been wonderful to me but now I must learn to take care of myself."

"I can't imagine why you're talking this way, Rose. You will stay right here with me until I'm married, or until you're married and then—"

Rose sat down on the edge of the bed she had shared with Emily since she was six years old. She patted the place beside her. Best to get the talking done immediately. Set her own mind at rest. Determine her own course before the reins were taken from her hands.

It could not be said that the long conversation that followed brought the two young women closer. If anything, it accentuated their separation. Emily cried at the idea of Rose going away to work—and as a housekeeper! "Oh, Rose, you can do better than that."

Rose was dry-eyed. "Indeed? The last night I was in this house, Emily, the man who fathered me turned and walked away the moment I mentioned the connection between us. The man I thought would claim me, disappeared almost as soon as he appeared in my life. In all the time I've lived here, I haven't had a single white friend besides you and your parents. And though you all have treated me so well that I imagined I could be part of your world, I am quite disabused of that notion now. Nothing remains but for me to find my own place. Surely you can see that."

Emily stared at her, spots of color rising to her cheeks. "You want to leave us, then?"

"I have to leave. Truly, Emily. I love you all, but I have to leave. It will be—it may be a month or so before I hear from the Academy but Dr. Connie thinks I'll get the job. Oh, Emily, please be happy for me. I couldn't bear to hurt you when I know you only wish me well."

Maxine was equally distraught, though she understood the necessity better than did Emily.

She assured Rose that "your home will always be here when you want it," and "you mustn't feel you need to leave because you're always welcome." But in the end, Rose felt her aunt was to have the matter taken out of her hands. And as for Clarence, he merely nodded and wished her well.

"Did you enjoy the party?" Emily asked her when they were lying in bed together again that night. There was an unaccustomed shyness in her voice. "I mean, I know it was hard for you with Uncle Benjamin, but. . . ."

"It was a lovely party," Rose fought to keep the coldness from her voice. "And you? Did you have fun?"

"It was nice. Everyone was nice, but oh, Rose, you know who I liked the best? I mean, the very, very best was Mr. de Zavala. You remember him? That kind Mexican in the diplomatic service? So very charming. And a beautiful dancer."

"He's a little old for you, isn't he? Quite middle-aged, I'm sure. And isn't he married? I thought he mentioned children. A son your age, wasn't it? There must be a wife, too, somewhere in Mexico."

"She's rather sickly," Emily murmured. "I mean, of course I'm not interested in him in that way but he is a charming man, Rose. And I do hope we see him again."

"You liked the idea of Texas?"

"It seems a very interesting place. A frontier, but civilized, I think by the Mexicans. They were settled there long before the British settled here."

"In Texas?"

"No, not in Texas, I think. There were only Indians and a few Catholic missions there until recently. It seems to be as much a frontier for Mexico as it is for the United States."

"I do not much like the idea of frontiers," said Rose. "I would think they would be very dirty and uncomfortable."

"But to be somewhere altogether new! To take the hand of Destiny and step into the future!"

Rose laughed. "Is that how Mr. de Zavala talks?"

She could not see her cousin's face but she felt the burn on it as if it were her own. Emily shifted under the heavy quilts, turning to face the moonlight that streamed through the lace curtains against the tightly closed glass. Rose noticed that her chin was up.

"He was quite the nicest man I've ever met. I don't think I shall marry until I meet someone as nice as he."

"You might as well aim for the best," Rose agreed and then the girls fell silent, each lost in her own thoughts.

A murmur from across the pillow brought Rose back from the edge of sleep. "If I go to Texas someday, you shall go with me. It will be an adventure. We can write a book."

Rose did not answer.

The Wyman Female Academy was housed in the former Wyman mansion, a substantial three-story brick house surrounded by gardens and garden walls. Beyond the entry, a wide, tiled hallway opened on one side into a parlor with a dining room and kitchen behind it. On the other side were doorways into three large rooms, each fitted for classes with desks, chairs, tables, bookshelves and chalkboards. The school employed two teachers, one for sciences and math, the other for English, literature and languages. Behind the classrooms, Headmistress Ellen Goodwin lived in a small suite of rooms that opened onto the garden.

Miss Goodwin answered the bell the afternoon that Rose presented herself, clutching her portmanteau in both hands, her trunk beside her on the wide brick porch, and the rattle of the taxi wheels fading to a cobblestoney echo on the street behind the high iron gates. She felt very small, facing the tall carved wooden pair of doors. Very small and very much a stranger. The look on Miss Goodwin's face as she scrutinized her closely did not help at all.

"I wasn't expecting—" she began. "That is—You would be—"

The lady looked quite at a loss, Rose thought. But the face was kindly enough. Grey hair, loosely piled in a bun softened the rather stern wrinkles on the woman's brow and the lines at the corners of her mouth were definitely given to laughter.

"I am Rose West, your new housekeeper. Dr. Connie wrote—"

"Of course. Of course. Come in. Come in."

She led the way past classrooms into her own small parlor. "The front is so formal and we must get to know each other a bit if you are to work with me.

Now just put your bag down and have a seat, please. I'll have Cook make us tea and you must tell me all about yourself. We have a dozen girls here now and we have been without a housekeeper for almost three months. I've been overseeing the maids myself so the dust is not piled up in the corners, but. . . . This is quite a job you are taking on and I am not sure. . . . That is, I expected. . . ."

Again she seemed at a loss for words

"A colored woman?" Rose filled in the sentence.

"Why, yes. When I wrote to Connie, naturally enough I expected. . . ."

"I am colored," Rose said shortly.

"I see."

The silence stretched.

"Well, let me see about that tea. I'll only be a moment." Miss Goodwin disappeared in a swish of good grey woolen skirts.

Rose looked around, noting the still life watercolors grouped here and there on the damask striped wallpaper. A portrait of a jovial gentleman graced the fireplace mantel and a miniature of a very pretty young woman stood near it. Her parents, perhaps. The pictures looked old enough. And there was a definite resemblance. Rose wondered, briefly, why a woman like Miss Goodwin had never married. There was beauty still in the lines of her aging face. An unrequited love, perhaps, or some great tragedy. She remembered, suddenly, that Dr. Connie had mentioned she was "one of my former patients." She wondered. Not that it was any of her business. She was the housekeeper. That was all.

She stood and crossed the room to the tall windows that looked out on the back gardens, bare now, except for half-melted drifts of snow along the bushes and the walls. In a large fountain basin, a cherub poured out an empty bowl. Dead leaves littered the flagstones.

A swish of skirts announced Miss Goodwin's return. Rose returned to her seat and waited as the tea tray was placed on the little table in front of the settee. Miss Goodwin was obviously nonplussed. Not accustomed to pouring tea for the housekeeper, no doubt. Rose found herself smiling. Perhaps she should have worn something a little plainer, something that made the roles more clear. Her own good wool, blue as the sky, would have done nicely in any parlor in New York, she knew. Dear, dear, this was more complicated than she had imagined. She simply wasn't accustomed to being colored.

"One lump or two?" The silver tongs were poised above the sugar bowl.

"One. Thank you." She accepted the cup. Miss Goodwin settled into her chair.

"Now tell me about yourself," she said, brown eyes smiling over the edge of her cup.

Two hours later, Miss Goodwin knew her far better than Rose would have imagined possible, given the slow start of their interview. But Rose was determined to hide nothing, however little she wished to volunteer, and before Miss Goodwin was done she had discovered exactly who her parents were, where and how she had grown up, what and whom she knew, and some measure of her expectations for herself. She had even, probing deeply, uncovered the old connection with Luke. Rose felt quite drained, but Miss Goodwin looked increasingly at ease. She did not, however, look overly pleased.

"So that's it, then? You've grown up white though your mother was a slave and now you want to find your own roots. Your own self. And Dr. Connie felt our little Academy was a good place to start. You have not worked a day in your life and I am expected to train you in a job which will require not only considerable domestic skill but considerable diplomatic skill as well. The housekeeper is responsible not only for making sure the upstairs and downstairs maids keep everything clean and neat but also she must make sure the girls are always where they are supposed to be—in their rooms, their classes, or their meals— and on time. Some of these girls, Rose, are rather, shall we say spoiled? They do not take kindly to being told what they must do, even by their parents and their nannies. You are, obviously, neither, looking both young and white. They might mistake you for one of themselves. Do you think you can handle it?"

Rose's grip on her teacup threatened to break the fragile handle. She set it carefully back on the saucer, looking straight into the piercing sable brown eyes. Neither woman smiled.

"I have to handle it, Miss Goodwin. It's my only chance."

"You're very young to say such a thing," Miss Goodwin replied but the corners of her mouth lifted. Definitely laugh lines. Rose relaxed a bit. Sipped her tea. Waited.

"Very well," the headmistress said at last, rising. "You will sleep on the second floor with the girls. That way you can keep on eye on their comings and goings and be available when they need—oh, a button stitched or such things as young ladies are constantly needing when their mamas are not around. The two maids, Maggie and Janet, have rooms on the third floor, along with Cook and her husband, who does the maintenance and helps in the kitchen. We also keep a groom and a gardener but they have rooms near the stables so you need not be concerned with them. Cook is quite independent. She will not thank you for interfering with her work, and really, she does it quite well. Has been here forever or at least as long as I have been. As for the girls, themselves, they are all on Easter vacation right now, so you will have the opportunity to adjust yourself to our arrangements. You will meet the students soon enough. They're nice girls, if a trifle—well, silly sometimes." She shook her head sadly. "Most of these young ladies really see no need to prepare themselves for anything but marriage. However, we do what we can to see they are well prepared for whatever life may bring. Not all fortunes are kept, you know."

Rose did not know, having never found herself heiress to any fortune but remembering her dreams of sailing away with her father, she knew exactly what it meant to have one's hopes destroyed.

A quick glance from the headmistress left her feeling that her mind, once again, had been read. Really, she must watch herself. Smoothing her face, she picked up her bag and followed the woman upstairs. The groom followed with her trunk.

"You won't mind uniforms, will you?" Miss Goodwin opened the door to a narrow chiffonier. She took out a black dress, cut for someone smaller than Rose, and held it up to the girl. "Hummm. Can't say it becomes you. Unfortunately your own clothes—" She studied the sky-blue wool and shook her head. "There needs to be a little more clearly defined, shall we say, distinction?"

"We would not want there to be any confusion, would we, Ma'am, between me, the housekeeper, and them, the students?" The question was dry to the point of bitter. Miss Goodwin straightened her back and fixed her with a steady piercing gaze.

"Perhaps you have something more suitable for, ah, dusting? Only sometimes, of course. When the maid does not do her duty. But one must look a little stern, my dear, to assure that the maid will obey." She changed her stance. "You notice my own colors—"

Rose couldn't help smiling at the older woman who stood, arms akimbo in a most unladylike pose. The gesture was gone as quickly as it had come. Gracious and relaxed, Mrs. Goodwin moved towards the door. "I'm sure I'll find your choice satisfactory, Rose. As long as it's dark and practical. You might want a touch of lace. Perhaps we can have something made. I'll leave you now to unpack your things and send Janet up to help you. She can show you around afterwards. Though the students are out, we will have supper, as usual, at six. Sharp."

Rose stared after her a moment before kneeling to open her trunk. Perhaps she shouldn't have let Emily talk her into wearing her best. Her cousin had been so insistent. "You are not some dowdy, Rose, and I won't let you pretend to be for a moment! You told me yourself you were off to be real, and here you go, first thing, pretending to be some dowdy!"

And that was why Rose had not worn her good practical dress. Dark, of course. With a touch of lace. She had several of them. Indigo. Brown and a dark rich green. Mrs. Goodwin should be pleased. Rose wondered if she would be sitting with the girls at supper or would she be expected to eat with the cook. It had not been the sort of question she wanted to ask Miss Goodwin though the only alternative would be to ask someone who might well take advantage of her ignorance. Oh, dear. Oh, dear.

At least she knew her own room. Closing the lid to the trunk, she unbuttoned her gown, unbraced her corset, unlaced her camisole and removed her shoes. A luxurious sigh escaped her as she lay back on the feather bed, her head pillowed on satin. Yes, this might not be so bad. Certainly, she would learn a great deal.

A light tap on the door was preceded, before she could answer, by Janet's dark face. The woman looked as if she could not decide whether to curtsy or stare. Rose swung her feet off the bed and pointed to her trunk. "There," she said, "If you would be so kind as to put those things away and then perhaps bring me some water to wash." She lay back down, wiggling her toes, as Janet immediately went to work.

For the next few days, Rose followed Miss Goodwin around, learning the lay of the house and the duties required for each room. She received a ring of keys and lengthy introductions to each servant. She learned which china and linens were required and where the supplies were kept and how they were ordered. She accompanied Cook to the market and Miss Goodwin to the tailor and the bank. She walked through the gardens with the gardener and discovered what was planned for springtime color and summer fruit. She visited the stables with the groom and watched while he hitched up the surrey for the headmistress's ride to the Commons, a social visit on which Rose was not invited.

Rose applied herself diligently and learned all she could. When the week was over, she felt almost prepared but she stayed in her room as the great front doors began opening, admitting giggling groups of schoolgirls, kissing parents and friends goodbye in the parlor, then rushing upstairs to their rooms, their squeals penetrating the walls. A knock on her door brought her to her feet. Miss Goodwin smiled at her.

"Supper at five after six tonight, Rose. Do be prompt." Rose nodded and the woman strode briskly down the hall, knocking on every door, though Rose could not hear what she said as they were opened.

The girls were in place, standing behind their chairs in the dining room when Rose appeared in the door. The headmistress gestured toward the empty seat at the other end of the table. "Students, I want you to meet Miss Rose West. She will be our housekeeper for the remainder of the year and she will be dedicated to keeping you all on your appointed schedules. You are to mind her or she will be reporting you to me."

There was a noisy chorus of yes Ma'ams' as the girls, aged about twelve to eighteen, pulled out their chairs and Cook's husband passed the steaming dishes around. Except for requisite greetings from the students at her right and left hands, no one spoke to Rose. She ate steadily, taking time between courses to study the faces around her. Spoiled and silly. Miss Goodwin was right about that. Yet there was also an innocence, a lack of fear, an impartial practicality, a sense of fun that charmed her. Girls that had not known suffering, might lack sensitivity, but they showed little, if any, cruelty. Their company was almost pleasant.

Miss Goodwin's voice was raised above the clatter of a dozen forks on china. "Please girls, show Miss West your manners. If you quite behave yourselves, I shall be able to retire to my room for supper in the future and she will be your hostess. Would you like that?"

The sidelong glances came thick and fast. Rose set her face in stern lines. She'd have no one thinking she was easily pushed over. She eyed down the challengers and found herself smiling at last. The girls shuffled in their seats, sitting up straight, dropping left hands into their laps. "Yes Ma'am," came the chorus. It sounded like music to Rose.

She did not discover until much later that former housekeepers always ate in the kitchen. She only knew, watching her new mentor, that Miss Goodwin longed to share the responsibility for twelve strong-minded girls. Rose was determined to prove herself worthy of it.

The rest of the spring semester passed quickly. The problem, Rose discovered, was not in lacking intimacy but in allowing too much. She shared no confidences with the girls, though she received theirs, recognizing she must needs be involved with their lives but wanting none of their input on hers. Only Miss Goodwin knew the secrets of her parentage and Rose had the feeling that the secrets shared so freely with a peer whose family had "fallen on hard times," as the story was whispered about, would end abruptly if the girls knew who she really was.

The girls came readily to her room, drawn perhaps, by her exotic looks, her good manners, and the style that showed even in the simple gowns she wore. She listened as they sat in her rocker, telling her their love stories and crying, sometimes, over their romantic heartbreaks. She rousted them out of bed and down the stairs in time for breakfast, checking out their dress as they rushed past and sending them back to straighten stockings or change smudged blouses. She scolded them if they left their rooms a mess and confined them to their rooms without supper if they were late to meals or classes. They submitted with good enough grace. They liked her, she could see that, and she gladly sewed on their buttons and mended their hems when they protested they had no time, "not a minute, oh, Rose, please–" to take care of such things.

The girls called her Rose, soon enough, though Miss Goodwin protested vigorously. It would erode respect, she insisted. It was essential that the housekeeper be addressed by some title. Rose refused to agree. She was not comfortable with "Miss West." That name belonged to Emily and though she'd shared it, it never felt her own. "I see," said the headmistress. "However, proprieties require–"

"I'm not sure you see at all," Rose interrupted. "You have a full name. I do not. The name I was given–the only name I have– is Rose. They can call me Miss Rose, if you wish."

"You need a passport, Miss Rose," Miss Goodwin said, smiling. "You will have to settle on a name then, even if you have to make it up." The smile faded. "You really should do that, my Dear. If anyone were to learn of your parentage. . . . I find it unpleasant to mention such things but the Slave catchers from the South have been very active lately in Boston–thugs and kidnappers who would not hesitate to seize a defenseless free woman and declare her escaped. And there is virtually nothing one can do about it, the laws being what they are. You do need a passport, Rose, that will declare you free."

"I will speak to Emily about it when I return to New York for the summer."

"You will be coming back, will you not? About mid-August, to help us prepare–"

"You are satisfied then with my work?"

"More than satisfied, my Dear. Delighted."

The days were full but sometimes at night, cushioned on her satin pillows, the loneliness would strike her, though no tears came. She looked forward to summer and a return to the West family.

Her homecoming was a joyful occasion with Emily and Maxine making much of her. Even Clarence beamed when she appeared at supper that first evening.

"We have missed you, Rose! Emily has been quite out of sorts since you left and Maxine mopes at least one day a week. But you look well. I understand you've become quite good at keeping the girls in hand. Miss Goodwin had written us a glowing report."

"It's not so hard, Uncle Clarence. They think I'm a fine lady, impoverished by circumstances, and they are ready enough to keep me out of further trouble." A smile took the tiny sting from the words. Clarence cleared his throat and resumed eating.

"You've not told them. . . ." Maxine began.

"Of course not! Emily interjected. "Why should anyone know any more than what they see? Rose is a fine lady, no matter." She hesitated, wrinkling her fine, white brow. "Though I suppose a husband would have to know."

"I talked with Miss Goodwin about everything," Rose said. "She was surprised at my appearance, you see, having received my application through Dr. Connie's efforts."

"She was expecting. . . ." Maxine began again.

"Someone colored, of course," said Rose.

The meal, begun so noisily, ended in near silence.

It was a measure of Rose's newfound independence that she refused to share the bed with Emily when they returned to their room that night. Rummaging through the chests in the nursery, she pulled out two large quilts and folded them into a pallet on the floor.

"Whatever are you doing?" Emily asked, pausing in her undressing.

"I've gotten so accustomed to sleeping alone. You don't mind, do you?"

The small face developed a pout. "But I was so looking forward to snuggling up and telling secrets, as we used to." She slipped into her nightgown, slid between the sheets, threw Rose a pillow. "I have some wonderful new secrets but I must confess, I'm afraid to tell them in the light, across the room."

Rose blew out the lamps and sat down on the edge of the bed, reaching for the small hand, feeling so much older, suddenly, than her friend. "All right Emily, now tell me all your secrets and I will tell you mine."

"You first."

"I'm lonely," Rose said, simply. "That's all. And I find I need a passport. It seems that slave catchers are especially active in Boston because there are so many freedmen there. And the defenses against them are very limited. That's why—that's part of why I say nothing of my history. The girls are good but they talk. And who knows where talk can lead when the wrong ears overhear."

"Oh Rose! Oh, my dear, dear Rose."

"It's nothing really. Now let me hear your secrets."

She was answered with silence. It was as if Emily were mourning her. "Enough of that," Rose snapped. "I will be quite all right. Tell me what you're planning. And with whom?"

"Do you remember Mr. de Zavala?" Emily answered at last. Rose grunted a surprise affirmative.

"The married gentleman from Mexico?"

"I told you his wife was sickly. She continues so."

"You've been in correspondence with him? I'm surprised at you, Emily."

"It's all very correct. The letters come and go with Colonel Morgan. Or Uncle Benjamin." The words shut off suddenly. Rose waited.

"You've seen him, then?"

"Oh, Rose, I'm sorry. I didn't mean to bring it up, but yes, he's come twice this spring. He's a captain now, with his own ship, *The Glacier*."

"Has he asked about me?"

"Aunt Maxine told him you were working at the Academy. We did not discuss it."

There was another silence.

"Mr. de Zavala, then," Rose prompted.

"As I said, his wife has been quite ill for years. She and the children—there are three, almost grown—stay with their mother while Lorenzo travels. They have not spent much time together, ever, though they've been married almost twenty-four years. He has been so busy all his life in government service and diplomatic endeavors. And he has written a great deal. Oh Rose, he is such a fine person with such high ideals. He reminds me a little of Luke, though age has tempered his passions considerably. I do admire him so.

"And he, you, no doubt."

"It would appear. He does keep writing. And he says such lovely things."

Rose lay down beside her cousin, still holding the small hand. "There's no one else, then? Not one of all the rich white cream of New York society who tempts you? Surely, you could have your pick."

Emily made a sound of disgust. "They are all so—so shallow, Rose. Nothing but horses, games, the latest plays and entertainments, and the latest gossip from here and abroad. Nothing real." There was another long pause. Emily's face was turned to the window, eyes open to the moonlight. "I don't understand it quite, Rose, but I have no interest in such things. I want to do something that matters—or at least support someone who is doing important work. There is so much pain and evil in the world. How can I sit and prattle endlessly about nothing? To be married to someone like that would be death." A shiver touched her shoulders. "I don't want anyone but Lorenzo," she whispered. "Oh, Rose, what shall I do?"

"Wait," said Rose, taking her friend in her arms. "We just wait, Dear. And go on."

7

Luke came at Thanksgiving to see Rose at the Academy. She was not expecting him. She had not encouraged him. There was no place in her life for a colored romance. Though she had renewed her visits with Dr. Connie during the summer, she had first made sure Luke would not be present. She did not propose to engage her heart in the discussions with her mentor.

It was enough to love and be loved by a black woman who had known her since birth and understood her better than anyone else on earth. Emily, as dear as she was, could only see the African half of her background as something less. Something to be overcome. And to her Aunt Maxine, generous though she aimed to be, Rose remained a charity case.

With Dr. Connie, Rose could be simply herself.

With Luke, she was pushed to be something more.

He would begin his senior year at Bowden College in Maine, that fall of 1829. Still on full scholarship, he had been doing very well, Dr. Connie told her on their very first visit, a few days after she returned to New York for vacation. But no, he would not be home that summer. He had accepted an internship with a journal in Philadelphia—an abolitionist paper—and though the pay was meager, board was provided and he could earn enough for a suit of clothes. A young man had to have decent clothes, Dr. Connie said, chuckling. "The white folks who make decisions do not pay attention to people in rags. And most especially, not to colored people in rags."

Rose smiled, changing the subject. "I would have to trust your opinion. The dark clothes you advised me to have made up were exactly what Miss Goodwin had in mind." She described her first wardrobe conference with the headmistress. "She was rather questioning my youth, I think, until I showed up for dinner the very first evening dressed just as you suggested. I'm afraid Emily's suggestion—that beautiful blue wool that I wore on arrival—had quite the opposite effect."

"You're happy there?" Dr. Connie leaned forward on the couch, demanding an honest answer.

"As happy as I have a right to be, I suppose."

"That's no answer, girl. You have a right to be happy as any angel in heaven. What I want to know is, are you?"

"I'm learning a great deal. I've learned how to manage a household, how to manage servants, and how to manage the students. It has been a very productive time. My relations with Miss Goodwin are excellent. She appears to be very pleased with my work. And the girls like me, I do believe. They certainly spend enough time in my room."

Dr. Connie sighed. It was not going to be easy to get an answer from her young friend. Whatever else she had mastered, Rose had certainly learned how to avoid exposing herself. "And for fun?" she probed gently. "Are you going out at all, my Dear?"

Rose laughed. "You mean with men? Oh, Dr. Connie, I really do live in a no-man's land, you know. Those that might seek me out would necessarily discover my parentage. Indeed I would not hide it. And how would they think of me, then? The way my father did, no doubt! They would run as fast and as far as need be to get away from any respectable liaison. And really. I could not bear even the suggestion of any other kind."

"It can be rather limiting, being raised to be a lady."

" My raising did not exactly prepare me for my life as I must live it, unfortunately."

"You must not say that, child. You must not. God alone knows what He is preparing you for and you must accept every part of your experience as part of that preparation."

"That may be easier for you to say than for me to believe."

'What do you mean?"

"Well, look at you, Dr. Connie. You are clearly an African American free woman. You have been prepared for life as a healer, both of body and soul. Though you minister to both worlds–the colored and the white–you clearly inhabit the Negro world. You could not choose otherwise."

"And you can."

It was not a question and Rose did not answer. It was all she could do to meet those amber eyes–so like Luke's–straight on. She lifted a shoulder in a minuscule shrug. Dr. Connie looked down, fingering her apron.

"Luke loves you," she said at last.

"Still?" Rose's voice held an unaccustomed archness.

Dr. Connie's dry tones matched it. "My son can be a fool sometimes.

Perhaps he read too much of the English romantics. He seems to think that a promise made and received with a 'maiden fair' is binding until death."

"We were only children," Rose protested, feeling the color rise in her face. "I mean, I was, at least. Surely he cannot think he would hold me—"

"So you do remember!" Dr. Connie chuckled. "Very well, I shall not trouble you any more with your memories. I understand that you are in difficult circumstances and that only you can decide on your direction. I only wish—I can only pray that your choices will be based on what is good for everyone whose life you touch and not solely on your personal ambitions."

She stood, straightening her apron. "Shall we make some cookies? With no children about—and it doesn't look as if my son is going to gift me with grandchildren any time soon—I rarely make sweets. Given the weight I put on last winter, I simply can't indulge myself without a good excuse. But you're quite thin. You wouldn't mind a treat, would you?"

Rose followed her into the kitchen. The dimple in her left cheek, rarely seen these days, was clearly visible. It was a good thing Luke wasn't going to be around, thought Dr. Connie. Poor boy.

At the West home the atmosphere was not as comfortable. Too many questions were unasked. Too many subjects avoided. Though Emily was often teased by both her parents about her single state, no one dared to say a word about Rose's lack of beaus. And it was only with great caution that the subject of her work was broached. Neither Maxine nor Clarence wished to call attention to the very different circumstances the two young women would inherit as a matter of course. Emily, of course, wanted to know all about her life and laughed gaily over Rose's stories of "her" students. But Emily, an incurable romantic—just like Luke, thought Rose—could only see her cousin as passing time until "something better comes along."

As far as Rose could see, the "something better" may have already arrived. It was a relief to return to the school. To be the housekeeper of a well-regarded female academy was, after all, quite a success story for a young colored woman, however white she might appear. As for the "something better" Emily envisioned —marriage, of course, to a socially acceptable and materially successful white man—Rose could not imagine the possibility unless she were willing to practice a deception she was incapable of pursuing. Luke had quite ruined her illusions, she thought sometimes, not without bitterness. Dr. Connie was easy. Dr. Connie could be any white girl's black nanny. Wise and witty, stern and demanding without ever forgetting her place. But Luke was different. Even after three years of not seeing him, his challenges, his promises—oh God! Even his eyes still haunted her.

She took up her chores with gratitude, extending herself more than ever on behalf of her young ladies. At night she embroidered or sometimes slipped back down the stairs to play softly on the parlor piano, picking out the melodies by ear, tuned to the memory of the old church songs her mother sang.

"Rollicking lullabies," Miss Goodwin called them, coming out one night in her nightdress and wrapper to listen silently for a while before making her presence known. It pleased Miss Goodwin to see Rose enjoying herself.

The rollicking lullabies served to keep the blues away though they were never far around the corner. Thoughts of Luke, unbidden, claimed her mind at the oddest times—a political opinion someone might venture, a line of poetry in a book, a Negro looking either proud or bowed, a gusty day like the autumn day they sailed kites off the high porch of Dr. Connie's house. She would not linger with such thoughts any more than she would choose to wonder when or whether her father might return. She wished to be rid of her past. But she could not.

All the girls had left for Thanksgiving vacation and she was downstairs by the fire, reading *The Pioneers* by James Fenimore Cooper, lost in the tale of danger and daring at the far edge of the forest when she heard the knock. She expected a messenger, the knock was so definite. Or perhaps a parent returning for something left behind. Smoothing her hair and sighing a little at the interruption, she took her time in opening to the blustery day outside.

To see him standing there was to see a ghost come to life.

His cloak, a fine black wool, was covered with snow. He doffed his tall hat, bowing. Standing still in the doorway, stunned, Rose watched the snowflakes gather on his hair, white melting into the crisp black curls. He wore it long, slicked and tied back with a black suede bow but there was no way to smooth it out. His shoulders had broadened since she saw him last. And his face—she had seen that African face so many times in dreams she refused to remember. She couldn't speak. Could only stare as he stamped the snow from his boots, smiling at her, hat still in hand.

"It has been a long time, Rose." His smile broadened over even teeth, so white in that dark face. "Would you believe me if I said I happened to be in the neighborhood?"

"Luke!" she managed. "What a pleasant surprise. Forgive me. Do come in. The weather is quite frightful. You must tell me all your news."

She could hardly face him. Seating him in the front parlor, she hurried to the kitchen to make tea, grateful Cook had left a few small cakes for her before going to be with her family for the holidays. In fact, all the servants were gone, except for the gardener who seemed to want no family beyond his precious plants. The students had left the day before, delighted with the prospect of a very long weekend before the rigors of school reclaimed them the following Wednesday. Rose suspected the headmistress's desire to spend Thanksgiving with her own family in New York might have played a part in her decision to extend the usual vacation by three days. Not that she would have gone if Rose had not insisted on staying. It was simply too much trouble to close the house for the long weekend and she did not like to leave the servants alone.

Rose had given them all a vacation as soon as Miss Goodwin was gone, wanting to be left alone with her thoughts and projects. She had books to read and clothes to mend. She was even considering a shopping trip to the markets near the docks where prices on everything from cloth to kitchenware were much better than in the downtown shops. Having charge of the household purse was a responsibility she bore with pride and she economized on the school's behalf where she could. Of course, the company at the docks was much rougher than downtown. She had hoped the gardener might accompany her.

Such foolish thoughts, she chided herself, pouring the boiling water into the teapot. But she could not bring herself to think about Luke. Not yet. What could he be doing here? And what response was he expecting of her after all these years?

She felt him watching as she returned to the parlor, tray in hand, but she would not look up. Busying herself with the silver service, she poured, inquired about sugar and cream, offered cakes. Handing him the china cup and saucer, she realized with a tiny shock, that she had known exactly how he liked his tea and had prepared it so without noticing his silence. He did not speak until she met his eyes.

His smile was almost gone. "You are well, I see. Though a trifle thin. Are they working you so hard, Rose?"

She did not like his use of "they." As if she were not in charge of her own life! She was not, after all, a slave! Her lips pursed. "I enjoy my work," she said. "Miss Goodwin has set me in charge of running the household and appears quite satisfied with me."

"I see."

Silence lay like snowfall between them, deadening the tinkle of china, the small sounds of breathing, the slide of boots on the rug as Luke crossed and recrossed his legs. Rose stared at the tea table, wondered whether to reach for a cake, and cursed her self-consciousness. Except for the one night of her party and the brief exchanges in church with the Wests, she was utterly without experience in relating socially to men. Or did a black man count?

No. That was hardly fair! Luke was her friend, after all. She must remember that. It was not hard to inquire about his mother and his school, to answer politely about her present work and her summer vacation, to engage him in small talk about the weather, to tiptoe gingerly through the garden of conversation they had once romped passionately together.

"It's good to see you, Luke," she ventured at last, calmed by the mannerly distance between them. "You finish at Bowden this year, I understand. And Dr. Connie said you had an internship with *The Messenger* in Philadelphia last summer. She's very proud of you, of course. Have you determined where you will go when you graduate?"

"You mean what I'm going to do when I grow up?" The old smile was back. Teasing. Familiar. "No more than you, Rose. I'm learning a great deal, of course, but I'm not very clear on where it will take me. And sometimes, given the situation in our country, I'm not at all sure that school is not a waste of time." The fire was burning low and he stretched long legs, rising to place another log on it, and remaining to lean on the mantel. "I may be dodging the battle front."

"Not you, Luke!" The words burst from her before she could think. Perhaps it was the sight of that body, poised like a panther beside the flames, all tension and ease. "You! Of all people. I could not imagine one who could care more about others. Who would be more willing to battle for justice. You—"

She stopped herself. Oh dear, she had forgotten the magnetism he had, that ability to pull her right out of her own safe world into the thick of wherever his interests lay. And she had forgotten how extraordinarily handsome he was. Perhaps it was the clothes. The white faces usually seen above collar and cravat seemed pale, almost sickly by comparison. Really, she must not think this way! She felt color rising to her face as she bent her head to the teapot. He was watching her.

"You're very beautiful, Rose."

"You mustn't. You mustn't say such things."

"Why not? Why can I not make an observation with which any man would agree? Have we grown so very far apart you cannot receive so much as a compliment from me?"

"I did not. I did not mean it that way."

"No, of course not." There was a cynical edge to his chuckle, an unfamiliar sound. He was standing, now, behind her chair. She did not look up as his hand came to rest on her shoulder. "Do you remember that day I told you about leaving for college, Rose?" Long hard fingers tightened their grip. "Do you remember what I said? What you said?"

She would faint if he did not move. What could he be thinking! What could she be thinking?

"It was a long time ago," she said. "We were children." She remembered using the same words on Dr. Connie. She hoped Luke would receive them with equal grace but she doubted it.

"Children? I was twenty-one years old, Rose. And you, nearly sixteen."

"So much has changed," she murmured.

"How? Have you given your affections elsewhere? Or have you simply determined to shut me out of your life because I am a Negro? Is that what has changed, Rose? You have determined that you do not wish to be a part of the Negro world, at least insofar as you can manage to escape it?"

Rage gave her words. "Be fair, Luke! I am doing the best I can! I take your mother's advice as if she were my own mother. I live in the world I was given neither black nor white nor any fixed place between. I am not socially acceptable for the climate in which I was raised, and I hardly know, I hardly know the other side."

"The dark side?" He was relentless.

"All right! The dark side! If that's what you must call it."

"How dark must it be before one should call it dark? Chains? Whippings? Lynching? Slave traders still stealing our people from Africa though the trade has been internationally outlawed for more than twenty years. The traders simply bring them from Africa to the Islands, now, give them new names, put them on some plantation owner's roster, and ship them here as born bondsman. Then everyone gets a cut when they–our people, Rose–are sold as animals are sold."

He had loosed his grip and stood facing her. She cringed from his anger, tears starting in her eyes. "I cannot help that, Luke! I cannot help any of that."

He was back by the fire, pacing like a caged man. Head turned away, she could hardly hear his whisper. "You could love me, Rose. You could help me help them."

The sky was darkening outside where the snow still fell. She really must light the lamps. But she could not seem to move. Why did he come back to torment her? Forgetting had seemed so easy.

Luke resumed his seat. The silence lengthened.

"I'm sorry, Rose. Please. You must forgive me. I did not mean to demand anything of you. I only wanted to wish you well. To see what friendship still remained. To offer whatever service I could render for the few days I will be in Boston." He sighed, offering a rueful smile. "My tongue does get me in such difficulty sometimes. Mother used to warn me, often enough, that I must curb it but I do keep forgetting."

Impulsively she reached out to touch his hand. "You must forgive me also, Luke. Without you to prod me, I have probably grown much too complacent. It's easy to ignore what one does not wish to contemplate. That is, unless one has a friend who keeps insisting ignorance is not bliss." She smiled at him. "Let's start over. You tell me what college is like. What you are learning and doing and what you are planning. And I will tell you whatever you ask."

But he did not ask again what she most feared to answer and in her gratitude she listened happily as he recounted his adventures in the all-white college where he'd spent the last three years. It had not gone ill for him. Those few who disapproved had left the school altogether and among those who remained, he was, apparently, something of a hero. The lads vied with one another, he told her, laughing, for the opportunity to sit next to him or accompany him to the taverns on their occasional nights in town. His society of late, he explained, had been damned near as white as hers had been since birth. Nor had he minded.

"Know your enemy," he said, and laughed again. "Now, Rose, don't look so! I know those white boys are no more my enemies than Emily and Mrs. West are yours. But they are part of a larger society which condones a crime I'm duty bound to fight and it helps to understand the workings of that society since those are the people whose minds I want to change."

"You will write, then?"

"I will write. I will teach. I will talk. And if need be, I will take up arms. Do you remember that old hymn, Rose? Or perhaps they never sang it at your fancy church ." To her surprise, he threw his head back and began singing though the rich voice rolled out softly: "*Ye that are men now serve Him; Against unnumbered foes; Let courage rise with danger; And strength to strength oppose.*" He was smiling when he stopped. "I am not very religious, you know. It seems to me the church is much more interested in preserving the status quo than in obeying the radical message of justice and mercy that Jesus Christ lived and taught. But I do attend meeting sometimes with the Society of Friends—the

Quakers. There is little room for hypocrisy since we all sit silent until one feels bidden by the Spirit to speak." The smile became a chuckle. "Not that all speeches I've heard sound Spirit-guided but they've often enough to keep me coming. And the Friends have gone out on several limbs to hasten the abolition of slavery though they refuse to make emancipation a doctrinal plank of their belief."

"There are Quakers in Boston?"

"Indeed. I am staying with a family of Friends about a mile from here, lacking funds to let a room for the weekend, and being determined–"

"You never told me the nature of your business in Boston, Luke. What must you do?"

Luke stood, hat in hand. "You must forgive me. It has gotten quite dark while we sat talking and I'm afraid I have subjected you to great impropriety by remaining so long. Only please agree to allow me to return tomorrow and I shall take my leave and let you rest."

"Tomorrow?" Rose retrieved his cloak from the pegs by the door. He put it on and bowed deeply. A stage bow.

"Tomorrow." He stood shock still as she approached him, placing a hand on his arm, her face, for a moment, so close to his. "My business here is to see you, Rose, as much as you will allow it in the few short days I have."

The amber eyes regarded her, unblinking. Rose looked into them, giddy with an altogether new feeling. "Perhaps you would like to join me for dinner tomorrow? I cannot guarantee the results of my cooking, not having done much but our cook left food to prepare along with specific instructions and I did learn a little about the kitchen from your mother." Her dimple showed. He laid a finger on it. "You will come then? Two o'clock?"

"And Rose, you must forgive me if I fail to notice what I'm eating."

She stifled the giggle that rose in her throat. Really! How unladylike. But she leaned against the door for a long time after he had gone, her eyes dreamy. When she went upstairs to bed she was singing softly to herself.

Luke came Thursday, Friday, Saturday and Sunday. He came early and left late. On Thursday he laughed at her meal–a roasted chicken, burnt on the outside and still pink in the middle–and ate it with gusto. On Friday, he walked with her to market at the docks, enjoying her purchases as much as if they were his own and taking her to eat, afterwards, at a tavern nearby where so many nationalities were jumbled together no one seemed to notice the black man and white woman who were so engrossed in one another.

On Saturday he asked for a tour of the house and garden and spent a full hour listening to the gardener's plans for the coming spring plantings before preparing the fish he had brought for supper. He was, as it turned out, a better cook than Rose. On Sunday morning, she accompanied him to the meeting of Friends. All but one besides Luke were white, she noted, but if any thought her hand on Luke's arm amiss, no face revealed the question. It was an altogether pleasant time.

They had potato soup together afterwards, sitting in the kitchen and laughing over forgettable nonsense. Luke made a hoecake on the hot wood stove top. It was mandatory training during his internship, he explained. That and bacon, not the lean bacon, mind you, but the fatback were the slaves' whole diet, he said. The intern reporters were supposed to experience those things they intended to write about. "So that's what we lived on for the summer–fatback and hoecake, cooked by ourselves. Too bad we can't send them some of this soup, Rose. It tastes just like my mother's."

"She taught me."

Rose cleared the dishes and went into the pantry, returning with the fruitcake Cook meant to save for Christmas and a bottle of French burgundy. "Miss Goodwin keeps a few bottles for special guests so surely you would count. And Cook can't get too angry over two tiny slices, do you think?" Her dimple flashed as she set out saucers and goblets, sliced cake and poured wine. She raised her glass. "Here's to–"

"No, no," Luke tapped her goblet aside. "You must allow the gentleman to make the toast. At least the first one." He laughed at her frown. "Here's to the most beautiful lady a man could know. And, here's to the hope he will know her much better still."

Rose sipped her drink slowly. The dark wine was almost bitter on her unaccustomed tongue. Luke drained his glass quickly. She poured him another. It disappeared almost as rapidly. She poured him a third, finished her own and started over. Luke sat still, the laughter quite faded from his eyes. When he spoke, his voice was thick.

"I have to leave tomorrow, Rose. Very early, I believe. Dawn. I shall be late for classes, even as it is. But I had to have this last afternoon. And I had to tell you–" he waved his glass, spilling a drop of red on the polished pine tabletop. "Even if I had to drink myself into the words, Rose, I had to tell you I love you."

The words hung in the air between them.

"What do you mean by that?" The woman's voice was very small.

"What do I mean!" The man leaned across the table, reaching for her hand. "I mean I want to marry you. I want to come home to you every night–"

"I did not think you intended to do very much coming home." Rose removed her pale hand from the brown one that encircled it. "Are you not already married to your work?"

"Oh, Rose," he groaned. "Would you make me choose?"

"I cannot. Nor would I. Nor does it matter, Luke, because, however fond we are of one another, it will not work. It cannot. Surely you can see that."

He put his face in his hands. "I can see nothing," he whispered, "but what I must do and what I must have. My work. And you."

"Let's go in to the fire," she said.

His arm was about her waist as they walked to the parlor. She could feel his breath, the wine heat against her face. Sinking to the rug in front of the fireplace, he drew her down to his side. A giddiness was in her head, an unaccustomed warmth in her belly. He took the glass of wine from her hand and set it carefully on the tiles. His body, crouching, was a panther's, golden eyes aglow. It made her feel quite dizzy.

"Rose."

And then both of his arms were around her and her face was buried against his shoulder. The smell of him–so clean and somehow strong, even with the bittersweet wine on his breath as he turned his face, his mouth seeking hers, his hands moving across her back, tightening. Her skin was suddenly alive, her loins melting as he leaned against her, pressed her down, his arm pillowing her head, his hand unlocking her bodice, pulling at the laces of her stays, caressing her nakedness. Ancient rhythms possessed her body, rocked her gently through and furiously beyond the sudden pain as past and future surged into an overwhelming now.

She surrendered, hardly knowing what she did.

Afterwards, sobered, she wept.

A groan escaped him. "Darling, oh, my darling Rose, how can you ever forgive me? God knows I never meant–Oh God–"

She turned her back, twisting in his arms, struggling to sit up He loosed her as she reached for garments that lay scattered where he had flung them. She pulled his shirt around her, shivering.

"I cannot, I cannot altogether blame you." She managed a smile. "I certainly, ah, participated."

He lay still, an arm covering his face. "You must not blame yourself at all, Rose. All that happened was entirely my fault. I should have known. I should have never– But you are so very beautiful and I have dreamed of you so long. And then the wine and the fire and not knowing how long it will be before I see you–Oh God, Rose, I do not know how I shall go on."

"As you always have." Her voice was a whisper in the gathering dark. "And I shall go on as I always have."

"You cannot mean that. This changes everything. You must. Surely you will marry me, Rose, and permit me to erase this stain on your honor."

The thin smile she offered was cold as the wind against the windows. "Is that why? So I would marry you? Is that what you thought?"

"Never! Believe me, Rose, I never thought at all that we would come to this. Not now. Not until–unless–you were my wife." He stood in one swift movement and pulled on his trousers. Bare-chested, he knelt in front of her, offering a shawl in exchange for the shirt she still clutched around her. "I will stay a while or I will go immediately if you wish. But you must tell me. I love you, Rose, with all my heart. I have loved you for as long as I can remember. But I make no claims on you." A smile flickered and died on his lips. "I can only beg for mercy."

"Mercy," she murmured. "Yes, mercy and justice are the heart's desires." She would not look at him as he finished putting on his shirt and buttoned his collar, tied his cravat. She could not move. The wind was still rising outside. Another gale blowing in. His travel tomorrow would not go easy. She wished him gone already. She wished him to stay forever.

He knelt again, taking her limp hands into his own strong ones. "You must tell me, Rose. You must let me know what you wish me to do."

"Go," she said thickly. "It would be best, I think, if you go now."

He waited a moment longer, silent above her. She did not turn her head as she heard his footsteps cross the room. Nor when the doorknob turned, admitting a rush of frigid air. Nor when it clicked softly, closing behind him. Nor afterwards. She did not move until the clock had sounded out the hours twice. And then she rose, gathered up her clothes, washed herself, went to bed and stared into the dark.

The next day the servants returned and she was grateful for the job of putting everyone to work. Classes would commence on Wednesday. By Tuesday evening, the students would be back. There were preparations to be made. She was glad to have something she must think about besides Luke.

But at night, in her bed, he haunted her.

His first letter came less than a week later. He had written it in the coach on his way back to Maine. He declared his love and guilt, her innocence and beauty, his hope for their future. She read the letter twice, alone in her room, and hid it away in the dresser. She did not respond.

Nor did she respond to the next. Or the next.

"Another letter?" Miss Goodwin said, finally, having waited more than long enough for Rose to introduce the subject. "You obviously have an admirer, Rose."

"I suppose so."

"An old friend? Or a new one?" Miss Goodwin was not easily deterred.

"I've known Luke since–since I was born. His mother was my mother's midwife. He's Dr. Connie's son."

"Oh, Luke! Of course. She has spoken of him in every communication. He's in college now, is he not? In Maine?"

"Yes." There was no escape from those piercing brown eyes.

"He came to visit you, I take it. Over Thanksgiving?"

"Yes."

"And–"

"Nothing!" She turned her back. "Nothing! Please Miss Goodwin, I cannot talk about him." Gathering her skirts, she ran for the stairs, escaping to her room before the tears started again, leaving the headmistress staring after her.

She did not go home for Christmas that year, pleading too much to do in a long letter to Emily and Maxine. She was afraid to write to her cousin only. Afraid the pen she held would speak for itself and say far too much. She could never admit her fear of seeing Luke again. So alone in the building once more, she spent the Holy Days reading listlessly and staring out the window at the browning snow. It was a great relief to welcome the girls back to school and take up her duties once more.

Rose missed two periods before she could admit that there was something wrong. She had managed to ignore the slight queasiness in the mornings and the fatigue that seized her every afternoon. But when her blood did not let down for the third month, she knew. Dr. Connie had instructed her, long since, in all the facts of birth.

She seriously considered flinging herself off the dock into the icy February seas. Death should not be long in coming. She considered going home to Aunt Maxine and Emily. They might be terribly upset but they would adjust. She considered running away, packing her trunk, taking the money she'd carefully saved and going, perhaps, to Ohio. Perhaps she could teach. Perhaps she could present herself as a new widow, without family.

But she did not consider writing to Luke. And she rejected the idea of going home because then, of course, Dr. Connie would find out and she would be drawn inexorably into the family she did not want to join. As for death, it was too final a solution. And so she waited. The letters came a little less often now but they persisted, at least twice a month, each sounding a little more desperate than the one before. She stopped reading them altogether.

Spring came. She was having trouble lacing her stays. In fact, her dresses hardly fit though she let out what seams she could. She no longer stopped in for cozy chats in Miss Goodwin's parlor. The headmistress watched her, asking nothing though an occasional frown creased her brow. Rose managed her work with her usual efficiency and tended the girls who still gathered in her room, chattering away with no idea that their confidante's world had completely altered. Rose ordered two new dresses, complaining about "getting fat on this good food."

It was mid-May before Miss Goodwin laid a hand on her arm as she was hurrying away after dinner. "We must talk, Rose. Will you stop in for tea this afternoon? Around three?" There was no way to deny the request.

And so the story finally came out. All of it. The promise at fifteen. The decision not to abide by it. The reasons. The reunion. The attraction. The wine and the fire and the wind on the windows. Luke's world and hers and the gulf between.

"Only the one time, then?" said Miss Goodwin, when she had finally run out of words and tears.

"Only that last afternoon. I could not stop myself."

"And Luke? He pushed you into this?"

"I cannot say that. I was willing enough at the moment, ashamed though I was afterwards. And he, too. He said he had never imagined such a thing happening until we were married. And I know he meant it."

"But you do not wish to marry him? It certainly seems to be the simplest solution."

"It is not simple, Miss Goodwin, to be a Negro in the United States. And to be married to Luke would be very complicated, indeed. He is an educated and very intelligent Negro and he plans to use that intellect fighting for emancipation. No doubt he will go south. And no doubt he will be killed soon afterwards. He is not a man to hide away from trouble."

"As you are? No, forgive me, Child. I have no way of knowing what trials you face, whatever your choice. But I do know you and I am sure you want the best, not only for yourself but for your child. Would you deny the baby a father?"

"Miss Goodwin, I do not wish to sound cold, but you must understand that I was not raised to be a colored woman. All I know about the Negro world I learned from Dr. Connie and Luke, who were certainly not typical of their class. I never associated with the servants except to instruct them. I was raised to be white. And the more Luke has told me of what black people suffer, the less I want to be part of it."

"But the baby, if Luke is very dark, as you described, the baby will certainly—"

Rose nodded, fresh tears gathering.

"So you do not wish to raise the child? Would you give it to Dr. Connie? After all, it is her grandchild."

"I am not going to tell Luke." Rose was vehement. "I do not want him, ever, to know about this. I will not be bound—"

Miss Goodwin shook her head sadly. "I must take time to think about it, my Dear. I must tell you it is not the first time I have had to deal with such a problem though this particular situation is certainly the most complicated."

"You will help me?"

"Of course."

The solution, as Miss Goodwin presented it at their next private teatime, a week later, was simple enough. Rose would stay with her for the summer since the baby was due in August. They would hire a wet nurse who would keep the child with her for the time being. Rose could continue working to support the infant. And if she decided, after another year or two, that she did not want to keep the baby, Miss Goodwin would find a foster home, "a good one, assuredly, with a couple who would treasure the child."

Emily was severely disappointed to learn that Rose would not be home that summer. "I have so much to tell you," she wrote. "Lorenzo de Zavala's wife passed away early this year. As I told you, she was sickly. He has since been to see me. I fear you will not approve, but he has asked Father for my hand and we plan to be married on November 12. Dear Rose, how can you stay away right now when I need you so to help plan for our wedding! Only promise me that you will come for that, at least. No one else could be my maid of honor."

Tears filled the blue eyes as she read and re-read the letter, longing to talk to her friend. But there was nothing Emily could do besides pity her. And she could not face that. Nor could she face her aunt and uncle. To have a child outside of marriage. What status could she ever hope for were the fact ever discovered? She would be seen as no better than any slave. She could not allow it. What she had to bear, she would bear alone.

She wrote to Dr. Connie, explaining briefly that she would have to work that summer and mentioning that she had seen Luke. "It was a rather sad time for both of us though he is doing very well," she wrote, offering no further explanation.

The baby was born in mid-August, 1831, a healthy boy with a lusty cry at being thrust unwelcome into a brand new world. Holding him afterwards, when the midwife and Miss Goodwin had finally left the room to her and the colored wet-nurse, she could not believe how beautiful he was. Black curls lay plastered against the high forehead and the tiny nose and mouth looked just like Luke's. The wide eyes, staring mistily at her, looked almost amber, though his color was more café au lait than chocolate. He nuzzled against her breast. She fought off the desire to enfold him and gestured for the nurse.

"What you going to call him, Ma'am?"

Funny, she had not even thought about a name until now. She held onto him a moment longer. It would not matter. Whatever she named him, his father would never know.

"His name is Luke," she said, giving him into the nurse's arms. "Luke Junior."

8

The autumn semester began in a swirl of poplin skirts and bright faces. Miss Goodwin moved among them with the same serenity as before. Rose followed the example.

It was not always easy. A new spirit had possessed her—the one contained in a milk-brown baby boy who lay a few short blocks away, cradled in the arms of someone not his mother. Even so, with Miss Goodwin's encouragement, she managed daily visits to the little house that she had rented at three dollars a month for the child, his nursemaid and the nursemaid's widowed father. Her son was thriving, a strong and healthy boy who strongly resembled Luke except when he smiled. Dimpling, he looked like a colored Benjamin.

Rose reached for him when she could. Miss Goodwin granted her permission to leave every day after lunch for the hours before she had to present herself at the head of the table for dinner. On Saturdays and Sunday night, she was relieved of that chore. There were many hours, as it turned out, to be spent happily with her son.

In November she took a week away to be at Emily's wedding. If she could have gone and returned to her son on the next day, she would have, but decency demanded she assist the bride with laying out her trousseau and packing her trunks for a wedding trip to Maryland where Emily planned to spend a month or so acquainting her new husband with her grandparents' way of life. Lorenzo de Zavala, anxious to relate to his new wife's culture, was more than glad to agree. In the meantime he stayed with Clarence during the day and out of the way in the guest rooms at night while the women busied themselves with matrimonial preparations.

It was not a large wedding. The gentility of New York City were a bit surprised by the suddenness of the announcement, not to mention the nationality of the groom. Beyond the small cluster of family members in the front, along with a score of friends and business associates, the huge sanctuary of the Church of the Transfiguration stretched away empty when Emily came slowly down the aisle to meet Lorenzo at the altar on November 12. Benjamin did not attend, pleading an urgent and unavoidable sail to London. The senior Mr. West was too ill to be present and his wife, sitting stiffly in the second pew, looked somewhat ill herself. "The girl takes after her mother," she was heard to sniff. "Irish! No class at all. Marrying that middle-aged Mexican!"

Clarence, releasing Emily's arm to return to his wife's side, wore a look of longsuffering tolerance. Maxine's smile was tentative and tears stood in her eyes. She wished her husband understood her fears. Would the man take her daughter far away forever? Would her darling Emily be in danger in the raw new world to which her husband called her? And what about Rose? What friend would she have left?

Only Maxine's parents, beaming at the bride, seemed perfectly pleased with their granddaughter's happiness, having perceived that Mr. de Zavala was both wealthy and intelligent as well as charming and obviously in love. "What more could one ask for, after all?" Eldon whispered to his wife who nodded, remembering another wedding long ago and praying her granddaughter would find the joy in marriage that seemed to elude her own daughter.

Standing beside the bride, holding Emily's bouquet while she bared her finger to receive the ring, Rose tried to think of nothing at all. She felt, for the first time, completely unrelated to everyone present. Dr. Connie had not been invited. Emily had pleaded for her, but in the end explained to Rose that it just could not be done. "Grandmother West would be dreadfully offended and I must admit, Rose, that Mother and Father are not overjoyed at the marriage either, though they agreed with reasonable grace. At least Mother did–she understands about the heart–and Father finally went along. But I do not wish to stir up trouble and I'm afraid the sight of Dr. Connie would do that."

Because she's black? thought Rose. Like me?

But she agreed. She had no wish to stir up trouble, either.

The priest fell silent, finally. Emily's whisper brought Rose's mind back to the church.

"I do."

"And you, Lorenzo de Zavala, do you. . . ."

Firmly. "I do."

It was done. Very gently, the groom lifted the veil and kissed his bride. The senior Mrs. West looked unnerved, Emily noticed, with a giggle rising like hysteria in her throat. She stifled the sound before it escaped. Laughter would be even more out of place than Mrs. West's near anxiety attack.

Afterwards, back at the mansion, there was music and dancing, champagne and cakes of every description. The rooms were full of flowers and decorations of silver and green reflected candlelight everywhere. The appropriate toasts were offered. The appropriate words were said. The bridal couple did not appear to notice that they, along with Eldon and Kate Sturn, were the only ones having a wonderful time. Lost in their own new world, the pair paid no attention to the strained conversations around them.

Rose stood alone near a window. She did not want to dance any more, did not recognize nor wish to converse with any of the cousins and captains of industry who were willing to waltz her around the room, asking questions she had no desire to answer. Her own grandparents barely acknowledged her, though Mrs. Sturn had smiled at her several times with a peculiar mixture of pleasure and pity. Rose wanted none of it. She was lost in thoughts of the only other dance she had ever attended, the one held in her honor, in this very room. And though that occasion had obviously brought great joy to Emily, Rose could only remember meeting her father for the first time and losing him within the very same hour.

As her son had lost his father within an hour of conception?

No. She would not think about that now.

Eldon stood in front of her, bowing stiffly, asking for a dance. His wife—my grandmother—must have sent him, she thought, seeing Kate's smile of approval. But she and Eldon had nothing to say to one another beyond the required pleasantries. She had only met him once before, briefly, before being hustled away to Dr. Connie's house where she always stayed for the duration of family visits. Eldon released her with another bow and returned to his wife. Rose longed to run away. To escape to Dr. Connie and sit by the fire with a cup of tea, a real conversation, and the comfort of being loved for exactly who she was.

Except that she no longer knew exactly who she was and the only two men who could name her were impossibly far away. Her father and the father of her son. The very fact that those two men would never know each other—would never want to know each other—left her feeling desolate.

She was startled when Colonel Morgan appeared in front of her. She had not seen him at the wedding and was not particularly pleased to see him now. His eyes were far too bold and the man was entirely too sure of himself.

"May I have the pleasure, Miss West?" he said, bowing. "You are much too beautiful to be standing alone on such a festive occasion."

"Thank you Colonel, but my feet have quite worn out. These little French boots I'm wearing do seem to cut off circulation."

"Then perhaps we had best sit down." Without waiting for an answer he guided her to a settee and settled himself beside her. "I understand you have been working in Boston as the housekeeper for the Wyman Female Academy." A smile creased his sharp features. "Not the sort of work I would expect to find you doing."

Really, the man was too familiar! As if it were his business! "I have enjoyed my responsibilities," Rose said coldly. "The girls are very good and the headmistress has made my life with them most pleasurable."

"You enjoy Boston, then? You would not consider relocating?"

"I have not considered it, no."

"But perhaps if you found something more beneficial? Higher wages, perhaps, and greater responsibilities and opportunities? You appear to be a woman of intelligence as well as beauty."

"Perhaps you should tell me what you have in mind."

Colonel Morgan leaned back in his seat, crossing his legs. "As you may remember from our last meeting, almost two years ago, I believe, I have long had an interest in Stephen Austin's efforts to develop an American colony in northern Mexico. The Indians are being pushed back to the west and the population there is growing steadily with immigrants coming in from the United States as well as from southern Mexico and Europe. Texians, they all call themselves. The land is rich and our political prospects are excellent. In fact, some believe that we may soon have enough settlers to liberate Texas from Mexico altogether, either to become an independent republic or to annex ourselves to the United States."

Again the thin smile. "Mr. Austin does not favor this plan, of course, being troubled by undue scruples, some feel, about rendering due loyalty to the Mexican government. However, we must thank him that our relations with Mexico have been well maintained, as you can see by our close association with Mr. de Zavala, a statesman who has served in many capacities with the Mexican government since they won independence from Spain. Unfortunately, due to the instability of that government, Mr. de Zavala is currently in exile. It seems he was not in accord with the imperialistic policies of the current leadership. However, his loss has been our gain, as he has allied himself with the American colonists while awaiting a return to the fold of Mexico City. His diplomatic skills have been supremely useful, given that, overall–" The smile was broader. "The Texians are a rather rough group."

Rose was growing restless. "And how does all this concern me, Colonel Morgan?"

"Business, my Dear. If you will indulge me, I felt you would want a little background. Before Mr. de Zavala's, ah, fall from grace, he received an *empresario* grant to a very large tract of land along the Rio Bravo. He has recently transferred his interests to the Galveston Bay and Texas Land Company with which I and your, ah, Mr. West are associated. We are seeking five hundred new settlers. With so many people, much is possible."

He leaned forward. "Texas is ripe for trade. To this end, I went into partnership with Mr. John Reed of New Orleans last year and we have purchased a schooner, the *Exert*, which promises to be a great asset to our business. In addition, I intend to purchase a quantity of land near Galveston Bay in Texas and establish a town and a port. I will need help. Mr. West has assured me that you would be a great asset to us, Miss West."

"But you have not yet made this purchase?"

"Not yet."

"Then there is really no reason for us to have this discussion."

Morgan blinked. "I beg your pardon?"

Rose stood up, forcing the man to rise as well.

"It is I who must beg your pardon, Colonel Morgan, but I am currently well situated and neither the politics of Mexico nor the ambitions of the Texians hold interest for me. Perhaps when you have a more definite plan...."

Morgan stared after her as she left the room. He had never wanted a woman so much nor been rejected so coldly.

Later, in their room together for the last time, Rose helped Emily out of her wedding gown and into her evening dress. "I'm glad you will not be leaving us too soon, Emily. Your mother is beside herself with worry, you know. And your father is none too happy."

Emily laughed. "Mother would be worried if I were moving next door. Truly, Rose, I would not mind going anywhere with Lorenzo, regardless of her fears and father's terrible sense of propriety, but it seems we will have to be here for a year or two. They will have me well in sight. I am so very glad we can, at least, escape to Grandmother and Grandfather Sturn's for a month or so. It will be lovely to be in the country with them, to show Lorenzo the place where my mother grew up." She sighed. "It would be foolish, I suppose, to insist on having our own house when our future lies in Texas."

"You will be going there, then?"

"That is what Lorenzo intends. And I am his wife." She flung her arms around her friend. "Oh Rose, to be his wife! I cannot yet imagine it! Dreams do come true!"

"For you, perhaps."

"You must not talk that way! Do you not have what you wanted? The job in Boston—"

"Is hardly the same as marrying the man of your dreams."

"Oh my dear Rose! But you have never had a man in your dreams, have you? Which reminds me, what were you and Colonel Morgan discussing so intently? He certainly seemed interested in you, though I cannot say you looked as if you were returning the compliment."

"Colonel Morgan is a married man as you well know. Nor would I like him overmuch if he were not. But he was offering me, I think, a job."

"A job?"

"In Texas. He intends to purchase land there—apparently he already has considerable trade with the Texians—and build a town. He wanted me to work for him in some capacity though he was not very clear on the details. Of course, he does not yet have the land."

"In Texas! Oh my dear, you must do it! Then we could still be together! Only think—"

"I'm awfully tired of thinking, Emily. As far as the job goes, we'll have to see. I cannot imagine it, myself, but if the timing is right—"

Rose left the next morning, slipping away with small goodbyes as the wedding couple greeted their first day together and began the final preparations to embark for Maryland. Clarence was home to help and Rose lifted a hand to him in farewell as she left for the station, a new trunk stowed beside her in the family carriage. She had brought only her carpetbag but Emily had insisted on having dresses and new undergarments made for her, "for the festivities, of course," as well as giving her linens of which she insisted she had a surfeit. Rose received them gladly, imagining sheets re-made as small white shirts and glad to offer towels, napkins and tablecloths to grace the tiny home where her son was living.

She did not return to New York at Christmas. It was Luke Jr.'s first and she could not bear the thought of missing it. As it turned out, Emily and Lorenzo remained with her grandparents for the holidays so her absence was not much noted. After a pleasant letter to her Aunt Maxine about the joyful weight of meaningful work, Rose made special arrangements with Miss Goodwin to give all the servants a two week vacation. As soon as they were gone, encouraged by a few extra dollars of traveling money, she moved her baby into the big house along with Jenny, the wet-nurse, and Jenny's father who kept the fireplaces fed and entertained the baby while Jenny took over the kitchen.

Rose spent the best Christmas season of her life watching her son crawl about in this house that was entirely hers for a little while. The newly made-up family, all dressed in their finest, sat together in the dining room on Christmas Day with white-haired "Grandpa" at one end and Rose at the other while Junior securely perched on Jenny's lap, burbled happily and grabbed at the silverware. Surrounded by candles and Christmas greens, a golden roast goose dripped juices onto its spiced apple bed in the center of the table while the fire roared in the fireplace and the wind of a gathering storm rattled the windowpanes. Pausing to remember the reason for their celebration, Rose asked for a moment of silent thanks and a prayer for peace on earth, goodwill to all mankind. Shushed for a moment, the baby stared at the candles with eyes so bright they might have been stars.

Playing Christmas carols for Jenny and Grandpa afterwards, as the baby curled sleepily into his blankets by the fire, Rose was certain Emily herself could be no happier than she was at this moment. Her heart lived in Boston with her son and New York was a former life, impossibly removed. Except for occasional visits, Rose could not imagine returning.

Luke Junior had just passed his first birthday when Rose visited New York again to see Emily's first child, born late the next summer. By then Lorenzo was back at work in the diplomatic fields, Mexico having once again shifted its leadership policies. Unfortunately, he was traveling so much she had little of his company during the pregnancy. But he arrived from Mexico in time for the birth of his son and in the joy of that reunion, the family scarce had time for Rose. She hovered around Emily's bedroom for a few days, feeling herself more in the way than not, then gave up her place to Maxine and returned gratefully to Boston.

The de Zavala's named their little boy Augustine, expecting great things of him. Hoping for proximity more than anything, Maxine rejoiced in each day her daughter remained with her and did her best to be indispensable to the comfort of the new mother and child. Clarence suggested more than once that the living arrangement should be permanent. After all, with Lorenzo so occupied both with politics and with the business of the Galveston Bay and Texas Land Company, he scarcely had time for a family.

He did not mention, except to Maxine, that it was bad enough their daughter had married a Mexican. He could only hope the man would not follow through on his plans to drag her away to his own strange land. Maxine, with less prejudice and more pain, agreed. As the year came to an end and Lorenzo remained in New York working and socializing in the milieu of his in-laws, the Wests came to believe they might keep their daughter close, after all.

But Emily longed to escape her parents' walls. Marriage to Lorenzo had changed her, had broadened her horizons. Love required stretching herself out into new understanding and a less self-centered sociability. Acknowledging the bigotry to which her husband was subjected, albeit covertly, among her father's friends, she made herself useful as his charming and socially impeccable companion among New York's elite investors. Following her husband's example, she developed the tact which can put a positive face on the most negative characters.

Lorenzo noted teasingly that she was becoming a true diplomat's wife—and she had not yet set foot out of the country. She laughed and said she hoped so—and was it not about time for her to join him on some foreign shore? If not Mexico, then Europe. Paris perhaps? He said he would see what he could do. He was gone before the end of March, leaving Emily newly pregnant with their second child. When she sent him word, he wrote back asking if she preferred he return immediately or continue with preparations to bring them all down to Mexico. "Come for me when everything is ready and not before," she answered. "Otherwise, it may be another year before we leave here."

The birth of Barbara Marie just before Christmas was a subdued occasion unlike the birth of their firstborn though Emily could not say whether that was due to Lorenzo's absence or her mother's anxiety, or the sadness she sensed in her cousin Rose, home for the first time since Augustine's birth. Even Dr. Connie carried a strange air of wistfulness, holding up the new baby. She must want grandchildren, Emily thought with sudden insight. Luke is of an age to give them to her, and I suppose he will not. Because of Rose? Could he be still in love with her? And she won't have him, of course.

But Rose would not discuss it though she remained with her cousin for a month, missing the holidays with her own son in order to cheer up the young mother who was missing her husband profoundly. When Emily finally dared to ask again about Rose's relationship with her old friend, Rose answered only that she had not seen Luke in more than three years. He had come to see her once at the school and she had decided it was best not to pursue the friendship. Emily sighed and said she wished her friend could find the happiness she'd found as Lorenzo's wife, and even though Luke was a Negro, if she loved him, why not be with him? Rose smiled and said that marital happiness was not for everyone. Indeed, it was uncommon even among the couples they knew. "Not many people would take the chances you are taking to marry the man of your dreams."

"Would you consider going with me, Rose?" Emily asked, prepared to rescue her friend from a loveless life. "I'm sure Lorenzo would be glad to have you as part of our household, wherever we go. You can help me with the children. And it would be so wonderful to have family from home. Besides, you have been working so hard these past few years."

"I cannot."

"Are you so married to your school? Or is there something you're not telling us? A beau?"

"Nothing like that. It's rather hard to explain."

Emily sighed, knowing her friend would not elaborate further. "Just promise me you'll think about it," she said at last. "It might be very good for you to move about a bit and it's difficult for a single woman. But if you were with us—"

"If I were with you, I would feel like a child again, Emily. I do enjoy my independence."

"Then you must broaden your horizons. What good is freedom if one doesn't use it? And Texas, Lorenzo tells me, is a land of many opportunities. No, don't shake your head at me, Rose. Just promise me you'll think about it. I'm not going there myself just yet—Lorenzo tells me he may be appointed to Paris—but Texas, he says, is where we're bound eventually. Perhaps by then—"

"I'll think about it," Rose promised.

But all Rose could see was the face of her son. Texas might as well have been the moon. Attractive, but out of reach.

She only came close to telling her secret once. That wistful look on Dr. Connie's face, laying Barbara Marie in Emily's arms, had brought Rose almost to the point of confession. But by the time the bustle of birthing was done she had overcome the impulse. Nor did she speak of the boy when she went to visit the midwife before returning to Boston though the two women spent a long and somewhat strained afternoon together. When the small talk was done there was little left to say. Dr. Connie respected her reticence at first and secrets have a way of clogging conversation. But she could not let Rose go without an honest word.

"You have not seen Luke?" Dr. Connie asked as she was leaving.

"No."

'He tells me he writes to you."

"Yes."

"And you never answer."

"That's true."

"Forgive me Rose. I know you don't wish me to pry but Luke is my son and he suffers a great deal over you. What would you have me tell him?"

Rose paused with her hand on the doorknob. "To forget me," she said.

"That's all?"

"Isn't that enough?"

Dr. Connie laughed. "You must not know my boy as well as I thought you did. That's not nearly enough! Now perhaps if he heard you were married—"

Rose bent her head. "I am not likely ever to marry, Dr. Connie."

"And certainly not to Luke, is that it?"

She could not meet the older woman's eyes. "Luke is a fine young man," she managed. "He would make any woman very proud."

"Any colored woman, you mean?"

She looked up despite herself, "Well yes, of course. That is—"

Dr. Connie was not smiling. "I must not know you as well as I thought I did, either. Time was, I imagined you could see deeper than the color of a person's skin." Her lips twisted. "People do change, I know, though I try to be optimistic about it. I like to imagine good children will stay that way but mostly they just grow up and turn out like the folks they associate with."

"I associate with very nice people, Dr. Connie."

"White people. Nothing but white people now. Isn't that the truth?"

Closing her eyes against the accusation, Rose seemed to look into her son's face. Amber eyes in the brown skin. Thick lips stretching into dimples.

"No!" she burst out, tears stinging. "That's nothing near the truth!" Turning she ran down the steps, leaving Dr. Connie staring after her.

Rose cried herself to sleep the night before she returned to Boston. "Whatever shall we do?" she murmured to the son whose small face floated in her mind.

Miss Goodwin told her to go on over, "of course," as soon as she arrived back at the school. Kneeling in the door of the cottage that Sunday afternoon, she held out her arms as her son ran to meet her. "Mama! Mama!" he cried, chortling as he reached for the sweet she always brought him. Really, she must make Jenny stop him calling her "Mama." She loved and hated the word though

Jenny almost encouraged it. "He forget soon enough," she would say. "If you wants him to, Ma'am." There would be time, Rose thought. Time enough for him—and her—to forget.

"You've been good?" she asked, holding on to the warm little body, smelling the tender scent of his shoulder as she stretched an arm away from his grasp. "I'll ask Aunt Jenny so you must tell me the truth. If you've been good you can have the sweet." She hugged him closer. "Can you say sweet?"

He nodded vigorously, dimpling. The nursemaid smiled. "He's a case, he is, Ma'am. Aren't you, Junior?"

"Sweet," said his mother. "Can you say sweet?"

"Sweet," the little boy said, reaching as he tried out the new word. "Sweet, Mama. Sweet."

Rose held him for a long time. "Mama gone," he said once, reproachfully, then laid his curly dark head on her shoulder and sucked at his candy as he stood still in her arms. Rose stayed with him that evening until after he went to sleep.

Miss Goodwin pointed out, a few days later, that Rose's heart had gone out of her duties at school and lived, it seemed, in the cottage with the boy. It was time, she said, for Rose to make a decision. "Unless you intend to leave the child in limbo until he's grown up, you really owe it to yourself as well as him, Rose. He will be three this summer, my Dear. If he is to gain new parents we must find them for him soon. But first, you must decide whether you want to keep him or give him up."

"I don't know. I just don't know."

Perhaps she had cried too often. Miss Goodwin was unmoved by the tears. "You had best make up your mind. The older he becomes, the harder it will be to keep him a secret. And what are you going to say when he begins asking questions? You would not want to lie. A poor example that would be!"

"What do you suggest then?"

"I made my suggestion long ago. That you marry the child's father and make a home for him. Give Dr. Connie some grandchildren and yourself some happiness."

"Happiness was never my goal, Miss Goodwin."

"And what is?"

"To make something of myself. To be somebody."

Miss Goodwin snorted, a most unladylike sound. "As if you could remake what God has made! As if you were not somebody already!"

Rose lifted her chin. "Indeed I am. I am the bastard daughter of a slave and the master's son. That makes me both illegitimate and a Negro. Not an admirable somebody in our society, Miss Goodwin. And besides that unfortunate beginning, my mother is dead and my father, no doubt, wishes I'd never been born. And you're suggesting I find pride in that heritage? Forgive me, Miss Goodwin, you have been very kind to me and often very wise but in this instance, you do not understand my situation at all."

Miss Goodwin was undeterred. "I do understand, Rose. All humans, whatever their status, have similar feelings. I do not believe you are uninterested in happiness. I believe you think it unattainable and are willing to settle for ambition. If I could change your course I surely would because I foresee a great deal of misery for you if you cannot change your way of thinking. And not only for you–"

But Rose could not listen anymore.

It was not that she did not long to be with her son. Had she not had a job to do, she would have spent every waking moment just watching him grow. She had not imagined one could be so charmed by so small a person. She longed to show him off, to take him proudly home to Emily. Take him to see his Grandma Connie. Take him to meet his father. And hers.

No, it was all impossible.

Lorenzo returned to New York for Emily and the babies soon after Rose had left. He stayed only long enough to ready his little family for the journey back to Mexico. For the next few months they waited in Toluca, his family home in the Yucatan, for the official word that he was named the Mexican minister to France. Safe in a civilized city and entranced by their excursions into the countryside, Emily could have remained there indefinitely. She loved the warm and milky-blue waves of the Caribbean Sea, the tiny twisted trees that outlined its sugar-sand beaches, the crystal green waters that pooled in the forests nearby fed by underground rivers deeper down than the hardiest native swimmers could reach, and the brilliant flowers that bloomed throughout the winter she had left behind. The neighbors were fine and their house was lovely. Briefly relieved of politics, the few months there were as pleasant as the best of dreams.

But the inevitable word came down from Mexico City and by the end of November, 1933, they were on their way to Paris. Given her husband's pleasure, the only disappointment Emily dared voice was that they had not remained long enough for her to learn Spanish.

Her husband assured her she would not need it. English was the language of the future, he said, particularly the future in Texas where they would be settling when the present work was done. The prospect still excited him. The Americans might be lacking in grace, he said, but they were certainly blessed with energy. If it could be directed wisely, a great deal could be accomplished in *Tejas* for both the United States and Mexico.

He was a little concerned about the direction of the Mexican government, he confided. Though the new Mexican president, General Santa Anna, was an early advocate of the Constitution de Zavala had helped to write in 1824, there were signs that he was slipping back from its republican principles to the imperialism of his predecessor in the Capitol Palace. If Santa Anna upheld the right of Mexican states to help govern themselves, all would be well, he told his wife. The strength of a representative form of government was being aptly demonstrated by the United States. Two such republics, side by side, could only prove themselves good neighbors.

And if not– "What then, darling?" she asked him.

"Then it will be a very sad day for the losers," he responded. "But I do not intend to be among them."

Emily wrote to Rose again before they left. "We will likely not be in Paris more than a year or two," she confided. "When we return, Lorenzo still plans we shall settle in Texas. I trust this gives you time enough to settle your affairs and make arrangements to come with us. I miss you, dear friend."

Rose focused on her work, anxious that Ms. Goodwin find no cause for complaint. Still refusing to make any firm decisions about her son's future, she avoided personal conversation with the headmistress. Another year passed. Emily wrote from France that she and Lorenzo had another child, a boy. She asked if Rose was still considering Texas. Rose avoided the subject when she responded with congratulations.

As for Luke, she avoided thinking of him as she avoided reading his dwindling letters. And she was surprised at her reaction when Dr. Connie wrote, in the spring of 1835, that he was courting someone else. "Or being courted is more like it. He claims to be too busy to think of marriage but he has brought her home to introduce us and she was quite nice. I trust you are relieved by this news. Perhaps I shall have grandchildren after all. I must, however, warn you that he will be coming to see you in the near future. He would not say when, lest you refuse. Surely, my Dear, you will allow him. It has been almost five years since you saw him, has it not?"

Rose stared at the words on the paper for a full two minutes before crumpling it in her hand. That day she did not go to see her son. Pleading a headache she went to her room to lie and stare at the ceiling. However far away she'd stayed from Luke, he had remained a doorway in her mind. An open door through which she could always retreat with her—their—son. And if that door were closing. . . .

Two things she knew. She would have to make more permanent arrangements for their son, and something would have to take his place.

As if God heard her cry, the following week brought another letter, this time from Emily who had just returned from Paris. She insisted that Rose come home for a visit that summer. "School will be out soon and Lorenzo is returning to Mexico immediately to prepare our new home in Texas at a place called Buffalo Bayou, of all things," she wrote. "I will be joining him this winter with the children. Perhaps the timing will be right for you to come with us. At any rate, you must allow me to attempt to persuade you."

Rose explained her situation to Miss Goodwin, arranging her facts as carefully as in a ledger. She told her of Colonel Morgan's offer and Emily's wishes and even included the fact of Luke's new courtship. She did not talk about her feelings.

"What do you want?" Miss Goodwin asked, quite simply, when she was done.

"Want?" Rose's voice was startled into wistfulness. "I want so many things and they are often contradictory. I cannot possibly have all of what I want or even most of it. I want both to be acceptable in society and to have my child with me. I want to be a mother, raising my son at home, and I want to make my own way, make something of myself by working in the world. So you can see, Miss Goodwin, that it does me very little good to think of what I want. I must think, instead, of what is best."

"What is best for you? Or what is best for your son?"

"I will not raise my son as a bastard.'"

"That is your choice, then. So you must decide how to give him a different raising."

"I will not marry Luke."

The older woman smiled with only her mouth. "Well dear, you can see how each choice defines the next one you must make. It is simply a process of defining our limits, would you not agree?"

Rose was silent. Miss Goodwin prompted her. "So you will not raise the child a bastard and you will not marry Luke. So then—"

"I cannot raise the child," Rose whispered.

The headmistress's tone was brisk. "So it remains to decide who best can do that job."

"Not Jenny," Rose said. "I mean, I want Jenny to go with him because Junior knows her but I want someone stronger, more intellectual, more aware, wiser—"

"Someone like Dr. Connie?"

"No!"

Miss Goodwin's liquid brown eyes were cold. "You are being extraordinarily selfish, you know. I have kept relatively quiet on the issue for these four years since your child was born but I cannot allow you to make a decision that will forever cut him off from his father, as so many of his people have been cut off. As you were cut off, Rose, for all you pass as white. I cannot, before God, sit quietly while you sacrifice your son's heritage on the alter of your ambition. Forgive me, dear, but it has to be said."

Rose bowed her head. "I cannot make a decision yet. I have put all that behind me."

"Your son is very present, Rose, and he comes out of your past. Luke deserves the chance to know he has a son. And even if you cannot bring yourself to tell him now, perhaps seeing him will help you make up your mind."

Rose did not want help in making up her mind, at least not help from Luke. But he arrived without notice before she could flee.

She returned from her Saturday visit with Junior to find him waiting in the parlor. She almost passed him by, imagining the figure sitting in the shadowed room was a visiting father to one of the girls. Her mind was full of a nearly four-year-old's antics. His laughter. His movement. His quick intelligence. She was aching with the pressure of making a decision and eagerly awaiting an escape to Emily as soon as school was out. Perhaps from a distance it would be easier to decide.

Luke's voice stopped her as she reached the stair.

"Rose."

She turned around slowly. "Luke."

They were both silent, staring.

He had risen. She moved towards him. "I did not expect— That is, your mother wrote me that you—But I—"

"I was afraid if you knew I was coming you would have run away."

She could not help smiling. "I was about to."

He said nothing, his hands circling the brim of the hat he was holding.

"Would you like tea? Have you been waiting long?" Rose remembered her manners.

The man nodded, "Yes on both counts. But I did not mind the wait. It gave me a chance to brace myself."

"Unfortunately, I have not yet had that opportunity. If you'll excuse me, perhaps while I am in the kitchen–"

But he followed her. Turning from the stove to see him standing by the table, she had a flash of no time passing at all since the time he had stood there while they toasted one another with Miss Goodwin's Christmas burgundy. She turned back to the business of making tea. A great deal had happened since then.

"You remember, don't you Rose?" His voice was faintly teasing. "You and I right here one snowy afternoon."

"It is not kind of you to mention it."

"Not kind?" His voice sharpened. "Not kind, Rose? Did you think I had no feelings that you should so ignore me afterwards? Knowing how much I cared for you, you could, at least, have written what was on your mind. Do you understand that I have thought of you every day since?" He smiled, softening. "And far too many days before that, too."

Rose stayed busy with the tea, arranging the cups carefully on the silver tray. "How can you say such a thing? Dr. Connie writes that you are courting. 'A very nice young lady,' she says. One who may give her grandchildren."

"And you believed her? My mother wants grandchildren so badly she is ready to have me marry anyone." The teasing look was back. "Well, that's not exactly true. You were always her favorite. Sometimes I thought she loved you even more than me. But we have both given up on you, or at least she has. The woman she mentioned is someone I work with at the journal. She has become a good friend but that's all."

"It doesn't matter."

Luke came around the table, took her shoulders firmly in his hands, turned her to face him. "It matters a great deal, Rose. It has been four and a half years since I saw you last. I have come, several times, to this very street and stood, watching your door, before forcing myself to turn away because I knew you did not want to see me." He tilted her chin up with a long finger. "Look at me, Rose. You may not see me again for a long time. Perhaps never. I am not a man to pursue futile causes but I am a man blessed with the faith that love can overcome all obstacles. How else could I be part of the movement for emancipation? How else could I have dared to love you?"

He took a deep breath, releasing her. Rose stood shock still. He paced and whirled. She remembered, suddenly, the light of the fire on a panther's grace, golden eyes glistening as a wind full of snow howled against the windows. As he moved towards her.

"Do you think I have not regretted loving you, Rose? Do you think I have not regretted everything about you—your whiteness, your family, your wealth—that has kept you from loving me? And everything about myself as well—my blackness, my poverty—"

"I am no richer than you, Luke. I live on my wages." And support a child, she almost said.

He sat down, putting his head in his hands. "Forgive me, Rose. I don't know what I'm saying anymore. We are preparing for an educational mission to the South. The sides are so polarized surely we will soon see civil war. By choice, I shall be in the middle of it and what man knows whether he will escape the violence he faces?" He groaned. "I should be laying out strategies and making plans and instead I'm drifting and dreaming and feeling consumed by a rose. A yellow rose."

She poured their tea there in the kitchen. Neither spoke, but their silence was strangely companionable. At least he had suffered, too, she was thinking. At least she was still talking to him, he thought.

"It cannot work, Luke. We both knew that."

It made him angry. "You knew that, perhaps. I never did."

"Better you should realize it."

"Is that all you have to say?"

She returned his stare. "That's all."

He set his cup down very carefully. Stood up. Bowed. "I will take my leave then, Ma'am. Begging your pardon. Ma'am."

He turned at the door. "Do remember me to my mother. If you see her again."

Then he was gone. Shocked into sensibility, Rose remained where she was, staring at the stark emptiness where he had been standing. If she could have called him back she would have but it was too late for that.

When Rose awoke the next morning she knew what she had to do. A hasty letter went out with the morning post along with a note to Emily, advising her to expect her imminent arrival. Then she sought out Miss Goodwin. Two hours of conversation left Miss Goodwin looking puzzled but reasonably pleased and Rose pale but determined. She hurried over to Jenny's cottage. Entering without a knock she embraced, then disengaged herself from her son.

"Jenny, what would you think of going to New York? With Junior?"

"New York? Well Ma'am, I can't rightly say I want to go there. My folks are all here. My pa counts on me. Can't say I could go or couldn't go. Why? You thinking of taking the boy?"

The boy was listening, wide-eyed.

"You go play now, Junior. You go out and play with your Grandpa, you hear? Your mama and I got to talk."

But the boy edged closer to his mother and Jenny's father did not move from his place in the doorway. The story, after all, included them. Rose reached an arm around her son, drew him close as the two women seated themselves at the small kitchen table. Junior, holding tight, held still.

"We have—I have friends in New York," Rose said. "If I were to take Junior to them, would you be able to go with him? Your father could go too."

Jenny stared down at her hands, deep brown sculptures on the white wooden table. "My family here," she said finally. "My sisters. My brother." The deep brown eyes looked into hers beseechingly. "I take good care of him, Miz Rose. You leave him with us, even no money, we find someway to feed him." The pretty round face was sad, earnest in its simplicity. "I love him like my own. My own that died and never had a pa."

Rose pushed herself back from the table. Outside a pink and purple twilight was descending. Perhaps she and Junior could take a walk before darkness fell. Best to enjoy what she had while she could. It was a foolish idea, after all. Best perhaps to leave him here, with what he already knew. It would be much less confusing to everyone. And she could certainly send money.

"It was not a good idea," she said, smiling at the darker woman. "People like me, we don't have family anywhere." The smile curved downward for a moment, then righted itself. "As for the boy, you and Grandpa are about as much family as he's likely to get."

9

The small brown face was puzzled. A leather-shod foot kicked at the bare patch of earth. "You're going away?" he asked. "When, Mama? When you going? When you coming back?"

"When *are* you going," she said automatically, correcting his grammar as she always did. "When *are* you coming back."

"When, Mama?" A tear trembled on a curly lash. "When are you, Mama?"

She had not meant to let him call her Mama, and had continued to scold Jenny when she used the word to refer to her. But Junior had clung to it as he clung to Rose on every visit. And the sound of it was sweet. She'd grown accustomed.

She sighed deeply. She would do what she had to do. As she had always done.

She had cherished this four years in secret for long enough. It was time for each of them to get on with their lives.

He tugged at her skirt again. "When are you going, Mama? Why?"

"I have to go to New York," she explained, kneeling in the grass beside him. "I have business to take care of there and it may take me all summer."

"I can go with you." Small fingers pressed into his eyes, a little trick he used to hold back tears. His lip quivered. "Aunt Jenny won't mind. You can take me with you. I'm big now. I can go." His face brightened.

She put her arms around him. "I wish I could, Junior, but I don't have a place there for you. I just—I just can't, that's all."

Tears spilled out of amber eyes as his fingers went into his mouth. "Don't cry, now," she snapped. "You're a big boy." Grief roughened her voice. And she was thinking of leaving him forever!

There was no moon and only the flare of an occasional streetlight broke up the darkness as she walked back to the school later that night. She felt her way along the street like one walking blind. She felt disconnected, remote, though her mind raced with details which must be attended. She put the matter of her child resolutely behind her.

"So you've reached a decision?" Miss Goodwin asked, facing her across the small table in her parlor the next afternoon, her eyes on her own fragile teacup.

Rose tried out a laugh. "More as if I have found another way to avoid the issue," she said. "At least for a little while. A summer."

"You intend to come back to us then? I want you, of course, but I had the feeling—" The blue eyes met the brown ones. Neither woman dropped her gaze.

"The years here have been very good for me," Rose said at last. "You have been very good to me and I have learned a great deal. It is not something I would want to give up."

"Nevertheless—" Miss Goodwin prodded gently.

Rose laughed again. "There's always the nevertheless, isn't there?"

Miss Goodwin sighed. "It would be easier for me to help you reach a decision if I knew your mind on this matter, Rose. You have become adept at hiding your feelings, you know. Not that I wish to pry but when you asked to talk with me, I assumed you wanted to tell me what you have already decided. It seems however, that you are still vacillating." She shook her head. "For four years, now, I have watched your vacillation. It is sometimes a strain."

She took a deep swallow and carefully replaced the delicate cup in its saucer. "I would be glad to help you in anyway I can, my Dear, but if you are not willing to share your thoughts, there is really nothing I can say that would help."

Rose also put down her cup. "I cannot share what I don't understand myself, Miss Goodwin." The full lips curved in a tiny smile. "It is not so much my thoughts as my feelings that give me trouble. The fact is, I could go on as we are quite cheerfully—enjoying my work, enjoying your company—and most of all, enjoying my son."

She took up her cup, sipped slowly. Miss Goodwin waited, watching her. Rose smiled again. "Nevertheless," she said, "as you have been telling me for the past two years, it is hardly fair to the boy to grow up in secret. And, as you have also been pointing out, the longer I keep him nearby, the harder it will be for both of us to separate."

"I can see your mind has not changed on that point, at least," said Miss Goodwin.

"Which point do you mean?"

"Your resolution to separate yourself from him."

Rose's lips tightened though she said nothing.

"Very well, then," said Miss Goodwin. "Tell me, at least, what your immediate plans are. Do you wish me to look for a new housekeeper? Or will you be returning to us from New York?" Rose said nothing. Miss Goodwin continued, relentless, but gentle. "It does take some time, Dear, to locate a good assistant. And, having become accustomed to your level of service, I fear I shall be more particular than ever."

Rose put her cup down very carefully and stood. Moving to the fireplace, she picked up the miniature of a woman about whom she had often wondered, but never asked.

"Your mother?" she inquired.

The older woman nodded. "She died when I was seven." She indicated the other picture on the mantel, a jovial gentleman with a large mustache. "My father raised me. With the help of my grandmother." A smile softened her face. "I used to think I should feel sadder about it all, you know? Not having a mother, I mean. But my grandmother was so wonderful there never seemed to be anything lacking in my life."

Rose returned to her seat, facing her mentor. "I have the offer of a job in Texas," she said.

"Oh?"

"It seems a good job though the details are not clear. A gentleman–one of the captains who has had a long association with the Wests and the Sturns–has invited me to assist in a new enterprise. He is involved in both land speculation and the shipping trade and he intends to establish a town there, a shipping port, I take it. I presume he will need managers for his various businesses."

"What sort of business, exactly?"

"Well you see, I told him I was not interested so we did not discuss it further."

"But now you are?"

Rose looked down. "Texas is a long way from New York," she said. "And Boston. It would be– It would be an adventure."

"And a place to start over?"

"That, too."

"Would you take the boy?"

Rose looked up, surprised. "But how could I? I would have to sail down with Emily and her children. She and her husband have returned here from Paris this spring after a political disagreement with the Mexican president. As far as I can understand from Emily's last letter, Mr. de Zavala has now resigned as

Mexico's minister to France and, apparently, intends to throw in his lot with the Texians. The family is in New York now but he will be leaving this month to prepare a place for them in Texas. Emily writes that she intends to follow in the fall. She wants me to go with her. And she tells me Captain Morgan continues to inquire about me."

"Captain Morgan?"

"The gentleman who offered me a job there."

"I see."

The pause lengthened between the two women. Miss Goodwin broke it at last.

"And the boy?"

"I am not sure what to do about the boy," Rose said, simply. "Jenny and her father would like to keep him. They are the only family he has known."

"You could take him to his grandmother," Miss Goodwin said. "I thought you were considering it at last."

"It is much too complicated," Rose answered.

Miss Goodwin stared at her. "What of his right to know his heritage? Connie is a wonderful woman and I know she would cherish the boy as much as you do, if not more, because she would not be distracted so much by life's possibilities, as you seem to be."

She settled her cup in its saucer, clinking hard against the china. "Forgive me, but I cannot stand by silently while you deny your son the most important gift you could give him."

Rose said nothing.

"You will let me know, will you not?" said Miss Goodwin, rising.

"About Texas, I have decided already to go. About Junior, I will decide this summer." She got to her feet, a smile twitching her mouth. "You must not think you have not made an impact, Miss Goodwin. You have shaken my mind in the place I believed myself to be most unshakeable."

"Would that I could," Miss Goodwin murmured, opening the door. She remained there, watching as the slim young body retreated in a gentle swish of dark rich cotton.

Lorenzo de Zavala had already sailed for Texas when Rose arrived in New York. In his absence, Emily was more than delighted to see her old friend and show off her children. And the news that Rose had decided on Texas brought cheers of joy.

"You are coming with me! Oh my dear Rose! We can all be a family again!" Emily seized her friend around the waist and waltzed her around the room. "We must call in a seamstress," she exclaimed, pausing for breath. "The Texas climate is quite different, you know. Extraordinarily hot! It would be lovely not to have to wear sleeves or stockings at all, but we can, at least, purchase lighter materials. Oh Rose, I can hardly believe you are going to come though I must say, you do not seem nearly as excited as I."

"It's a big step," Rose murmured. "And I must confess, I still suffer from doubts about Captain Morgan. Not that I doubt his intention to hire me," she went on hastily. "But quite honestly, I do not like the man though I have no reason to question him."

"As you say, it is a long step. And you are more accustomed to the company of women, Rose. But I assure you, Uncle Benjamin, ah, I mean, I hear tell that Captain Morgan is an excellent businessman and a gentleman in all respects."

Rose heard her father's name without a cringe. She had finally accepted his never coming back for her though she wondered to herself if some small hope that he might visit her in Texas—far away from the rest of the family—might be influencing her decision. Regardless, the die was cast. "We shall see," she told Emily, still smiling.

She spent the summer in preparation, accepting Emily's guidance in her choice of clothes but adding the serviceable dark things she knew would be expected for a person of her station. Determined to set up housekeeping on her own, wanting dependence neither on Emily's nor Captain Morgan's households, she accepted the gifts that Maxine and Clarence offered her: bedding and linens, lamps and glasses, pewter, silver plate, coarse china and iron cookware. Maxine even gave her a small Turkish rug she had long admired. "Was there anything else?" Maxine kept asking. As if she were planning never to see her again, thought Rose, and regretted the thought instantly. Maxine had never been less than kind. And Texas was indeed far away.

Texas was still a wild country, Emily told her. Nothing was being manufactured there, except such things as pioneers made for their own use. Captain Morgan would be filling his warehouse with imports from New York, Europe and New Orleans but she would do well to be ready for settling when she arrived. Rose added a year's supply of soaps and other toiletries to her lengthening list, comforting herself with the thought that Emily's list was far longer. But then Emily had three children, the youngest not yet a year old.

Rose could hardly play with Emily's children without pain, thinking of her own. If her reticence puzzled her friend, Rose hoped she put it down to a lack of rapport with little ones. But she caught Emily watching her sometimes, a sharply curious expression on her face. It did not lessen as Rose pretended not to notice.

"There's something you're not telling me, Rose," she said one day, coming in with that look of stubborn determination Rose recognized so well. "I know it's not my business or you would have discussed it but I'm just as sure it's something that's very important to you. It colors your action, your expression, everything. As you value our kinship, I must beg you to confide in me."

Rose said nothing. Emily's expression softened. "Please, Rose."

Rose sat down. Emily waited.

"It's a long story."

"We have time."

"It's very hard to give up a secret one has carried for so long."

"I'll keep your secrets, Rose. You know I will."

"Even from your husband?"

Emily's gaze did not waver. "Even from him, if I must, for your sake."

There was a long silence after Rose finished her story and there were tears in both women's eyes. Rising, Emily came to kneel beside her friend, her arms around her. "Oh Dear. My dear, dear Rose. And you have carried this all alone, all this time."

"Miss Goodwin helped."

"Yes, but she's not family, is she."

"I have no family," said Rose.

The hurt on Emily's face was almost palpable. "You have me. You have my mother. We're your family by blood as well as by upbringing."

"Forgive me," Rose murmured. "Of course you are. But surely you understand what I mean." She shook her head at Emily's puzzled air. "Or perhaps you don't understand, after all."

"There are many things I do not understand, Rose. You're quite right about that." Emily got up to walk around the room. "But I do know children need parents. They need a family. And you have the capacity to give that to your child. If you're determined not to marry Luke, then let us take the child with us! Let him grow up in Texas! You can always claim to be widowed. I'll certainly agree with whatever story you need to tell."

"It's too late for that," Rose said, holding her face in her hands. "There are too many links to New York. I will be working for Captain Morgan, remember? He would certainly know better. And what reason would he have to protect me? Indeed, his knowing would strip away the small protection I have as an honorable, woman of good reputation. Who knows what he would expect of me, then? He has a certain eye for women, I've noticed, and he knows my origins. And, innocent and good as you are, Emily, even you must know that Negroes are not regarded in the same way as whites, however cultured a few of us have become in your society. Neither our morals nor our souls are considered very important. Considered of value." Oh dear, oh dear, thought Rose, I really must shut up! I am sounding just like Luke.

"I see what you mean," said Emily, slowly. Then the chin came up again. "But there must be something we can do. We cannot leave that child, your son, with strangers, Rose. There must be something. What has Miss Goodwin advised?"

Rose's laugh was short. "That I marry Luke. And that I will not do."

"Was that the only advice she gave? Nothing more?"

"Well, yes. She recommended I take him to his grandmother. To Dr. Connie."

Emily sprang up from the bed where she was sitting and seized her cousin's hand. "Of course! Of course! Silly me! Why did not I think of that! She would be so very happy to have him and then his father could get to know him. And you could see him any time you wanted. And no one in my parents' circle would ever have to know." She added an afterthought. "Unless you married, of course."

"I cannot see him any time I want to if I am in Texas," Rose said, ignoring Emily's last comment.

"No, you clearly cannot have everything you want. But then, who can? I cannot live near my parents and my husband both, however much I love them all. And though I won't presume to equate that with being away from one's own child, I do understand that one choice usually rules out another. But it appears you have already decided not to raise this child yourself. Why deny him the other half of his family at the same time?"

"That's what Miss Goodwin said. Only, the last time we discussed it, she added words like selfish." Rose's smile was faint but something had lightened in her heart. Perhaps there was a way, after all.

For the first time since putting it into the mail, she was glad of the letter she had written to Dr. Connie from Boston. Though she had not explained the matter, she had, at least, alluded to the subject. Had said, at least, that they must talk.

"You what!" Dr. Connie's voice was as sharp as her eyes, staring, widened by shock. "You're telling me that you and Luke– you had a child!"

"He doesn't know. I never wanted him to know."

"You never told him! You just told him to go away! As if that would solve everything! You had his child and you never told him! And him loving you all these years!" The voice was as accusatory as Rose had imagined it might be. She kept her head down, waiting for the words to run down. Run out. She waited a long time. Dr. Connie had a great deal to say. A great deal had to do with the selfish instincts to which all humans fall prey. "Survivalists," she called it. "Everybody trying so hard to save themselves, that nobody can manage to work together."

When she fell silent at last, Rose had nothing at all to say. Dr. Connie waited. "You know Luke's been thinking of marriage," she finally resumed. "Nice girl. He's brought her here a time or two. My guess is that his feelings for her aren't all that strong. He's really more married to his work than he ever will be to a woman but he knows I want grandchildren and this girl is very respectful of him and of me." She cast a sidelong glance at Rose. "Very pretty, too. Dark and very pretty. And very much in love. You'd think the sun rose and set with Luke to see her follow him around with those big eyes of hers. And he likes her well enough. She's quite intelligent. He met her working with the journal in Philadelphia."

Rose braced herself not to care. Why should she care what Luke did with his life? She was doing what she pleased with hers. "He told me about her," she murmured, not adding that Luke insisted the woman was merely a friend. Dr. Connie stopped pacing, her face showing the hint of a smile. She moved towards Rose, put a warm brown arm around the slender shoulders.

"You know I'll always love you, no matter what you do or don't do. And I suspect Luke feels the same way." A brown finger lifted Rose's chin, dark eyes stared into her own. They were like her son's, both sharpened and softened by age. "In my heart of hearts, Rose, I pity that girl if Luke marries her. She will always be in second place and she's bound to feel it though he's too much a gentleman to admit such a thing." The older woman shook her head sadly, "Child, child. I do not understand why you do this to yourself. Though you may deny it, I believe you still love Luke. You have a child with him! Why not marry him and allow all of us to be happy?"

"I'll never marry Luke," said Rose, finding her voice at last. "But I can bring your grandchild here if you wish to raise him."

Dr. Connie sat down abruptly. Stared up. "And what about Luke?"

"I presume Luke will soon find out. By that time I hope to be far away."

"In Texas? With Emily?"

Rose seized her mentor's hand. "Promise me you will not tell him. Promise me that, Dr. Connie, on your honor. I will not have him pursuing me. Let him find happiness with someone who can appreciate him for who he is."

"Someone who does not mind his being black?"

Rose sat down beside her. "First of all, I beg you to forgive me. I have been selfish. I have also been frightened. I have not wanted to lose what little I had as far as my reputation. And I did not want–" Her voice failed. She could not tell Dr. Connie that she did not want to become part of the Negro world, that her aspirations were higher. She could not so insult the woman who had mothered her from infancy. But she could see that Dr. Connie already knew.

"Did not want to marry Luke," the older woman ended the sentence for her. Rose nodded.

"So you kept the child with you? Miss Goodwin knew, of course?"

"He stayed nearby. With a nursemaid. A very nice woman named Jenny whose father came to live with them. I thought it would be good for the boy to have a man around. I used to visit every day." Tears filled her eyes, suddenly, remembering her son running to the door to meet her, holding up his arms. No, no, she must not think about that now. She was making other arrangements. "Miss Goodwin knew, of course. She helped me a great deal. But she never let up on me either."

"Never let up?"

"She thought I should marry Luke. And when she saw I was determined not to she tried to convince me to bring the boy to you. She said many things you have said."

"So she convinced you?"

"It was Emily who convinced me," Rose said slowly. "I finally told her last week after swearing her to secrecy beyond the grave. And she was worse than Miss Goodwin. Would not hear of my leaving him with strangers, as she put it."

"True enough."

Rose shrugged. "Yes."

"I suppose you do not want anyone else to know about the child?"

"Indeed not. Will you promise me that too?"

There was a long moment of silence. "My Dear," said Dr. Connie at last, "you cannot imagine how much I wish to proclaim this grandson created by the two people I love best. But I will give you that promise for the present. If you love me, you will release me from it soon.

Rose said nothing.

"Well now," said Dr. Connie, pushing herself up from the settee to begin a mental tour of her small house. "I'm sure we can make room. The child can have Luke's old room. And we will put another bed in there for—did you say Jenny? It would be a pity to separate him from the only other mother he's known, especially if you are determined to go off to Texas. A poor idea if you ask me, which you aren't, of course." She paused a moment to pat Rose's shoulder. "There, there. I shall not implore you or chastise you anymore. I shall concentrate on the gratitude I feel in the discovery of a grandchild. And the father—Jenny's father—would he want to come? I can clear out that little attic room I've never used. It's really quite nice, finished off with a gable window. No doubt he could be useful here. It's always nice to have a man around the house."

"Jenny may not come. She has family there and may not be willing to leave them."

"We shall see," said Dr. Connie. "I feel capable of caring for him myself."

The two women discussed particulars until long after dark. The only subject avoided was Luke. He did not come home often, Dr. Connie mentioned, almost casually. No, she did not expect him home at all that summer. Perhaps at Christmas.

By Christmas Rose would be in Texas. "You will not write him about it?" she begged. Dr. Connie shook her head. "I'll respect your wishes," she said, "much as I disagree with them."

Rose hung her head. Dr. Connie sighed. "Someday you will change your mind, Rose. I believe I know you well enough to know that."

"Perhaps," Rose whispered. "But I cannot imagine it."

"It's a simple path from here to there," the midwife said. "All you have to do is to keep on wanting to be good. The way will open. You'll see."

"I'll send you money for him."

"That's totally unnecessary," Dr. Connie said briskly. "I have yet to meet the little boy but he's my own now."

"I'm not giving him away. I'm only giving him up. For a while."

"I understand that. And I'll take care of him for you as well as for myself. And Luke."

It was enough. By the time Rose curled up in Luke's old bed for another night in the house she'd visited so often for so long, she was half-satisfied that her son's future was in good hands. Dr. Connie would not let her down. As for the other half–her own plans to leave–she closed the door on her heart and went to sleep.

Her eyes were dry when she left Dr. Connie's house the next morning to walk back to the Wests. She would wait another week before returning to Boston. There was much yet to do. Captain Morgan was briefly in port and she must see him before he sailed. Texas was her next step forward but she must make her own plans for the move. She did not intend to live in Emily's shadow.

As for her son, the matter was finally resolved. The family she could not have for herself, she could still give to him. And what she could not give of herself, his grandmother could. It was an altogether satisfactory conclusion. She ignored the pain that attended it.

Dr. Connie persuaded Rose to take her along when she returned to Boston for her son. It would be easier for the child to have the trip as a time to get acquainted, she said. Besides, she was eager to see her old friend, Miss Goodwin. And she had not taken a trip in a long time. "Even New York can be very confining," she laughed with an eagerness in her eyes that Rose, resistant at first, could not deny.

They did not talk much on the journey, swaying together in the wide old coach, conscious of the way the other passengers drew their skirts aside when Dr. Connie heaved herself on board. Conscious also of the curious glances that darted their way and busy with their own thoughts, they did not mention the child at all until they were walking away from the coach stop in Boston the next morning, approaching the little house where he lived.

Dr. Connie suddenly stopped. "What's his name?" she asked. "All this time and I never asked his name!"

Rose smiled. "Junior," she said. "Luke, Junior."

Dr. Connie's smile grew broader with every step. By the time they reached the stoop her face was split wide open. Behind the door they heard the pounding of little feet racing to answer the knock. Rose scooped the child into her arms, tears spilling over. He clung to her neck.

"Mama! Mama! You came back!" He pulled back to look at her, very serious. "I was afraid," he said. "I was scared you never come back. It was bad dreams. You won't go away again, will you? You won't leave me again, will you, Mama? You back now?"

She set him carefully down on his feet, looked up to greet Jenny standing in the door, glanced at Dr. Connie, waiting behind her, then turned her attention back to her son.

"Junior," she said. "I'd like you to meet your grandmother."

She left the two to become acquainted as Junior showed Dr. Connie the yard. The tree he liked to climb. The bushes where he played hide-and-seek. The fence he was not allowed to cross. She went inside to discuss arrangements with Jenny. Jenny had decided she would rather leave her sisters, grown up, after all, than to be separated from the boy she loved as her own. If her father could go with them, she told Rose, they could be packed and ready within two days. The matter was settled within an hour. Grandpa, raising his white brows a bit at the sight of Dr. Connie, looked delighted by the prospect.

Rose explained their plans to Junior when he brought his grandmother back from their tour. "New York!" he said, eyes wide. "We're going to New York! Aunt Jenny and Grandpa and Grandma and me and you! All of us! Where will we live? Will we have trees?"

"I have trees," Dr. Connie replied. "And a room for you. Your daddy's old room." She avoided Rose's eyes. "And room for Jenny, too. And for your grandpa. We'll all be together."

"Daddy?" the child said, wonderingly. "Who's my daddy? I never seen him."

Rose turned away, leaving the grammar uncorrected for once. Dr. Connie took the boy on her lap. "It won't be for a while, Child, but you will. And he'll be very happy to see what a fine, big boy you've become."

"When?" he insisted. "When will I see him?"

"Maybe we'll all have Christmas together," said Dr. Connie. Right now he's in Philadelphia, working with a newspaper. Maybe he'll take you there someday. When you're just a little bigger."

"My daddy!" the little boy breathed in amazement, then jumped down to run to his mother. "And Mama? You be there at Christmas, too! We all be together!"

No one said anything. Time enough later to talk about Texas. Time enough later for tears.

Miss Goodwin was very happy to see them both. Miss Goodwin approved of the turn of events. Cozy in the little parlor, the two older women talked most of the night. Rose excused herself early, explaining that she needed to pack up her room. But once there, she found herself sitting, almost dazed, in her chair unable to move forward on anything. Giving up and climbing into bed she twisted and turned but could not sleep for a long time.

10

Though she had not yet left him, his loss was a stone on her heart and a mist in her head.

The time was very near.

Captain Morgan, now promoted to colonel, would be docking the *Exert* in mid-October. They would sail by the end of the month. Not the best of seasons, Clarence West kept saying, regarding his daughter with a disapproving air. Dreadful enough that she was following her Mexican husband off to the wild lands of Texas and taking all three of his grandchildren. But to be sailing in the hurricane season!

Maxine fluttered nervously about, attempting to calm the storms at home. Emily held her chin up and kept tight reign on her temper. Rose rushed through her morning tasks, helping her cousin now that her own wardrobe and supplies were packed and ready and then rushed away to Dr. Connie's to spend a few more precious hours with her son.

She prepared him the best she could, knowing that nothing she could ever say would make a difference to either one of them. Things were settled, it seemed to her, before either of them were born but she could not stop trying to explain.

Dr. Connie watched, disapprovingly at first. And then accepting that she could not turn the young woman's head, she surrendered to the inevitable and offered what comfort she could. Mostly she minded the child, showering him with all the love she felt for both his parents.

The *Exert* docked. Colonel Morgan called on the Wests. Arrangements were made to transport the women's crates to the shipyard. Emily was "trying to get New York into a box," said her father, attempting rare humor over his daughter's insistence on shipping everything necessary to set up a proper home. The Colonel, refusing to take sides, suggested subtley that anything that could be shipped to Texas would certainly prove useful, "there being little there at present, though of course I am remedying that situation as quickly as I can."

Rose, after a pressing invitation, sat stiffly in the parlor while the Colonel discussed his plans with Clarence West. A hotel was being built at Morgan's

Point, port for the sizeable tract of land his company had purchased on Galveston Bay. The hotel, along with various other enterprises, would be the heart of a township Morgan was developing, called New Washington. The port, at the northern end of the Texas coast, was only three hundred miles from New Orleans. A prime location.

The past two years had brought undreamed success, said Morgan. The population of Texas was growing fast, swelling from both the north and the south, doubling in the past year to some 25,000. Land was available as low as twelve and a half cents an acre. The price was pulling people in as fast as they could walk there, many coming from west of the Appalachians.

Morgan laughed a bit shortly. "Rather an uncouth group for the most part. It takes a certain bluntness, a certain weight and passion of temperament, one must suppose, to trudge a thousand miles or more to set up a house they have to build themselves with whatever is at hand and then set themselves to digging up the ground and planting what food they want to eat someday. Living, meanwhile on whatever they can kill or grub out of the bushes."

Again the short laugh. "You can well imagine their countenances. Rough as any you might find on the docks. The children are wild, though well-trained to work. And the women are weather-beaten as mastheads and about as thin."

He shrugged, glancing at Rose. "Of course, those men who can, run cattle or plant cotton. Their families are a different sort and form the beginnings of society there. There are occasional balls and the social graces are observed, if roughly. There is not much concern with one's parents or place in society. There is not so much sense, you see, of custom and culture; so many cultures and classes being mixed with all of them, more or less, dependent on one another for survival. For instance, everyone is involved in politics, though many can neither read nor write more than their own names."

His eyes returned to Rose, lingering. "It is a most fortunate beginning for some," he said. "If one has the money or the energy, the horizons are very broad in Texas. One can go far. Even the dirt farmers will see dreams realized."

Clarence West, listening attentively, was not satisfied. Dirt farming, after all, was nothing he had ever wished to consider. Emily would certainly never have to sully her hands. But there were other problems.

What was the situation with Mexico now? he wanted to know. "Emily says Mr. de Zavala has written that there is a considerable stir among the American colonists. Something like a Declaration of Independence seems to be afoot. Does that mean war?"

"It means commerce, sir," said Morgan briskly. "There is a great deal of money to be made in times of war. All for the good of the country, I mean. More food must be imported, since farmlands may be overrun. Guns and gear are needed for the soldiers. And a little something for their women who wait at home."

"It was my understanding from my conversations with Mr. de Zavala this spring that the colonists were reconciled to being a part of Mexico."

"Mr. de Zavala is an optimist," said Morgan. "A good thing, of course, though not always in line with reality. I'm afraid the political alliances between Texas and Mexico continue to deteriorate. We had looked to the President, General Santa Anna who has been most helpful in the past, to promote the status of Texas as a separate state, populated as it has been by English-speaking people. But he has completely gone in the other direction and is demanding closer judicial ties to the Capitol along with trading limitations we are ill disposed to meet and taxes which we are ill disposed to pay."

"Mr. Steven Austin, who has cared more for the American colonists than any living man might be expected to, undertook the lengthy journey to Mexico City in order to negotiate a more favorable relationship but it appears he offended certain authorities with his requests and was arrested and imprisoned before he could return."

"He is not still in prison!"

"He was released this summer, after more than a year. I have not seen him since his return, but I understand he is quite weakened, physically. And mentally, he is more than a little rebellious."

"So it will be war, then?"

"The Texians are already arming, Spanish and English alike. What they lack in style, I must say, they make up in determination, sheer strength and stubborn wit. They are, after all, frontiersmen, whether from the United States or Mexico."

"And who will be leading this—rabble?"

Morgan smiled. "Mr. Austin has done an excellent job of holding them in check but he is hardly a general, though I believe he has been so designated. He is more diplomatic, shall we say? His nature inclines towards collaboration rather than confrontation and the tactics, as you can imagine, are quite opposite. It appears that the colonists' hopes for independence are being pinned on General Sam Houston, a former governor of Tennessee and something of a hero in the French and Indian wars. I seem to recall that he spent some time as a youth living among the Indians himself, before he returned to civilization and took up law and politics. A rather rough sort, I must say, but intelligent, well spoken and capable of command."

"Mr. de Zavala did not go into such detail."

"He would not wish to worry you nor his wife, I am sure," said Morgan, as one who suddenly remembered his mission. "Nor is there reason for worry. Indeed, you must forgive me if I have caused you concern for your daughter. I assure you, the Mexican force is concentrated far south of the land we now hold in Texas and the passage between Mexico City and San Antonio is dry and deadly. The colonists are well armed and determined to defend their homesteads. We see little cause for concern."

"Your ships, then, are being used for this revolution?"

"My ship is at your service, Sir, to transport your daughter to her waiting husband." He acknowledged Rose with a small bow. "And her friend to her new tasks."

Before Clarence West could recover his questions, Morgan had brought the conversation back to New Washington and the burgeoning business there. As many as a dozen ships might ride at anchor in Galveston Bay these days, he explained with a note of pride, not mentioning that more than one might be run by a crew of the buccaneers who had long used Galveston Island as a hideout. But they had not damaged Texas trade. Preferring to prey on Spain, they were proving themselves allies in the conflict with Mexico.

His ranch, along with others in the region, was prospering and he had already planted a grove of orange trees there. In the new township, one warehouse was already finished and another was being built. One would receive local goods for shipping out–mostly cotton, beef, and animal skins. The other would store the goods being shipped in. The town could certainly support the business. A dozen families had already settled there with more arriving on every ship.

"You will manage it all for me, Rose," he said, tapping his cane on the warm wool carpet. His smile was as narrow as his face. "I intend to keep you very busy."

Rose did not return the smile. "The hotel? Or the warehouses?"

"Why, both, I should imagine," said the Colonel. "In the warehouses you will have to keep close accounting. The hotel–you will live there and offer general oversight, though someone else can look to the day-to-day operations." He gave a short, sharp laugh. "There should be no problem with workers. I have labor enough and to spare."

Rose sat quietly while Colonel Morgan detailed his operation. She learned that the plans included a half-dozen Negroes to help in the hotel and another half-dozen to work in the warehouse. "I can get more should you determine there is need," he finished, mistaking the question on her face.

"These Negroes," she said, hesitating on the word, "they are slaves? I did not think slavery was allowed by the Mexican Constitution."

"Why yes! That is, no!" Morgan regarded the darkening eyes staring into his own for a full half minute before pulling an embroidered silk handkerchief from his pocket and touching his forehead. "I mean to say, Miss West, that I have a number of black indentured servants who are working for me in Texas. Building and so forth. They will be available to do your bidding."

"You do not pay them?"

Morgan stared at her. "I will be paying you, Miss West. I will be paying you five dollars a week as we agreed and your room and board, of course. If your work is satisfactory, I will raise that to six dollars a week within six months. And when you are ready to settle, I will help you build a little place of your own. Is that satisfactory?"

"That is quite satisfactory for me, Colonel Morgan. But that was not my question. Are your other servants paid?"

A small snort of exasperation escaped Morgan. He rose to his feet, thumping his cane down hard. "I do not see that being any of your affair, Miss West. Now if you will, pray, excuse me, I must return to my work."

She said nothing, remaining stiffly on the parlor settee as the two men moved towards the door. He turned before opening it. "Yet, since you will be overseeing the help, I suppose I must tell you now that most do not receive wages although their accommodations are certainly more than adequate. As yours will be."

"They are slaves, then," Rose murmured half to herself.

"And I paid plenty for them," Morgan said, settling his hat before reaching for the door. "Goodbye, Miss West. If, as I trust, this conversation has not taken away your appetite for this new adventure, I shall expect to find you ready to sail a week from today. My men will be here tomorrow or the next day to take your boxes to the ship. If you wish to accompany your friend, you will have to make certain choices." Again the thin smile. "So you will not have very much time to think things over, Miss West."

"I shall keep that in mind, Colonel Morgan."

He hesitated a moment longer. "There are papers you will have to sign.

We are traveling, of course, to a foreign country however Americanized our own settlement. You have a passport, I presume?"

"No," she said. "I do not."

"It will be necessary," he told her. "I will see to it for you." Then he was gone.

If the doors behind her had not seemed so firmly closed, Rose might have changed her mind in that moment. But she could not. She saw no where else to go.

And having made the decision to go on, she could not flee at the sight of the name on her passport.

"But it's not my name!" she said, staring at the document Emily brought to her room two days later. "It's your name! Surely you cannot mean–"

Emily sighed. The realities of life were always, somehow, darker when she was attending to her friend. Little was as simple as it should be. And it was all so very difficult to explain. Embarrassing really. Especially when Rose's pride more than matched her own. But she must try.

"Your birth certificate is, ah, inadequate, it seems, for you to travel as a, ah, free woman. It was so much simpler, given our present time constraints, to have you use my name." She tried on a smile. "Now that I'm not using it anymore."

Emily did not smile back. "Like your old clothes," she said, staring at Emily. "Something I can have when you're done with them."

"That's not fair!" The small face puckered in angry frustration.

"No, of course it's not. But I simply can't believe–I mean, it's almost too much–" Rose sat down on the bed abruptly, burying her face in her hands. "Do I have to give up everything, then, to gain this new experience? Even my name?"

Emily slipped down beside her, putting an arm around her shoulders. "It's only for the officials, Dear. It will not make a hoot of difference to anyone else. You'll introduce yourself as Rose and that's who you'll be. The other– It's just to make the passage easier. So there will be no mistake."

Rose would not lift her head. "You mean so I will not be mistaken for a slave? You mean if I used my own birth information–even though all Negroes born in New York have been emancipated for the past seven years–the emancipation might not hold in Texas? I thought Texas was part of Mexico, not part of the Southern slave block."

"It's very complicated, I'm afraid," said Emily. Getting no response, she patted her friend's shoulder and got up. "I beg you to trust me, Rose. It will ease both our minds." She paused at the door. "The important thing to remember, Rose, is that you must be able to return to New York when you wish to. I cannot, in good conscience, let you leave your son behind here without making certain you can come back to him." She stopped talking, getting no response. Better not to explain too much. Better that Rose not know about the argument with her father who wanted to follow Colonel Morgan's advice and use Morgan's name on Rose's passport, sealing her identity as his servant. Who knew where that might lead! Whereas, by sharing Emily's own name, Rose would also carry Emily's white identity. Or, at the very least, the identity of belonging to her.

But it would only hurt Rose to explain such things. Not that she didn't understand already. Emily sighed audibly as she left the room.

Rose stopped re-packing her travel trunk and carpet bag–everything else being already en route to the ship–left word with the maid of her whereabouts and went to see Dr. Connie and her son. She spent the next three days there, sharing Luke's old bed with the small warm body she would soon be leaving behind. Forever, she kept telling herself. Preparing herself. But her heart would not acknowledge her rationales.

"You know Mama is leaving day after tomorrow," she told him the last day of their visit. "I don't know if I will be able to come tomorrow but I will see you before I sail."

"I'm going to stay with Grandma," he announced repeating his instructions. "I'm going to stay right here and be very good and at Christmas my daddy will come." He paused, gnawing at his thumb for a moment before dimpling up at her. "And then you'll come back and we'll all be together. With Grandma and Aunt Jenny and Grandpa and you and me."

"I will not be back for Christmas, Junior." Sorrow roughened her voice. "Texas is a very long way away and I will have a job there that I must do before I can come back."

"Is it a long job, Mama? A very, very long job?"

"It's a long job, Junior. But I'll send presents."

The amber eyes blinked steadily, willing away the tears. They spilled anyway. Small arms clung. "I don't want presents, Mama. I just want you."

She could not, must not cry with him. "You'll have Grandma," she told him, loosening his grasp. "And you'll be very happy."

"I'll be very happy," he repeated solemnly. "And you'll come back."

"I'll come back," she promised at last, catching him up for one more hug. "I will come back, Son."

Dr. Connie came to hold the little boy as his mother left. Matters rushed on to conclusion. The last short morning in New York, the last short visit with her son, the last long ride to the docks passed in a blur of tears and confusion. But they were all on deck finally, along with a sizeable crew and the sizeable families of thirteen artisans and tradespeople who were accompanying them to start new businesses at Morgan's Point. With much creaking and groaning of wood and canvas, the sails went up and the *Exert* backed slowly out of the harbor. Side by side against the rail, Emily and Rose watched the figures on the dock get smaller and smaller. Maxine was still waving even while the other hand held a handkerchief to her eyes. Clarence, one arm around his wife, extended the other in a long salute.

And then the ship turned into the wind, the sails billowed full, and the dock with its people and the city behind them slipped slowly down into the water.

Rose remained on deck while Emily took the children below to explore their cabin. There was nothing but ocean around her now. Ocean and the wind.

"You are enjoying your first sail, Miss West?" The voice beside her brought her mind back to the ship with a start. She turned to see Colonel Morgan staring down at her.

"It's quite wonderful out here, Colonel. So– So free."

"Indeed it is." A smile played over his thin lips. "Though business must go on as usual for some of us." They stood in silence for a few minutes, sharing the wind. "If the weather holds, we should be making New Orleans by early December and be in Galveston Bay well before Christmas. I believe Mr. de Zavala plans to have a house prepared for his family by then. And the hotel at Morgan's Point should be completed."

"New Orleans?" said Rose. "I did not realize we would be stopping over."

"Well of course, my Dear. One cannot miss New Orleans either coming or going from Texas if one is in the business of trade. New Orleans is almost as good a market as New York, better in some things. And much closer to home."

"You think of Texas, then, as your home, now, Colonel?"

Morgan shrugged. "Close enough," he said. "Sailors really have no home, Miss West. We live for the wind and the newest ports."

"I do not think of you so much as a sailor, Colonel Morgan."

"What then?" His glance was penetrating. Curious. And strangely personal. It made Rose uncomfortable. "Pray how do you think of me, Miss West?"

"Why, as a gentleman, first. A family acquaintance. And my employer whom I hope to satisfy with my work."

"It should not be too difficult. I find you, already, most satisfying, my Dear." Rose said nothing. Morgan waited. "I will see you at dinner, then," he said at last. "And, should you need anything, do not hesitate to let me know."

With a swift, small bow, he was gone. But Rose was uneasy with the feeling that lingered in the air behind him.

In the days that followed, she often found him watching her. Not wanting his attention, she kept herself surrounded by the children and when they were abed, stayed close to Emily. It was, overall, a most pleasant voyage. The water remained calm except for a few rainy squalls, soon over. The children adapted well to the motion of waves and after the first few days, did not experience seasickness. Emily was so delighted to be going to her husband that she was a constant source of optimistic cheer. And Rose was finding that she loved the sea. Removed from everything, time and space for everything were opened-up. She held her future lightly in her hands, along with her past. But she was neither. She was now. She breathed in freedom with the sharp salt air and never wanted it to end. Even the thought of her son, further and further away, could not erase the joy in her adventure. As for the work at the end of the ride, there would be time enough to think of that when she arrived.

They were two days out of New Orleans when Colonel Morgan found her alone by the rail one evening after dinner. Emily was below with the children and the deck was deserted except for two men on the ropes. Leaning out over the water, Rose was lost in the thought that the voyage was drawing to an end and she was soon to be thrust into a whole new world. A world populated, she remembered with a tiny shiver, by slaves and masters. What a strange irony that she descended from both categories.

"Enjoying the evening, Miss West?"

The voice was close. She turned slowly to avoid bumping into the figure who loomed behind her. "Why yes, Colonel. It's a lovely evening. I was regretting that our sail would soon be over."

"You will enjoy New Orleans, I think, Rose." He bowed pleasantly enough. "If you will permit me to call you Rose. Perhaps you will allow me to show you New Orleans. It is a most enchanting city. Very French. With a touch of the American wilds, of course. But charming. And not dangerous in the company of a gentleman."

"I will have to see what Emily and the children intend," Rose murmured.

"We have not yet discussed New Orleans at all."

"I'm sure Mrs. de Zavala will not begrudge you my company," Morgan said, his eyes fixed on her face.

Rose said nothing, wishing him gone. She would have to get over it, she thought to herself. He was her employer now. She would have to be in close communication along many lines. She did not have the luxury of excusing herself from his presence.

"Before we dock there are a few more papers that must be cleared, Rose. I hoped, perhaps, you would indulge me this evening since tomorrow will be extremely busy with preparations for landing and the next day will be quite impossible." Again the thin smile cracked his face. "I would have spoken with you sooner, but I have not wanted to interrupt your time with Mrs. de Zavala and the children."

"Very well, Colonel. This evening will be fine."

"If you will follow me, then."

She had not been in his cabin before though Emily had responded to his invitation to bring her oldest boy in for a visit. It was a surprisingly large room with a desk, a table and several chairs. There was only one bunk but it was a double size. Two oil lanterns fastened to the wall shone softly yellow, their brass fittings gleaming under fire. Morgan reached into a cabinet and pulled out a bottle of wine and two glasses.

"You will join me, Rose," he said, not questioning as he drew the cork and poured. "Quite a nice wine. From France." He lifted his glass. "To prosperity." He smiled at her. "And adventure."

She sipped slowly. She had not drunk wine since the day she drank it with Luke. Tasting the sweet bitterness again, she pushed away the memories that rushed at her, overwhelming her consciousness. Really, she must concentrate. She willed herself to look across the table at the Colonel who watched her over the edge of his lifted glass.

"You are very lovely, Rose," the Colonel said.

"There are papers, Colonel, that you wish me to sign?"

His smile broadened. "All business is it? Well then." He rummaged in his desk for a moment and handed her the sheets. She read carefully, eyes widening. When she put the papers down, it was with a small gasp of horror.

"What is this? What can you mean? Surely you do not intend! Why, sir, this was not my understanding at all. I am to be an employee. Not– Not an indentured servant! That is no better than being a slave! I am a free woman, sir!

I never imagined such misunderstanding! If I had, sir, you must know I would never have embarked."

"No. No, I suppose you would not have, Rose. But before you determine evil of me, I beg you to review the papers you are holding once again. The period of indenture, you will see, is only for one year. And the amount of your wage is included, so you may charge me with breach of contract if I fail to satisfy my portion of the agreement."

"As a gentleman, I trusted you already, Colonel Morgan. Why should such a thing as this be necessary? Have you reason to trust me less?"

Morgan sighed, pouring more wine, "As you have pointed out, Rose, I am a gentleman. Unfortunately, though you were raised as a lady, your parentage. . . ." He let the sentence hang in the air, heavy as a sword on the thinnest of strings above her head.

"I am no lady by birth," she said flatly. "But I am, indeed, a lady by character." The thought of her son, of Luke, of the fire and the wine and the long-ago winter night came unbidden. She dropped her eyes, knowing somehow, that Morgan also knew—or guessed she was no lady, even in character.

He finished his second glass. "I could not take the chance—the expense of bringing you here and having you decide it was not to your liking. Texas is very short on women. Lovely women in particular." His smile was unpleasant. Cynical. "Who knows what other offers you might receive. I am only doing what any businessman must do, my Dear. I am guaranteeing the return on my investment to the best of my ability."

She said nothing, looking down at the paper, longing to be away. Back in New York. Back in Boston. Back where everything was safe, if not secure. She was afraid of the man who measured her across the table. She was also afraid to move.

His tone softened, wheedling almost. Surely you agree, my dear Rose, that a year of guaranteed service is a minimal investment for your passage. And you will be paid, exactly as we have agreed."

"And if I refuse to sign this?"

He poured more wine, swirling it, deep red, in the glass. "Then I'm afraid I cannot let you disembark in New Orleans. Or perhaps," the smile was even more unpleasant, "I shall send you back to New York from there. There are always ships. And an attractive woman would surely be accepted in some captain's quarters . Your services would render a ticket unnecessary."

"You cannot mean that!"

He rose and came to stand behind her chair. "Oh, but I do, my Dear. I am absolutely serious." He bent over her, dipping the quill and placing it in her hand. "So please sign your name and let us put this rather unpleasant business behind us."

The sword above her head trembled. She signed and stood up. "If you will excuse me, Sir."

But he was waiting for her. "Not so fast." His hand closed on her arm, firm as a vice. "I have waited for you to approach me. I have hoped to get to know you better on this voyage. But you have eluded me thus far. Now I find I can no longer restrain myself."

She could not scream. Who would hear? Who would care besides Emily and what could she do? What dreadful unpleasantness for everyone! And yet to bear this! To bear this! "Sir." she protested, struggling to remove her arm from his grasp.

"You can make it easy or hard as you wish," he said, shrugging. "To be perfectly honest, I like it both ways. There is a certain pleasure in overpowering a woman, just as there is pleasure in mutual enjoyment." He shrugged again, his eyes glittering in the lamplight. "I will leave it up to you."

He tripped her when she tried to run and he was on her before she could rise from her knees. He was much stronger than he looked. Holding her arms in a hammerlock with one hand, he unbuttoned her bodice with the other, loosened her stays, pulled at her skirts. Hopeless, now, she allowed it, imagining more trouble than she could ever hope to cope with if Emily were to find out what had happened. And though Emily would believe her, who else would care? And what difference could it make? She had already signed the papers. She belonged to the Colonel for the next full year.

With the sword at her throat, she was laid on the floor while he had his way. Silent as death she backed herself into the farthest corner of her mind, her soul curled into a ball. She did not move or speak until he was finished.

Afterwards, as he watched, lounging on the bed, she arranged her clothing, awkwardly and fast, hating the time it took with his eyes on her but even more terrified of what awaited outside that room if she were seen as he had left her. Her reputation. Her precious reputation. Much good had it done her to guard it so zealously. Much good had it done her to pretend. Yet, though her virtue had left her at Luke's hands, until now she had never felt she had lost it entirely. She had never felt filthy before now. She had never felt hopeless.

Slipping away from his door in the dark, she made her way to the deck.

Kneeling there by the rail in the shadows away from the moon, she wept until she no longer could tell the difference between her tears and the salt spray that cooled her face. Then she went to the washroom and washed herself. Creeping away to the cabin she shared with Emily, she changed into her night clothes without making a sound and waited for sleep until daybreak made patience futile.

11

In New Orleans, the talk was all business and war. Not that the gentlemen in their silk coats and bow ties appeared to take either state of affairs seriously. In the better taverns to which Colonel Morgan insisted Rose accompany him, the gentlemen passed along news of fortunes and battles lost and gained as one might mention what one had for breakfast or was expecting at dinnertime.

Chastened into silence, Rose listened, gathering information for Emily as well as herself. Her cousin, fearing the streets and not enjoying Morgan's company, remained cloistered with the children in the hotel where the Colonel insisted they remain for the week he needed in the port.

Morgan called for them every morning and though Emily always pleaded the children as a reason for not stepping out of doors, there was something in his eyes when he insisted on Rose's company that made her reach for her wrap.

Unable to escape the daily excursions, she gave herself up to the study of New Orleans. Accustomed as she was to Boston and New York, the city was as alien as any foreign country. French was more often spoken than English and though, in polite society, Rose could hold her own in that language better than Emily, she could not understand the more common street dialect at all.

It added to the strangeness of the place. A sultry air hung over the wrought iron railings that lined balconies, still bright in December with vines blooming red and yellow, pink and white. The streets were a jostling mass of bodies, black, brown and pale in all stages of dress and undress. Rags dripped sweat under burdens that nearly hid black men from sight as frilled petticoats passed by, showing lace in the shade of French parasols. There were shops of every sort, selling everything from Chinese silks to French and English books, Mexican herbs, muskets from Tennessee and voodoo dolls from Africa or the islands. Taverns abounded, along with vendors, hawking their wares and foodstuff through the crowded streets. Passing a slave market the first day, Rose paused in horror, then turned her head and hurried on, unable to bear witnessing what she had, hereto, only heard about from Luke. And passing certain balconies, she stopped again for an instant shocked by the beautiful women who draped scantily clad bodies over the rails and called to the men below.

Colonel Morgan remained at her side though he spoke little and she, even less. Bound to him now in ways that had once been inconceivable to her, she held her head high and pretended otherwise. To see her hand placed lightly on his arm one might have supposed them courting though the coldness in the air between them would have led one to imagine they had quarreled.

But the company kept was not in vain. For the first time, listening to the banter of sailors and the well-laid plans of businessmen, many of whom had come and gone from Texas, she learned what to expect at her destination. The air was full of politics and money and if she sat quietly, eyes turned down to the admiring glances, the men soon forgot she was there and spoke freely of the things that were usually kept from the ears of delicate women.

It was here Rose learned that Mr. de Zavala had been threatened with arrest that summer. That he had lost all sympathy for his own nation and was now considering a position in the new Texas Government. That Texas had, indeed, declared its independence, and that General Santa Anna, the on-again, off-again president of Mexico, had declared his intention to utterly subdue the rebellious Yankees. That war had already broken out in Gonzales over a cannon, once given and recently demanded back by Mexican troops. The Texians, apparently, had won that round and kept their cannon. She learned that a Texian force had captured Goliad and defeated the Mexicans in San Antonio and that a hot-headed group had plans to push their victory down below the Rio Bravo into—so far—uncontested Mexican territory.

She heard that the political splits were many and deep and the only point of agreement was the desire to be free of Mexican rule. That while Austin and Houston apparently trusted each other, there were many who trusted neither of them. It seemed that Texians were, above all, a fiercely independent, hard-headed lot. She heard that the would-be new nation was futilely seeking military aid from the United States and that most of the new army volunteers were hot-tempered sharpshooters from the frontiers of Tennessee and Kentucky who, presumably, would go anywhere for a good fight and good land. She learned that the Texians had desperate financial and manpower problems but were not lacking in will and wit.

She heard about the Peace Party and the War Party and the many Mexican leaders who, like de Zavala, had allied themselves with the Yankees for philosophical as well as personal reasons. The range of difference in opinions was apparently great in Texas but on one point all seemed to agree. There was abundant good land to be had there and it was worth fighting for.

Land was the beginning and end of many conversations. It seemed that Texas was a place for dreaming land. The potential was incredible, they all agreed. Nowhere was land so plentiful, so rich, and so cheap. An asset to the nation, they all agreed. Unfortunately for the rebellion, the nation was presently resting on its recent purchase of the Louisiana Territory and did not wish to be bothered with the war of the unruly Texians. If Sam Houston could not talk Congress into helping them out—and him a former Congressman and a personal friend of President Andrew Jackson—Texas was likely to remain on the outside looking in.

There was a great deal of talk about Sam Houston, much of it somewhat libelous. It seemed he had been an up and coming Tennessee statesman when he married unfortunately and was divorced the same year amid clouds of secrecy. Whatever may have occurred, his wounded pride had driven him back to the Cherokee he loved as a child. He lived with them several more years, was adopted into the tribe and married Tiana, the Chief's daughter though he left her when he finally rejoined polite society.

Of course, the men said, laughing, he had to come back into society at the Texas level which was low by any standards. Sam Houston's nickname among the Cherokees was "Big Drunk" and it followed him back to Tennessee where, apparently, he could not rouse much confidence. Those who knew him insisted the name was well-earned. No one questioned his motivation, but many seemed to doubt his competence. But Austin knew him, liked him and talked him into coming down to Texas. The Texians were willing to let Austin name him Commander-in-Chief though they weren't likely to follow him anywhere.

With Steve Austin it was the opposite. No one questioned the competence of a man who had successfully settled almost a thousand families in a foreign country. But after spending the past fifteen years leading the colonists into cooperation with the Mexican government, many doubted his ability to lead them to independence.

There was a great deal more to politics than Rose had imagined. It seemed each man was fighting his own war for his own rights, all under a banner called "Independence." And among the many rights of independence, according to men of New Orleans, was the right to own slaves.

The names and power plays meant nothing to her though she memorized them as she had once memorized her history and French, prepared to quote when called upon. She shut her mind to the issue of slavery, unable to bear the pain it evoked. She took comfort in her one-year contract and concentrated on the feeling of a raw wild west just beyond the confines of the silkily civilized city of New Orleans. The idea of a new frontier captured her imagination and lifted her, almost, out of her misery.

She shared her information with Emily every evening, believing that the wife of a man as often mentioned as Lorenzo de Zavala in this Texas saga, should know as much as possible about the situation she was entering. Quivering lips and a paling face would have little impact on unruly mobs at the gate. Best to be prepared. Privately, Rose decided to learn how to shoot a gun. But that plan she did not share with her friend.

Delighting in adult company after a day of keeping her children confined, Emily kept the chatter going, hardly noticing the silence in which Rose wrapped herself when she was done with telling the news of the day. Though she absorbed every word about Texas, Emily had little interest in anything New Orleans could offer. She awaited only the word of sailing on to reunion with her husband. But for Rose's sake, she, too, pretended.

"You are enjoying the Colonel's company?" she asked toward the end of the week, "And the sights of the city?"

"Not much," Rose answered shortly, then regretting her loss of composure, she hurried on to share the day's news of Texas.

"So there will be war."

"It appears it is already in process."

"And my dear Lorenzo must be involved."

"He is solidly aligned with the Americans, Emily. He must stand or fall along with us."

"Oh, but we must stand, mustn't we, Rose? The Americans cannot lose this war. It will mean our independence."

Rose laughed. "You are talking as if you were Texian already, my Dear."

Emily looked up at her, surprised. "But I am, of course. I am his wife. Whatever he is, I must be and what matters to him must, of necessity, matter to me."

"But he is Mexican."

"Not any more! Not if Texas becomes independent."

"You think, then, that nationalities are so easily shed? That a government can be overcome or a province torn away and everyone living there, whatever their origin, is immediately at one with the victors?"

"Pray don't confuse me so, Rose. I only know that Lorenzo and I are one and if he has cast his lot with the Americans, surely that makes him one of us. Or otherwise, I should have to become one of them and I am not happy to call myself Mexican."

"Nor might he be happy to call himself American," said Rose, surrendering to her sense of irritation. "Surely you realize that every country has its own pride. Mexico has an older history of civilization than the United States and her statesmen and scholars, such as Mr. de Zavala, must be equally proud of what they have accomplished as Mexicans in winning her independence from Spain."

Emily covered her face with her hands. "There's a great deal I do not understand, Rose, and you must tell me what you think I need to know about politics and so forth. I only know that I love my family as well as my husband and though I have already chosen to live my life with him, I should hate to spend it as a citizen of a country at war with my own."

"It seems the Americans started this war," said Rose, feeling no pity for Emily's confusion. "There are many, at least in New Orleans, who are particularly anxious to join Texas to the Union as a slave state."

"Oh!" Emily dropped her hands, staring, her face gone pale. "Oh my dear!" She recovered herself in an instant. "But that can have nothing to do with you!"

"It already has," said Rose before she could stop herself. She took the words back as quickly as possible. "I mean, one thinks about these things, of course, given the circumstances. I have not thought much about it since Luke used to bore me with stories of the South when I was much, much younger. I did not like to listen then, nor do I now. But, it appears the issue of slavery will be unavoidable."

"Colonel Morgan has brought this up?" The blue eyes were sharp again. Focused. "He is aware of your parentage, I suppose. Has he attempted to use it against you? Has he insulted you in some fashion?"

Rose said nothing. Emily pressed on, alarmed by the silence. "Because if he has, my Dear, we must tell my husband. Someone must defend your honor. Much as I hate the very idea of duels, he will not allow you to be–"

"Mr. de Zavala has much too much to do to concern himself with anyone's honor besides yours and his own," said Rose, finding voice immediately to break the flow of thought. "I have no need of protection, dear Emily. Colonel Morgan is a gentleman, of course. An American gentleman."

"I'm not sure I believe you, Rose. And I am newly acquainted with your capacity for keeping secrets even from me."

"You must believe me on this. You really must." Rose smiled, coaxing. "Any suspicion might be misunderstood. It could make matters most uncomfortable for all of us."

Emily looked unconvinced. Sighing, Rose moved to the balcony, feeling the sea winds stir over the mass of humanity in the street below. The crowd parted suddenly and a line of Negroes walked by, chained neck to neck in a sinuous line that moved towards the marketplace. She shuddered and stepped back into the room, stilling her face and emotions before she turned to face her cousin.

"Everything will be all right, Emily. Soon you will be with your husband and I will be at my new job. Texas awaits us, full of promise as they say. A land of opportunity for all of us. We must be patient and trust in God, as Dr. Connie would say."

"But you will tell me, Rose, if you are mistreated, will you not promise? I could not bear to imagine you treated as less than a lady."

"Who could I call on besides you?" Rose asked, embracing her friend. "For better or worse, you're my whole family now."

When Colonel Morgan came the next morning, desiring her company, Rose refused to see him, sending word that she was indisposed. She had quite enough, she told Emily, of seeing New Orleans. Though Emily looked a question, she did not ask it, and Rose thankfully turned the subject back to the problems of frontier homemaking.

So the women and children remained in the hotel together, passing the next two days in housekeeping chatter and awaiting word of passage on to Galveston.

They sailed on Saturday. The Colonel assured them with a jocular air that they would be "home" in plenty of time for Christmas. Apparently business had been good. The hold was filled to bursting and the ship sat noticeably lower, in the water. Emily prayed there would be no storms. Rose merely hoped.

They had picked up several new passengers in New Orleans, among them an itinerant preacher come lately from Ohio. His name was Luther Collins and he was, to all appearances, a dedicated man and a sincere one. His speech was brief and to the point. His eyes, blue as an October sky, were clear and focused and his forehead wore few lines though his untrimmed hair and beard were grey. Dressed entirely in rusty black and none too clean, he was a bit lumpish in form and somewhat stern in countenance. He drew no attention to himself but those who watched him, as Rose did, were surprised by the stillness they saw in his face and comforted, somehow, by his long gazes.

So it was with a startled sense of expectancy, that Rose saw him at daybreak the first morning out, catching the dawn, as she had made a long habit of doing. Coming closer, she was taken aback by the rapture with which he greeted the sunrise, standing alone by the rail, his face transfixed with joy as his lips moved silently.

It was almost too private a moment. She slipped back into the shadows. His eye caught the movement.

"An awesome God!" he called across the deck. "An awesome God, indeed, Sister!"

"It is a beautiful sunrise," Rose murmured, stepping forward to meet him. And indeed it was. Spires of gold rose straight out of a golden sea, tinged with the wide-sweeping purple-red of the horizon. Above and below, near and far, blue air met blue water with nothing between.

The two stood still, watching, unable at first to intrude on the morning with words. Rose was the first to break the silence.

"You will be staying in Texas, Sir?"

"My first time," the man said. "A rather wild place, I hear tell. It has been illegal for anyone outside of the Catholic Church to preach there while Spain, and then Mexico, ruled but I understand that the colonists are in the process of declaring independence. I have heard tales of other missionaries traveling there now. A rough land, I hear, and a rough people. Certainly a land in need of the light."

"Surely we all are," said Rose, half to herself.

The preacher caught the words.

"It is within thee," he said. Thee has only to attend it."

"There is light enough around us here and more beautiful than stained glass windows," said Rose, smiling to hide her discomfort with the turn of the conversation but somewhat emboldened by the intimacy of dawn. "I must confess, Sir, that religion means little to me. It would seem we have more need to be saved from one another than from the fires of hell."

The man chuckled. "I cannot but agree with thee, Sister. Man's cruelty to man would seem to know no limits. Our hell may be here on earth, as well as our heaven. But we cannot blame God for that, nor is it reason enough to deny the power of the inner light."

"What do you mean? What is the inner light"

"The light of the spirit of truth and love, Sister. The simple consciousness, imparted by our Maker, that draws us into love for one another, recognizing that we are all children of the same Father. It is a lack of attention to that conscience that gets mankind in trouble, time after time."

"So if one listened to conscience, one would not need churches?"

"To what purpose? If thee were attuned to the inner voice that breathed from the Father Himself, what need would there be for churches or preachers or books? Hand in hand with thy Maker, thee would dance through life in joyful harmony. But I do not speak of conscience as it might be generally understood. There are those who call themselves conscience-stricken because they break a rule." The smile drew laugh lines on his roundish face. "I am not among those. Indeed, the Friends were once regularly arrested for breaking all the rules of the church as it stood. The Friends would say, perhaps, that the rules of man and the laws of God are not at all the same thing."

"You are a Friend? A Quaker?"

"Thee knows of us?"

"A friend took me once to a Quaker meeting. It was very different. Very peaceful, with no pretense or snobbery."

The man laughed out loud. "Thee must not think that! There's pretense and snobbery enough, wherever one might go. Even now, the Friends have split over some nonsense begun by those who would disown members who will not declare a certain theology—the infallibility of the Word, the divinity of Jesus Christ, and so forth. It smacks of inquisition trials! And to what end? Christ is no less divine for any theology declared or undeclared. And I would think Him far more interested in our correct actions than our correct words."

"And how would you define correct actions, Mr. Collins?"

The blue eyes twinkled with the rising sun. "Why, sister, the instructions are in the Word. 'Love God with all thy heart and soul and mind and strength. Love thy neighbor as thyself.'"

"What does Jesus have to do with such a concept?"

"He showed it could be done. He, a man of flesh and blood, lived out the teaching that giving unstintingly of oneself for the sake of others is the way to please God. But when he declared that love is a *commandment,* the powers of the day determined to kill him most horribly. And he forgave them from the cross! Perhaps I am a heretic, sister, even to my Friends, but I cannot but believe that act of forgiveness shows more divinity even than the resurrection! With that word, he brought a light into the world that cannot be quenched."

"I do not understand such things," murmured Rose, looking away. A strong wind was coming in with the new day and the salt spray stung her face. But she was unable to leave.

The man sighed, leaning on the rail. "The resurrection I can almost understand, sister, because that, I believe, would the reward of perfect obedience. But the forgiveness–that remains the mystery of divine grace. The only key for imperfect humans to enter into the perfect world, leaving the ill-done dead and buried underneath the cross."

"But forgive me, Sister, those are words said by preachers in pulpits and I cannot explain them otherwise though I have come to hate the rituals of religion while cherishing ever more the Father the churches purport to worship. Indeed, I have come to believe a cup of tea and a plate of biscuits shared with those who love God dearly is a far better communion than kneeled at a gilded rail to drink from a gilded cup. But people must seek comfort where they can and to believe in God a little may be better than believing not at all."

"I think not," said Rose.

The rising sun caught the man full in the face, leaning into it on the rail. He hardly blinked. "And why not, Sister?"

"Because that little belief gives one the comfort–or delusion, I would say–of believing that, no matter what one does, everything will be all right because God will forgive it. It would be better not to believe in God at all and have to contend with the reality of consequences for one's actions."

A quizzical eyebrow lifted in her direction. "What if one believed in the Father a great deal?"

"Why hardly anyone does! That would be very difficult. One would have to behave, I suppose, rather like Jesus, since the Bible says he is the firstborn son."

"The consequences he faced for honesty were certainly not to everyone's liking."

It was too much for her. "If one does good and evil follows, how can you speak of salvation? One is delivered into evil! If God is controlling everything, how can such things be?"

His gaze sharpened, flashed briefly over her black hair, blown into frizzy ringlets by the rising breeze. The brilliantly blue eyes analyzed her skin tone. She submitted, knowing, suddenly, that he knew. "I do not believe in salvation," she said. "I believe in myself."

His laugh was a chuckle, deep in his throat. "Did I use that word, Sister? It would be difficult, seeing that the devil rules this earth. Hate, lust and greed invade the minds of men and a soul that loves God and his neighbor has a long struggle ahead, no doubt. But it will be the same for everyone here in the end. We will never get out of the world alive."

He shook his grey head. "A Friend's discipline is to turn the other cheek. But we are not speaking of embracing evil, of submitting to evil. We are speaking of embracing God, of submitting to God even—or especially—when evil has overtaken us."

"Then why not live for what is offered, seeing there is no reward for right-doing?"

He lifted a hand and swept the skyline, turning away from her to face the sun again. The red glowing ball was riding well above the waters now. His face reflected the light, glowing both inside and out, it seemed, quieting Rose in an instant.

"Because of Him," the man almost whispered. "Because He's the Creator and whatever torment He allows, He has His reasons and I do not question them. Every man and woman will learn what they must on earth and teach whom they may. But I do not believe our Father forgets us when He drops us here for our lessons in pain and desire." He sighed. "One must learn compassion while keeping hope alive. Eternity is very long, Sister, and earth life very brief."

The discussion ended there. Rose left him shortly afterwards and went to breakfast with Emily. But she felt his eyes on her from time to time as she moved about the ship. And from time to time when he did not see her, she watched him.

The wind sprang up that evening and Morgan, busy with the crew, did not appear for dinner. Due to arrive in Galveston early the next morning, the two women retired with the children. "Soon," Emily whispered to Rose as they settled in for the night. "I shall see him very soon."

It may have been past midnight when a sudden jolt of the ship flung Rose against the wall and startled her to wakefulness. Rain pounded against the portholes and the ship was wallowing, bucking the waves like an untamed animal, all sudden whirls and pitches. Curious, but careful not to disturb her still sleeping companions, she wrapped herself in her hooded cloak, slipped out of the cabin, and made her way towards the steep steps onto the deck.

She was insane she told herself, struggling to keep her balance, as the ship heaved, rising and falling with a steep suddenness that seemed to rocket her stomach from her throat to her knees. Yet she could not stop herself until she had crawled up the steps, pushed through the door of the cabin above and stood pressed against the outside wall, grasping a rail with both hands as the wind whipped past her with a high thin scream.

The night was wild. Black water merged with black sky so thoroughly that only the frantic motion of the ship told where one left off and the other began. Above the scream of the wind, the screeching creak of wood, and the pounding crash of waves breaking over the deck, she caught the occasional shouts of men working frantically to reef the sails and hold the ship into the wind. Excitement filled her, though she chided herself for a fool. Her bare feet were ankle deep in water and waves washed over the cabin itself, drenching her where she huddled, leeward to the wind.

She must not continue in this foolishness! In a moment of calm, she turned back to the door but as she grasped the handle the wind caught her cloak, throwing her off-balance as the ship rose sharply, flinging her to the deck. At the same instant, a breaking wave lifted her, sending her careening, end over end through bottomless water, helpless even to reach out a grasping hand from the heavy folds of the sodden black wool that enveloped her.

With a crash like the breaking of bones, she struck wood as the ship righted itself for an instant. Without thinking, without seeing, without feeling anything, she rose and raced back up the deck, finding herself suddenly with her hand on the door. It opened, miraculously, and closed behind her as she fell inside, just as the ship lurched upwards in its mad dance with death and the sea came down like a river across the roof of the sturdy little cabin.

Through the blackness, like a ghost in the crash of the elements, she heard the voice of Luther Collins. "Thee's been dancing with the wind, then, Miss Emily? And the angels have brought thee back! Thee must not forget this moment."

She found her breath but not her voice for a moment. Rasping, gasping, she could only frame a question. "Why do you call me Emily?"

A chuckle came through the darkness. The man was apparently totally unmoved by the storm. "Why that was the name the captain gave me when I asked, Sister. Emily Morgan, is it not? A relative, perhaps? Would that explain thy love of the sea?"

"I am called Rose, and I am not a relative of the Colonel," she said, amazed that she could reach for dignity from the small sodden space she occupied on the floor. Indeed, she was not at all sure she could rise. Everything trembled and she had no strength in her limbs.

A large hand was laid on her arm, grasping it firmly. "Indeed thee must forgive me, then, Sister. And if they have taken away thy rightful name, thee must forgive them as well, though it must be a bitter pill to swallow!"

"I did not know," she murmured, feeling caught in a dream that was almost, but not quite, a nightmare. "I did not know he had changed my name in fact."

Collins asked no more questions. The grip on her arm tightened. "If thee can stand, Sister, I will help thee to thy cabin." The chuckle again filled the darkness. "We would not wish to see thee saved from the sea and lost to pneumonia."

She could not stand but she could crawl and with his hand to hold her steady, she made her way down to the steps. He remained on his knees beside her as she crept back to the space she shared with Emily. But at the door of the compartment, he stopped her for a moment. Through the darkness, his whisper came clear as distant lightning, each syllable outlined against the night. "Thee must not forget that God has saved thee. The work now is to keep a hold on that salvation. To do good and help others." Again the chuckle. "So that our Father will not regret the time wasted on a foolish child."

He was gone before she could answer.

She could not find dry clothes in the heaving dark. Indeed, she was trembling too hard to try. Slipping out of her soaking garments, she got into her bunk naked and lay still, warming slowly, feeling as if she had died and come again to life.

She was not entirely certain life was a blessing. So Morgan was calling her, by a name he himself had given to her! Was there to be nothing left of her past? Nothing left of her freedom to choose?

But she was almost warm now, and felt, somehow, entirely safe. The past receded like a dream, awakened from and then forgotten in the comfort of covers. Had there indeed been angels with her on the deck? She wondered for a moment, feeling sleep steal over her. Had it been God, indeed, who kept her on board to the end?

And if so, to what purpose?

And then she drifted away into thinking of Luke. In her dreams, he was both man and child and he came to her walking across the waters. He stretched out a hand to where she lay sinking but though she tried, she could not reach it. Down she went without a struggle and found herself, to her amazement, breathing the water easily in and out.

12

The sky was blue the next day and the seas settled. The mad waters of the night had passed like a dream, leaving only a bitter cold and a mad tangle of ropes and broken spars in its wake. By the time Rose had dragged herself from bed and onto the deck, the sun was high and all hands were on deck and hard at work. Above, half the sails snapped and billowed under a brisk easterly wind.

Rose shivered, missing the woolen cloak that still lay soaked in her cabin. But the Colonel stood near the bow, turned out in full naval uniform and watching her. She had to approach.

"Good mornings" were spoken. Rose watched alongside as the sliver of land in the distance slid up through the water. "The storm has thrown us about," said the Colonel, "but we shall arrive at the Point before nightfall. You shall see the entrance to our bay in good light."

He raised a finely blue-coated arm to point. "Yonder lies Galveston Island. It would be an excellent port if crossing the bar were not so treacherous." A small laugh. "Though Jean Lafitte, the privateer, was quite adept at it, I understand. The island served as headquarters for his band of buccaneers for some five years following the Battle of New Orleans."

Pausing at her puzzled look he went on to explain. "Mr. Lafitte joined forces with the French and Americans to repel the British attack on the city some twenty odd years ago. Apparently he and his pirate band displayed considerable nerve. Some say New Orleans would have been lost without him."

His eyes were on the island which appeared ever more clearly to port. It was a curiously flat land, its misty grasses barely broken by the occasional skeleton of a twisted tree. A few rough buildings gave evidence of habitation though no movement could be seen. Rose restrained a small shiver. A raw land indeed!

The Colonel resumed his discourse on the pirate. "I understand his fondest illusion was to become a respectable American citizen. It is said that he was in love with a lady of society. He cut an elegant figure–rich, I suppose, with stolen goods—and was a gentleman, by some accounts, though it hardly suited his trade. The family would not have him, of course, nor would the government. Rather a pity, perhaps. It seems he was a man of courage and considerable loyalty though one must wonder what he had to gain. It is said he came to the island to await acknowledgment for his service in New Orleans. Instead, his men were finally cleared out by American forces in 1821. He disappeared into Mexico they say, and, presumably, died in the Yucatan some ten years back."

The Colonel's eyes remained fixed on the island, slipping away to leeward as the ship slid forward into the broad inlet under wind-whipped sails. Blue-brown water frothed at the hull.

"So the pirates are gone, now?" Rose asked, finding the silence heavy.

Morgan turned to look at her. "Quite gone, my Dear," he said smiling. "But there shall be troubles enough without them. You heard the news of war, of course, and though the Frenchmen of New Orleans see it only as a game—and the United States government may see it as no more than that—I can assure you that the Texians take it very seriously."

"I heard some talk, of course," said Rose, cautiously. "It is serious, then?"

"Serious as death. It seems the climate has shifted in the past few months since General Santa Anna assumed a sort of dictatorship. He fancies himself a western Napoleon of sorts. It was not always so. When he took the reins of government from General Bustamante three years ago we regarded him as something of a hero. Import taxes were repealed though that may well have been because the colonists refused to pay them. And immigration, which had been abolished, resumed. Some movement was made towards establishing Texas as a Mexican state with its own state constitution. But it was not to be. Texas remains part of Coahuila with the state capitol in Zacatecas where few Americans live."

"The efforts came to nothing?"

"Apparently they had an opposite effect. Mr. Austin was imprisoned when he went to Mexico City to present our petition. It came as a surprise to everyone, believing as we have lately that we can work out our differences while co-existing as a part of Mexico. Certainly no one has been more in favor of maintaining the peace than Steve Austin. And he was not disappointed, at least at first. Though he suffered an initial setback from Santa Anna's deputy, his conference with the president himself went well. The General would not concede the separation of Texas as a state but he agreed to a number of improvements in federal services to our colonies."

"What happened?"

"Unfortunately, as Austin was on his way back to Texas with his good news, someone discovered a letter he had written in a fit of anger at his earlier reception. It smacked of sedition. They arrested him then, and he spent over a year in jail. It was a foolish move if Santa Anna expected cooperation from us. The Mexicans have had no stronger defender than Steve Austin. He has held an unruly crowd in line for the government for many years now. But I suspect his patience is exhausted along with his health. He has not been well, they say, since his imprisonment though he continues to shoulder the burden of leadership. Whether or not General Houston will share it remains to be seen."

The thin smile re-appeared. "The Texans are not an easy lot to manage, I assure you. The immigrant mix here can be volatile, coming as they do from Ireland and Germany as well as from Mexico and from the mountains of Kentucky and Tennessee. A hardy lot, over all, and the hardships suffered from Indian wars and the deprivations of frontier life have forced a real cooperation. But communication remains a problem. The Americans are as blunt as the Mexicans are subtle and the mountain men are loud-spoken to boot. And all are prepared to fight for their rights. There are many who would like to repeat the Revolutionary War. Santa Anna has become a King George."

He laughed lightly, adjusting his jacket as he turned his back to the wind. "No, it is not an easy mix nor well designed for diplomacy. Mr. de Zavala has been of utmost service in that regard, though, apparently, Santa Anna has decided he is a great danger to society. His imprisonment was ordered this summer though he has escaped so far. He is not, of course, the only Mexican gentleman to join the rebels but he is the most highly placed."

A small sigh escaped him. War might be good for the economy but he was not eager to fight. "Reconciliation might be possible, but there are so many hotheads among us. William Travis has led several forays against small federal forces lately, though he was roundly condemned by those of us who favor peace. But Santa Anna grows ever more imperialistic in his demands for subservience. It is not easy for worthy men to bear. The arrest of several Texas leaders has been ordered and rejected of course. I hear he is now sending General Cos with several thousand troops to enforce his will. There have been engagements already with the advance troops. So it seems the war is truly upon us now."

His lips tightened. "Quite unpleasant, really. The import taxes were most unfortunate but there are more ways around them than there are ways around the guns of war. And it does not help that the Americans are unwilling to organize under particular leadership. Sam Houston has been named the Commander-in-Chief since Austin removed himself to go and seek aid from the United States last month. But Houston is a general without an army as I understand it. Texas is full of volunteers who have no wish to be led by anyone. And Houston, though he commands a certain respect, is regarded as somewhat cautious for the tastes of the War Party, while the Peace Party no doubt, is still hoping that the entire conflict will dissipate. So whatever strategies may be in effect, they are likely also to be at odds."

He paused again, still looking out to sea. "Mexico has been good enough to me, I must say, though there are gains to be made from independence. Less control is usually translated into more money from the trade. And I have many plans yet to realize."

Rose said nothing, fearing to break the stream of confidences.

"There will be privations," the Colonel murmured as if to himself. "I would not delude you, Rose. We are somewhat upwind from the battle which I hear was just fought—and won—in San Antonio but I do not believe General Santa Anna will give up so easily. The Texians have shown great enterprise under Austin and the other *empresarios*. The colonists number some twenty thousand now. What was once a wild country—so far from the civilized Spanish cities of Mexico as to be given over to the Indians and a few intrepid Catholic missionaries—has become very valuable. The shipping trade has increased dramatically. There are a few industries: sawmills, cattle and so forth. And with the advent of the Southerners, whom Travis best represents, considerable land is under cultivation. Cotton grows very well here."

She stiffened. Slaves, she thought. Slaves are cultivating Texas! Careful with her face she was glad he had not noticed her reaction.

Neither spoke for a long time. He was facing forward now, leaning into the prow, looking ahead as if he could see already their landing at his own port. Morgan's Point. "I am planting oranges," he said, in an oddly dreamy tone. I have always wanted an orange grove. They should do well if the Santanistas don't destroy them."

"They are coming this way?"

Morgan's briskness returned in an instant. "Well, my Dear, that remains to be seen. Certainly they shall not if General Houston can muster enough men to stop them. And I have every confidence in the General. If not—" He gestured towards the bowels of the ship. "I would certainly not be investing my life, my fortune and my sacred honor."

The smile he turned on her was unpleasant. Feral, almost. *You have no honor*! The words almost rose to her lips. She swallowed, turning away.

"I must see to the children," she said, slowing her feet as she crossed the deck, trying not to run, feeling followed by his eyes.

Guns, she thought. Of course! That was the weight in the belly of the ship. Wheat, of course, and fabric, and who knew what small items welcomed in this desolate place. But guns would be the weight and bulk of this particular shipment.

So the war was close. Closer than she had imagined, even listening to the stories in New Orleans. Morgan was right. They told the story there as one would describe a hand of cards and she had not imagined the reality. She must speak to the Colonel about a gun, she thought as she went down to the cabin below. She must learn to shoot.

"Good morning Miss Rose," boomed a voice directly in her ear. Luther Collin's face loomed over her in the narrow hall. "Thee is hurrying," he said. "Recovered, then, I take it."

She found a smile to meet his own. "Thanks to your help, Sir. And the angels."

"Thee does not look as pleased as so miraculous a rescue might lead one to expect."

Perhaps it was the way of preachers, this peculiar intimacy with which they approached one. Well, she could meet it. She had no reason not to trust him. "It is the war," she said. "Have you heard about it?"

He laughed out loud. "They speak of nothing else in New Orleans. Taking bets. The Americans are favored, I believe. But the people of Louisiana do not care much about the outcome except as the trade is affected. Among the gentlemen–with whom I do not much associate–they say Texas is populated by an uncivilized bunch who would be welcome neither at their tables nor in their councils. The ship captains and land speculators, of course, are an exception. They bring in money rather than requesting to take it out."

"So the men of New Orleans are not backing the Texians?"

His shoulder lifted in a bear-like shrug. "Perhaps they made a good bargain with Colonel Morgan. I understand he is bringing in supplies."

So she was right! The thought brought a smile. "For an unworldly man, Mr. Collins, you are well informed."

"The unworldly are the most in need of information, perhaps." He peered down at her in the shadowed hallway. "We have nothing else with which to protect ourselves. Particularly if one does not believe in bearing arms."

"You bear no arms? You would not fight for a worthy cause?"

He did not speak. She did not move. The blue eyes were very close.

"There are many ways to fight, Sister," he said. "I have chosen the Sword of the Spirit. It reaches into all the corners and casts everything into light."

"What do you mean—" she started to ask, but as quickly as he had appeared, he was gone, disappearing up the steps onto the deck without another word.

Emily was struggling with her stays when Rose entered the small cabin. "I'm so glad you came back," she said, flinging down the laces and whirling on her heel. "I try and try and I still look like a mutton chop with a ribbon around it." The light voice broke into a giggle. "Do you think he will still love me?" she asked. "Three children is no light burden to put on a body and add no weight." She turned helplessly toward the small square mirror mounted on the wall. "You shall have to be my mirror Rose. I must look my very best and one alone can never get these tight enough." Her dress, laid out on the bed, was dark blue velvet, lace collared and satin-bowed. Rose had helped her choose the pattern., "A homecoming dress," Emily had called it. "Homecoming because wherever he is, is home." Rose had refused a new garment for the landing. She would be arriving into a job, after all. Not into the arms of a husband.

"You're beautiful as always," said Rose, stopping for a moment to admire her friend. "How could a sane man think otherwise? And Lorenzo de Zavala is a very sensible man." Or at least she had once thought so. He was not the sort of man to invite his wife and children into a war zone, she would have thought. But there they were, with no turning back. She wondered if Emily had any understanding of the danger into which they were venturing. The unmentionable possibilities.

The children, ready-dressed and restless, watched by the door as Rose tugged Emily's waist back to a semblance of its pre-childbearing state. Finally arranged, Emily pirouetted, preening. Blue eyes glowed above pink-flushed cheeks. "Will he like it, do you think?"

"He loves you so, my Dear, that he may not even notice the dress. You look beautiful. That is what he will see."

Rose could not share her news. Love, not war was all that Emily needed to know at the moment. And Emily, after all, would not be alone. Emily had a husband to guide her. Unlike herself. And unlike Emily, Rose was not eager to land. As the shores came closer she felt herself stiffening though she tried to believe it was only the cold that had seeped into the very marrow of her bones. But the chill deepened with every glimpse of the Colonel, hurrying now about the business of preparing to dock.

And then, in the creak of wood and slapping of canvas, the ship turned to port and the noise of shouted orders swelled over the wind as a settlement came into sight on the nearby shore.

So this was to be her new home—this wild place into which they sailed, bearing guns. And Morgan, a man, it seemed with little conscience and considerable greed, was to be her conductor through it. It was too much. Better to be entirely alone. She retreated within herself, pretending it all a dream. Time enough, later, to awake and take note.

As in a dream, they approached. As in a dream, she saw Lorenzo de Zavala's face among the small crowd at the dock, though he saw no one, it was clear, besides his wife at the rail. Emily lifted her arms, her children momentarily forgotten, tears running down the smile lines on her face.

As in a dream, they went ashore and Emily moved into her husband's arms, their children clinging to her, alarmed by the sudden emotion, whimpering a little as children do, until their father bent to them, lifted them, welcomed them.

Rose watched, forgotten for a moment.

De Zavala was the first to remember. His arm around Emily, he moved forward, extending a hand and a welcome. "You will come with us, of course," he said, exercising a bow made awkward by his hold on his wife. "It is good to see you again, Miss Rose."

Rose glanced at the Colonel, busy with an official of some sort. De Zavala caught the glance and smiled. "I am certain the Colonel does not expect you to assume your new duties today. If you will come with us, we will proceed to the hotel. We will rest there tonight, and then tomorrow—" He turned back to Emily. "Tomorrow, Dear, I shall take you home."

As in a dream, the afternoon and evening passed. Rose received impressions, that was all. A dozen houses, roughly built but substantial enough. More trees than were to be seen on Galveston but except for oak groves, heavy with moss, they were spindly things, dried by the weather and bent by the wind. Not at all like the tall, proud greens of the Northeast. But the low land was not without beauty, shining with marshes and covered with grass, golden in the deep slant of the lowering sun. The land's horizon reached as far as the ocean's and was nearly as uncluttered.

The town itself was no more than a rough dirt wagon track with a hotel, store and saloon alongside a few wooden houses. The hotel, a two-story, wooden affair, was shaded by a wide veranda furnished with a few roughly made chairs. It stood in the center with a large warehouse close behind it. A number of horses were tied in front of the warehouse with several rough carts which were being hitched for a pull to the docks. Bearded white faces contrasted with black ones and among them, more smoothly, moved a few smaller brown men and women. There was movement everywhere along with shouts of the Colonel's landing and his intentions.

Rose and the de Zavala's did not approach the warehouse. Time enough for that, soon enough, Rose thought, as they crossed the veranda and passed through the wide doors into the downstairs tavern. Wooden benches filled the room in front of a long polished bar. At the far end of the room a huge stone fireplace, decorated with the longest horns she had ever seen, kept the cold at bay.

The men at the tables—there were very few ladies among them—were not so rough a lot as she might have imagined though a few coonskin hats were to be seen, pressed tight down on their owners' untrimmed locks. There were a number of uniforms, some very fancy, though no particular pattern seemed to have been chosen. It would appear each man had made his own decision on the dress to wear to war.

De Zavala, she was strangely relieved to note, wore his usual dress coat with its high embroidered collar. And he had not mentioned the war at all. Were it not for the bristle of muskets along the wall and the fervent faces above the motley array of uniforms, she might have imagined the talk of war was but another part of the dream.

Their entry brought a pause in conversation. It seemed a hundred eyes were fixed on Rose and Emily as de Zavala led them to a table. Restraining the urge to look around, the women kept their eyes cast down and little by little the noisy talk picked up again. The serving girl took de Zavala's order and brought thick steaks on thick china plates more rapidly than could have been expected. They ate in silence, mildly stunned by the reunion and the ambience of war. The children stared about, wide-eyed, too interested to eat or even talk. Secure on his daddy's lap, baby Richard whimpered for a moment or two, then commenced gurgling happily, waving his arms at one and all.

The childish babble provided strange contrast to the voices all about them. In low-voiced drawls and loud stentorian tones, battles were being discussed and plans being laid. Rose concentrated on her plate. The food was plain but well prepared. Emily had also noticed the weapons. And the uniforms.

"The war is close, then?" she whispered.

De Zavala lost his smile for a moment. The pleasantly round face shadowed with something like pain. "It is on us, my Dear. Had I known for certain before you set sail, I would not have allowed you to come. But I cannot be sorry you are here."

"Nor I," said Emily.

Rose said nothing, watching the door for Colonel Morgan. He did not appear.

The meal was over at last. The children, calmed by the heavy food, slumped in their chairs. It was hard for Rose to believe the journey was over, that this was the place, in fact, toward which she had been coming for so long. She glanced around the room again, careful to meet no one's eyes. The crowd was growing. She would not have been surprised to count a hundred people there. Or fifty, at least. And except for herself and Emily, no women remained. It was surely time to retire.

Would Rose mind sharing her room with the children that night? Emily asked, hesitating with a small blush as her husband went to see to the arrangements. Glad for the company of little ones, Rose offered an instant "of course."

There was no fireplace in the small room to which they were led though a brick in the foot of the feather bed took the chill from the covers and made it comfortable as any nest. Snuggled in with the children, Rose remembered Boston and her first night there and the pleasure she had found in her work. Perhaps.

It was always best, at any rate, to think positively, she told herself firmly, imagining Miss Goodwin's face for an instant. Rise to the challenge. Do your best. And always look forward. But the future was shadowed by more factors than she could name. Staring at the ceiling in the dark, she could not picture the morrow, let alone the next week, the next month, the next year.

Beside her, the children breathed deeply into sleep, relaxed and totally trusting. Rose sighed and closed her eyes, remembering the past, holding her own son in the arms of her own imagination. The future would come as it would come. But if she forgot her past, she could see no reason at all to look forward to whatever lay ahead.

She remembered, as she drifted into sleep, that she had not seen Mr. Collins in the dining room. She wondered where he went. And she wondered, too, why she should care.

The children woke her early, chattering like morning birds, eager to get on with their new day and their daddy. Barely remembered, he had been the source of many imaginings and they were full of anticipation for the reality. "Come on, Rose. Let's go. Come on, Rose. Come on."

Feeling the weight of Texas already on her shoulders, Rose pushed back the covers and got everyone into their clothes, herself last. The sun was already yellow in the sky, though still close to the horizon when she took them all downstairs.

Morgan was waiting in the dining room though Emily and de Zavala were nowhere to be seen. He rose as she approached. Busying herself with settling the children, Rose evaded his eyes after wishing him good morning. But he was quite undeterred.

"So Miss–Emily," he said, smiling. "You do not mind if I call you by the name on your passport, do you? It makes things simpler, don't you think?"

Rose could not look at him. "No sir," she said. "I don't think so at all."

"Ah. But that would be because you do not yet see things as we see them here in Texas."

She had forgotten. How strange that she had forgotten about his cruelty!

"I shall never forget again," she murmured, keeping her face down until the hot flush of anger could subside.

"What did you say, my Dear?" The Colonel leaned forward and raised a deliberate finger to lift her chin. "Did you say something, Emily, about forgetting?"

And ancient pain rose in her like a red and yellow flame. Screamed in her, as if of ancestors, dead and buried and still burning alive. A brand new rage threatened to engulf her. It was no longer hard to meet his eyes.

"I shall not forget your cruelty, Sir," she said.

He slapped her. Lightly as if with a glove.

The room–though there were no more than eight or ten men there besides the cook and the serving girls–was utterly still. The children sat still, frozen in amazement and fear.

Almost–almost the anger exploded. She could feel the flames licking out, rising, consuming the mockery in those eyes, consuming the skull itself, the brain, the body, the very soul of its enemy. And in the burning, she felt herself consumed. Unreclaimable. Unexplainable. Gone beyond possibility.

Facing that thin smile, it seemed worth it. And then over his shoulder, she saw the movement of Luther Collins.

His eyes were on her. No, not on her. In her. His lips moved, but barely. Like the whisper of breeze on a pond in the northeast trees. Maybe Ohio was like that, she thought suddenly, irrationally. Trees, tall and straight. Meadows and streams and gold and purple wildflowers near the pond when the sun is slanting silver shimmers across the stillness.

Her lip twitched at the sweet sibilance in her mind. Unbelievable! And she had just been slapped!

She dropped her eyes.

"If you please, Colonel Morgan, I will do my best for you, whatever you choose to call me. You can depend on it."

She could feel his tiny startle of surprise though his pride covered it quickly enough.

"That's better, Emily."

She dared to look up then, her question boldly stated in the glance.

"And I, of course, shall keep my part of the agreement," he responded. "You will be paid."

"Perhaps you will show me to my new duties, Colonel, as soon as I breakfast with the children. Their parents appear to be sleeping in and my responsibility to them is not quite finished."

Morgan nodded. "I will return in an hour. I trust you will be finished at that time." The thin smile had altered into an attempt at humor. "War waits for no man. Nor woman."

When Rose thought to look again, Luther Collins was nowhere in sight. Strange. That image of the sun on wildflowers near a pond in–Ohio? And the indescribable peace of it! No, she would not go to war. It might flame about her but she would not give herself to the flames. She had something to live for. Someone. Somewhere else. She would have to go back there. Sometime.

The food was served finally. Augustine, the eldest, ate in silence as Barbara Marie pushed food around her dish, obviously unhappy with the turn of events. Rose tried to entertain them with stories of their new house, their new life, their new adventure. But Augustine was not done with the old.

"Why did the Colonel slap you, Rose?" he asked at last, pushing away his empty plate, his small face both puzzled and angry.

"Well, he didn't slap me hard, now did he?"

"Why did he slap you at all?"

"Because he wanted to show me who was boss."

"What's a boss?"

"A boss is someone who can tell you what to do."

"Like Mommy?"

"Not exactly."

"What is it then?"

"Well, a boss doesn't love you like a mother or a father or a grandmother or me. A boss—that means someone you work for. They tell you what work to do for them. And then you have to do it."

"Why would you work for them?" The boy really had an inquiring mind.

"To make money," Rose said shortly, gathering the children up from the table. "So we can pay for this nice breakfast and hotel room and all the nice things we have. They cost money, you see. So, when you're big, you'll have a boss, maybe, and you'll work for him and he'll give you money."

Augustine was not quite finished. "And sometimes he'll slap you?"

"I hope not," Rose said, pushing him ahead of her up the stairs. The hour was almost up.

13

The day passed in a blur of detail. More than grateful for her experience in managing food cupboards and linen closets, money and maids, Rose followed Colonel Morgan through the crowded warehouse, finding everything in disarray but paying close attention to the order he envisioned. The warehouse manager, a full-bearded husky Negro called Tom, walked with them, glancing at Rose surreptitiously now and then but never daring to meet her eyes. An intelligent man, she noted, and with a certain sense of pride. He seemed to know exactly where everything was and should go. With any luck she'd have little to do beyond keep the books.

"Do you write?" she asked him in the moment Morgan stepped aside to speak to a driver unloading yet another cart at the door. More guns she noted. And the heavy boxes must be ammunition.

"Write?" Behind the beard, the thick lips pursed. Light reflected in the black marble eyes, glancing up. "No Ma'am. I don't write."

"Perhaps you can learn," she said softly.

He looked at her full for an instant before dropping his eyes once more. "That would be nice. That would be real nice, Miss–"

"Rose," she said, more softly still. "But he calls me Emily. It's the name on my passport. Perhaps you should use it, too."

He stared at her then, frankly and with curiosity. She returned the look, silent. Morgan was on his way back.

"I'll do my best, Miss Emily," he said, loud enough to be heard.

A muscle twitched in the Colonel's cheek, drawing a corner of his mouth upward as he approached them.

"Tom is also an employee as you may have learned," he said. "Forgive me, Miss Emily, for not introducing you more properly." He gestured to the stacks of boxes that surrounded them. "One is so preoccupied with the details of order that the people become secondary."

She said nothing. The tour continued. At a small desk in the back, he opened a drawer, produced a ledger, and added the fat sheaf of papers he carried.

Everything would have to be entered, he explained, leafing rapidly though the sections. Foodstuff here. Soft goods there. Hardware on these pages. And another ledger for military supplies, also divided by type. Money out in this column. Money in on this one. Origins—by ship or tradesman, he explained—were to be noted along with listing buyers or distribution points. Running short was to be noted over here. Over-stocked noted there.

"Never put anything much on that line," he said. "It seems everything I bring is used up before we can restock."

She nodded mutely, trying to take it all in. A much bigger operation than the school but the same basic principles, she thought. It should not be too difficult. And if Tom could learn the books. . . .

"Shall I start now?" she asked the Colonel.

"What? Oh no. There is much yet I must show you. Tomorrow will be soon enough to get to the actual work of it when I must also move on to other business. But today is dedicated to informing you. I do trust you are able to absorb it all for I am hoping to leave these details in your capable hands." Again the bow, barely mocking. "Miss Emily."

The girl lifted her chin. "I shall do my best, Colonel Morgan. I trust you will be satisfied."

They left Tom hard at work, with a half-dozen other broad shouldered blacks, bringing a semblance of order out of the chaos. It was a big warehouse, she realized, but hardly big enough. The boxes of guns were crammed almost to the ceiling and more were on their way.

"They will not be here long," he said, catching her look. "The Texians have been on short rations with guns and munitions. General Houston will have these out of here by the end of the week unless, of course, another of the Texas commanders-in-chief arrives here first."

"There is more than one?"

His smile was cynical. "Texians are an independent people. Not likely to settle on a single leader whatever the council may have decided. Besides, fully half are volunteers and firmly believe in the right to choose whom they'll serve. As for the regulars—the colonists—they'll be heading home to plant their fields soon enough, those that haven't already left for the comfort of a Christmas fire. Not many have lined up behind Houston, I fear, though he's the government's choice. Unfortunately, down here that is as likely to be a liability as an asset."

"There is not agreement, then?"

The smile gave way to gentlemanly snort. "Agreement! The Texians cannot even agree on whether they want independence or reconciliation! War or peace. Though I must say, the voices for war get stronger as you must have noticed from the supplies that have been requested."

"Guns for Christmas," she said softly. "Mr. Collins would not approve."

"Mr. Collins?" He raised an eyebrow. "The preacher? You became acquainted?"

"On the boat," she replied, wishing she'd kept silent. "He informed me that he is a Quaker. They do not believe in carrying arms."

"He will, doubtless, find himself quite uncomfortable in Texas then. There is no man here not armed and many of the women, as well. Long before the war there were rattlers to shoot in the brush. Or the bandits that come down from the wild lands across the Sabine River. Or perhaps a renegade Indian striking a blow against civilization. You do understand we are on the frontier, Miss Emily."

"I thought perhaps I should learn to use a gun," said Rose. "Now you have convinced me of the necessity."

"I should not think it necessary for a woman. But if you insist." His smile was almost friendly. "I have a small pistol. Perhaps I can give you a lesson or two before I have to leave. We will do what we can in the little time I have. There are matters at the ranch I must attend to as soon as possible.

He showed her the hotel, top to bottom, proud as a parent of the structure he had created. It was unusually fine for the area, she realized. Most of the other buildings in town were simple two room structures of raw wood and shingles with a sort of porch—a dog run he called it—running between the rooms providing for maximum ventilation during the intense summer heat. The hotel, however, was Eastern with Victorian carving gilding the eaves and porches and high gables rising in the attic. The help slept up there, Morgan explained, not offering to guide her up the steep back steps.

"Not you," he said shortly, catching the question in her eyes. "I had special quarters prepared for the manager, of course. We hope to keep you comfortable during your stay with us, Miss Emily. It may induce you to remain and there are privations enough already to bear."

The twelve rooms on the second floor were small but adequate. Only two, somewhat larger and in the front, contained fireplaces. The de Zavala's were in one. The other was kept for the Colonel.

Two bathing rooms at the back end of the hall completed the floor. "There is also a bunkhouse in the back," he said, pointing from the window at the end of the hallway. "There are many more men who stop here, of course, than we could possibly fit into these rooms and we do our best to accommodate them all. Certainly there has been no shortage of business. And with the only decent restaurant and saloon right here, there is no reason why it should not continue to grow." He laughed lightly. "The war has been good for us so far."

In the kitchen, big and busy, he introduced her to the cook, a large and light-skinned woman with a friendly smile whom he called Sally. The other servants, more sullen but equally lively, were not mentioned by name. The saloon was run by a white man named Fred Gaines. Lean and taciturn, he acknowledged the introduction with a barely puzzled glance.

"Miss Emily will be managing the hotel," Morgan told him. "That will include keeping the books, of course." His tone was dry. "No doubt you will be relieved to have the matter out of your hands. I see the customers are keeping you busy."

"Morning to well past midnight," the man muttered. "And getting livelier every day."

"No trouble?" said Morgan.

"None I can't handle."

"It will be worse before it's better," said Morgan. "I believe the General will be coming this way soon. I have a shipment here for him."

"Sam Houston?" Fred Gaines was clearly surprised. "Here?"

"You foresee a problem?"

"Ahh, to listen to the talk. . . . There are some, you know, do not think highly of the General. Afraid to go to war, they say, and him the commanding officer! It could get ugly, Colonel, though, of course, it can all be handled."

"See to it, then," Morgan said. "We can bring in extra men if you need help. We have enough fighting on our hands with the Mexicans. Among our own people–"

"Crazy!" said the man, shaking his head. "Sober men mind their manners and their business, but in their cups–who can tell what will happen?"

His eyes lingered for a moment on Rose's face. "You will be managing the hotel then, Miss? I fear you will find us a rough lot."

She smiled, liking him. "With your help, of course. It is hardly a thing one can do alone."

At the hotel desk, Morgan introduced her to Mrs. Mittlestet, a large German woman in charge of the housekeeping but doubling as clerk. She showed her where the keys were kept and the books in which were recorded the names of their guests and the dates of their visits. They discussed regular prices and special prices, both higher and lower than the usual. They discussed the regular services and the special services and the costs involved.

"You will be in charge then, Miss?" said Mrs. Mittelstet, regarding her with suspicion. Her lips, a thin line to begin with, tightened as she turned toward Morgan who was engaged in conversation with a new arrival. Another soldier, Rose presumed, though he wore the rough garb of a settler and carried no gun. But there was something about the still face enlivened by eyes that saw everywhere at once that made her wonder. Catching Morgan's glance in her direction, she turned her attention back to the housekeeper, attempting to set her at ease by mentioning her own experience as housekeeper at the academy.

"You will find this quite different, I'm sure," the woman said.

"No doubt," said Rose. "But with your help. . . ."

"I shall be very busy, myself," she replied. "I am only too happy to turn the record-keeping over to you." Turning away, she busied herself with the books. "Whenever you are ready, Miss."

"Not quite yet, Miss Mittelstet," said Morgan, returning to his charge. "Miss Emily will be occupied with entering the warehouse shipments for the next few days. If you will continue the clerking duties this week, Monday will be soon enough to see to her training."

He led her back along the hallway, past the kitchen and pushed open a door near the back wall. "Your quarters, Miss Emily. I trust they meet with your approval."

She could hardly believe her good fortune.

A fire burned in the grate of a small fireplace, warming up a little parlor, furnished simply, but elegantly enough with a settee, two straight chairs and a table. The silverplate tea service she had brought as a gift from Maxine was set on a sideboard, along with a bottle of wine and two glasses. Beyond the parlor, another room contained a double bed with a high carved headboard, a dresser, a clothes cupboard and a water stand. Her boxes, delivered from the ship and half-opened, crowded the room, and a maid was already busy unpacking her travel trunk.

A door from the bedroom opened into the back yard. "So you can have a bit of privacy," said Morgan, catching her glance. She wondered exactly what he meant. But she didn't ask, turning instead, to lead the way out of the room.

Back in the parlor he uncorked the bottle with a slow deliberation and filled both glasses. She moved to the window, watching a wine-red sunset beginning to form in the cloudy distance.

"To the future," he said, raising his glass. "May it satisfy us all."

Her mouth twisted on the bitterness of the wine. She set it down after a small sip. "I am not quite acclimated, I fear. The very smell of this makes me quite dizzy, Colonel Morgan. I pray you will excuse me from celebration."

His eyes narrowed. "You do not wish to celebrate with me, Rose? After all we have been through together?"

"Rose, is it now? After being Miss Emily all day?"

"We are alone now," he said, as if that explained everything.

"It makes no difference to me, Sir. I am who I am, whether alone or with a roomful."

"You do not wish to celebrate with me, Rose?" he said again.

She stared back at him, refusing to sit down. "Colonel Morgan," she said at last. "I am your indentured servant and though you pay me, you have already described very well the bond in which you hold me at your pleasure. But my own interest here is not pleasure, but work. Should you choose to use me otherwise, there is little I can do, but I assure you, Sir, that you will find more pleasure in my work than I will ever give you otherwise." Her smile matched his own for thinness. "It would not be good for business, Colonel Morgan, to confuse me overmuch with personal matters."

The man had the grace to bow. A dry chuckle escaped him. "Well spoken, Miss Emily," he said, draining his glass. "Perhaps I should leave you alone to dress for dinner. There are still a few people I must have you meet before I leave you. Unfortunately there is not much time."

Emboldened, she pursued her gain. "I was hoping to dine with the de Zavala's. They will be leaving tomorrow, I understand."

He turned with his hand on the doorknob. "That will be impossible, Miss Emily. I must require your company this evening. At least for dinner."

He was gone before she could reply.

The evening passed in introductions. Coonskin caps and broad-brimmed hats were swept from trimmed and untrimmed heads as strangers passed by their table for a word or two with the Colonel who greeted most of them as old, if somewhat shallow, friends. Most, as it turned out, were newcomers, known only by gossip and reputation, recently come from New Orleans, Georgia, Alabama or the Appalachian frontier. A few had come much further. A Frenchman, two Germans, a half-dozen Irishmen and several Englishmen all made their way over to greet the Colonel. Most spoke of the Texas Navy, asking questions about available ships and shipping routes. And all, it seemed had come to fight, though few seemed entirely sure of who would command them. Some mentioned Houston and some Jim Bowie but most asked only where the action was to be, what stores were to be had, and where could horses and guns be found.

Not one mentioned Christmas, due in the following week, nor asked about families or news from the east coast. The war was on every mind, it seemed, and there was room for nothing else. She heard de Zavala's name mentioned often, sometimes with suspicion and sometimes with awe. But no one asked about his family, newly arrived, and no one asked about her, though bold eyes swept her body from time to time as Morgan mentioned her name and explained her place as his business manager.

"Bit young, ain't she?" one growled as if she weren't there. She stared him down. "Hard bunch to handle, Miss," he added, almost apologetically.

"She's quite experienced," Morgan said.

"But with the war and all. Hardly seems right for a young lady."

"She's quite experienced," Morgan said again.

The man turned to stare at her. "Ah well then, if we're to have entertainment. . . ."

"Miss Emily is to be my business manager," Morgan said slowly, emphasizing every word. "A difficult job in and of itself, I'm sure you'll agree."

The man backed away. "To be sure," he said. "To be sure, Colonel. We'll say no more about the other."

But she caught his eyes on her throughout the evening and she did not like their look.

The de Zavala's did not appear for dinner. Or perhaps, she thought, they had eaten already and retired. She was ready to retire herself. It had been a very long day.

But Morgan did not let her go until almost midnight. And she was afraid, for a moment, as he hesitated in the hallway outside her door, that he would not leave her even then. She faced him with her hand on the knob.

"I will be up very early in the morning so I can breakfast and go to the warehouse," she said quickly. "With so much traffic, it seems that would be the first order of business."

"Will you not celebrate with me tonight, Rose?" Morgan asked yet again, his voice thick with wine and the smoke of cigars in which he had been indulging.

"I fear I have no celebration left in me, Colonel. You must excuse me for a little sleep so I shall be able to concentrate on my work tomorrow."

"Your work, my dear, is for me. You must not forget that." He stepped closer, laying a well-manicured hand on her sleeve. "It would not go well, in Texas, for you to forget that."

Rose stood very still. "Indeed not, Sir. Therefore I beg of you that I be excused to rest so I may do the best possible job in the work I'm indentured to perform."

In the moment he loosened his grasp, before he could respond, she slipped into her room and closed the door. Leaning against it, she waited until his footsteps sounded, moving slowly off down the hall.

She did not realize until then that she had been holding her breath.

In her dreams that night she found herself sliding down a steep bank into deep and swirling brown water. She held a child in her arms, stretched up to keep him above water as her own body sank lower. But suddenly, her head below the surface, she was breathing, in and out, as if the water itself were air. And in her arms, snuggled again to her breast, the baby also breathed smoothly.

Greying light and the crow of a rooster awakened her and she slipped into her clothes and made her way through the back yard to a place where she could watch the sun rising over the bay. The town around her was silent but there were stirrings along the distant docks and behind her smoke rose from the hotel kitchen chimney.

She found Sally alone in the kitchen up to her elbows in biscuit dough. The cook returned her greeting with a broad smile.

"Morning, Miss. Coffee?"

"Yes, please."

Sally looked at her flour encrusted hands, shook her head and gestured towards the cupboard and the stove. "Cups in there. Pot of coffee already cooked there."

Rose helped herself. "You from around here, Sally?"

"Ain't nobody from around here, Miss. Except maybe the Indians. Colonel and Miz Morgan brung me from New Orleans two, three years ago. I cook there. I cook here. Make no never-mind to me, long as I cook family. But this—far way too much. I tell the Colonel I cannot do. And you know what?"

Rose wondered if everyone in Texas was quick with confidences. "What?" she asked.

Sally leaned forward, lowering her voice. "He pay me! Yes indeed. A dollar a week and leftovers. Share those with the other help but that dollar I save.

Don't nobody know but figure you the business woman so you gonna know so might as well say it out. Figure he paying you, too, for you be putting such good face on it."

She went back to patting the biscuit dough. "Dollar a week ain't bad but it ain't being free neither, is it? Wouldn't know nothing about that. Ain't never been free."

Rose said nothing. The older woman regarded her for a long moment. "You know anything about that, Miss? You born free?"

She must have seen the slap, Rose thought, restraining the urge to smooth her hair or find a mirror which could tell her if the traces of her buried African heritage had suddenly appeared. But that must be it! She must have seen or heard about the slap.

"I wasn't born free," she said. "But I was raised free. In New York. Raised by my father's sister and her family."

"What for you come here? You work there?"

"Long story," said Rose, rinsing the coffee cup carefully. "Challenge. Friendships. Things I wanted to leave behind. Not that I knew exactly what I was coming to. But the money was good enough."

"You sell yourself?"

Surprise stiffened her tone. "I beg your pardon?"

"You sell yourself? To the Colonel? He own you now for how long?"

"We have a year's contract."

"A year he own you?"

"I don't think of it that way, exactly. He's paying me. I have my own quarters."

The older woman pounded out the dough, turned it over, slapped it down and lightly started twisting off the biscuit balls. Rose waited until she looked back up.

"You want me to tell you something, Child? You want to get through that year, no trouble, no fuss? You just remember he own you. Ain't guilty for nothing that way. Nothing to think about. Nothing to do but what he say. No problem. Colonel's not bad man, long as he boss. You forget that, you done forgot your head, girl."

In the long silence that followed, Rose moved toward the door. The kitchen was stifling suddenly, filled with the sound of shuffling feet as other servants filed in and went to work. Sally called to her softly before she could close the door behind her.

"Didn't like you, girl, wouldn't say none of this. You and me, we get along." Holding her floury hands aloft she came up to Rose, leaning to whisper. "Tommy told me you said you teach him to read. That be something. That be something good. But mind you don't tell the Colonel."

"You know Tom?"

"He my husband. Colonel bought us together. He got half a heart, anyways." She was laughing as she returned to work.

Rose ate breakfast quickly, avoiding the few pairs of eyes that regarded her boldly as she sat alone by a window. The biscuits, she noted, were particularly good.

Morgan paused by her table only briefly. "You will see to the warehouse today," he said in response to her "Good morning." She nodded quickly.

"You will need to begin taking inventory. The receipts are in the desk and Tom can name every shipment. Amazing man! If he could read and write he could buy himself back." His laugh was short and sharp. "Might not be a bad thing. A good man is a good man, slave or free. And a bad man–" He shrugged, then turned up the corners of his mouth. "I'm trusting you will do an excellent job. That you have had an adequate rest."

"An excellent rest, Sir. For which I do thank you."

Crude aisles has been formed through the shipping crates in the warehouse so even though the place was more packed than ever, a certain order was emerging. Settling herself at the desk, she plunged into records and receipts, lost in the work until a soft clearing of throat brought her back to the bustle around her.

Tom was standing there, a bowl of soup in one hand and a large piece of cornbread in the other. "Sally sent these. Told her didn't look like you was aiming to stop for nothing and she said bring it along to you."

She persuaded him to sit with her a moment, indicating the numbers she had been writing. "Can you do any of these?"

He shook his head both ways. "Maybe so. Maybe no. I can try."

She lined them, one through ten, on a clean sheet. "All the other numbers come from these. You know these, you'll know them all. You practice a column of each one. Just like counting, only writing. You practice when you can. Show me tomorrow."

He folded the sheet very carefully into his pocket along with a stub of a pencil. "I'll do that, Miss." Taking her empty bowl with him, he left. She returned to the columns of figures.

Emily picked her way through the crates to the little desk about mid-afternoon. They were about to leave, she explained. A late start, unfortunately, but no longer to be delayed. She and the children had yet to see their new home. She only wished Rose could go with her. And really, she saw no reason why not. She had said as much to Colonel Morgan, indeed she had. What difference could a few more days make?

"And what did the Colonel say?"

"I'm afraid he insisted it would make a great deal of difference, Rose. In fact he refused to discuss the matter. But he told me where to find you and said he was sure you would agree with him that your presence here is required."

"He must be right, then. Perhaps at Christmas. . . ."

"Oh, but I asked him. And he said, he said Christmas was a very busy time and he could not imagine. . . ." The small pale face had reddened with withheld tears and irritation. "I cannot imagine he would hold you here against your will. And I cannot imagine spending Christmas without you. You are all I have of home now, Rose! You must not let them keep you from me in this way."

"It seems I have little to say in the matter," said Rose, rising to put an arm around her friend. "But there now, Dear. You are only a little ways across the water, and I'm sure we shall be together often. You must go home now and enjoy your husband and your children while you may. With the war upon us, who knows how brief those days might be."

For an instant, fear wiped every other consideration from Emily's face. She regained control quickly enough. "So many battles to live through," she murmured. "And I am so glad my husband is a survivor." Her usual cheer struggled to reassert itself. "Perhaps Santa Anna will not come so far north."

"I should imagine," said Rose, "that this is precisely where he would want to come." Her eyes swept the room, pausing on crates of weapons. Emily's followed.

"Oh!" she said in a small voice. "Oh dear!"

"I understand that General Sam Houston will be coming soon to pick up some of these munitions," said Rose.

"Forgive me, I almost forgot the message I was to deliver from the Colonel. If Lorenzo is not here when General Houston arrives, you are to send word to us immediately. And you must entertain the General until Lorenzo can arrive. It seems that Colonel Morgan may not be able, himself, to be here. There is a problem at the garrison in Anahuac. A Southern officer called William Travis led a band of Texians there in an attempt to take it over from the

Mexicans. Our men have been captured. Colonel Morgan must sail tonight to intervene or they may well be hung for traitors. Unfortunately, he said he is leaving considerable unfinished business but he trusts you will be able to carry on until he returns."

Rose was surprised to find herself regretting the Colonel's abrupt departure. At the same time she rejoiced in it. He was, at least, a known quantity in a sea of unknowns. With Emily leaving, she would be alone. But she must not burden her friend with her own fears and fancies.

"And how are you traveling?"

"By carriage to the Lynchberg Ferry and across." She put her arms around Rose for a long embrace. "Everyone is ready. I must go."

Rose left the books to walk her friend to the front of the hotel where children and nanny were already seated in the carriage. De Zavala appeared as his wife came in sight, offering a greeting and farewell in the same instant. Before goodbyes could be properly spoken, the carriage rolled off, followed closely by two heavily loaded carts of New York treasures. Rose, thinking of her own rooms so pleasant and close at hand, did not envy her friend's upcoming journey.

But even so, the small caravan, disappearing down the dusty trail, seemed to be taking her own heart with it. Around her, now, were only strangers. And so it would remain, apparently for the near future. There would certainly be no family Christmas this year.

Christmas! How long ago and far away the childhood days of opening presents underneath a tree. Receiving not quite what she wanted but close enough. I should have been more grateful, she thought. It seems that now there will be nothing at all.

Unaccountably, she thought of Luther Collins. He seemed a man to whom Christmas came all year long. Each day a present. Each sunrise a wrapping of the gift. She wondered how the sunrises of war would affect him. Perhaps he, too, would become a stranger to her.

14

She did not leave the warehouse until well after dark, working alone by the yellow light of the lantern Tom provided at sunset. She waved away the suggestion to stop along with the offer of food. By the time she wiped her pen for the last time and set it down, every shipment on the *Exert* had been entered. It was a start.

Bracing back her aching shoulders, she returned to the hotel. She was almost too tired to mind dining alone. Almost too tired to dine at all, in fact. But she must grow accustomed and the sooner, the better. Her second steak in two days did not look as good as the first though that was doubtless a matter of appetite.

"May I join thee, Miss Rose?"

She looked up with a start to see Luther Collins making a clumsy bow. "But of course! What a pleasure!"

Seated, he took a few moments to study her face. "Weary, I see. Thee has dived straight into the work, then?"

"It waits to be done. I am here to do it."

He nodded. "An honest attitude. It should please thy employers."

She said nothing. He essayed small talk. How did she find Texas? Was her work understandable enough? Were relations with the Colonel comfortable? And the people. How did she perceive them?

"I have made friends with the cook and the warehouse manager. Both slaves, I think, but paid a little. And not unhappy. A strange situation, Mr. Collins. Nothing quite fits."

"Freedom and slavery are equally strange, I believe. Few of us understand either state, though we all, as a matter of course, live in one or the other."

"I have the feeling, Mr. Collins, that your definitions would not be the usual ones."

"Perhaps not," he agreed.

When the serving girl came, Collins refused the steak and was offered a stew. Rose watched him move the chunks of meat aside, sopping up the gravy with his bread. "You don't like meat?"

"I'm no purist, the Father knows, but meat somehow sticks in my throat." He shrugged. "Been that way since I was small and had to help my father kill the chickens. Most unpleasant—all that blood and fear and pain. And then I saw on the first page of the Bible, in the Garden of Eden, that flesh was not the Creator's first choice for food." He shrugged again, plainly embarrassed. "It is not important. A very personal choice."

"You will find it difficult in Texas, I fear. There are many more ranches than farms as I understand it."

"Beans," he chuckled. "I eat plenty of beans." He looked down at his plate. "But tonight I neglected to order."

"Sally sent you her best, I suppose. Because you were dining with me."

"Best is like freedom and slavery, I think. Not many can speak to the meaning with clarity."

"And you are perfectly clear, Mr. Collins?" She cut and pierced a chunk of steak and chewed slowly, finding it unaccountably hard to swallow. Really, the man was having too much influence on her. And for a Quaker, he certainly talked overmuch.

The chuckle across the table broadened into a long, low laugh. "Hardly that, Miss Rose. I am as confused as the next man about this journey we call life. A poor pilgrim passing is all I know. Nevertheless, a pilgrim with a purpose."

"And that is?"

"To know my Father. To understand what little I can of the Creator. What other study could so profit a man? Or a woman?"

She glanced at the muskets that bristled against the wall, guarded by a tall Negro whose eyes were everywhere, watching. Behind the bar, Fred Gaines was also watching. Conversations clashed noisily as the calls for beer increased.

"There are many here who would disagree in fact if not principle," she said. "The study of war, the strategies of survival take precedence I think. Time enough for the Creator when one is too old to plan for daily life."

He shook his head. "There are many here who may be cut down in the midst of their daily life. Eternity, Miss Rose, is very long and life on Earth is quite brief. What better use could one make of it than preparation for what is to come?"

"Preparation?"

"The preparation to meet one's Maker. It would seem, by logic alone, to be a meeting worthy of diligent research, at the very least."

"And at the most?"

"Why, obedience to what one determines to be the Creator's goals."

"And those would be?"

"Peace on earth, Miss Rose. It is stated quite clearly in the Gospels."

Rose finished eating her steak. "It seems you may be in the wrong place at the wrong time, Mr. Collins. Peace is hardly the priority in Texas at this time."

"What better reason for such as myself to be here, then?" he asked, leaning back from the table with a smile. "But thee must forgive me. I have no wish to burden thee with either my philosophy or my preaching. Still, it seems I can hardly resist, thee listens so well."

"You might be hung for some of your opinions in this crowd, Mr. Collins."

"It is true I do not speak as freely to most as to thee, Sister. But one must give a true witness and to die to the flesh is but to rise to the Spirit."

"You seek martyrdom?"

"Indeed not! I enjoy life more than most, I think. To love the Creator can only increase one's joy in Creation. Sunrises. Sunsets. The ocean. The sweep of grasslands and the great green of the forests at home. Oh, there is so much! The sight of a river running over the white rocks of the desert or the green ones of the eastern mountains. A babe's smile. The true love of a brother or sister. That most of all." He paused for a moment, reddening. "I even confess to great pleasure in the company of a beautiful woman with a beautiful heart."

Weariness made her cold. "Would the pleasure be the same in an ugly woman with a beautiful heart?"

The flush deepened across his face. "Forgive me, Miss Rose. I do overstep the lines. Never having been married, there is much I do not understand about females and my skills of social intercourse are woefully inadequate. Nor am I a good Friend, in truth. It is simplicity itself to speak of God. When I speak of myself, I do err."

Before she could protest, he had risen and was gone.

How strange, Rose thought, signaling for a glass of wine. How strange that both Colonel Morgan and Luther Collins should want her! Much though she needed both material and spiritual guidance in this rough new territory, it hardly seemed right that her advisors had been drawn by something other than her mind and soul.

On the other hand, her desire for advisors was hardly pure altruism. And she was finding a certain satisfaction in facing that glittering look of desire, though the shifting of her world of women and family left her uncertain of herself. The future was unreadable, complicated by a thousand new variables. Oh for the simple credos of Dr. Connie and Miss Goodwin. Work well and do good.

Desires, half-formed and barely understood, made everything so complicated.

She was not approachable in this mood and the table where she sat remained empty, though the chairs were dragged away and a score of men stood against the walls at the far end of the room. The din grew louder. Near the bar, shouting had erupted. A heavily mustached Mexican, silver belted and spurred, was in a roaring argument with a couple of coonskin caps. Smooth as silk, the big Negro on vigil near the door slid in, the bulge of his pistol showing under his cowhide waistcoat.

"Kind of warm in here," he said, loud enough to be heard. "Reckon we might be needing some fresh air."

There were curses. Hands scrambled for knives. The black man was a whir of motion. A hard-heeled boot to the belly, the lead-weighted crack of a jaw and the fracas was over. Others backed away, muttering, picking up their beer and settling back, if only against the wall. At the bar Fred's right hand came back into sight.

The Mexican had disappeared along with several others who slipped quietly into the night. The Negro walked back towards the door as a maid brought water to the wounded.

Rose nodded to Fred Gaines as she pushed back her chair. No more! Her stomach twisted in revolt at the scene. Holding herself with care, she stood and made her way out of the dining area and down the hall to her rooms.

She realized, lying there in the dark, that she had never before seen anyone struck to bring blood. And then she thought of muskets and bullets and blood. Cannon balls, knives, pistols. And blood. She thought of war. She thought of lynchings. And she thought of Luke and Luther Collins. It seemed to her that the two men would like each other very much. Not that they would ever meet. Luke was likely home for Christmas, she remembered with a kind of panicked thrill. He was meeting his son for the first time. She hoped Dr. Connie had kept it a surprise.

The work in the warehouse passed more smoothly the next day. Shipments had stopped coming in and Tom was having no trouble getting everything organized. She noticed how smoothly the men worked with him, turning as a team. His wife, she remembered, had the same style in the kitchen which explained how smoothly the cooks managed to serve a great number of very demanding people. Rose could not imagine such cool competence in herself. For the moment she was grateful for her own small corner and the single focus she had to keep. Time enough later to learn teamwork. She was not accustomed to it, though she managed to reach a vaguely outlined state of cooperation with the warehouse, kitchen, bar and housekeeping managers. So far, none had turned against her.

The week passed. She spent the mornings with the warehouse ledgers. After lunch, she wrote in receipts from the restaurant and saloon. In the evening, sitting behind the desk after dinner, she recorded receipts from the hotel as she registered the increasing supply of guests. It was almost alarming, that surge. The rooms were never empty and in the bunkhouse in back men slept in twos and threes on the beds as well as spreading blankets on the floor. Hay for the horses disappeared as fast as it came in and the goods in the warehouse were dwindling rapidly.

Day after day, Tom argued with one person or another who demanded a share of the largest untouched crates.

"Colonel Morgan, he say that for General Sam Houston. Can't let you have none of that, Sir."

The men would glower. Tom would lower his eyes, his hands hanging open. Empty. Though they might stretch forward, he never stepped back. It was a thin line but the black man stood it well. The inquirers grumbled but they walked away.

"Do you know General Sam Houston?" she asked him at the end of the week as they worked together on his writing. He was progressing fast. Already he could put down numbers next to the words she wrote down to define supplies. Already reading the words, he would soon be able to write them as well. They were both very pleased.

"I met him once," Tom said, looking up from his carefully drawn characters. "Mighty big man."

"Big drunk, I heard." With Tom, she could almost giggle. It must be his casual certainties that made her feel so safe and sure.

"People talk. Half time, don't know what they saying."

"You mean he's not a big drunk? He's a good man? Not a coward?"

"Ain't no coward, that's for sure. That man go where devils scared to travel. Reckon that why he drink some, too much maybe. Can't stand all the little bitty hearts around him."

"He has a big heart?"

"Biggest and best, I always say. Don't wish nobody no harm. Not Mexicans. Not colored. Not Indians, even. He live with the Cherokee, he say. Went to Washington to represent them." He enunciated the words carefully. "That man want good. Not much good here, mostly speaking, but we got it pretty good, huh?" He laughed, changing the subject. "I get paid, he tell you? The Colonel pay me, though he buy me, too. No, never mind. Everybody got to work. I eat good. Got wife. Children. They gone now. Grown up and sold off." The dark face sobered. "Not for that, it be easy to think of yourself alone and your woman. But there be a lot of suffering out there."

Silence stretched between them. Tom bent back to his paper, took up his pen and resumed his careful work. "Reckon that why the General drink," he said.

It was not her intention but Rose was drawn to the door as inevitably as the crowd that formed ahead of her the next evening when Sam Houston arrived.

He galloped in front of a small group of men, riding a huge and ripplingly-muscled white stallion, dust rising well past his three-cornered hat. Not until he slowed in front of the hotel did she realize that he was older than she had imagined with lines in his face that had not come from the sun. But when the big man swung from the saddle, his head was high and the most arrogant of his detractors found themselves stepping aside.

He signed his name with a flourish of curls, saying nothing, though he stared her full in the face.

"We're very pleased to have you, General Houston. Colonel Morgan has offered you the use of his own room upstairs, if you're agreeable. He regrets he cannot be here himself, but his presence was required at Anahuac since–"

The General waved his hand, dismissing the commentary. "I know. I know." He softened the brusque tone to a pleasant rumble. "Most generous of him. I feared confinement to the bunkhouse. Not that I haven't done worse, and that lately."

The dust of the road was thick on his coat. "Perhaps a bath before dinner, General Houston?" She stood. "The boy will bring your saddlebags if you wish me to show you up now."

The dark eyes met hers unblinking. "Indeed not, Miss. Just see that Saracen is well fed and brushed down. I have ridden him hard today." He raised his voice enough to be heard above the murmuring of the crowd gathering by the door. "I am here to recruit soldiers to defend us from oppression and I must be about my business."

As if on cue, the men surged forward. "Drinks all around," shouted

Houston, moving towards the bar. "Pour them a round, Fred. Damn fine army we got here. Might as well get to know each other because there's a long ride ahead."

Rose sent a messenger racing through the night with simple instructions. "Tell Mr. de Zavala that the General has arrived. He will wish to come immediately." Then she set herself to minding the desk as every bed in the bunkhouse were spoken for, then doubled and tripled. And still the travelers kept coming. Not that any were yet thinking of sleep. The crowd pressing in around the General moved only to reach for more beer. Not that they could keep up with Houston.

The grandfather clock had struck four in the morning when Rose followed the three men upstairs, Fred and the doorman dragging Houston between them. Depositing him on the bed with surprising gentleness, Fred pulled off his boots and then motioned to Rose.

"You might bring him a glass of water, Miss. And wipe his face. Remove his waistcoat. The Colonel likes to see him well-treated and well he should be. I would attend to it myself but there's a mess below I have yet to clean away."

Tending to drunken men was not within Rose's experience. She stood staring down at the man on the bed for several minutes after Fred had closed the door behind him.

Houston opened his eyes. "Gonna tend to me, little lady? Gonna tend to Sam? You come here, little lady. I'll tend to you." A movement, an outstretched arm, laid him back groaning. "God I feel bad. Got nothing that doesn't ache. Damn this damn war all to hell. Gonna take them boys out and shoot them all. Blood all over the place. Make them die laughing. Damn it all to hell."

She held water to his lips, lifted his head. He drank greedily. "Put a little rum in that, would you, Miss? Don't want to think anymore. Gotta shut off the old brain works. No thinking is best, never mind." He laughed suddenly, then roared. "You think I'm drunk, lady. I'll show you drunk."

"There now, General." She moistened a cloth from the pitcher on the washstand and held it to his face. "There now. You'll be fine in a minute. There now."

Tears started from his eyes. "Take them boys out and kill them. That's my job. Don't much like my job, Ma'am. Don't much like this business. Ain't much of a hero myself. Don't much like the killing. Gotta be done, though. God damn, it's gotta be done."

She unbuttoned his waistcoat, loosed his cravat, patted his neck with the cool wet cloth. "There now, General." She was crooning to him as to a child. And like a child, he turned his head into the pillow, eyes drooping shut as he groped for her hand.

"Stay with me just for a while," he mumbled. "They're all gone now. They keep going. Me, I don't belong nowhere. Nobody owns me but you just stay, will you? Such a pretty lady. High yellow, it must be, but I'd have sworn you were white. Proud, too. Not my business, no, never mind. Just stay for a little while."

She stayed until he loosed her hand completely, a few hours later, it must have been. As the sky greyed into dawn and the roosters came to life, he awoke briefly, saying nothing, but she saw his eyes glittering in the moonlight and the pressure on her hand increased for an instant. Then he released her, twisting himself in bed. She waited until his breathing became louder, a slow rhythm, then she drew a quilt over the still body and let herself out the door.

She took a few hours rest. Tom and Mrs. Mittelstet could handle everything just fine. As long as she was up before the General.

At noon she sent the maid to his room with hot water and a message as to whether he wished the service of the barber who was waiting downstairs. He said he would also much appreciate a bath.

The man who appeared in the empty dining room two hours later was a transformed version of the evening's warrior. A velvet frockcoat was accentuated by lace at the throat and cuffs and his heavily brocaded waistcoat was rimmed with gold chains. Clean shaven to the long side-burns, his face was puffy, more lined than ever and a trifle grey. The General looked strong enough but not quite well.

"Perhaps you will join me for lunch, Miss," he said, approaching her desk. "Unless, of course, the kitchen is closed. Haven't eaten since yesterday morning and food would, be a good thing."

"I will see to it at once, Sir."

"Perhaps—" the broad man hesitated for a moment. "Perhaps you could serve me in my room." He gestured towards the men who had materialized in the doorway. "I am not quite prepared to face the crowds. They will be upon me soon enough."

"As you say, Sir." Rose wished his dark gaze were not so intense. Surely he remembered nothing of last night. And surely he could not be expecting anything from her.

A smile curved the General's lip. "Nothing for you to fear, my Dear. But a General must take some prerogatives, though his soldiers give him none. And the company of a lovely lady is a prerogative well worth taking though it lasts but an hour's lunchtime."

She felt as though she were being smiled upon by a bear. But a friendly bear, this one.

She smiled back.

"I will have the food prepared and come up directly. What would you like?"

"Steak," he fairly growled. "And potatoes, if possible. And pie. Don't forget the pie."

"Coffee?" she asked.

"Yes indeed. And ask Fred for a bottle of brandy to accompany it. With two snifters."

She brought a linen cloth and napkin when she brought the food, spreading the table that sat close by the window overlooking the distant bay. Settling himself only after she was also seated, the General attacked his food with no further thought for a full five minutes.

Rose sat quietly until he looked up from his steak. "Forgive me," he said. "Even the over-indulgence in alcohol has not dulled my appetite when good food is set before me. But conversation with a lady is a rarer treat. My head is a little heavy but if you will ask questions of me, Miss, I shall answer them all."

"I know little about you," she murmured. "I should like to know more."

And so, between huge mouthfuls of food, Sam Houston talked. Like a man unburdening himself from a near death fast of silence he laid down his history. His childhood in western Virginia, the death of his father, his mother's subsequent journey into the wilds of western Tennessee, his running beyond her into the Indian lands. He described his studies and quoted the Iliad to her. He spoke of ambitions and drives, fears and weaknesses and the contrariness of his love for both peace and war. He spoke of his love of justice and his utter cynicism that it should ever triumph. He told her about his time with the Cherokee and his time in Congress. The Indians, he said, laughing around a piece of pie, were considerably more civilized than the Congressmen.

As he finished his second piece of pie and poured brandy into the coffee cup, he mentioned women.

"Not many in my life, you might imagine," he said, leaning back in his chair. "Forgive me for overspeaking. It is not often, these days, that anyone listens to me without argument. And there is no time—forgive the language—for chasing skirts."

She said nothing.

"I was married once," he added. "In Tennessee. Didn't work. Might be why I'm not back in Tennessee. Or Washington."

He asked her about herself then, listening carefully as she offered a somewhat edited version of her own life. The bushy eyebrows went up. "You are a Negro? Free in New York? And you have agreed to servitude here? Slavery?"

Her head came up sharply. "I am well paid, Sir. Better paid than in New York. And the adventure is appealing, if only for the year's contract."

"Rather a strange thing, I should think. You were raised with whites, as a white?"

"I always knew," said Rose. "As did all of us."

"A very strange thing," said Houston. "It would be a most interesting study to see such a mind at work." The dark gaze seemed to search her brain. "And what have you learned, Rose, or should I call you Miss Emily, from your lifetime on the split between two worlds?"

"Why, that everyone inhabits his own world, Sir. And when one lives between two cultures, one has the freedom to select what customs one prefers."

"Free to choose slavery, then?"

"Those with no inheritance must work for a living. I am paid. What matters a piece of paper?"

His gaze, if possible, intensified. "A great deal, I should think," he muttered, then laughed. "No, Miss Emily, you are not being entirely honest with me. There is something you have left out. Something or someone from whom you are running, perhaps, so desperately that becoming a slave in Texas is the easier alternative."

She said nothing. He shook his head, dark eyes still fixed on blue ones. "Not a crime, no. You are much too well connected with Morgan and the de Zavala's. Something personal, I would imagine. A man, perhaps. A white man? One you are forbidden to love? Or a black man? One you do not wish to love? Or a child! Ah yes." He went on as the color rushed to her face. "Is it child to the black man or the white man? And where are you keeping it? Surely you have not brought it to Texas?"

The color had drained from her face, leaving it deathly pale. "The white man is my father and the black one my friend," she said, rising. "But really, Sir, it is most unkind of you to speak so. If you will excuse me—"

He was on his feet, bowing deeply. "Madam, you must forgive me yet again. I have been with the roughest of men for too long to presume to speak with a lady, as indeed you are, whatever your history. And I must confess that I had taken an interest in you afore now. If you will allow me, I will explain myself."

Rose resumed her seat as the General began to pace. "I will be blunt because I am a blunt man, Miss Emily Rose. I need a spy." He held up a hand to her start of surprise. "No, nothing very dangerous. It is a matter I had discussed with Colonel Morgan when this hotel was first built—that it would be useful to have someone working here who would check the wind, as the sailors say. Someone who could report on, shall we say the temper of the times?" His smile was rueful. "The Commander-in-Chief must needs know what is going on."

He paused for a moment by the window. "Morgan mentioned a likely wench, as he put it. A New York Negro girl, fathered by a ship's captain and raised by his sister, smart and well-educated, with a yen for adventure." He turned to look at her again. "Though Deaf verified for me that you had indeed arrived with Mrs. de Zavala, I could not well believe my eyes." The eyes were frankly appraising, liking what they saw. "You are—so much a lady. And you do not appear to be particularly—" An almost shy smile split the craggy face. "Adventurous."

He sat down heavily across the table, pouring more brandy and setting a snifter in front of her. "My dear, this has not gotten off to a good start though I have assured myself of several prerequisites in your character. You are an honest woman, a loyal one, and one with a strong will. Whether or not you have a sense or purpose—or would be willing to acquire one—remains to be seen."

She met his eyes. "What purpose would you propose, General Houston? I have no knowledge whatsoever of the intricacies of war. And no wish to be a spy."

The General sighed. "This is not the kind of war I would have chosen, Miss Emily. In the first place, I am not yet entirely convinced that we have just cause to be rebelling against Mexico. The Constitution they wrote in 1824 is a virtual work of art. The beginnings of a true republic out of an inordinately mixed population. No slavery allowed and though the natives have been pressed into a sort of serfdom, the conquerors are not at war with them as we are here. Of course, the Spanish have been down there for two or three hundred years. We are barely arrived and have not ceased our wars for more land.

"It should not have been so hard to cooperate," he added as if to himself. "This government, by and large, has been remarkably generous to the Anglo

Saxons who have flocked out here to settle on rich and nearly free land. And by and large they have left us pretty much alone. Until now."

He laughed. "Mexico has taken a viper to its bosom, Miss Emily Rose. What Anglo Saxon in the United States who has called himself an American is ever going to call himself by another name? We're a proud people. We might be the spit and the spawn of the earth—escaped here out of debtors' prison or just ahead of the hangman's noose but by God we're free now. We're free to claw and grind our way to the top of any ladder. We carry our own guns and no lords or ladies are going to stand in our way." His face fell, suddenly. "No Indians, either."

She could only look at him in silence.

"I suppose we aren't all free, either," he said after a while. "I suppose I'm sitting with a woman who isn't." His eyebrows rose again. "By choice," he said.

"It was not an easy choice," she managed. "But I will make an agreement with you, General Houston. I will not question your old choices if you do not question mine."

"I am in the more vulnerable position," the General said. "I must depend on both your responses and your reactions if you are to be my spy. And how can I know your reactions if I do not question the choices you have made?"

"You can see where the choices have led me. And you have, it appears, familiarized yourself with my life. You must know I enjoy a good reputation despite my lack of parentage."

He chuckled. "Oh, you have parentage enough, Miss Emily Rose. Benjamin Sturn, is it not? Newly promoted to captain of his own ship."

"He never saw my mother again. Not after I was born."

"But you have met him."

It was not a question. She did not answer.

He prodded. "On your eighteenth birthday."

"Yes," she said. "Colonel Morgan was there."

The General's eyes had not left her face. "He left. Your father left."

Again the rush of color, bringing tears with it, this time. She shook her head angrily, caught in the spell of a man whose eyes were wringing out her heart. He was ruthless.

"But that made you seek gainful employment. It did not bring you to Texas."

She said nothing. He shrugged. "You have your secrets. I have mine. But if there is someone you love in the United States, someone you wish to return to, you may wish to hear me out. We face a formidable foe. But one, we hope, with a fatal weakness."

He talked to her then about Santa Anna. He had studied the man in detail. Nor was there a lack of respect in his descriptions. Santa Anna had risen through the ranks through courage and intelligence, he said, along with an ardent ambition and an uncanny sense of the winning side. When he attained military skill, fighting in the Spanish army, he used it to move into leadership of the rebels who won Mexico's freedom from Spain. He had served the first Mexican Emperor well and then used his knowledge to bolster the next set of rebels who banished the Emperor in favor of a more representative Constitution. Moving from royalist to republican over the course of a score of years, he had become a champion of self-government and, not incidentally, a champion to the Anglo-Saxons settling in *Tejas*.

Then everything changed.

"It is because there are so many of us," said Houston. "And we are such a stubborn lot. No one wishes to send taxes to a government which has done nothing for us, or at least that is the way the people talk now. The land—well, the land was given years ago and now the settlers feel they have won it for themselves. And they have done it, to their souls, as Americans, not Mexicans. So now we're strong enough, we rebel.

"Santa Anna understands that mind. That is why he will march up here with as many thousands of soldiers as he can muster and utterly crush us. At least that is his plan. And he does not lack the capacity. For all that these mountain men wave their muskets and leap about, they have no comprehension of what they are facing. Santa Anna will have a disciplined army, executing classic maneuvers in throughly trained fashion with thousands of expendable peasants leading the charge. He intends to take no prisoners, mark my word. And what do we have here? A few hundred dirt farmers and ranchers along with a lot of excitable men and boys who love a good fight and don't want anybody telling them what to do. They'd chase down into Mexico after him, waving those muskets. And do you know what, Miss Emily Rose? They would never come back. Not a mother's son among them would get back."

He sighed heavily. "We have as much chance against Santa Anna, Miss Emily Rose, as a pigeon with its wings clipped would have against a gamecock with iron spurs. Except for one thing."

He leaned forward suddenly, tapping his broad forehead. "We have a mind, Miss Emily Rose. If we can think, we can think ahead. And if we can think ahead and if the enemy has become haughty, if Santa Anna has become convinced of his superiority and therefore not wary enough, why then, Miss Emily, we could, perhaps lay a trap."

"What kind of trap?"

"There are places a beautiful woman can go, Miss Emily Rose, that a man can never go. There are things a woman can do. . . ." He looked down at the table, traced a bead of moisture on his cup.

Her heart was freezing. Frying. "I'm afraid I don't understand."

"Neither do I," said Houston. "In truth, the idea is not even formed except in the knowledge that you are needed here to support the new Republic of Texas."

"And is this new nation to be slave or free?"

"Slave, no doubt. We have many Southerners here. And the land is rich for cotton."

"And why would I support a slave state?".

"Because you, too, are American, my dear. Because slavery cannot endure forever and your children will go on to be free. Because the United States is a great possibility, whatever its shortcomings, and because your own destiny is linked in a way it can never be linked with a Spanish government, thousands of miles across the southern desert."

He paused, as if weighing a gamble. "Because of those you left behind in New York," he said. "Because of your own desire to feel free. Because you understand that freedom is not a state of the body; it is a state of mind."

She did not move. He went on. "And because you will be rewarded with considerable acreage if you are able to play a part in the winning of this war." He laughed again. "Money we have none, but there's plenty of land for the giving."

"I can promise you nothing," she said at last. "But I will listen and learn and if you ask me questions, I will answer as fully and honestly as possible."

"That will be enough," said the General. "For now." He stretched, standing, then bowed. "It has been a great pleasure to make your acquaintance Miss Emily Rose. I trust I will be able to enjoy your company again in the near future. I need not instruct you, I'm sure, to share this conversation with no one except Colonel Morgan. He, at least, will understand, though it is not necessary that he know."

"I speak to the Colonel only as necessary, General."

"Very well then. He need know nothing of this from you but I trust you will feel more free with me in the future. Unfortunately, present duty calls. I must raise and furnish my army." He walked to the window where plumes of dust announced approaching horsemen. "Can de Zavala have arrived already?"

"I sent a message last night, Sir. As soon as you arrived."

"Good girl," he said, buckling on his sword. "We shall get along quite well."

He turned at the door. "I must introduce you immediately to Deaf Smith. You will understand why when you meet him. Best spy a man could have. Loyal."

She remained in the room to collect the lunch things. Loyal. The word echoed in her mind. It did not sound like a word that would describe her at all. She wondered what Sam Houston wanted from her and whether she would be willing to give it. At least he had made no forward advances. Perhaps the bear was a gentleman after all.

It was not until later that evening when the men at the bar burst into a rowdy rendition of *Silent Night*, that she realized it was Christmas Eve.

15

Emily de Zavala wondered why she had even come to Texas. The day outside was grey as oyster shells; the choppy waters of Buffalo Bayou were equally cloudy; twisted trees stretched out occasional bare branches, gnarly flutters against the distant horizon. The long dried grasses bent to the wind along the shore.

There was no other habitation in sight along the waterfront, nor behind it, either. And though there was a road in the distance across the narrow channel of Buffalo Bayou, she could not see it.

It was Christmas Day. Her husband had left her for Sam Houston. The children were unhappy and she had no friend to turn to. The life of a diplomat's wife was well and good in the civilizations of New York, Paris, and even old Mexico. But here in this raw land where talk was only of war and weapons and the strategies of victory and defeat, here where peace was mentioned only in passing and her husband must leave at the dawn of Christmas Eve to assist in plotting a revolution, here was not where she wanted to be.

Emily sighed as she stood on the porch that encircled the large house on three sides, scanning the bayou yet again. It was almost noon. The presents had already been opened. Lorenzo had said there was no reason to expect him back for several days and the children, bursting with anticipation of secrets hidden in the brightly wrapped boxes, were not about to wait. No company was expected. Mrs. Morgan, the Colonel's wife had called shortly after her arrival but she had made no mention of a Christmas visit. And she knew not a soul else unless one counted the rough men who had come to visit her husband day after day over the past week, talking an endless stream of politics and leaving him at last to walk the floor alone.

The talks did not make her husband happy, Emily knew that. Try though he might to join himself to these American comrades, these old business and new political partners, she knew his heart remained in the deep south of Mexico with his books and papers and the philosophies that had guided the building of a new republic on the foundation of the old Spanish empire. He himself was of pure Spanish blood, though born in Mexico at a time when such things mattered to the ruling class. He had made the best of it—not only for himself but others. He was not a destroyer, not a rebel by nature. He was the engineer of smooth transitions. And he had recognized long before most men of his class that the old lords of Europe must give way to the vibrant children of the new land. Even the Indians had a place in Lorenzo's plans.

He believed that all men, and possibly women as well, had the right to be represented by their government. And there were other rights in which he believed. "Unalienable rights," he called them, quoting the American Declaration of Independence. "The right to life, liberty and the pursuit of happiness." He did not believe in slavery.

In all other ways, Lorenzo loved the philosophies of the founders of the United States of America. Seeing his friend and fellow republican betray his own country into dictatorship, he was as ready as the next man to see Texas allied to a more democratic country. But even in his disillusionment with Mother Mexico, he found the irregular ways of freethinking frontiersmen hard to embrace. As did she. But Emily knew the thoughts that had kept her husband pacing through the past three nights came from a much deeper place than the irritation he sometimes expressed with the manners and moralities of his new neighbors. He had believed, almost until now, that reconciliation was still a hope. That the Mexican government could stretch itself enough to accommodate these brash newcomers whose entrepreneurial abilities had so enriched this empty land. And he had realized, finally, that it was not to be. Having won their sustenance from the Texas soil and sun without help from that government, the Anglos had no intention of sharing the wealth. And the Mexican government had no intention of tolerating such defiance.

A passion for justice along with a pleasure in the shared study of politics, economics, and social systems had taken Lorenzo to the seats of power in his own country. Economic expediency had brought him into cooperation with the Yankee financiers of the new territories in the north. He had not expected he would ever have to choose between the two. And had he not been so in love with Emily when the time for choosing came, he might well have retreated to his villa in the Yucatan, silenced for a time, perhaps, but waiting for the moment to be heard again, followed again by his own people. He was born, he told Emily, to be a reformer. Not a revolutionary.

Instead, he now found himself divested of his very heritage. His blood ties, his history and his Mexican holdings along with his old visions and the old friends who once shared them—all was being stripped away while Emily listened from their bedroom to the hollow sound of those footsteps pacing the wooden floor.

She knew Santa Anna had once been his friend politically. And even personally, the two men had shared ideals and abilities. But now, by all reports, Santa Anna had materialized into a ruthless dictator who had put a prize on his old friend's head and was even now approaching the Rio Bravo at Laredo, fresh from a blood bath of the rebellious government of Zacatecas and determined to annihilate the Anglo settlers and their Mexican sympathizers in Texas. The Mexicans, she had heard it said, would suffer doubly as traitors.

Her husband would not live out the day if he fell into their hands.

According to Lorenzo there was no doubt that Antonio Lopez de Santa Anna could do it. He had not achieved the highest seat in Mexico by being either stupid or cowardly. A disciplined soldier, a brilliant strategist and a charismatic commander-in-chief, he was a man who regularly checked the wind and led the people whenever the most powerful wanted to go—be it back to Spain or onward to conquer new frontiers. Born in Mexico, the son of a tradesman, he was not weighted with the bigotry of the old *peninsulars* who were born in Spain and regarded the native born as a lesser breed. Still, as the son of Spanish parents who had known neither poverty nor despair, he was not overburdened with compassion for the natives themselves and would sacrifice their bodies without compunction to win his battles.

Above all, Lorenzo had told Emily, the Generalissimo was a stubbornly ambitious man. Once determined on his course, he was not likely to yield to any diplomatic effort that might cast doubt on his power as supreme commander. As commander, he would do whatever was necessary to ensure surrender and Texas did not have the bodies to sacrifice however strong the will to fight. Face to face with such an army, the Texians would surely be overrun if the United States did not come to their aid, an increasingly unlikely event. The only hope, Lorenzo whispered in the night, was that Santa Anna's vanity might cloud his judgment and some trap could be designed to take him by surprise.

Emily could not understand any of that. Nor did her husband expect it. Often as not lately, he spoke of these things in Spanish, knowing how little she understood, not wanting her to understand, yet needing to speak. If she but held him when he stopped his pacing and came to lie beside her he was satisfied.

But she was not.

She wished she were back in New York. She wished, at the moment, that she had never met Lorenzo de Zavala or become in any way involved in this peculiar place with this peculiar experiment in self-government. The people here were no more polished than was her home here. Her New York furniture looked odd and out of place against the bare wooden walls. For all they had brought to grace the place, so much had been forgotten. There were no tapestries here, nor wallpapers and velvet hangings. Nor were there lawns outside, and flowers. Here, sand whipped under the door sills and through the windows and when the wind stopped, the insects were bad enough to wish one well away forever.

She thought of the snow blanketing all the manmade corners of New York and herself safe and warm in her father's house, her mother attending. And her friend Rose. . . .

Rose. The thought pulled deeper lines into the pale forehead. She would be working, of course. With Sam Houston at the hotel no one was likely to take it easy on Christmas Day. Poor Rose. The job must be a great deal harder than the management of a girls' finishing school. But if anyone could manage it with good grace, her friend was the person. But how must Rose feel, living in the swirl and backlash of a building war? Not that Emily was likely to have the chance to talk with her anytime soon. Morgan's Point, at the moment, seemed almost as far away as New York to a woman marooned on the far side of Buffalo Bayou and the San Jacinto River, alone with three children and an ill-equipped household to run.

It was time, she realized, to consider the serving of Christmas dinner. Lorenzo himself had shot the wild turkeys the cook was roasting and the chestnuts in the dressing had come with them from New York. Without him, she had no appetite for it, but for the children's sake. . . .

A movement on the water caught her eye as she started back into the house. A small boat had appeared with a man alone in the center, earnestly applying the oars. She stood watching, forgetting herself for a moment in the wonder of a Christmas visitor.

Luther Collins pulled up to the little dock and heaved himself out of the skiff and onto the boards. It took Emily a moment to recognize the heavy-set man with the ruddy face coming up the sandy path through the tall grasses. She had not seen, or at least not noticed him since they had been together on the ship from New Orleans. Nor would she have noticed him then except that Rose had taken a liking to him and pointed him out to her. A preacher, she recalled. Quaker, wasn't it? What could he be doing here? She had converted already to Catholicism as her husband required. Surely the man didn't expect. . . .

"A most happy Christmas to thee, Madam," the newcomer said, sweeping his broad, black hat from his head as he bowed a greeting.

"And to you, Sir," she said, inviting him in. "I trust it is not bad news that brings you here alone on so murky a day."

"Christmas Day, Madam, and Christmas greetings only," he said, standing awkwardly in the middle of the parlor, hat in hand and broadcloth coat gleaming with water drops. "Thee must forgive my impetuousness. I learned this morning that Mr. de Zavala had been called to council with General Houston and I imagined thee alone with thy children and out of sorts with thy situation on a day when all earth should be singing praises for the great gift of God."

There was a spot of mischief in his sudden grin. "So I thought myself to come over and bring thee a spot of cheer." From capacious pockets he produced oranges, a half-dozen of them, along with a bag of hard candies and, finally, a small and tightly wrapped fruitcake. "For the children," he said holding out full hands. "And for thee, too, of course."

"My good sir, there was no need!"

"Ah, but I felt one, Madam, if thee will forgive my impertinence. It cannot be pleasant for a wife's first Christmas in Texas to be spent without her husband." He colored, embarrassed, not moving towards the seat she indicated. "Not that I presume to stand in for him but if there is something I might do to cheer thee, I am at thy service.

Emily found herself smiling back into the reddened face before her. "Thee may come into the kitchen and help me sort out the serving of Christmas dinner," she said abruptly. "The servants must not be cheated of their celebration. And then you must join me and the children, if you will, at our own dinner."

Moving with him through the house and out back into the kitchen building, a new energy flowed through her. The impossible task of celebrating Christmas no longer seemed so. Laughing together at the big oak table while the cook continued basting the turkeys on a spit in the fireplace, Emily emptied out the sack of small gifts she'd selected for the servants and the two of them sorted them out, tying up each bundle with a ribbon bow and sprig of cedar. Her children, bringing their own presents, came to join them. The servants' children, a good dozen or so, followed soon after. The small black and white bodies intermingled on the floor, giggling and poking at one another, race and place forgotten for a moment.

Somewhere between the carving of the turkey and the making of ambrosia, formalities were forgotten. It was only natural, when the food was ready, to clear the big table in the kitchen and set it out. As the entire household crowded around, she found herself standing, plate in hand, at the head of a line that snaked out the door.

It seemed only natural, though it had never seemed so before, that everyone should eat together, the whites at the table, of course, and the blacks on the floor. Emily smiled at the fellowship, served the ambrosia herself at the end of the meal, passed out the gifts, one name at a time, and wished each one a happy Christmas. It was natural, when the bowls were washed, for all of the children to follow her and the Quaker back into the big house. And when Brother Collins found his place at the piano, it was only natural that all the children should gather around him and that their parents, finding no judgment at the door, should follow.

And then, of course, it was only natural that they all should sing. The dancing was a bare half-step behind.

The songs of that Christmas afternoon! The very sky lost its shades! They rollicked, all of them together through the sunset, golden as the day had been grey. Though she never took her shoes off, the children did, and her baby was entertained by other babies, dark as she was pale, while the nanny and the gardener danced an Irish-African Christmas jig. Then everyone joined hands and danced, Emily lifting her skirts as the blacks did, to stamp her heels and leap about on her toes. The movement was easy if one followed the music.

Brother Collins played like a man possessed. His left hand pounded rhythm like drums into the stately old melodies, while his right hand tinkled crystal flourishes that stood the grand old songs on their ears. *Silent Night* had never held so much appeal! The Africans danced and danced. So did Emily. She could hardly believe it was happening. The adventure of moving in strange new steps with her children and her—her friends, servants though they were—possessed her with a delight she had not felt since childhood. And better understood now, because she had never before questioned the arrogance—the separateness—of being white.

"It is not so bad, Mr. Collins, to be humbled," she said, sitting with him afterwards when the party was over and most of the guests had retired to the servants' quarters. A room there was being prepared for Mr. Collins. He insisted, despite the late evening dark, that he could not possibly stay; though he understood that was the way it was done along the frontier where both distance and danger often precluded same day visits. But he was adamant about not remaining overnight with a lady whose husband was absent.

He was only persuaded when the cook, still in the thrall of the day's showing of equality, announced. "He come back and stay with us. We make him plenty good room."

And that was that.

"Thee enjoyed thy Christmas, after all?" he said, sipping on the glass of water she offered him, having refused the wine. "I'm much too wound up, Ma'am. I would only get tipsy."

"It was the most fun—almost the most fun ever, Mr. Collins. And that's the truth,"

"Thee enters into the Father's love for a moment, love for thy brothers and sisters cannot be far behind. And there's the joy shared."

"I do not understand."

He looked at her curiously for a moment, blue eyes arching over his glass. "Thee understands," he said, and looked down again. "Thee does, indeed Ma'am. I could hear thee singing that understanding. I saw thee dancing with it."

He grinned again, reddening from throat to cheek. "I was a musician in New Orleans for a time, riding the river down from Cincinnati before I met the Lord. It's a long story, Sister, a long time ago. But sometimes the old rhythms get into my fingers and the Lord, I know He understands. It's good to dance and sing together on Christmas."

"I never imagined such a thing," said Emily. "With the servants! Dear Lord, what could I be thinking of!" She laughed out loud. "If Mrs. Morgan could have seen that, I should never make such society as Texas has to offer! She advised me to keep them on a tighter leash after all the trouble she had gone to collecting a suitable group for me. At least she kept families together. I suppose the Colonel had alerted her."

"These are slaves, then?"

"Oh no! That is, we pay them. Lorenzo would not have it otherwise. But they were sold as slaves and they know no better. Still they are happy to receive their monthly dollar or two. And we are happy to have them."

The pleasure had left Luther's face. "This war, thee must know, is about slavery."

"There is much more to it than that, Mr. Collins. It is about the right of free men to determine their own destiny." The words sounded right but they fell hollow on the ear. Mr. Collins was either not listening or not in agreement. His face held a faraway look while his hands still toyed with his glass.

"Freedom is not an easy word, Sister. Thee, myself, thy husband, General Houston, Santa Anna—we all have different ideas of freedom but in each one, it starts with freedom for oneself. Sometimes those freedoms block each other. My freedom to have slaves. The African's loss of freedom altogether. My freedom to settle this land. The Indians' loss of freedom to hunt here. My freedom to run the government. The Mexicans' loss of freedom to participate."

He shrugged. "Winners and losers. That is all it is. There is no love there. No kingdom of heaven consciousness. The kingdom we pray to come every Sabbath would have no contention. None better or worse, each in his place, serving the best, he—or she, Madam—can."

"Such a kingdom! A kingdom of perfect peace! Ah Madam, I think there we would have dancing sometimes, such as we had today. Yes ma'am, even that."

She remembered suddenly that Quakers had been so named because of their peculiar custom of standing silently together in meeting, in a circle usually. They would stand there, saying nothing, thinking God, until they began to shake. Quake. Dancing, she thought, was not so very different as one might imagine.

The clock struck ten. The cook must be getting tired waiting out there in the kitchen. She stood and Luther was immediately on his feet.

"Thee must forgive me, Mr. Collins. It has surely been a long day for all of us. Since you refuse the hospitality of my several guest rooms, I will let Orpha escort you to the room in back. I do hope you'll be comfortable."

She woke later than usual the next day, more refreshed than she had felt in a very long time. Outside the sky was blue already, fleecy with clouds as the red tint of the east faded behind the sunrise. A chorus of bird calls greeted her as she stepped from her bedroom onto the porch, facing Buffalo Bayou.

Already halfway across, she could see him, handling the big oars with ease, pulling himself back across the channel.

She stepped back to the kitchen and had coffee with Orpha. What should they eat today, she asked. And what did they all think about the Christmas celebration?

"Good party," said Orpha, emotionless this morning. "Good man bring good for everybody. Good music, oh Lord yes! Good dancing. Good food. Leftovers maybe all right? Got plenty 'nough."

They sipped their coffee in companionable quiet. Then by and by the children came and preparations for the day commenced.

Lorenzo would be pleased, thought Emily, holding for the first time the cook's tiny daughter. At the stove, Orpha entertained the children with drumming taps of the iron spoon on the iron pot in which she was stirring the oatmeal. With a sudden laugh she leaped, lightly for one so large, and brushed her heels together before landing solidly on the ground.

She would have good stories to tell her husband.

But Lorenzo de Zavala was not in the mood to listen to sweet stories of home when he arrived two days later, brought back across the bayou by the messenger who had brought him word of the General's arrival. He was not alone this time. James Bowie, the big, black-haired Louisiana trader had come with him along with Mr. Branch Archer, president of the November Consultation on Texian Independence. They were an unlikely pair. Like de Zavala, Mr. Archer favored independence as an autonomous state within Mexico, not as a state of total separation. Emily had learned that much already. Bowie, she had never met, but she had heard rumors of his wild and wicked ways with a knife and she presumed he had already cast his lot with the most radical of the immigrant soldiers.

It seemed the radicals had won the day. The conversations to which she was privy were void of the old cautions for restraint and reason. Her husband, like Mr. Archer, and Jim Bowie, saw no alternative to all out warfare. But unlike Mr. Bowie, Lorenzo would find no joy in the battle. Not only his emotions but his finely detailed sense of order was offended by Yankee independence. Orders by the Anglos were given to be argued, not followed. Every man represented only himself. The settlers fought only in defense of their own properties. And the immigrant volunteers fought for the love of battle, mixed, no doubt, with visions of plunder. It made an odd mixture. After the Texians won the first battle for San Antonio, half of them went back home for Christmas with no clear plans for return. And the other half, some five hundred volunteers led on by the ambitions of Frank Johnson and James Grant, were pressing the battle down into undisputed Mexican territory by planning an assault on Matamoros across the Rio Grande at the mouth of the Gulf. As it happened, General Jose Urrea was already on the march up the Gulf coast.

"Sheer folly," de Zavala snorted. "Sheer folly. It is a trap, of course. They shall walk into the pride of the Mexican army and never return. We have not men enough to lose in foolish maneuvers which gain us nothing."

"Reckon the boys want to enjoy some action," Bowie countered. "Reckon they felt pretty good after the whipping old Ben Milam gave the Mexicans there in San Antonio."

"Hardly the same stakes," said Mr. Archer. "San Antonio is crucial to Texian transportation and trade. We ship through Galveston while Matamoros has long been controlled by Mexican enterprise and shipping."

"Well now," said Bowie, "I reckon it might be best if they gathered themselves up and got themselves on back to the Alamo to help J.C. Neill hold the fort. Pretty slim band there now, I expect. And the Governor wants to defend it."

"Henry Smith is as strong-headed as the worst of them," said de Zavala, too tired to be diplomatic. "It is a foolish plan. With all our troops dispersed, the Alamo lies open to ravishment when the Generalissimo appears with his army. Even with a thousand men to defend it, how will it survive the encirclement of eight thousand? No! It would be best, as General Houston suggested, to set the place to the torch and free our men for a more mobile attack." His smile was a little grim. "It is how the Indians do it and how a small, fast-moving group can hold armies at bay. They strike like snakes and run away."

"But it makes no sense," Bowie told him. "We cannot afford to give so fine a fort to the enemy. We cannot give it up without a fight. White men don't do that. That's how we hang on to what we've got. We fight for it. We don't hand it over, for sweet Mary's sake!"

"Better than allowing it to become a death trap for our own brave men," de Zavala retorted. "Because I assure you, gentlemen, that is what it will become. And there will be no mercy, none at all. If you think the sacrifice worth the gesture, I suggest you join them."

Bowie's eyes flattened. "I shall do that, Mr. de Zavala. I only await my orders."

"You have them already, Sir, as I understood our conversation with the General. You are to go there at your earliest convenience to relieve Captain Neill, destroy the fort, torch the town, and organize the soldiers as a mobile fighting unit."

"You mean Sam Houston's orders? There are many generals now as you well know. I might even be one myself." Bowie's rich, low and easy laugh calmed the atmosphere in the room. Emily realized suddenly that she had been holding her breath. She let it out quietly, careful not to draw attention. Chairs shifted. Throats were cleared. By the time her husband started talking again the flush that always told his anger had receded from his scholarly face.

"And whom are we to trust for strategy if not General Houston?"

"He has not exactly made a career of warfare," said Archer. "I doubt sometimes, if he is up to the task we are assigning him."

"A good enough fellow," said Bowie, "but there are many who cannot abide him. They will only feel confirmed if they hear he has given orders to burn down our best fortress and run."

"The Alamo will never hold against Santa Anna," de Zavala repeated. "He will throw his forces against it like so many stones. And like so many stones, they will bury the place and all within it."

"Colonel Fannin is waiting at Goliad with five hundred men," said Bowie. "Were he to join forces with the band still at the Alamo and the boys who are headed off to Matamoros, we might yet stop the Mexicans. There may be a lot of them but they lack our spirit to survive." Teeth flashed white in his dark beard. "One good white man is worth a few hundred of those Mexicans."

De Zavala put his head in his hands. It was difficult enough to fight his own people. To hear them constantly degraded was almost too much. The *indiginos* marching with Santa Anna dragged out of their villages by force, no doubt, were probably natives of the Yucatan, his own home state. A strong and hardy people if such ever existed, able to march barefoot for thousands of miles in total deprivation through desert and mountains and the alien cold of winter and survive. Only to become targets for Yankee guns! Human pawns. The kind in use for millennia by kings and emperors. Win or lose, once taken for service, few would ever see home again. At least among the Texians each man made his own choice, his own stand. The pawns—the Indians—were eliminated before the game began. There was no more thought of winning them over than of winning over the coyotes. A sigh escaped him, a hollow sound in the deep silence of the room. And then a log tumbled in the fireplace, crackling sparks as another gust of wind shook the windows. The cold wind had greeted their return. It was not a good omen.

Emily, watching him as though her life depended on it, wanted only to cross the room and place a hand upon his shoulder. But she remained still. To catch attention might cost her the corner from which she contrived to listen to the conversation.

Raising his head, her husband caught her eye and straightened once again. He had but one future, after all, and one wife. His long ago friend, Santa Anna, had long ago betrayed him and many others. There was no retreat now. For the sake of his children and all he had yet to offer, he must offer himself to these Americans.

"Have beds prepared for Mr. Archer and Mr. Bowie," he asked his wife.

"Then you may retire, *Querida*. We have much yet to discuss and you must be weary."

She lay in bed for a long time, remembering Mr. Collins and the Christmas peace he had brought to her household. But the all-togetherness, the song and the dance, the music and the word all in one, seemed part of another world as she listened to the deep voices rise and fall behind the parlor wall, plotting the overthrow of an empire. There was something she must tell her husband before the die was cast, she thought, settling her head on the satin pillowcase and making room, unconsciously, to receive his body next to hers. She must remind him that she would remain with him no matter what; that she was his whether he remained in league with the Americans or not.

But by the time he joined her in the bed she had fallen fast asleep. And Lorenzo de Zavala, staring down at her pale face in the fitful streaks of moonlight as the clouds scuddered across the sky, listened to her quiet breathing for a long while before he turned away to remove his clothes and returned to wake her into his arms. Inside and then beside her, he held her as tightly as she held him and gave up his country altogether for love of her.

16

Now privy to the plotting of war, Rose was not certain what her friend's husband would do but Houston's intentions were clear enough. He had ridden south after Christmas after long conversations—sometimes very loud conversations—with Lorenzo de Zavala and half a dozen others who had remained closeted in Morgan's room upstairs for some forty-eight hours. She had brought beer, brandy, coffee and regular meals which she had regularly removed, barely touched. From the little she could pick up of the talk, it was mostly concerned with reaching agreement on dissolving all ties with Mexico. De Zavala was not happy about it but there was resignation in his face when the men walked out together to ride away in different directions. De Zavala was obviously not primed for battle though he would support it.

Rose wanted to visit with Emily, to discuss what was happening, to feel the stability of an old friend on a landscape which shifted with every new day. But Emily was apparently kept busy on the other side of the bayou and her own job filled every waking moment. Even the half-day break on Sunday was no longer possible. Morgan was rarely there, occupied with strengthening the tiny Texas Navy, and bringing in what supplies be could buy or beg in New Orleans. The shipments were coming in, sometimes faster than she could record them. Austin's efforts in Washington and other cities in the United States had some effect though far less than the Texians sought. A few hundred dollars here and there as well as donations of food and blankets and canvas for tents. A few extra boxes of ammunition. A few dozen muskets. Two cannon sent by sympathizers in Cincinnati. No official aid from the government. None.

Though the crates filled the warehouse there were hardly enough supplies for an all out battle with the Indians, let alone a war against all the forces of Mexico.

Well aware of the shortages both in men and material, the General left Morgan's Point to ride to Refugio just south of San Antonio where Johnson and Grant were preparing several hundred volunteers to cross the river and plunder Matamoros. It looked like an easy target to the sharpshooters but having watched the Mexican advance through the eyes of his spies that winter, Houston was well aware of the traps being laid for the Texians. With less than a thousand men prepared to defend the state, he did his best to discourage the squandering of half that number. Mistaking caution for cowardice, the officers ignored him, leaving each common soldier to make his own decision.

Attempting to lead where none would follow, Houston succeeded only in dissuading most of the men from following Johnson on to Matamoros. It was a good thing. The hundred and fifty soldiers who continued that journey were killed, almost to a man, when General Jose Urrea swept up the Gulf Coast in late February, leading a cavalry charge of several hundred men.

Still hoping to save lives, if not supplies, as Santa Anna marched inexorably on toward San Antonio, Houston formally ordered Jim Bowie to help command the regulars under Neill at the Alamo. His orders were to destroy the fort, torch the town, and organize the soldiers as a fixed fighting mobile unit, able to keep ahead of the six or seven thousand Mexican troops approaching from the south.

Bowie responded to the order while choosing his own aim. His unshaken desire to maintain the Alamo defenses was supported by Governor Smith who contrived to send William Travis along with him as well as the attorney James Bonham, Travis's old friend from Saluda, South Carolina. Some of the best of the rest joined them, heading for the hottest piece of action. Davey Crockett and his sharpshooter Tennessee boys rode in along with a few score other courageous—or foolhardy—souls. By mid-February there were about a hundred and fifty fighting men inside the walls. And none had any intention of leaving.

As February came to a close the atmosphere at Morgan's Point was fairly bristling with both muskets and anticipation. News and rumors mixed into stories that changed with each telling. But most agreed that Sam Houston had, once again, deserted the field.

In fact, unable either to coax the Alamo defenders from their fateful shelter, nor to persuade Colonel Fannin, relaxing in Gonzales with another five hundred volunteers, to join them for the coming battle, the thoroughly disgusted Commander-in-Chief had furloughed himself until the first of March and ridden off to the northeast to try for a treaty with the Cherokee who were threatening war from the other side of the beleaguered colony. In that, at least, he was successful. The Cherokee agreed, for the sake of their old friend, to leave the Texians alone.

Meanwhile, delegates from every Texas settlement were being called to gather for assembly in Washington on the Brazos on March first to declare their independence and write the constitution for the new nation of Texas. Returning early to the fray, Houston spent the end of February searching for troops from San Antonio northward and found none willing to follow him. And though he trusted the delegates would continue to endorse his command, he did not expect much political support for his plans. It was a dispirited man who stopped at the hotel in Morgan's Point on his way to the assembly.

Even the sight of her beautiful face did not cheer him as it had before. He was not happy about the role planned for Rose in the play for Texas independence. It was a dramatic role, desperate and dangerous. But these were desperate and dangerous times.

The crowds that gathered around him as he swung down from the big white horse did not share his pessimism. Cheers for the General went up along with a few mutters as he passed the stallion's reins to a stable boy. "Clean him up good. He's been under worse wear than myself and that's worse than bad enough." Then he surrendered to the press of people and led the way into the bar, head up though the smile on his face looked rather worn out.

He seemed to have aged considerably since Rose had last seen him two days after Christmas. From her post behind the desk she could see him at the bar, standing broad as usual though his speech could not be heard above the noise around him.

The louder voices at the bar held no hint of trepidation. To listen, one would imagine the war won already and the celebration of victory well begun. Still, the men sought news. How stood the Alamo? Had Bowie and Travis and Crockett whipped them all yet? Them Tennessee boys! Had anybody ever watched them Tennessee boys shoot! Knock off a Mexican at three hundred paces. Hell, knock off a couple with one load. And when you put the bayonet or knife behind it, hell, that's three or four.

With eyes as wary as his tone was flat, Houston shared his information. General Jose Urrea was advancing from the east with several hundred cavalry while Santa Anna approached from Laredo, bringing several thousand troops and heavy artillery to bear on San Antonio. There was no chance now of flight from the Alamo. Nor were there many willing to join the defenders. On Houston's direct orders, Colonel Fannin had finally started in that direction that week with some three hundred and fifty troops but made it a bare two miles out of town before turning back to Goliad. There were thirty-two men from Gonzales, the town Deaf Smith helped build, who had responded to Travis's call for help. As far as the General knew, that was all.

As for Bowie, he heard he'd just been taken with pneumonia though he'd refused to leave the coming fight. God knew they needed help down there, the stubborn fools.

"Any of you boys want some action, better saddle up now. Reckon you can still get through. Reckon they're going to need all the help they can get."

Silence descended on the bar. No one moved for a moment. Then, "How come you're not there, General?" came the slurred challenge and the rest took up the cry.

"Yeah General, how come you didn't stay down there?"

"Says they need help but here he is!"

"Gotta a little yellow streak there, Sam? Want to lift your shirt and show us that yellow streak them Indians put on your back?

And one, louder than the rest: "Don't let nobody say old Sam don't stand by his friends, no sirree. Old Sam will stand by his friends as long as they're standing at the bar."

"And paying!" came another yell.

"Can't fight and get drunk, too, I reckon," drawled a newcomer, earning points.

Houston put down his drink, straightened himself and faced the room. "Next person got anything personal to say to me about my conduct as Commander-in-Chief of the armed forces of Texas can meet me outside with a pistol. Or a hoe. Or your bare, bloody fists, by God! We'll see who's got a yellow streak up their chicken-livered backside."

The silence this time was absolute. For what seemed like eternity, Houston held them with an unwavering eye. Then he threw back his drink in one swallow and strode out of the room. Rose had to run to catch up as he stormed upstairs.

"The door's locked, Sir," she said, coming up behind him on the second floor landing. "I will have to open it."

He didn't turn but he stumbled a bit, stopping for her, though his speech was clear enough. "You do that, Miss. I've had enough of this crowd. Think killing people is some kind of goddamned game and they get to pick and choose just how they want to play it."

"Yes sir. They don't understand, sir." She unlocked the door.

He stared at her, not entering. "Miss Emily, is it not? Miss Emily Rose?"

"You might call me that, Sir."

"We have to talk, Miss Emily Rose. Won't you please come in?"

She hesitated. "I'll have to lock the desk, Sir. And try to find Miss Mittelstet to handle the latecomers."

"You do that, Miss Emily. And then you come back here. We have to talk."

He called out as she started downstairs. "And bring me a bottle of brandy. Make Fred give up that good one he's hiding. Tell him it's for the cause."

He had removed his coat and loosened his cravat by the time she returned. He took the bottle and poured a snifter, setting it before her on the table. Then he raised the bottle and took a long drink. "Don't mind, do you, Miss?" he said, as he settled himself across the table from her. "A man gets thirsty in this kind of atmosphere." He took another swig. "Hell," he said, laughing. "No use trying to fool anybody. I stay thirsty all the time."

Beneath the weathered brown of his skin the lined face kept a greyish tone, she noticed as the lamplight fell full on him. Deep lines pressed in between his brows and more lines crossed the high forehead. And those sad, anxious eyes held none of the laughter that came from his mouth. It was a generous mouth with one corner curling up and the other down but in repose he held it tight as he could. A drunkard he might be, she thought, but he was not one to lose control when control was required.

"It has been a hard journey you've taken," she ventured. "And one with few rewards."

"Insult after insult," Houston muttered, as if to himself. "If not for the Cherokee I might have fallen on my own sword." His laugh was bitter. "And never been missed for all of that."

She listened as he began to talk, describing his encounters over the past two months and the politics that had effectively nullified his uneasy command. "I command the regulars, they say, and the volunteers can choose their own command. But the regulars are about as ornery as the volunteers. Every man jack of them thinks he knows how and when and where and who to fight. Leaves me Commander-in-Chief of nobody. Got no idea, anymore, why they wanted anyone for this job nor why I took it." And then more pitifully. "How is a man to lead if no one will follow? And how can a war be won with neither strategy nor leadership?"

He shook his head like a bear coming into the sunlight from his cave. "It's as crazy a thing, Miss, as I've ever done, and I've done some crazy things. We've likely got less men in all of Texas than Santa Anna is marching up to San

Antonio right now. The settlements are spread in front of him like a feast and, believe me, he will eat until he's full and then some. He's not a man to give quarter. Barely half past thirty—my age!—and he's dictator of a nation. Napoleon of the West, they call him."

Again the bitter laugh. "Not like something anybody is ever going to call me! Me, I did pretty good making it all the way up to governor of Tennessee but I couldn't hold it together there, nor in Congress either, though I reckon I made a few points for the Indians. But I'm not ruthless enough, Miss Emily Rose, whatever you may think. Not able to twist the knife even when I can manage to get it in. Too soft for the Indians, too, though it's all sacred to those people. Even killing, torture—it's a sacred ritual to them though not one I can well accept. Couldn't live with it though I reckon I loved those people better than I'd ever loved before. Had to drink myself near to death to take them or leave them, either one. Finally left, of course. White man has his own destiny, like it or not."

He closed his eyes for a few moments. "But we're not the smartest people on earth, Miss Rose, for all we think we are. It'd be a miracle to win this war and I don't much believe in God these days, let alone in miracles."

"We do our best," she murmured, searching for a comforting word.

Houston picked up the bottle, drank, and slammed it back on the table. "Words! Those are just words, Miss Emily Rose. They've got nothing to do with the blood and guts that are spilled when men meet in battle. Try telling some dead son's mother that he did his best. Small comfort that when the field needs plowing or the roof needs mending or the cattle have got to be rounded up and the boys aren't there to do because they're lying somewhere, stone-cold dead because their best wasn't near good enough."

His head slumped forward and she thought he might have fallen asleep he closed his eyes for so long after that. But when she moved, softly as possible, to leave the room, a long arm reached for her and the voice that spoke was suddenly sober .

"I have a plan, Miss Emily Rose. It's the plan I've been searching for and I can see it now, plain as day, though you may wish, when I tell it to you, that it had remained in the shadows."

"I'm willing to listen, Sir, though I cannot promise. . . ."

He continued talking as if she had not spoken.

"Here is the problem. We have a present balance in forces of seven or eight to one favoring Mexico. Mexico also has the advantage of a commander who can demand and hold the attention of his troops. Those troops have been drilled and hardened by a thousand mile march up from Mexico City. And if Santa Anna wants more men, he has a half dozen top commanders who will get them for him and a large population to press into service. Soon as he speaks they're going to obey. Their lives depend on it."

His piercing eyes were intent on her face. "Now you're a smart girl. You can see nobody here is much interested in taking orders. I have to beg–and then be mocked by cowards who've come, it would seem, to watch me win the war by myself. The government's on me to act and what can I do? I refuse to ride those few who'll follow me straight into slaughter. What good would it do? With whom would we replace them? God knows we're few enough already. For every man we lose, a dozen women and children are going to be left defenseless. It's not feasible. It's insane."

She watched the slyness move into his eyes, still aimed into hers. "We need a trick, Miss Emily Rose. The only hope we have is to lure Santa Anna away from most of his army. He'll have to think we're even easier pickings than we actually are."

He sighed deeply. "Of course, after he's faced Travis and Crockett and that bunch at the Alamo, even with Bowie down and out, he's going to know that we've got at least a few good men. They'll reduce his troops by plenty before they go down but with any luck we can make him think the best of us died when he beats us out of that fort. Course that's pretty much the truth of it. Had I my say, I would not lose those men to gain Texas itself."

"He'll overrun them?"

Houston snorted like a bear pawing in the ground for vermin. "He'll kill every man jack among them, mark my words. Told them that to begin with but who was listening? There's no question they're doomed. They know it too, though Travis keeps promising they'll get reinforcements. What reinforcements are going to get through even if we had them to send? Which we don't."

Rose found herself drawn suddenly fascinated by the games of war. "So what's your plan, Sir?"

"Pretty simple. Simple works well, sometimes. The Cherokee taught me that though they're as complicated as a people can be. We're going to try an Indian trick. We're going to run. Oh, not really run, but we're going to look like we're running. Backing up. Slow enough for Smith and Burnet and that cursed crew who think they're running this government to leave us alone for a while. And fast enough to stay out of reach."

"But you will have to meet them. Somewhere."

His mouth hardened. "We will meet them. Somewhere near here, I think. After we see if he'll take the bait."

"The bait, General?"

"That would be you, Miss Emily Rose."

She reached for her untouched glass of brandy as he took another long pull on the bottle. The rest of the conversation did not come easily. The General was notably reluctant to continue. But continue they must. Rose's curiosity overrode her concern. If she was to play a role, she wished, at least, to know the meaning of the play.

"Bait, sir?"

He would not look at her. "The Generalissimo is a very handsome man by all accounts and wonderfully charming when he chooses to be. Those who know him also say he has a great weakness for beautiful women and will go to any lengths to win them. It is said he once faked a marriage ceremony in order to claim a particular beauty from her protective parents though he has a wife and family already in Mexico City. I must confess that I hope to exploit that weakness. With your help."

She said nothing. He did not look up. "I, too, can be a ruthless man, Miss Emily Rose, but I confess, I did not expect to find you so thoroughly a lady. I am finding it almost as difficult to explain my plan as it would be to prostitute my own sister."

The bitter laugh again. "Of course, given the right circumstances, the right stakes, I might do that as well."

There was nothing she could say. The room was stifling suddenly, the heat pressing in on her eyes, her ears, her throat. She wanted to rise, to run, but like one caught in a nightmare, she could not move. A prostitute? She was to be made a prostitute? For the Mexican army? Or at least for the Mexican General? And then what? Death?

Houston sighed and straightened in his chair, meeting her questioning azure blue eyes at last. "I am going to an assembly tomorrow in which we will declare independence from Mexico and proceed to write a Constitution for the nation of Texas. And then I must go out and find a thousand men whom I can drill into some semblance of military discipline. I do not imagine that to be an easy task. And then I shall have to persuade the people that we are marching off to war while in fact I take these men and keep them running for as long as possible so they will not all be destroyed, along with all hope of adding this great country to the greater nation of the United States."

He stared at her for an instant, then stood and walked to the window. He spoke with his back to her. "If Santa Anna had someone like you to distract him in the crunch, I might not have to waltz backwards across the whole of Texas only to lose in the end, leaving every soul here completely vulnerable to whatever punishment life wished to wreak upon us. We will make a stand, of course, as soon as possible. But if that stand is not to be in vain, the inequality of our forces demands the trick."

"And I am to be your trick?"

"If you are willing."

"And if not?"

"I have never forced a lady, Miss Emily Rose. And you are certainly a lady."

She could hardly believe she was engaging in such conversation. But she could not pretend to an innocence she had first given up with Luke.

Luke! How very far away he seemed. And her own son was distant as yesterday's dreams. It came to her suddenly, that if Santa Anna overran Texas, she was not likely ever to see her son again, let alone his father. What ships might be available for escape were not likely to have room for slaves. Emily might not be able to save her—or even herself.

She needed to understand herself in the light of what she knew now. And she wanted, for reasons she could hardly explain to herself, for this man to understand her as well. And so, after swearing him to secrecy, she told Sam Houston the rest of her story. All of it.

It was near dawn when she finished. The bottle had long since been emptied but the General still sat straight in his chair, his eyes fixed on her face as they had been since the beginning. He had said very little, only nodded from time to time in understanding.

"So you see," she said at last, "I have no claim to being a lady, even by character. Yet I was raised to be such and have never reconciled myself to the great distance between my raising and the realities of my life. I came to Texas to make something of myself, free of the claims and chains of an ill-gotten son. I had not imagined until that night before we docked in New Orleans that the chains had fallen around me when I first set foot on that ship."

A light breeze moved the curtains at the open window. Outside, the birds began to herald the coming of the sun.

Houston stood and took a turn around the room, pausing out of sight behind her chair. A large hand touched her shoulder.

"You are a strange woman, Rose. I have never in my life known such though I have known many strangers."

She did not turn around. "Is it so strange to wish to become something other than what you are?"

"It is only human nature, my dear. But few, I think, could live with such confusion about who that might be and still maintain the integrity you have brought to this place. It touches me deeply."

"Do not flatter me, General Houston. We are well past that, I should think."

"You imagine that statement flattery? I assure you, I mean it from the bottom of my heart."

She said nothing.

He went on. "I will tell you how much I mean it, Miss Emily Rose. If you do not wish to participate in this strategy, I shall never ask you again. I shall explain to Morgan that I found you totally unsuitable. That I felt you would be more likely to ride off with Santa Anna, having informed him of our plans, than to hold him vulnerable for us with your feminine wiles." His laugh was low, this time almost musical. "He might well believe that story, understanding something of your bitterness as well as your ambition."

"I am not bitter, General Houston. I have made my bed and now I lie in it. Someday I trust I can leave it behind and walk away whole."

"But you no longer wish to leave your son behind?" There was kindness in his question.

To her consternation, tears filled her eyes and fell. "I cannot," she said. "I have tried and cannot."

He knelt in front of her then, pulling a silk handkerchief from his vest. The large hands were surprisingly gentle as they touched her face, wiping away the tears. "Then I shall make you a promise, my dear. If you wish to return to your son, you shall be on a boat by the end of the year, all claims upon you dissolved. And if you wish to return with your son to Texas, you shall have a *labor* of land—that's one hundred and seventy-seven acres to give him for an inheritance. I give you my word."

She smiled, but sadly. "Your word, Sir, cannot overcome the law in a state which sides for slavery. A Negro cannot be free in certain southern states. Did you imagine one would be allowed the ownership of land?"

"I forget you are called a Negro." He shook his head, rising to his feet. "I seem to forget many things, my dear, when I am with you."

"High yellow," she said, refusing to be moved by his charm. "That is what I'm called now. It was a term I first learned strolling through New Orleans on Colonel Morgan's arm, at his insistence. The best prostitutes, he told me, were high yellow."

Houston paced again. "What can I offer you, then? How can I persuade you in this single chance you've given me to win your loyalty and help?"

She should not have expected him to understand. How could he, born to superiority and bred to freedom as he was? Yet, for a moment, she had imagined that he knew her now. And cared. That in exchange for the service he was asking of her he would offer her a name, a place befitting a gentle-woman, an official erasure of the history she could not otherwise escape.

How very naive she had remained despite experience! She would not falter again. He would see no more tears. But she could not imagine serving him.

He stood silent by the window, waiting. His shoulders had slumped and he looked old and tired. The burden of his men sat heavily there, she thought. And she remembered all those men, so young and eager. Uncouth, perhaps, and arrogant as only youth—white youth—could be. Yet they were human, as she was, and destined to die for the freedom she had run from, seeking something better. Something more material.

She remembered Luther Collins, suddenly, hearing again the earnestness in his voice as he declared, "Freedom and slavery are equally strange, I think. Few of us understand either state, though we all, as a matter of course, live in one or the other."

What, after all, did she have to lose? The only freedom anyone had was the freedom to choose from the paths before them. What those paths might be was left to fate. And were her choices, in truth, any more limited than those the big man at the window faced?

She came to stand beside him at the window and when he turned to glance, he saw the gold of the new morning reflected in her lovely blue eyes. Like a stage being lighted before them, the day came to life. Amid the small bird calls, a rooster crowed, and then another and another. Smoke rose from a nearby chimney as a woman appeared in the doorway, holding an infant in her arms, also watching the sunrise. From the stable came the sound of low nickers and scuffling hooves. Further off, the louder lowing of a cow.

The pair stood silent, not moving.

"I will help you, General Houston," she said at last. "I will help you if I can."

The face he turned to her was grave as death. He bowed. “I do appreciate that, Miss Emily Rose. And I shall do my best to be worthy of your assistance.”

17

On March 6, the Alamo fell without surrender, overwhelmed, as de Zavala had prophesied by forces thrown against it "like so many stones."

For eleven days they had held out—a band of some hundred and fifty men who dared to challenge the eight thousand soldiers commanded forward by Santa Anna. Like one man who holds the door against a hurricane while the children seek shelter underground, the men of the Alamo pressed their immovable bodies against the irresistible force of the Mexican army.

It was a time of dead reckoning. Fire and load and fire and load and fire and load for as long as the light lasted. Keep your head down. Mow down the front ranks. Watch the waves of bodies keep on coming. And pray to God their cannon won't smash through the wall. Then, in the dark, a little rest and a sharpened knife against the stealth-footed Mexicans being sent to fell the sentries watching from the walls and at the gates. During the eleven days the Texians held the fort, withstanding all the flesh and iron the Generalissimo threw against them, they killed some sixteen hundred Mexican soldiers.

Though escape routes were open at first, no Texian left except James Bonham, a young attorney from South Carolina who slipped through the invading army twice to carry pleas for reinforcements and returned at equal risk to take his place at the barricade beside his friend, William Travis. Thirty-two men from Gonzales responded to their cry for aid. That was all. But the defenders held on and kept firing as the food ran low, the ammunition ran low, and time ran out along with hope.

Until finally—stone piled on stone—the wall itself was broached by cannon fire. The roof collapsed, the invaders poured in like water, and the battle was hand to throat, to heart, to belly and bowel, shoulder and thigh as long knives and bayonets slashed and stabbed and the musket butts came down with brain-crushing precision and the courtyard filled with blood and bodies. James Bowie still holding his knife—cut down in his sickbed. Davey Crockett and his Tennessee Boys, hot-headed William Travis and the cool-blooded James

Bonham, soldiers and scholars, settlers and adventurers, pride of the pioneers and heirs to plantations—all gone.

Visible from the ramparts on the day of that final charge, a blood red flag was hung at the command of Santa Anna. And all day long over the clash and grunt and moan of conquerors and conquered came the high thin wail of Mexican bugles playing *deguello*, the cry of assassination, the funeral march without mercy. None was expected.

Santa Anna took no prisoners and not one defender escaped with his life. And when the last Texian had been shot or stabbed or clubbed to death, their bodies were thrown in a pile in the courtyard and burned like so much meat. A bare half dozen widows, slaves and children were spared and released to bear witness to the utter ruin of Texas' bravest warriors.

One such widow, Susanna Dickerson stumbled eastward towards Gonzales, leaving her husband's body burning with the rest of them in the courtyard, and clutching her small daughter to her breast in a daze best understood by those who have thought themselves dead by a natural or unnatural disaster, only to find themselves out on the road again, and walking. Walking and still holding a child.

Deaf Smith found her before she had gone many miles. Santa Anna's witness was delivered to the intended ear. Smith had just come from his home in Gonzales where Sam Houston had just arrived with the mission of recruiting soldiers to fight Santa Anna. He had ordered Smith past the enemy lines to determine immediately whether the Alamo had fallen.

Smith's talent as a gatherer of information was formidable. An upstate New Yorker, he had come to Texas to seek his fortune, married a native Mexican citizen, and founded the beautiful little town of Gonzales. The deaf man's courage, capability and loyalty were unquestioned. Strong, resourceful and at home in town or forest, speaking English and Spanish equally well—albeit in the strange, flat tones of one who cannot hear himself—he was adept at reading lips and far more alert to movement than one who can depend on hearing as well as sight. And with eyes that had been trained to hunt since childhood, Smith could see people's words well before anyone else could hear their whispers. He and Sam Houston had liked each other from the beginning, one silent as the other was garrulous. Trusting his general totally, the deaf man was willing to go into hell, if need be, to bring back whatever information was required.

Houston had left the Constitutional Assembly early and ridden directly to Gonzales in search of soldiers for his army. Quartered in Deaf Smith's house, his desperate efforts to build a Texian force had yielded some three hundred and seventy-five men eager to fight but woefully short on supplies. Searching further afield, he sent two messages to Colonel Fannin, still languishing in Goliad despite orders to go to the aid of the Alamo. The first ordered Fannin and the five hundred men under his command to meet Houston in Gonzales. The second, sent after learning that another Mexican general was approaching from the east, ordered Fannin to fall back immediately to Victoria with his troops. Texas had no extra lives to waste.

Houston had not neglected the study of Mexican history. De Zavala had told him that Antonio Lopez de Santa Anna was not prone to mercy though he had once been much admired for democratic thinking and a broad intelligence. Charming, clever and courageous–and blocked from power by the governing Spanish hierarchy–the ambitious young soldier had moved through the ranks of the army into the heart of government. Before he was thirty he had played a major role in Mexico's revolution against Spanish rule and in the adoption of the Mexican Constitution of 1824 which de Zavala had helped to author. But unlike de Zavala, Santa Anna was not a statesman by nature. Elected president, not once but many times, *El Generalisimo* usually left the business of government to his vice-president, preferring the heat of battle to the coolness of palace tedium. But as a defender of the state's absolute authority, Santa Anna had no peer. He was never less than ruthless when it came time to call rebellion to account. His strategy was both simple and terminally effective. Kill the rebels. Take their goods. Destroy their fields. Annihilate their towns. Allow no quarter from which they can rise again.

His military genius was his ability to do precisely that. His weakness was to underestimate the wisdom of his foe.

Whatever weaknesses Sam Houston may have suffered, he did not for a moment underestimate the Mexican commander. Amid his optimistic countrymen, he took no one into confidence. Noncommittal as a mountain on the Texian chance for victory, he waited for his spy. His new recruits had no such compunctions. Victory was the only word spoken or allowed. They were as eager for battle as only the uninformed can be.

And then Deaf Smith returned with Susanna Dickerson, a living witness to the Texians' utter defeat.

The loss of those fighters, "bravest of the brave" the General called them, shaking his head like a wounded bear and swallowing the curses that rose to his lips at the thought of the needless waste, was the saddest news but it was not the very worst of the information Deaf Smith brought. The Mexicans had fanned out, prepared to completely overrun the upstart colonists. General Urrea was moving in from the south, while General Antonio Goana approached from Nacodoches in the north and General Sesma was hurrying to join Santa Anna to the west with yet another division of troops, preparing, no doubt to follow Houston's trail.

Houston kept his host at the table until long past midnight, studying the maps before them and tracking the advancing forces. Beautifully deployed, he had to admit. "Sweep us out like a broom!" The Generalissimo obviously knew his business well. "Plenty to work with, too," he muttered, reaching for another long pull on the bottle of brandy that Smith had brought him. Smith said nothing, watching his lips.

Houston's strategy reduced itself to a single word. Run! He mouthed it. Smith's toneless chuckle filled the void. The General looked up. "Like hell," he said out loud. "We're going to run like hell, Mr. Smith. We're going to run and we're going to hide and we're going to stay ahead of the devil if it's the last thing we do." He pulled on the bottle again. "Because if we can't, Mr. Smith, it will indeed be the last thing any of us left in Texas will ever do."

The wide eyes, curiously trusting, that watched his face turned slightly quizzical. "Sometime, of course, you will fight?"

"My time, Mr. Smith," said Houston. "My time. No way to win a battle like this on the enemy's time." His chuckle was dry as a bone. "You've seen their armies, Mr. Smith. And you've seen ours. What chances would you give us."

Smith took the questions seriously. Thought about it. "Fifty-fifty, maybe," he said. "He is big but we are better. We fight for ourselves. Our homes"

Houston laughed again. "Fifty-fifty? You are very optimistic, Mr. Smith. I would put the odds much lower, but then I aim to equalize them if I can." He thought of Emily Morgan. Beautiful Emily Rose with those high-planed Indian bones, those lips like an opening rose against pale skin that held a dimple on its cheek, and the wild dark hair that curled away from its ladylike bun and escaped into tight little ringlets when the sea damp caught it. Ah, she was a winner, that one! Seemed like the mixed bloods were often the strongest in mind and body, though as to heart, they were as likely to get the worst of both worlds as the best. Loyalty was not common to those whose parents had shared nothing but a bed. He was not yet sure of Miss Emily Rose.

He shook his head to clear it. No time now to think of women except as pieces of the puzzle he had yet to put together. "I got a plan, Mr. Smith. Can't say it's much of a plan but it's all I can do at the moment." He smiled slowly. "Leastways, it don't involve dying. Not yet."

"I would not want to die, General," said Smith carefully. "Not if I can help it. I have four children. And a wife. But I will go where you tell me and do what you ask and trust God to take care." A rare smile touched his lips. "I do believe, Sir, that you care near as much for others' lives as for your own."

"Mighty little that might be," said Houston, drinking again. He leaned forward. "I dammed near stayed with the Cherokee this last visit, Mr. Smith. For me, a white man, that would be a kind of death, though an easy one I warrant. But if I thought my staying there would stay the death in store for the tribe, I would have done so. I owe their people more than I owe all of Texas. And they're a damn sight more loyal than any of my white brothers will ever be."

Smith stared at him. "I shall take care, Sir, to prove you wrong on that one point. A good man is a good man under any skin. Same with a woman." The large and grave somber eyes never moved. "Texas is good for that. Everyone gets a new beginning."

"Or a new end," said Houston, draining the bottle.

Smith moved his finger along the map, tracing the route past the rivers to Harrisburg and beyond, stopping at the edge of the Sabine River and the no man's land between *Tejas* and Louisiana. "I will prepare my family for travel tomorrow," he said.

"Whole town–whole state better get prepared and moving. Not going to be anything left of them if Santa Anna catches them sleeping. Going to be like ten thousand Indians coming in on us. And he's coming fast."

Houston rose heavily then turned at the door of the small bedroom vacated by husband and wife for his use. "We're going to have to burn the town behind us," he said sorrowfully. "I do regret it, Mr. Smith, understanding you helped build it but war is no more a respecter of civilization than it is of life. Best to leave nothing here for the invaders. Best to burn our houses, fields and stores that they be of no use to them. It's the one small edge we have, Mr. Smith. They are a thousand miles from home with nothing much at all between here and there. While we, good Sir, are here among friends and just across the river from the United States of America."

"Will they help?"

"I don't believe so," said Houston slowly. "Time was, I would have thought it but no longer. Not yet. Not until after we've won."

Again the small smile stirred the muscles on the watching face. "We will win, then, General Houston?"

"Damn right, Mr. Smith. We're going to win all right. We've got no choice and no place else to go."

Houston wasted no time in conveying his wishes to his new army. The fledglings, eager to march on Santa Anna for revenge of the Alamo, lacked the talent of the Alamo guard and were nearly as much outnumbered. It was unthinkable to waste themselves in such a way, if indeed their goal was Texas independence, he told them the next morning, persuading all but a few. Calling the townspeople together afterwards, he announced the need to move out of the way of the advancing Mexican forces. Immediately, he said. Next week would be far too late. For those who dithered on the line, he painted a gruesome picture of what awaited if they refused: pillage, plunder, rape and slaughter. He convinced them.

And then, faced with their panic, he ordered they be given most of his wagons as well as some of his personal cash. To those who questioned his leadership, he gave short answer. "I am leading you away from here," he shouted. "We are not yet prepared to fight on such unequal terms and I will not stay to see us all cut down."

Understandable perhaps, for civilians, but unseemly behavior for soldiers, some thought. Some twenty men, bristling for a fight in San Antonio, deserted the army as soon as orders to retreat were given. Houston let them go. He had not time to chase fools, he said.

He mustered his men to move back to the Colorado River, "to await reinforcements and supplies as we prepare to face the foe." But before they marched he called Deaf Smith aside and asked him to wait for the evacuation. "You must torch the town before you leave," he said. "There must be nothing left for Santa Anna. Nothing."

The still eyes never blinked. "I will do it," Smith said.

Speed was uppermost on Houston's mind as his men moved out. Like a rabbit on the run from the hounds, he prayed only to gain enough distance for breathing room, for a hiding place in which to train his soldiers for a battle they were ill prepared to fight. Texas had men enough for one major battle. That was all. There would be no second chances when that effort was expended. They had lost too many men already—hundreds cut down from their few thousand. Like the dead heroes of the Alamo, the rest of the newly dead had found that Texian pride was no match for the numbers against them. And with Santa Anna, the

"Napoleon of the West," at their head, there was no lack of discipline on the Mexican side.

Faster and faster, Houston urged his grumbling men into retreat. Finding the wagon wheels too often mired, he even sacrificed his cannon to the Guadalupe River in order to pick up running speed.

Behind him the people of Gonzales loaded what they could onto what wagons they had and headed east, pressing for the Louisiana border, leaving their homes burning behind them. The Great Runaway Scrape had begun. Following Houston's example, if not able to match his speed, the settlers poured out of their homes as if they were already on fire and ran on foot, mule or horseback. Pulling wagons, oxcarts, travois, or with nothing at all, they fled the advancing armies.

Unfortunately, when Colonel Fannin undertook to move his men from Goliad, a week after receiving orders to do so, he was too late. General Urrea's cavalry surrounded him a few miles from safety and he was forced to surrender with all his troops. Whatever rules of war the Colonel may have been expecting, he had reckoned without knowledge of the Generalissimo's mind. One week later, on Palm Sunday, on Santa Anna's orders, every prisoner was shot.

Houston was camped on the Colorado near Beason's Ford when he received word of the massacre. Across the river, almost in sight, was General Joaquin Ramirez y Sesma who had followed his trail from Gonzales with some seven hundred and fifty troops, including cavalry. Calling for reinforcements from San Antonio, where Santa Anna still remained with his wounded soldiers, Sesma had begun building the boats he would need to cross to confront his reluctant foe. Not that Houston's men were reluctant. Only the General hesitated, measuring the pros and cons and yet-to-comes of the conflict. Though his army had grown, bolstered by the notion of a pending battle, the Texians were still outnumbered and untrained. He had no cannon left though two were promised. He had no wagons to remove the wounded from the proposed battlefront and he had no doubt at all that the seven hundred and fifty Mexican soldiers he was facing immediately would be reinforced by thousands more within days of the first grand roar of rifles. Then, indeed, the war would be over and Texas the certain loser.

Still, pressed by the government on the one hand and his men on the other, he hesitated, hoping for a way.

The massacre of Fannin's men at Goliad erased that hope. He ordered Smith, who brought the news, to keep it to himself and on the afternoon of

March 26, he ordered his army to fall back to the Brazos River. With much complaining most followed.

Behind him, the word of the massacre spread like brush fire. Fear possessed the settlers and the Texian army cried out for revenge. The General might as well have been deaf. With less than a thousand troops—having lost about half that number already to desertion and disease—he ignored the demand, passed through San Felipe and left it burning, then continued on to the west bank of the Brazos to rest and drill his men at Groce's Plantation.

Ahead and all around him the Runaway Scrape accelerated. If Santa Anna's intent was to frighten every settler that he couldn't kill right out of Texas, he appeared to be succeeding. By early April almost everyone was on the move, with thousands pressed up against the San Jacinto River. Lynch's Crossing across the bayou from the de Zavala home and a bare day's march from Morgan's Point was a sea of bodies waiting for the ferry that would put them on the road to the safety of Louisiana. Children wept and mothers cowered as the men cursed reluctant animals and frantic families forward into the melee, near sinking the ferries that plied steadily back and forth across the broad San Jacinto.

General Houston also had plans to approach the San Jacinto crossing,

Word of his plans brought the troops to the edge of mutiny. They were tired of looking like cowards, they said. They wanted to stand and fight, they said. They were duty bound to protect the towns from which they were retreating, they said. And Sam Houston, they said, was not worth the salt on his beans.

A letter reached him from newly elected President of the Republic of Texas, David Burnet: "*The enemy are laughing you to scorn. You must fight them. You must retreat no further. The country expects you to fight The salvation of the country depends on you doing so.*"

"*I consulted none,*" Houston wrote back to Thomas Rusk, Secretary of War. "*I held no councils of war. If I err, the blame is mine.*"

He informed Rusk that he had taken command of the steamboat, *Yellowstone*, and was prepared to descend the river at a moment's notice. Meanwhile, however, measles had broken out and scores of his men were down.

And he flatly refused to step out in search of the enemy.

"We have but one good battle in us," he told Deaf Smith, sitting in his tent with the bottle his spy had brought back from a recent visit to Morgan's Point. "They can afford to lose as many men as we have altogether and still fight on. We have but one chance. One good battle."

He tipped the bottle. The hour was late and he was tired. Tired of battling mutinous soldiers, impetuous governments, panicked settlers, bad weather, bad habits, and bugs. The mosquitoes were already thick enough to carry off his entire army were they so minded. And now to be stricken with measles!

"Did you see Miss Emily?" he asked Smith. "Did you convey my regards?"

"Yes sir. She was over occupied. Mrs. de Zavala was with her, awaiting passage to Galveston on Morgan's ship along with a few hundred others who will never have a chance to board. There was much pleading and pressing of hands, though Mrs. de Zavala seemed more concerned about her husband who is at Harrisburg than about herself. She demanded to know what you were doing to protect them. I told her we were keeping them advised so they could be got out in time. She sailed with her children the next morning. Yesterday."

"And Miss Emily? Did she respond to my instruction? Did she understand? Did you explain? What did she say?"

"Delay him a day." I gave her the message, and added, if possible, seeing that things are not always possible though they may be promised. She said she would do it. She said to trust her." The thin man hesitated, shadowing his eyes.

"Did you not believe her?"

"There is something there. A question. A concern. Some kind of doubt. I know not. There were too many people about to press for an answer so I had to be satisfied."

"And did you deliver the letter?"

"Yes Sir. She was surprised. And pleased, I think, though her face went pale at seeing the lettering. She did not say a name. Only 'Thank you.'"

The letter had arrived the week before, addressed in a broad and elegant script to "Miss Emily Rose, in care of General Sam Houston." He had suspected for God knew what reason that it came from the father of her child; that the man was somehow attempting to make Houston his ally. The presumption of it forced a smile. If the man dared use such tactics he might yet win his lady. He was glad, at least, that it was now delivered.

Deaf Smith stood and stepped outside, seeming almost to sniff at the salty air, checking the wind. Houston moved his stool to catch the view of the late rising moon through the tent flap "That moon will never care whether we stand or fall," he said, pointing. "It will go on, exactly as it has, whether or not we live another day, whether we attain our dreams or are destroyed by them, whether we maintain integrity or sink like slime to the bottom of any pit."

"That it will, Sir," said Smith. "But that is the moon and we are ourselves. There is no escape from one's own conscience."

Houston sighed, lifting the bottle once again. "Never say I haven't tried, Deaf," he told him. "I have tried and tried and tried to escape the voice of my conscience. It is so very often completely at odds with what I am ordered to do."

"I imagined, Sir, that you must give the orders."

"There's where you're wrong, Deaf. I have no such authority. My job is to read the minds and make the orders fit."

"Whose minds, sir? You mean the government?"

"I mean the soldiers' minds, Deaf. The center piece of their minds that wants to live."

Some two hundred miles to the southwest, Santa Anna had removed from San Antonio to the burned out site of Gonzales where he waited, restless, with General Vincente Filisola, his second in command. Convinced the war was already won and trusting his generals for the mopping up, the Generalissimo was toying with the notion of returning to Mexico City and his presidential responsibilities. His generals, wanting to see the rebels completely broken, urged him to remain.

Into this divided state of mind came Sesma's request for reinforcements against Houston.

Santa Anna was elated to learn that Sesma had the elusive Texian Commander almost in his sights on the Colorado. It would be good to destroy the tiny rebel army before it could escape across the border. Though Sesma could certainly do that without his help, it might be interesting to observe this coward foe in action. Most strange, he thought, that men as courageous as those he had faced at the Alamo should countenance such a person as their chief. There was the possibility, of course, that the man was crafty rather than cowardly, but the Generalissimo doubted it. He had not been much impressed with Texian military strategies. Still, it could be interesting.

He ordered his carriage, a sumptuous affair, to be prepared for travel though he left it the second day out to ride horseback with his men. It was good to be moving again. Good to shake off the weight of his losses at the Alamo. Good to be planning a battle again.

Arriving in Sesma's camp near San Felipe on April 6, he found that Houston had already come and gone, leaving little to plunder. The town was in ashes and the crossing guarded by a desperate band of sharpshooters under Captain Mosely Baker, a stubborn man who had been saved from desertion only by receiving Houston's disgruntled blessing on his determination to drop out of the army and fight. Houston even granted him the band of volunteers. One who was captured revealed the General's hideout on the Brazos, some twenty miles away, but managed to convince the Mexicans that the Texian army awaited only the opportunity to join the flight out of Texas.

Reassured, Santa Anna took five hundred men and fifty cavalry on to Fort Bend where he was joined by Sesma and his forces. There another captured Texian was forced to reveal that President David Burnet, vice-president Lorenzo de Zavala, and the rest of the Texas government, were at Harrisburg, some fifteen miles away. Temporarily abandoning his pursuit of Houston, the Mexican generals set out for Harrisburg, cannon in tow.

He found the town abandoned, except for three printers, still working on the last issue of the *Telegraph and Texas Register*. They informed him, with the kind of courtesy practiced by those facing armies alone, that the entire government had just departed for Galveston, pulling out in a steamship headed for Morgan's Point where they would doubtless board a schooner for the Island. Determined to capture the traitors, particularly that old friend and new arch-enemy Lorenzo de Zavala, Santa Anna sent an advance guard of cavalry under Colonel Juan Almonte hurrying on the port. He lingered only long enough to burn down Harrisburg.

Galloping up the shoreline with fifty dragoons, Juan Almonte almost arrived in time. The little boat being frantically rowed towards Morgan's waiting schooner–the escaping seat of rebel government–was still within easy reach of his rifles. They had them in their sights. He could have destroyed them all and earned his commanders's gratitude if he had not been burdened with a gentlemanly nature.

Along with the men who lined the boards in the escaping craft, sat a woman, Burnet's wife, clinging to the president's arm as she cast terrified and pleading eyes towards the men whose guns were leveled on them from the shore.

And Juan Almonte could not give the order to fire.

Instead, his hand moved to his heart in salute.

18

With the spyglass given by Colonel Morgan pressed to her eye, Rose watched the shore from the upstairs window of the hotel. She stood in Morgan's room, the one she had shared for one long afternoon and another long night with General Houston. And she had promised him—What? That she would prostitute herself to the Mexican commander for the sake of the Texas army? That she would give away her soul as she had given away her body?

Texas! She had not imagined the land would claim her so entirely. Had not conceived of its demands.

The hotel had been overflowing for weeks though paying guests were few. In Morgan's absence, though she hoped with his blessing, she made room for as many as possible and ordered that beans, at least, be offered everyone who asked. It was the least she could do for the thousands of suddenly homeless settlers fleeing toward the safety of the Louisiana line. It seemed all Texas was on the move, running, terrified, dragging what little they could take of their precious things in their desperate flight from the very man she had promised to seduce in the name of independence.

She stepped back from the window, glancing around the room. Houston's presence seemed to linger there, a powerful presence though the man himself seemed vulnerable as a child. It had been easy, in those unguarded hours, to lay their souls bare to one another, to confess their desperate needs for success. "You just want to be somebody," he had told her, teasing her gently as he left the hotel a few hours after securing her word. He had reached down from that big white horse to touch her chin with a long, broad finger. "You are somebody already," he said. "You are someone very special."

For a moment, looking up at him, she had been a child again with the father who had touched her only once, in a dance. She wanted, absurdly, to put her arms around the rough-hewn man above her and hold on. Perhaps forever. She had been very much afraid.

She was not afraid any more. Everything was settled, though the irony of it curled her lip into an ugly line. She touched the letter she still carried in her pocket, delivered less than a week ago by that strange man the General had sent. Deaf Smith, they called him, the man who watched for movement as a hawk might watch and yet maintained so still a face. "Delay him a day," he'd murmured in her ear during the moment she stood near him in the crush of people at the bar. Such an odd voice he had or perhaps she only focused on it to avoid the message itself! "Delay him!" As if the matter were fully resolved. As if, in the General's mind, she were no more than a pawn he could move on the chessboard, bringing it up as planned to checkmate.

She had glared at Smith. He looked straight back with no change in his expression. "If possible," he murmured, toneless, shrugging. Before she could speak, he was gone. And she was holding a letter she could not remember having taken though the bulk of it astonished her.

It was from Luke. She had recognized the handwriting immediately, the delicately curving letters contrasting strangely with the strength of the hands she suddenly remembered. And he had sent it, the presumption of the man, "In Care of General Sam Houston, Commander of the Texas Forces."

She wondered if the General had guessed the identity of the sender. It seemed, sometimes, that the General was literally prescient though he claimed it was not the future that he saw, but the past. "Humans," he had told her, "often repeat themselves."

It was the sort of thing that Luke might say, she thought, returning to the window. Out in the channel, Morgan's schooner lay at anchor. The glass would not show it but she could imagine him on the deck of the Flash, watching and waiting to make good the escape of the new republic's government. He alone among the captains—and most of the people as well—had not given up on Houston's promise to win. But then, he alone knew of the strategy being employed.

At the dock, Governor Burnet and his wife along with de Zavala and a half dozen other men had just scrambled into a skiff and picked up the oars. Their horses, winded from the ride from Harrisburg, stamped on the beach where Tom walked with Chico, the Mexican stableboy, gathering up their reins to bring them back to the hotel.

Was Santa Anna right behind them? There had not been time for asking. Morgan, out there in the channel for two days now, had told her to be ready with the skiff and when the Governor raced up, shouting for a boat, Tom took charge immediately. "They're close, very close," de Zavala called, smiling a brief apology in her direction before he galloped off after the others.

At least Emily was safely in Galveston with the children. And it looked as if her husband, against all odds, would live to see her again. But as for Rose's own fate–

She was seized by a sudden longing to see Luke again. Both Lukes. The father and the son. The letter he had sent with a note enclosed from Dr. Connie had brought him back to her more vividly than she'd imagined possible, especially the pages he had spent on their son. Reading it over and over in the night times since, she could almost hear him speaking, telling her again exactly what he was doing and why.

"To be free, dear Rose, that all men and women may be free, that our son grow up in an altogether free country."

And the song! Who would have imagined he had it in him to write such a song! She had thought him so serious, though caught in the rush of memories his letter brought, she remembered his sense of romance and the playfulness that softened his philosophies, if not his politics.

"There's a yellow rose in Texas
That I'm a'going to see
No other darkie knows her
No one, only me."

It was his tribute, he explained, not only to her but to the southern culture he was infiltrating. Oh! Take care, Luke, she thought, remembering the lynchings and whips in the stories he'd once told her. But at least in Tennessee the oppression was not so great as further south. There were freedman in Memphis and in Chattanooga where he was both teaching and linking a line on the Underground Railroad to freedom. "The most rewarding work I've ever done," he wrote, "but it is nothing compared with the thought of seeing your dear face again."

Could he be coming? Could he be coming here? And to what? From what she heard, Santa Anna destroyed everything in his path. God only knew where she might be, if she were even still alive.

Again the ugly curl of lip. What would he think if he knew her present situation? Her plan to cooperate with the authorities who would make Texas a slave nation. No, not only cooperate, but play a crucial role in bringing about that very outcome. Could he bear it? Could he love her still? Could he ever respect her again? It had not mattered for so long. She had closed him from her mind since she first set foot on Morgan's ship in New York. And now at the crucial hour, to have him intrude! If God indeed were watching as Mr. Collins kept insisting, He must be laughing fit to kill.

But Luke, it seemed, was capable of anything. His gratitude for his son had overridden his anger at her hiding him away for so many years. "I try to understand why you made that choice," he had written, three months before the letter found her. "I cannot say I have succeeded. Nevertheless, I find I cannot love you any less for deceiving me nor more for making me the happiest father that ever was. The reason for this state of mind is simple, dear Rose. I already, and always, have loved you as much as it is possible for me to love." He had signed it, "Your darkie." Knowing Luke, it made her want to laugh and cry at the same time. If God could work a miracle—she smiled briefly to herself—and lift her out of here, she would go to him and be his wife and never think again about the white folks she had left behind.

But now it was the white folks who were leaving her behind. Leaving her and Tom and Sally and fourteen-year-old Chico who wanted only his chance to fight. Well, he might get it soon enough. The Mexicans would arrive momentarily. And, no doubt, they would be angry. Poor foolish boy. As if he could pit his childish courage against a whole army! One would not think he would fight his own people but as he explained it, he was Texian now. Texian as anybody. And indeed there were many former Mexicans among the revolutionaries. A desire for freedom and the bond of frontier life had, temporarily at least, erased the issue of nationalities. The line of color, however, was harder to cross.

Morgan had taken most of the servants to Galveston; she had told the rest that they could leave, linking them with white families where she could. Free blacks were suspect to the point of being virtually illegal in Texas though once across the border they might have a chance. She provided papers, signed by Morgan, explaining that, as his indentured servants, they were being sent out of Texas until such time as return was safe. Most left gladly. A few protested but in the end, only she, Tom, Sally and Chico were left.

The skiff had moved out past the waves though barely a hundred feet from shore when she caught a movement down the beach. Riding hard, plumed helmets regal against the waterline and blue and white uniforms brilliant in the sun, a company of dragoons materialized on the sand. Oh God! The Texians were not going to make it! And Morgan's cannons could not help. The little boat lay directly in line with the Mexicans on the shore. As if in a play, a theater by the sea, in uniforms more dashing than anything she'd seen, the men drew up beside the dock, raised their rifles, aimed at the heavy-laden boat still struggling through the water, and looked to their commander.

She watched in amazement as he lowered his gun, then pointed at Mrs. Burnet, whose terror registered minutely through the spyglass. The faces of the soldiers registered something close to shock. The commander's gestures were adamant. There would be no shooting.

Tom and Chico, mounted now and holding the reins on a small train of horses, were immediately surrounded. She was glad to see them staying calm. Chico looked merely awed as if, for half a chance, he would have ridden with the dragoons himself. Rose put the spyglass in her pocket. It would be her turn soon enough. Not waiting to see the skiff reach the schooner, the soldiers were leaving the beach, spurring towards town, keeping Tom and the horses in the center of their file.

So these were the slayers of children? The bloody handed barbarians sent to slaughter everyone in sight? Could not fire on a woman! Perhaps miracles were not so unlikely as she had imagined. Sam Houston would appreciate that. Rose smoothed her hair, took a slow deep breath, and went downstairs to receive them. Imaginings of Luke would have to wait. There was no time now for any thought beyond the moment. She opened the front door.

They halted, all fifty of them, in double file in front of the hotel, filling the muddy street with a shocking elegance. An aide swung down and approached her. His English was perfect.

"In the name of his Imperial Majesty, Generalissimo Santa Anna, you are ordered to deliver your stores for the use of your government's army. Resisters will suffer the punishment of traitors."

Her eyes slid past the underling and moved up to the leader, watching from his horse. Could this be Santa Anna himself? She allowed her lips to curve upward, lowered her lashes a moment. She hardly imagined he would shoot her. "Your wish is my command, Sir. How may I serve you?"

He responded in English, though more heavily accented. "We will eat and drink here. You will show us what you have."

"The cook is an excellent one, Sir. And the warehouse manager will do everything you say." She lowered her lashes again, gesturing towards the other servants. "Her name is Sally. His name is Tom. My name is Rose. By your leave, Chico will tend your horses as you eat. We await your orders."

He bowed, hand over heart. "Colonel Juan Almonte at your service."

He barked an order in Spanish. The men dismounted and followed him inside, dispersing quickly through the hotel. She found two dragoons guarding the cook in the kitchen though Sally seemed completely unintimidated and the soldiers looked almost happy. Within the hour food was on the tables and a barrel of wine had been opened. Were it not for those high-plumed helmets and the buzz of Spanish everywhere, she could almost have been witnessing any other night at the bar. It was easy, for a little while, to feel no fear.

But there were differences. Most patrons did not help themselves. She made herself useful, bringing provisions, attempting to maintain order even as her small empire crumbled.

The sun was reddening against the western plains of San Jacinto when she moved to Almonte's side. "Will you look at the warehouse today or will you wait until after you have rested?"

"*Mas tarde,*" he said. "Later, *Senorita.* The men sleep here. You prepare a room for me."

He called her back as she walked away. "You occupy it with me, yes?"

Her hands fluttered, surprised in motion. "Sir–"

His eyes were bold, appraising her. "*Yo, no?* But perhaps my commander?" A smile grew on his face. Broadened. He spoke carefully. "Ah yes, *Senorita.* I will not molest you with my presence, but *el comandante* will appreciate the diversion." Without waiting for an answer, he directed a few staccato sentences to a nearby soldier who rose from his bench to loom over her. "Juan is your bodyguard," he said. "We will not wish anything to happen to you this night. You may lock your door to sleep. He is outside."

She stared at him, flushed with anger. To go willingly was one thing. To be delivered under guard like an animal was quite another.

"You are beautiful, angry, *Senorita,*" Almonte chuckled. "Maybe *El Generalisimo* will forgive my error in not shooting the woman on the boat if I bring to him a woman so beautiful as you." He drank deeply of his wine. "True, *Senorita,* you will not mind much. *El Generalisimo* is a handsome man and an excellent lover, certainly."

"*Y de mas,*" he called as she walked away, "you will not have to be here when it burns."

In her own room, enjoyed for a bare four months, she surveyed her precious things: the furnishings, the rich draperies made to her order, the velvet dress she had worn only once, and that in New Orleans. Perhaps for this occasion– Sighing, she replaced it in the wardrobe. She had arrived with a great deal. She would leave with nothing unless Houston kept his promise or Santa Anna made a better one.

The crackle of the letter in her pocket brought her mind back to Luke and to her son. Would she ever see him again? Would she be more likely to see him if she went to Mexico than if she attempted to remain in Texas? Sam Houston must think he knew the answer to that or he would not have forwarded the letter to her. But he had not witnessed the chivalry she had seen in Colonel Almonte. Though he might be treating her as a prisoner of war, he obviously had no intention of abusing her. Might not his commander be the same?

Fully dressed, she stretched out to sleep. When she awoke, a few hours later, she found she was still clutching the letter in her pocket.

She did not recognize Luther Collins when she first saw him coming up the street just after breakfast though the set of the newly tonsured head and the bulky body underneath the rough black robes was instantly familiar. Before he reached the hitching posts, she knew him. A priest! What an excellent cover, though she had not imagined Collins lending himself to the efforts of war! Stifling a smile, she listened from the door as he approached, asking one of the guards if there were captives he would be allowed to bless. He was referred inside to the Colonel's aide. Rose inclined her head as he passed. "Father," she murmured. "Bless me for I have sinned."

The aide was willing to provide a private corner for her confession. Only a few dragoon were in sight; a dozen others were ransacking the rooms and emptying the pantry. The Colonel had gone to the warehouse where Tom was helping him load a line of wagons that stretched across the yard and into the street. Mules, horses and donkeys knickered and brayed in the dust. There was obviously no shortage of transportation though all of it, as far as she could see, had been made in Texas. She repressed a shudder at the fate of their former owners.

The Mexicans were winning. They had won everything so far. How could Houston's paltry little army stop them now? And who was she to stand like a dam of pebbles in that flood?

Facing the wall, Collins was silent. She bowed her head, conscious of Juan watching from across the room. "Who would have thought it!" she murmured. "And what is your mission, sir?"

"Thee must speak, Sister. Thee must speak, even as I do, a murmuring to cover my words. Understand?"

She nodded and began to tell the story of Almonte's arrival. He stopped her, raising his finger in a priestly way. "Thee must confess, Sister, lest one of these, walking close, hears and discovers us. Then we will both die." He hesitated. "It is a good thing to confess to one another."

She nodded and began. Catholicism was the official religion of Mexico and every Texas immigrant had been required to convert. She had learned the rudiments at least.

"Forgive me, Father, for I have sinned. I have not–" She hardly knew where to go from there.

"I have not thought as I ought. I have been selfish," Collin's voice prompted her. "Run on in that fashion, though 'twould be blasphemy not to be honest. Never fear. I must speak and cannot listen."

And so she presented her litany of fears and fancies, doubts, deceits and desires to the God who might or might not be listening. And all the while, with his back to the room, Luther Collins informed her of Houston's movements. The General had crossed Buffalo Bayou on the steamer *Yellowstone* with some nine hundred soldiers, leaving his baggage and two hundred sick soldiers under guard at Harrisburg. They had acquired two cannons, the Twin Sisters they called them. The force was well prepared and they were moving today to camp on the Plains of San Jacinto near Lynch's Crossing past Vince's Bridge. Tom Rusk, Secretary of War was with Houston, supporting the General's strategy against the army's desire to charge the enemy. Deaf Smith had captured a Mexican courier, carrying William Travis's old saddlebags, and they had learned that Santa Anna was coming with only eight hundred men, besides the fifty cavalry with Almonte. Timed correctly, it would be a fair fight. And if Santa Anna surrendered, the war would end there.

"Thee need not participate, Sister," the priest whispered, his words a bare stirring of the air. "That is the message from the General. We need no tricks. Thee need not cast thyself down."

Astounded, she stopped her confessions. Aloud, he said, "You have fears, Rose? You must confess your fears to the heavenly Father."

She stumbled on. "Death overlooks me, Father. Forgive me for my lack of faith."

His bare-breathed whisper continued, insistent. "If thee is captured, the General said, and thee wishes to help him, place a kerchief on the tent where it can be seen. Delay with Santa Anna as long as possible. Deaf Smith will try to bring a message."

"To the Generalissimo's own tent?"

"He has done more. He is fearless."

"I am not," she whispered. "I do not know what to do."

"Thee must choose, Sister." His voice dropped to a breath in her inner ear. "Everyone must choose their own future as the Spirit moves them."

The room had emptied as they spoke. Only Juan remained, still watching from a safe distance.

"I cannot run away," she said. "I have no choices."

"Thee must choose whom thee will serve. That is the only choice one can rightly make," he said and raising his hand made the sign of the cross over her bowed head. "In the name of the Father and the Son and the Holy Spirit." The words were in Latin. Together, they stood.

"I was Catholic before Quaker," he murmured, catching her glance at the shaved center of his head. "To be a priest was easy. Natural." He raised his voice a little. "Are there others?" he asked her.

"Only three, Father," she said aloud. "But they are servants and not Catholic, I think.

He extended his hand again. "God bless you, child."

She noticed, watching him walk away, that he wore no shoes. Taking note of the penitential attire, the soldiers on the street outside stepped back, allowing him to make his solitary way past them. She stood watching as he grew smaller, a moving dark speck in the dust of the road towards San Jacinto.

"You are confessed, now *Senorita*?" Almonte had come up beside her. "An Irish priest?"

"They speak English," she answered, finding a smile to offer him. "It is most useful."

"It is good to be confessed." The dark eyes stared at her. "Later, one can confess again."

She bowed her head. "As you say, Sir."

He looked her over, appraisingly. The dust, carbon and sweat of the past few days clung to her. "You will need a bath," he said. "And then, afterwards, a pretty dress. You have one, yes?"

"Obediently she heated water and carried it to the bathing closet. He watched until she turned to face him. "Please sir—"

With the door locked against him, she enjoyed the half hour of freedom. Soaping her hair, she allowed herself to forget the future. She was with Emily again, upstairs in the big house in New York and they were preparing for a party.

It was to be her party, this time. All the generals were attending. She would choose one to marry.

Ah, such nonsense! She settled into the water to rinse her hair and came up shaking her head like a dog. She would do what had to be done to save her own life. All the rest would have to take care of themselves. Collins, at least, had set her free from her promise, though free to do what, she was not quite sure.

There was a knock on the door. "*Senorita, ya llega El Generalisimo!*"

She understood enough Spanish to leap from the tub. Drying herself, she slid the velvet over her head. There was no time for stays and corsets. Considering the heat already rising on this morning in mid-April, she was glad to leave them off. Outside she could hear shouts along with marching feet and the occasional clang of metal. Her hands trembled as she pulled a comb through tangled curls, smoothing her hair down and back. She was almost ready.

The knock on the door was sharper. "*Senorita, abre la puerta! Pronto!*"

There was nowhere else to go. She removed the envelope from yesterday's dress and left the dirty clothes on the floor. The letter she slipped into her pocket. It betrayed nothing to the Mexicans if it were seen. And if it were left, it could only be burned.

There was a shout of salute from outside. Swords clanked as heels came sharply together on the floor. She peered in the tiny glass, loosened a curl at her forehead and another at her ear, noted the pale arc of her bosom—no sun had touched her there—swelling from the creamy lace insert that covered her breasts. She lifted her chin and touched perfume to her throat. And opened the door.

The splendor of the man who faced her almost took her breath. Glittering gold epaulets, heavily fringed, bordered a richly embroidered tunic hung with golden medals that covered his chest. A long jeweled scabbard held his sword against the sleek white line of his trousers, its tip against the high black boots that were clinched with long silver spurs. Close-cropped black hair framed his head like a picture she had seen in a history book of Julius Caesar. Dark eyes in a boldly handsome face appraised her, approving.

At his side, Almonte watched. She curtsied, glad for the long ago practice with Emily. "*Senor Generalisimo,*" she said. "We welcome you."

He raised a finely arched dark eyebrow. "Indeed?" he said. "We welcome you, also, *Senorita.*" Lace showed at the velvet cuffs as he waved a hand towards the kitchen. "We will eat now. You will accompany us."

"The best we have," she told Sally, waiting nearby. Sally shrugged. Not much was left from the soldiers' plunder. "There is not much, Sir," Rose said.

A few sharp sentences and several soldiers disappeared, returning with hampers of meat and potatoes. Stone-faced, Sally returned to the kitchen while Rose joined the Commander at the table where he sat with Almonte. He turned his full attention on her. She felt naked as one does in dreams, trembling with shame, but she met his eyes when he raised them and controlled herself. Lightly, he touched her hand where it lay on the table.

"You have, no reason to fear us, *Senorita.* I am a gentleman, first of all. *Y entonces*—" His laugh was short. "*Entonces soy El Presidente, El Generalisimo.* You understand?"

She kept her eyes on his face. The short black hair curved forward around it, framing aristocratic features, firmly drawn. He was the most handsome man she had ever seen. "*Si Senor,*" she responded.

"You speak Spanish? That is good."

"Very little, Sir. I am learning."

Again the eyes swept her body. "That will be useful. You will, *como no,* come with us."

"To Mexico, Sir? After you have won the battle for Texas?"

The flick of his hand conveyed disdain. "There is nothing to win here. Here we have only to subdue the rebels." The full lower lip curved up. "Simple, *Senorita.* I thought to meet this Ooston *pero* who runs before me like a dog." He tapped a glass, motioning for wine which an aide instantly supplied. "Now I think I will meet him here. The dog is running but we will catch him before he escapes us, no? So that he will not return." He sighed. "It is a long march to chase cowards. Many men have died. He must be punished."

The food appeared. He ate with gusto. She took a bite. Chewed. The meat tasted of ashes in her mouth.

"You are not hungry? You must eat." He raised his glass which was instantly filled. "*A la victoria!*" he shouted. A hundred glasses clinked around them. "*A la victoria!*"

She sipped at her water.

"You do not drink to victory? You must drink!"

A glass appeared in front of her. "To victory," she said, raising it. But whose?

By noon the ranks and files of men were ranged along the street, trailed by the line of wagons. Carrying nothing, she was escorted to a finely furnished carriage by two soldiers who mounted up beside it. Through the silk curtains she could see Santa Anna moving to the head of the line on a glistening black stallion, its trappings almost as rich as his own.

"*Adelante!*" came the cry and the carriage jolted forward along the rough road. A thin rain had begun to fall and she felt an unnerving flash of pity for the men outside as the dust turned into mud beneath their feet. They followed the road down which Collins had earlier disappeared. She hoped there had been a horse waiting out of sight for him. She hoped he was long gone.

The shrill of bugles marked cadence for the marching feet. Well past the edge of town, she peered through the curtains and she saw smoke rising behind her. The warehouse and hotel were in flames. There would be nothing there now. Nothing for her to return to. She wondered if Sally and Tom and Chico were also marching or if they had been left. As if in answer, Chico appeared, running up alongside the carriage. "Tom say not to worry," he said. "He and Sally be all right. You be good, he say, and you be all right, too." His voice dropped. "You need help, you find me. I come. I watch you." He ran on. The soldiers beside the carriage paid no attention.

The weather turned colder as a late blue norther blew the April day into ragged grey fragments, wind-whipped and wet. She dozed and woke again to a different sound from the bugles. It sounded like a funeral dirge, high and shrill in a way that made the skin crawl and the belly retreat into knots. Far ahead she heard shouts, then shots. A cannon boomed, followed at some distance, by another. The line had come to a halt. One of the guarding soldiers galloped away. The other gestured in response to her questioning face in the window. "Ooston," he said, pointing. "*Por alla.*" He whipped a hand down like a hatchet, chopping. "*Le terminamos.*"

Terminate. Had Houston been routed so soon and so short of victory? She retreated into the cushions and closed her eyes.

How long she sat there, willing away all thought, she could not say. The air was greyer and there was still no sign of the sun though the rain had stopped when the carriage started to move again and the cadence of the march picked back up. The bugles were silent. Another hour passed, or perhaps two, before they stopped again. They were near the Lynchburg Ferry Crossing on the little peninsula bordered by Buffalo Bayou to the west with the San Jacinto River on the north and marshlands to the east. Along the waterlines live oaks pressed close against the central grassy plain. Already soldiers were throwing up a barricade—a rough affair of sticks and branches some five or six feet high. Well behind it, sheltered in the trees near the river, a white silk tent was being pitched. The Generalissimo himself stood near it.

He turned as she stepped from the carriage, not far away, and moved towards him. "Welcome *Senorita*," he bowed. "Here we meet the enemy." He reached for her hand. "*Y tambien*, here we meet our friends."

She controlled a tremor. "The battle is over?"

He laughed. "*Ah no, Querida*. It was a play act. It was nothing. *El Cobarde* can only hide though a few of his men are brave enough. We will not preoccupy ourselves tonight with him. Soon General Cos will arrive and between us we will take no prisoners. But tonight we will enjoy ourselves, no?"

"Yes Sir," she said.

"Your name is Rose?"

"Yes Sir."

He smiled. "*La Rosa*," he said gently, placing a hand on her arm. "Come with me, Rosa. Let us explore this ground where the rebels dogs must be buried."

She kept her face very still. "May we go to the water? It is very beautiful there."

"Ah, the *Senorita* does not like burial grounds? *Esta bien*. We will look at the water."

The sounds of camp and cooking filtered through the trees as they moved back to the river a few hundred feet behind the tent. Above and below them the marshland crept to the edge of camp, filling all but the high ground where they stood and the grassy plain before them.

"He is hiding over there," Santa Anna raised an elegant hand to point, lace trailing from his cuff. "We will bring him out soon enough." The dark eyes narrowed, measuring the distance. "Then we will make him dance," he said. "They will not like the dance, I think. It is the dance of death."

In her mind's eye, she saw Houston bending from his huge white horse, touching her face. "You are special," he had said. How could she wish him death? But the kerchief, the kerchief Collins had mentioned to her. She had none. She had nothing.

She stepped away from his grasp on her elbow as they approached the river. With a small exclamation, she slipped on the bank and caught herself, jamming a hand in the mud. He stood still as she went down to the water and washed herself, then returned to his side, holding out her dripping hands. "Have you a kerchief, Sir?"

He laid a square of red silk in her hands. "*Como no, Querida*," he said.

She held it tightly as they stood together on the bank, silent with thoughts that could not be shared. By the time they returned to the camp, the tent was well up, a three room affair, draped and carpeted with oriental rugs. The outer chamber, a meeting room, was complete with a dozen cushions and two low tables, one covered with a linen cloth and holding figs, oranges and wine, and a covered dish that smelled like chicken. On the other lay a map and papers with numbers on them. She was careful not to look closely as Santa Anna watched from the door, half-smiling. Emboldened, she moved deeper into the tent, lifting a flap to see his wardrobe neatly arranged in its own small room. Beside it, the silken canopy covered another room filled by a large bed resting on a Turkish carpet and made up with a red embroidered velvet quilt. She turned, still holding the kerchief in her hands and smiled back at Santa Anna.

He stepped back as she moved past him through the door. "You will permit me?" she said, shaking out the blood red square of cloth. Before he could answer, she stretched up to tie it to the corner stake.

"Our flag of non-surrender," she said.

"You do not like the Texians?"

"They would make me a slave," she said. "How could I surrender to that?"

Surprise crossed his face. "A slave? *Pero. . . .* "

"I am a Negro," she said shortly, "though I do not look it, being of mixed blood. High yellow, they call it."

"Yellow! Ah, *La Rosa Amarilla.* More perfect than the pink. Most beautiful of all."

His smile was dazzling. "*Ven, Querida,*" he said, taking her hands to draw her back inside. "Come."

19

With one long leg, Deaf Smith felt for the branch beneath him on the giant oak tree. It was a long stretch from the perch where he had kept his spyglass trained on the Mexican camp all the long wet afternoon. But the wait had been rewarded.

In the gathering dusk beneath the canopy of leaves, Houston waited.

"She is there, General. She has put up the kerchief."

A brief smile creased the thin man's weathered face as he dropped from the last branch. "It is a red one. Looks to be Santa Anna's own. Silk, I would say."

"You don't think it's a trap?"

"No. The look on her face when her back was to him– No, I do not think it is a trap."

Houston mused, beginning to pace. "Mr. Collins believes she will help us. I will have to trust that it is so, though truth is, I can understand her doubts. What reason has she? What does Texas hold for the likes of her? There is only the closer link with her son. We will have to trust it." He turned to face the scout. "You gave her the letter?" Smith nodded. Houston went on. "You think you can get through that line?"

"There are ways. Which one will work, I do not know yet.

"But you will try?"

"I will try."

A few birds still hanging on to their invaded territory shrilled bravely to one another as the sky darkened into night along the banks of the bayou. But mostly the sounds of camp came through the live oaks, the crackle of fires, the clanging of pots and pans. Rough voices split the heavy air with laughter interspersed with curses. The air was charged with violence, sharp as lightning flashes.

"They would be fighting now if I allowed it," said Houston, careful to keep his face towards Deaf. "They have been ready for a long time. If I can only hold them off tomorrow morning. By late afternoon the sun will be in the Mexicans' eyes. And if our plan goes well, their eyes might not even be open."

"I do not think of you as a gambling man, General."

Houston's laugh was harsh as barbed wire in the throat. "You do not know me, then."

"We could charge them tonight while they are still in disarray. If General Cos arrives according to his message we will have five hundred more men to fight tomorrow."

The big man shrugged. "If the kerchief were not there, we might do so. It helps to even the odds. But look you, Deaf. Our men see no better than theirs in the dark and ours are doubtless less of a team. Santa Anna is no fool. He will not be unready for surprises. And if Cos arrives in the midst of battle with fresh reinforcements, the surprise will be ours and they are likely to win not only the night, but Texas."

Smith was silent. Houston paced. Turned back.

"Man, I would not fight at all could I but escape it. We have, however, arrived at the point of no return. If the girl performs—If you can reach her—If all goes well—You are quite certain Santa Anna is an opium user?"

"I have seen him myself. Though he does not allow it to interfere with battle."

"Recreation, then? Well, we shall have to hope that Miss Emily Rose provides fine recreation."

"It is a long wager, General. She is not the type."

The General was not listening. "I must speak with Rusk," he said, staring blindly across the plain that separated him from the Mexican army. "Together we must compel the men to wait." He turned back to Smith. "At dawn tomorrow, you must go and destroy Vince's Bridge. We will not allow retreat and who knows what reinforcements may be following."

"Besides General Cos?"

"Besides General Cos, General Sesma is waiting near San Felipe. And Filisola may be on his way from Gonzales with another few thousand troops. We must delay them any way we can."

"There will be no retreat for us, then?"

"We are done retreating, Mr. Smith. To retreat now is to lose Texas. Now I must return to camp."

Smith called softly after him. "And the girl, General? What is to be done with the girl afterwards?"

If there was an answer, he did not hear it. The General's back disappeared through the dark trees. Grey as a ghost, Smith moved in the opposite direction. Slipping out of the wide shadow of the oak, he dropped to his knees, then to his belly in the tall grass, sliding like a snake across the plain. Alone, perhaps, among the soldiers there, he thanked God for the clouds that lay on the night like a huge black blanket.

Beneath the silken canopy, Rose lay quietly next to the man who had touched her as she had not imagined possible. The Generalissimo's passion was more gentle, more controlled than Luke's had been. And the feelings he aroused in her! Raw lust, she supposed, but undeniably exciting. He touched her like a treasure, touched every part of her until she wanted him as she had never imagined wanting anyone. They had spoken very little. Had not needed to. Even now, in the dark, with him asleep beside her, she did not want to move beyond the shelter of his encircling arm.

She did not know what had awakened her though it seemed a voice had called her through the strange bright dreams in which she walked as one might walk on sky or water. But now there was a heaviness in her head and she felt a raging thirst. Perhaps it was the opium he'd insisted on putting in the wine. She had never tried it before. The wine itself was rarity enough.

She must have water. Moving carefully, she loosened herself from the man's arm and slipped into the outer room. It was too dark. She could see nothing. Reaching blindly, she found cloth—a blanket—and wrapped it around her naked body as she edged towards the remembered door. Kneeling, she lifted the flap.

There was no one by the tent though a few campfires still gleamed and a few voices spoke quietly in the dark. She found the jug set near the door and raised it to her lips.

A pebble struck it with a tiny ping. Startled, she almost dropped it, then caught herself and replaced it slowly on the ground.

There was a faint stirring at the edge of the marquee, no more than a mouse might make. But she knew it was a man.

Still, she was not ready when lips were suddenly pressed against her ear and the familiar toneless voice, breathed words. "Cos will come tonight. Tomorrow, at midday, the officers must eat and drink together. You must find opium and dose the wine." The breath of a chuckle warmed her ear. "They will have pleasant dreams. God willing, they will not wake up."

She neither saw nor felt his retreat.

Across the San Jacinto Plain the voices around the campfire grew louder. John Wharton, Houston's adjutant general, was shouting, red-faced. Some listened. Many shook their fists and shouted.

"Tonight! I say we get them tonight! Slit them bastards' throats and leave them bleeding like the boys at the Alamo bled. Like the boys at Goliad, shot in cold blood! "

"Sneak up on them! Get them in the dark! Slash them!" The chorus swelled. Men stood, flexing muscles, buckling down their knives. A few picked up their guns.

"Fools!" It was the General's voice. A lion's roar. Red firelight flamed across his face as he leaped forward, every hair on end. "We are a breath from victory and you would spoil it! Falling over friend and foe alike on the blackest of nights! You think yourselves witches to see better than they do in the dark! You think to disgrace yourselves and kill each other in some blind murderous brawl? Where's the reward in that? Where's the merit?"

Absolute silence reined when he stopped speaking. He looked around the campfire, seeming to meet every eye. A few heads dropped. A few stared back, rebellious. When he spoke again, it was in a conversational tone, man to man in the back room of the tavern.

"If you want vengeance more than victory, then where's the mind for battle, men? Chasing its emotions as some girl might do?"

Even Wharton had little to say as the General walked away. One by one the men followed to their own tents or wrapped themselves in blankets under the trees. As the campfires died, the dark of the cloudy sky descended, absolute and silent.

When Rose awoke again, it was to the sound of voices just beyond the partition where a candle glowed a halo through the silk. She listened avidly to the rapid Spanish, scrambling for what words she could understand. "*Soldados. Tres cientos. Nada mas.*" Three hundred. Nothing more. Yes, it must be General Cos who arrived.

The low voices went on and on. She caught the word *cobarde* and Ooston and *manana por la manana*, an odd turn of phrase that meant early morning. There was more discussion. *Tarde* was mentioned. Afternoon, then. The voices slowed, stopped. *Buenas noches* moved them outside the marque, footsteps fading in the soft crunch of grass. She lay still, breathing deeply as Santa Anna returned, reaching for her.

But it was good with him. Even quickly, like this, as he sheathed himself in her and began the dance in which she could not help but follow. "*Querida,*" he said, guttural into her ear. "*Mi querida.* My love. *Eres muy especial, mi amor.*" You are very special.

The sun was up, the tent lit like a lamp when she awoke the next morning. Alone, she looked around the room, her eyes caressing the fabrics, delighting in the colors. Gold and silver gleamed where she was used to wood and brass or enamelware. She sighed, twisting away from the sight of bygone promises. To live in such luxury! Adored! To be consort to a president! His touch, his look alone would have been enough. But to bring such honors with him! To her!

What, in all of Texas, could compare? Its best was less than this and now there was so little left at all. Morgan's Point was burned along with every major town from there to San Antonio. She'd received no invitation to Galveston, not even from Emily who was too white-faced with fear to manage more than a greeting and farewell as she ushered her children aboard the boat to safety. Whether the Texians won now or not, there was nothing left here for her.

The scene from the night before was a bad dream. How could she betray the first man in whose arms she had found shelter? It was not something Morgan could ever give, nor Luke, both of whom knew her, first as a Negro. But to Santa Anna, she was simply "woman." What luxury to be woman first of all!

As for Sam Houston, she might as well be "warrior" as "woman" to him. She did not think he had ever seen her except in terms of usefulness to the cause. When a man like that called one special, one could only conclude he meant specially useful. She sighed again and reached for the purple dressing gown near the bed.

Alone at the table in the next room, jacketless, but otherwise fully dressed, Santa Anna sat studying a map while an aide stood at attention in the open doorway. He looked up, smiling as she entered. "Good morning, *mi Rosa*. You look rested."

She did not feel rested. She felt buried in rock. But she smiled lightly. "It was a good night, Generalissimo. It promises to be a good day."

He leaned back. "Why not. Today we meet the enemy and finish him. As for you, *mi querida*. You and I will begin as the rebels end. There will be a home for you in Mexico City. You will be my wife."

Surprise slowed her movement towards the door. "Are you not married, Sir?"

His voice was sharp. "Who told you that?"

"Why, you are much talked about, Sir. There is much envy of your position both as a warrior and as a man."

"They will envy you, *mi Rosa Amarilla*," he said, accepting the homage gracefully. "You may go now but return to me quickly."

He returned to the map as she picked up the gown that lay still where it had been discarded the night before. Through the folds of cloth, the bulk of Luke's letter could still be felt. Ill luck or God's grace to receive that letter now. She could not say which, only that it made her personal decisions less personal. Was there no end to giving up one's way for the sake of others?

Chico came up behind her as she approached the river past the marsh. He slipped out from behind a large tree trunk like a brown shadow, shirtless like many of the Mexican boys who followed with the women behind Santa Anna's army.

"*Senora*," he whispered. "Miss Emily, I must go, Tom say. He say run to General Houston's camp and tell three hundred soldiers come last night with cannon and nine wagons and forty-three mules."

Her doubts evaporated in the eagerness of the bright young face. Right or wrong, one must stand for something. No need to shatter the boy's illusions. "Three hundred," she said, glad to have understood correctly. "And eight hundred with Santa Anna besides the fifty horse soldiers. You will remember? If you cannot get to the General, tell Mr Smith. Remember him? The thin man who is deaf but speaks and sees everything with eyes like glass?"

"I tell him." The brown eyes sparkled, brilliant, as smiles flickered like quicksilver across the slim face. "I be a scout now like him."

"Be a good one or you will be dead," she said, apprehensive for more reasons than she could name. Voices were approaching. He darted away as she continued towards the river where she washed her face and hands then tarried a little while on the bank. She heard voices raised near the tent from which she'd come. Santa Anna's was among them. And then she heard a shot. The apprehension deepened.

He was in conference when she returned, engaged, apparently, in an argument about the location of the tent. His aide, Colonel Pedro Delgado seemed to think the entire camp was too much exposed. Nor was he happy about the marsh that encircled their flank. General Castillon apparently agreed. She caught the words, "Vince"s Bridge, *mas alla*." Further off. Adamant gesturing indicated the need for an immediate move. General Cos, looking from one to another, shrugged.

The Generalissimo held up his hand for silence as she approached. "Did you hear the shot?" he asked pleasantly.

A thin shudder passed like ice strands through her veins. She guarded her face with great care. "I did."

"One of your friends tried to run away across the plain. He is dead now."

"Chico!" she gasped, forgetting.

He rose in a single motion, lithe as a whip, circling her wrist like an eagle talon. "You knew."

I only knew he dreamed of such adventures and spoke to me of them. The very young think they can never die. I warned him."

"When did you warn him?" The grip on her arm tightened into pain. She looked up at him, tears stealing from beneath her lashes. "Only this morning, *mi general*. He stopped me on the way to the river and said he was going to run away. I said no, he must not. Tom and Sally, they want to stay with you and I want to stay with you, and could he not see there were advantages in every way to remaining. The courtesy with which you have treated your servants."

She was babbling and she knew it but she could not stop the stream of words. Perhaps the tears would help explain it. A woman might be emotional, even over the unexpected death of a servant boy.

"He was Mexican," she mumbled, head down against the surrounding stares. "He was a child. I thought he would find a home behind you."

"More a traitor, *pues*!" he said, loosening her arm, though the dark eyes bored into her. "He was fortunate for a traitor. Most must die more slowly." He looked around at the men who waited, watching her, silent. "You may go now," he said to them. "*Aqui nos quedemos hasta el adieux*." He looked at the sun, already well above the trees. "*Antes del medio dia, quisas*." The men moved away. "*Estan cansados*," she heard Cos mutter, loud enough to be heard.

Midday, then. An attack before midday. Perhaps. They were tired.

"But you, my *querida*," the man said, taking her wrist in an iron grip as they moved into the tent. "You will not want to go anywhere, will you?"

Again the icy jab of fear. "Only with you, Sir," she whispered. "*Mi general*."

"*Digame*," he said, settling on a cushion. "Do you know this Ooston?"

"I have met him at the hotel. We spoke."

"What did he say?"

She lowered her lashes, lifted a slender shoulder. "Pleasantries, *Senor*. One hears them often in a bar."

"Ahh."

"He was very drunk, *mi general*. He is often very drunk in the evening. He starts, they say, around noon."

"Ahh."

She pressed on. "They talk of him all the time, of course. Some think he is very smart. More think he is a coward."

"*Porque?*"

"He will not attack. Some say he learned it from the Cherokee, to fight on the defensive only. Others say he is afraid. They say by evening, when he is drunk enough to overcome his fear, he is incapable of leading an army. And in the morning, when he is still sober, he reasons against it.

"You have heard the reasons?"

Again the lowered lashes. "One hears everything, *mi general*, if one listens. General Houston himself explained, standing at the bar there, that it is better to lay a trap in hiding for the enemy. He imagines, some day, if he waits long enough, the Mexicans will charge in blindly and he will have them, neatly, with few losses. The men laughed at him in the bar. 'The enemy will never come to you,' they told him. 'Why should they stick their necks, like rabbits in a trap when they can wait and flush you out?'"

"The men are more smart than their commander," said Santa Anna. "And now his back is to the river while our army and supply train grow." He smiled, stroking his chin. "It is a pleasant place to camp, is it not? The view is pretty with the water so near. We will enjoy ourselves." He raised his voice to summon the aide who stood a discreet distance away from the door. "You will inform the generals to meet here at noon. The men may rest. We will not attack this morning. We have adjusted our plans."

"And now, mi Rosa," he said, turning to take her in his arms. "We shall dance again, no?"

The pleasure she felt was different this time, separated, as it were, from her heart and soul, distant as the sound of a shot across a morning meadow. She worried about the opium. She had not seen where he kept it. How much would it take? How much could be added before someone complained of the taste? And how ever was she to get it into the bottles that were delivered along with the meal?

Those were the things she thought about as Santa Anna slumbered beside her. When he no longer stirred with her movements, she slipped out of his arms and dressed herself, ignoring the mud that clung to the hem of her gown. "I am to order lunch," she told the aide who regarded her, unblinking. "He said the generals will be coming."

The man jerked a thumb towards the kitchen shelter.

"Tell them."

"We will need wine," she said. "A cask."

He raised his eyebrows. "*El Presidente* means to celebrate! I thought first he would destroy his foes."

She dimpled for him, allowed laughter to ripple across her tongue. "I think he means to do it afterwards," she said. "By evening General Houston, if he runs true to form, will be far drunker than anyone will become at noon."

White teeth beneath the dark mustache flashed a growing confidence in her. "I will bring a small cask," he said.

She hesitated on her way to the kitchen, then turned back. "Perhaps you can set it inside the tent before the soldiers gather to eat," she said, marveling at her own nerve as his eyebrows lifted. Any moment now, she would be found out and killed horribly. Slowly. Like traitors die.

He was staring at her. She lowered her lashes. "I am being foolish and most presumptuous," she said. "I imagined the soldiers would not like to see wine when they had none themselves to drink."

His voice was hard. "*El Presidente* does not concern himself with such feelings. It is for the soldiers to respect his wishes, whatever they may think. Complaints are punished, *Senorita*. We do not have many."

"Of course," she said, and moved on to confer with the cook, mostly by gesture. Two huge catfish had been caught this morning. Would *El Presidente* and *los generales* enjoy them? Oh yes, surely. At midday, then? *Muy bien.*

She lingered in the little shed behind the fires, finding comfort in the stout Mexican women who reminded her of morning coffee with Sally at the hotel or of tea in Dr. Connie's kitchen. But here, a dozen children scrambled around their feet, picked up routinely, scolded or petted and set back down. They were no different from any other children. Some were the age of Junior. She hoped that General Houston would be merciful. Children should not die for grown-up wars. What did they care about a nationality? What did she care? What did it matter what side she were on as long as she stayed alive?

But when she stepped back into the tent and saw the cask of wine, its cork already pulled, she breathed a deep sigh of relief. Behind the partition, Santa Anna stirred, waking. Frightened she stopped where she stood, staring around the room. Where was it? She did not remember him searching for it when he dropped it in the wine the night before. The silver box was simply there in his hand. She did not see it now.

"*Rosa?*" The voice was querulous, still full of sleep. She went to her knees by the table, lifted the cloth. Ran a hand underneath.

"*Rosa! Donde esta?*" His voice had sharpened. Ah! Her hand touched a cold metal edge. Clutching at it, she drew out the silver box, opened it. The white powder was inside.

"*Rosa!*"

Shaking now, she tilted the little box over the mouth of the open cask, spilled some in. Hoped it was enough and not too much. She was putting it back, beneath the table, when he stepped into the room naked, finding her on her knees.

"*Que haces?*" His eyes were full of suspicion.

"I dropped my ring somewhere." She dimpled up at him. "I hoped to find it while you still were sleeping so I would not have to confess my carelessness."

He regarded her for a long moment. "I shall get you another," he said at last. "What else have you done while I was sleeping?"

"I ordered lunch " she said. "The habit of a hostess is still with me, I'm afraid. But I was walking about and stopped at the kitchen. They had caught some large catfish. I said you would enjoy them with the officers at one."

"Why did you do that?"

She stood and went to him, winding her arms around his waist. "I wanted to do something for you," she whispered. "You have done so much for me and I can do nothing."

He grunted in half-pleased acknowledgment, reaching for his dressing gown. She rushed on. "I asked the aide to bring some wine. So everything will be ready."

"You wish to join us?" he asked in some astonishment.

She lowered her head. "Whatever pleases you, *mi general.*"

He stepped into his wardrobe, opened a trunk and handed her a yellow dress. "*Para la Rosa Amarilla,*" he said, reaching for his own clothes. "But I cannot allow you to sit with my generals. You may wait here in the bedroom until we are finished. You will wear this dress only for me."

It was the most beautiful gown she had ever seen. The skirt was of deep gold velvet with a waist richly embroidered with leaves and flowers set on pale yellow satin. Lacework, shot with golden threads, adorned the low neckline and cuffs. She slipped into it, settling herself on the bed.

He called in his aide to help him dress in the wardrobe while she worked on buttoning the loops of twenty pearls that closed the front of the gown.

Outside she heard the men begin to gather. A clink of dishes told her the food was also arriving. "You will be silent," the Generalissimo told her, pausing to stare down at her before leaving the room. "I do not wish anyone to know you are here. After they leave, you may eat." He looked her up and down, approving. "You are too beautiful, *Querida*. I do not expect you to be difficult."

"No, *mi general*."

But she discovered, after he was gone, a tiny peephole in the partition close to the outside wall of the tent. Careful neither to move nor breathe too loudly, she watched the proceedings on the other side.

The fish was served on silver platters, the wine poured into crystal glasses. Santa Anna reached beneath the table for his silver box and dropped a pinch of opium into his, then raised the glass. "A *la victoria*!" he said, drinking deeply. His officers followed suit though one or two noses twitched.

"Strong wine," the Generalissimo said, wiping his mouth. He smiled around the room. "Strong wine, soft women and smart soldiers. It is a good combination."

Then the talk was all in Spanish. Rose no longer tried to follow it though she heard the syllables begin to slur as drowsiness overcame the assembled officers.

But the sun was well past its zenith when Santa Anna finally stood. "*Nos retiremos*," he said. "*Una siesta, y por la tarde, ya!*" He laughed. "O *quisas manana. O pasado. No hay apuro. No hay apuro.*" There is no rush. There is no rush. The men stood also and filtered out the door, a look of confusion on a few faces. Delgado and Castillon who both had confined themselves to a single glass, spoke angrily in low voices. Only General Cos, loser of the first battle for San Antonio, seemed much relieved. His men had been marching for days. A day of rest could hardly suit him better.

"*Muchas gracias, mi general*," he said. "*Appreciamos el descanso*."

They will not long appreciate that rest, thought Rose, slipping down to lie against the pillows as Santa Anna returned to the bed. The Generalissimo struggled out of his coat and pants. Stripped down to his silk drawers but with the diamond studs still fastened to the french cuffs of his fine linen shirt, he also fell back on a pillow.

"You will be happy in Mexico," he said, reaching for her. "But if you do not wish to go, I will give you the lands of de Zavala to manage here. You are good manager, *Rosa Amarilla*. I give you the land of Morgan also. Morgan and de Zavala. First the slave, then the master. *Te gusta, mi querida?* I give you all that." His voice slowed, rough as he struggled against sleep, pulling her towards him. "Or perhaps I keep you all for myself. You are good in my bed, *Rosa Amarilla*."

She closed her eyes and lay against his chest as his breathing slowed into the rhythm of rest. It did not take long. And it was not long afterwards before she, too, fell back into sleep.

With the dawning of the day, the war of nerves renewed itself between Sam Houston and his men. He should be used to it, he thought. His words, however beautifully declaimed, whatever honors and positions they had won for him, had never been law to anyone, even his wife. That situation had near killed him. This one could be much worse. His own life he could fling away. But the thousand men behind him—some of them sick and helpless—he could not drop that burden until it was removed. He was tired beyond weariness but he must not falter now.

"Fight! We're ready to fight! Now is the time!" The shouts resounded through the trees though it was too early for most soldiers. The urge to grab a gun and do some killing had not yet surged in many breasts. There was no point in arguing before it became essential to prevent mayhem. He hoped he would have a few more hours.

He sat alone in the opening of his tent, overhearing the arguments without effort. Wharton, silenced for a little while last night, had resumed his war cries with the morning light. "What is he waiting for?" came the question, again and again. "Does he think Texas can be won without a war?"

If he could have it his way, certainly. As it was, given the indisputable numbers in the game, he had chosen the Indian way. A trick of terrorism. A massacre, thinly masked as a battle. It was enough to make a man sick. There was no one, of course, to whom he had breathed the word and those few who knew his plans—Morgan, Deaf Smith and Emily Rose—had their own reasons for not judging him. Morgan because winning was all that had ever mattered to him. Deaf because his loss of hearing had made him, somehow, more Indian than the Indians themselves. And Emily Rose because, like him, she was first of all a survivor. As to whether she believed that her survival was best tied to him or to Santa Anna, of that, he could not yet be sure. The kerchief itself might be a trick to lure him into ambush. But it was too late to question.

As to the truth of it—what might be best for the beautiful yellow girl from Morgan's Point—that was not his concern. He had been as honest as possible when he asked her help. He would indeed assure her of some land though how to manage it was a question for the peacetime that would follow if today's ploy succeeded. Certainly he could never acknowledge her role openly and add the charge of hiding under a woman's skirts to the other judgements arrayed against him. No, if Emily Rose chose him, chose Texas, chose the United States, she would be on her own afterwards. It might not be fair but it was expedient.

Still, there might be something he could do to help.

His thoughts pursued one another like squirrels in a box, leaping for an exit where there was none. Sighing heavily he rose and began to walk among the campfires where the men were gathering for breakfast. He paused by each to speak a few words of encouragement. "Today we'll fight," he assured them all. "This afternoon when the sun's in their eyes we'll attack and win."

The faces turned toward him registered the range from disgust to determination. But all looked ready for battle.

He ignored the arguments summed up in "Why not now?" and moved along the line collecting his officers and assigning them. Sidney Sherman, a fearless, if somewhat excitable warrior, would command the regiment closest to Lynch's Ferry, a stone's throw from General Cos's men on the other side. Edward Burleson, a former commander of the Texian forces would lead his unit down the center. George Hockley would command the artillery just forward to the right with Henry Millard's regular infantry holding the right flank which alone remained exposed. Sidney Lamar, who had joined Sherman the day before in attempting to steal the Mexicans' cannon right out from under their noses, was rewarded with the command of sixty cavalry to be partially concealed by a stand of live oak at some distance from that exposed right flank. Isaac Moreland was in charge of the cannon fire. Three fifes and a drum were assigned to beat cadence for the advance.

A smile twitched Houston's lips as he assigned the tune: "Will You Come to the Bower I Have Shaded For You?"

Drawing the leaders into his tent, he marked positions on the map. They would move out thus in rank and file. Halfway across the mile-wide field of grass they would advance to a double line some nine hundred yards wide, fanned out and facing the Mexicans. They would raise their weapons. They would stand and fire at a distance of no more than sixty or seventy yards. Further back would be a waste of time and ammunition. Further forward, they might be shot first.

Houston went over it carefully, refusing any argument.

By the sun it was not yet ten o'clock. In the distance a single shot rang out. The sound struck Houston like a blow but nothing followed.

He called the troops together and joined Tom Rusk in a rousing speech on the battle to come "Remember the Alamo," they roared in unison. "Remember Goliad." In Spanish, Juan Sequin, captain of a Tex-Mex unit, echoed the cry in language the enemy could understand. He ended the meeting with instructions to the officers to drill their men.

There was to be no shooting. They were to remain out of sight. When the sun was in the enemy's eyes that afternoon, then they would strike. They were fewer than nine hundred men facing twelve hundred or so with more reinforcements coming behind them. They must pursue every possible advantage.

He had said the words so often they were dust in his mouth. From the look on their faces, his words were dust in their ears as well. But commanded, they obeyed.

It was not enough. By noon, incited by Wharton, the call to battle had reached crisis proportions.

Houston did what he had sworn to never do. He called a war council. "I make my own decisions," he had told Rusk as Secretary of War, "Any blame must fall fully on me." He had not mentioned praise. It was all very well for the dead heroes of the Alamo but he could see no way to remain simultaneously alive and praiseworthy. To remain in charge was the very best he could do and he had seriously been doubting that ability of late.

But today, a war council would take up precious time that might otherwise be spent despoiling the perfect battle plan. He gathered a half-dozen of the cooler, or at least less mutinous heads together, excluding Wharton, his second in command. The theoretical question of attack or defense was broached and debated for almost two hours. The majority favored defense.

Outside the tent the men still howled for battle. Houston watched the sun.

20

Sunlight slanting in from the west, brilliant in the fresh-washed sky, glared through the silk of the white marquee and pressed against her eyes. Rubbing them, Rose sat up. In the distance she could hear music.

She recognized the song as one of those the men at the bar might sing on a particularly rowdy night. "*Will you come to the bower I have shaded for you.*" Frontier romance. But who could be playing such music now? And was that a shot she heard? Or was she still dreaming those vivid dreams?

The shots were unmistakable now and memory rushed in. Nearby she heard a shout, sharp with alarm. A bugle shrilled and there was an answering shout. It sounded like Pedro Delgado and Manuel Castillon. She heard a clatter of voices and she could hear the sound of running feet.

And then, from further off, she heard a roar rapidly growing louder. Deep voices thundered in unison. Even at the distance, she could make it out. "Remember the Alamo! Remember Goliad!"

An immense volley of fire seemed to shake the ground.

Outside the tent there were screams.

Even above the boom of muskets, the roar of men and the shouts and shrieks of the hunted, she could hear Houston's bellow. "Hold your fire! God dammit, hold your fire!" But the firing went on. Coming closer. Someone else was shouting, "Give 'em hell! Give 'em hell! Cut 'em down! Don't stop!"

Beside her Santa Anna sat bolt upright, staring wild-eyed. Without a glance at her he was out the door, still in his underclothes. There was more shouting just outside the tent. A panicked argument of many voices. She could hear Santa Anna's voice above the others. Other voices shouted other orders. More yells. And above everything, the screams and the roar.

"Remember the Alamo! Remember Goliad!"

Weighted by the heavy dress she still wore, Rose crawled to the doorway. Santa Anna was running, racing for the corral with death at his heels. He leaped on the huge white horse she remembered from Morgan's ranch. With neither saddle, bridle nor spurs, he wrapped himself to the animal like a centaur, dug in his heels, and was away from the fray in an instant. Around her men were racing to grab their guns, stepping over the bodies of the fallen. Through the trees nearby she saw General Castillon struggling with the cannon as men jerked and collapsed around him, blood spurting from the holes that suddenly opened in their bodies, in their heads. But he stayed at his post with the cannoneers, loading, aiming.

Fire exploded from the cannon's mouth. A fast reload and it exploded again and was answered by twin explosions from across the field. The screams intensified as shards of glass, nails, metal struck all around. Once more the Mexican cannon roared and then shattered as the Texian cannon found its mark. The cannoneers fled. Castillon turned to face the foe.

The Texians were upon them now, a torrent of terror hell-bent on destruction, striking the camp from one end to the other. They were shooting point-blank, muzzles jammed into bellies and chests. Long knives ripped through cotton shirts and heavy uniforms alike and the raised and emptied muskets became clubs, splattering brains and blood on the trees and on the ground.

Just past the breastworks now destroyed by the oncoming army, she saw Houston go down, his big white horse shot out from under him and a bullet through his boot. A cavalryman was at his side in an instant, leaping off his horse to help him up. Then he was astride again, sword still in hand, blood trailing from his boot as he raced the lines shouting encouragement. And all around her the unarmed Mexicans along with the women and children fled back into the swamp.

The Texians followed, firing, hacking, clubbing.

She saw Tom Rusk approaching Castillon where he still stood beside the demolished cannon, loading his rifle. Rusk's hand was out as he shouted, "Wait." But a red-haired soldier who was closer rushed in with a knife roaring "Remember Goliad!" And Castillon went down, his uniform and his body split, his entrails showing greyly through the blood.

She felt nauseated. How was it that she had never imagined the actual scene of war? How could she have forgotten it was meant to end in death? Surely, she too must die for her part in this slaughter! The screams felt a part of her soul though she could never have said, afterwards, whether she ever opened her mouth.

A booted toe lifted her almost off the ground and she fell, gasping on her back. The butt end of a gun was over her, poised to smash, but before she could cover her face with her hands another hand seized the weapon and a voice spoke roughly.

"He don't like you killing no women and children. You heard him."

"She ain't no woman. She's his whore. Traitor bitch."

The other man, more weathered and turning grey, laughed. "Looks like a woman to me." He bent closer, peering through the filth on her face. "Hey, ain't you that girl from Morgan's Hotel? How'd you get out here? They capture you or something?"

The first man kicked her again. "Traitor bitch! Look at that dress! She ain't here like no captive, nossir. She come to him because she liked it. Liked what he done for her." Another kick. "You like that, bitch?" And another kick. And another. He raised the rifle butt again.

"I wouldn't do that, Clem. Old man knows this girl. I seen them together once at the hotel. Talked a long time. Wouldn't want to have to tell him you was the one took her out, if he asks." He slapped the first man on the back. "Go get yourself some Mexicans, son. Got plenty of them still alive."

With a scowl, the first man walked away. The other leaned down. "Best get yourself out of sight, girl. Ain't nothing to nobody much to murder you right where you lay." He looked up at the tent. "Can't say I'd blame them, neither, you dressed like Jezebel right here in his tent."

Groaning, unable to move through the pain, she stared up at him. He shrugged and unsheathed his knife. She covered her face. Oh God!

The billow of silk folded over her as he slashed the ropes that held up the marquee, already full of bullet holes. Dazed, she remained where she was, hidden, still and silent. An occasional boot came down on her. She made neither movement nor sound. Around her the noise of slaughter went on and on.

She had never imagined such noise. Groans deeper than a grave. The screams without language. The growl in the throat of the attacker. The whimper, loudest of all. The unexpected calls for "mama," oddly the same in either language. A difference in emphasis, that was all.

How much time had passed? Fifteen minutes? Thirty? Why had she never imagined this ending? What had she thought? That battles were clean? Bloodless? That Sam Houston would swoop in and carry her away before the carnage?

"Gentlemen!" she could hear him shouting nearby. "Cease fire! Cease fire! The battle is won! The battle is won!"

But the fire and the screams and the roar went on. Even in Spanish came the shouts. "*Recuerden el Alamo! Recuerden Goliad!*" And the plea cut off in the throat. "*Mi no Goliad! Mi no Alamo!*"

"Parade!" shouted Houston. "Gentlemen! Gentlemen! Cease fire! Parade! Parade!"

A scuffle, a grunt and a cry just above her. A body fell heavily on top, blood seeping through the silk to cover her face and hands. She didn't move.

"Gentlemen! Gentlemen! I applaud your bravery but damn your manners!"

The silence came down at last, broken only by the sounds of dying men and the more distant sound of rough English voices. Moving with the caution of an injured cat, she dragged her body from under the dead one above it and pulled back a corner of the covering silk. There were bodies everywhere, lying twisted in pools of blood, open eyes staring at nothing, faces frozen in hate or terror or pain. The aide who had brought her the wine lay nearby doubled on his side like a man asleep but his eyes were blindly open and blood still trickled from his mouth and a knife wound in his chest. She wondered if he had blamed her before he died. If he had guessed about the wine. The blood looked like wine congealing.

A child lay further off. She thought she recognized the cook's son and wondered what happened to his mother. A musket blast had taken off most of his head.

From her place on the ground she stared about, catching no movement beyond the twitchings of the nearly dead. The Texians were not within her line of vision. Then carefully, she edged her way back towards the marsh behind her away from the vengeance that had rushed across the plain. Head down, she inched along on her stomach, slipping here and there through pools of blood. It might have taken an hour but only when the underbrush had closed around her did she dare to look around.

Still on his horse–though it was not the one she had seen him mount when Saracen went down–Houston was surrounded by a rough and bloody clump of men a few hundred feet away. Approaching them, encircled by Texians leading horses, was a large group of prisoners, their tall plumed hats still in place. Their uniforms matched the cavalry she had first seen on the beach at Morgan's Point. Marching alongside Tom Rusk who led them, she recognized Juan Almonte and marveled at the rush of relief she felt that he was not dead.

Others were coming out of the swamps now, men with muskets herding groups of disarmed Mexicans, a few women and children among them. She saw Juan Delgado there, soaking wet, his uniform in tatters, his feet bare and bloody. But there was no sign of Santa Anna.

They all approached Houston, a crowd swelling past a thousand. She could see him giving orders though she could not hear the words. Then, followed by a few of Santa Anna's wagons, the General led the men back through the waving grass. It crossed her mind to go to him but fear and better sense held her back. What could she claim there in his hour of triumph that would not diminish it for him? No, he would not want to see her now. Against the reddening sky she watched the tall horse and rider disappear into the valley that crossed the plain. Moments later no one could be seen. And then in the shadows of the underbrush she wept.

Nearer noises brought her back to herself in the waning light. Not everyone had left with General Houston. The noises came from among the bodies where a few soldiers scavenged, using their knives to rip open pockets and sacks. Dead fingers were examined for rings. She saw one body's unblemished pants removed though there were no jackets or shirts that were not stained with blood. She stared in horror as one man bent over Castillon, using his knife to pry a gold tooth from his mouth.

At Santa Anna's tent a small group paused to argue. Three stalked away. The others, furtive, bent to their task, stuffed what they could in their pockets and followed them.

There was no more light to see. She put her head down in her arms and closed her eyes. In the distance, a few birds sang. The furtive scuffling died away.

A touch on her face and the sound of her name awakened her.

"Shhh, there. Shhh, now. You're all right." It was Deaf Smith's voice. "I've brought you some food."

She sat up, feeling her way in the darkness. The man must have eyes like a cat. She could see nothing at all. But strong hands touched hers, leaving behind a bone with meat on it. She gnawed at it, feeling like an animal, starving. She drank half the jug of water he handed her and by the time she finished she could make out the shape hunkered down by the bush. He passed her another fleshy bone as she flung away the first one.

"Feel better." It was not a question and she did not answer, knowing he could not hear and doubting even his eyes could see her lips move in the darkness.

There was a toneless chuckle. "I am glad to find you. I was afraid—" A long silence. "I cannot take you back with me but I will send someone for you tomorrow. The General said maybe Captain Isaac Moreland, a good man. He will take you safely off the battlefield."

"And then? And then what?"

The voice droned on. "Much has been destroyed but aught yet remains. A place will be found for you. You have greatly aided the cause and though the General cannot thank you in person, he is most grateful." There was another long pause. "You must believe that, Miss."

A blanket was laid over her feet. "Stay here so we can find you tomorrow. Do not show yourself, our men are likely to shoot first and ask questions later. Hidden, you will be safe."

He sat with her for a while, patting her hand from time to time as one might pat a dog. The comfort of his presence overwhelmed her, brief though she understood the meeting would be. They did not speak but when he rose without a word and started away, she could not stop herself from calling after him.

"Did General Houston really send you?"

He melted without a sound into the dark.

Leaning heavily on the stout hickory stick he had used as a crutch more than once, Houston made his way very slowly to the foot of a giant oak in the center of camp. It was well past noon. All morning he had been receiving officers and men alike in his tent, grateful not to move. The ball had passed through his leg, breaking two bones which had been clumsily set by the field surgeon. But he had one of his boots back on, at least. Hurt like hell to move the other leg but it was more than worth it. The euphoria around him held him up, lifting the spirit he had feared was permanently cast down.

They had won the day! Had won the battle with only two casualties and twenty-four wounded though the surgeon said that six of those would die. The carnage was awful on the Mexican side. According to the morning reports some six hundred and thirty soldiers were dead. It could have been worse. If he had not shouted himself hoarse trying to stop the slaughter, if Juan Almonte had not rounded up his cavalry and others for surrender, if a few of his officers had not halted the target practice on the Mexicans swarming out of the marshlands to leap into the water, swimming for their lives—God knows there would have been a thousand dead. As it was the hastily jammed together stockade held some seven hundred prisoners.

The victory on the battlefield had exceeded his wildest dreams though Texas civilization had been virtually destroyed in the process of waiting for it. No doubt he would be blamed for that, too. It did not matter. When he concluded the coming business with Santa Anna he would wash his hands of Texas and go visit New Orleans for a while. Might have to get another doctor to look at his ankle which still hurt like all bloody hell. And if it healed, well New Orleans was a fine enough place for rest and recreation. At least—he permitted himself a smile—until they called him back to govern the rowdy state. Or nation, as the case might be. He was not sure the United States would take them, even now, with independence surely won.

The victory he had lived for through the past six months of abuse—months of running and waiting, running and waiting, drilling his men without pause while ignoring all suggestions to engage the enemy—had almost escaped him. Santa Anna was not found among the prisoners or the dead and reports from Henry Karnes, his scout, as well as from Almonte had him fleeing the scene on a big white horse, seconds before the wave of Texians washed over his camp and annihilated most of his men. Cowardly, it would seem, but perhaps the head of a country might justify the need to save, first of all, his own skin.

That skin was worth a great deal. Another smile escaped the lips drawn tight against the pain. He was grateful to God, yes indeed. Grateful, finally, to the God he had not trusted since the church in Tennessee refused him sanction—refused him baptism—after his divorce from that girl who never wanted him. He had always suspected God was much more broad-minded than the church. And surely God had guided Henry Karnes and Deaf Smith through the swamps where they had finally flushed the Generalissimo out, sloshing along, barefoot and masquerading in the rough clothes of a slave. They found out later he had tried to take Vince's Bridge, hacked apart by Deaf that very morning. Trapped and turning back, the Generalissimo's horse had finally dropped him in the mud. They had not even recognized him at first—surprising, perhaps, but even faces change with fright and circumstances. If the prisoners had not called out as the scouts brought him back to the stockade, "*El Presidente, El Presidente,*" he might even now be skulking among them, laying plans for his next battle when he re-joined the thousands of Mexican soldiers still in Texas.

Yes, God was good. Houston wondered about that shout of recognition from the Mexican soldiers. One might imagine it an error in judgement. Stupidity, even, to give away their leader. But there must have been at least a few who had seen him leave unscathed and were infuriated, given that his negligence had cost so many lives. *El Presidente* had not even posted sentries! The girl had done a fine job on him, after all. He did not imagine Santa Anna was often so careless.

When the guards laid hands on him, ripping away the old cotton clothes he wore, his status became more clear. There were diamond studs on the fine linen shirt he wore underneath and his underpants were silk.

Reaching the giant oak, Houston allowed the men to help him get down to the blanket they'd placed for him. Leaning back against the tree he took a deep breath, restraining himself from shaking his head to clear away the pain that seemed to film his eyes and ears. More than six hundred people were dead, he reminded himself. All he had was a busted leg. He looked up.

Santa Anna stood before him with Almonte at his side to translate, closely surrounded by a half-ring of Texas soldiers, guns at ready. A few hundred more were packed noisily behind them, rough voices raised in suggestion of how to treat their illustrious prisoner.

"Hang him!" came several shouts. "Got plenty of trees and rope!" Houston said nothing, watching the face in front of him grow paler under its layers of dirt. "Hell, don't hang him," came another voice. "Cut him up in little pieces and feed him to the dogs!" "While he's still alive and watching!" someone else shouted. "Do it like the Comanches! Fingers first!" Then the hanging chorus started up again.

By God, the man was trembling though his head was as high as it would go! Houston stared at him, silent. But when Santa Anna began to speak in Spanish the General held up his hand to quiet the crowd. Almonte translated the full-blown words.

"That man may consider himself born to no common destiny who has captured the Napoleon of the West. It now remains for him to be generous to the vanquished."

"You should have thought of that at the Alamo," said Houston, evoking more shouts for a hanging.

"My government demanded that the enemy be destroyed. I, myself, am a gentleman born. I am distressed by such orders but as a soldier, I must obey." said Santa Anna.

Almonte translated.

Houston leaned forward, jabbing a finger at his foe. "As dictator of Mexico you are the government. And you were personally responsible for ordering the massacre of the men who surrendered to General Urrea at Goliad. I have it on authority that he pleaded for their lives and you denied him."

"Hang him! Hang him right now! Hang him" The shouts grew louder. Santa Anna's face grew paler. The hands he lifted in supplication trembled.

Houston could swear the man spoke English. But it was not a point worth making at the moment.

Houston kept him there for more than an hour, almost enjoying watching the waves of fear that washed across his face as the shouts for his death grew more and more insistent. Indeed, the men around him would have cheerfully swung him from the very tree above him but the General knew he was worth far more alive than dead. He could only hope that none of his stubbornly independent soldiers would decide to take matters into their own hands.

"I will spare your life," he said at last, "in exchange for the everlasting freedom of Texas. You are, after all, the government. You will be held prisoner here while we secure your written promise on several issues and convey them to your generals." He took a piece of paper from his pocket and read:

"You will swear never to take up arms again against Texas.

"All hostilities between your nation and ours will cease immediately. Your armies will immediately withdraw below the Rio Grande.

"All Texas prisoners of war will be released immediately."

He handed the paper to Almonte and continued. "Furthermore, should we ever allow you to return to Mexico you will be pledged to work with others in your government for diplomatic recognition of Texas as an independent nation, bordered by the Rio Grande. You will develop a treaty of commerce with us and in all ways respect us as your equals."

"Equal, hell!" came a shout. "Dammed superior, if you ask me!"

"I say hang him! Cowards never keep their word nohow!"

Almonte was translating.

"I will do all that," said Santa Anna. "And more."

"You will write a letter immediately to General Filisola informing him of the terms of your surrender and ordering him to immediately command the removal of all Mexican troops in Texas. Your life will be forfeit if he does not obey."

"I will do that," said Santa Anna.

The soldiers, wanting blood, would not be quieted. "Take him away," said Houston. "Keep him away from the other prisoners and post sufficient guard to protect him. And provide him with paper and a pen. In my tent, if necessary." He leaned back against the tree and closed his eyes. His leg throbbed like hell. But the job was done. At least, he would consider it so when the courier was on his way to Gonzales. Ah yes, one more thing must be done.

"Send Almonte with the courier and a guard to General Filosola," he told

Wharton who stood nearby. "That officer's word will be good in any case. We want no misunderstanding of our action, today."

"Yes sir," said Wharton. "It's a good day, Sir. Excepting your leg, of course."

Houston did not bother to answer. A little longer he could linger underneath the tree and then he must go back to the tent for the final bit of business with Santa Anna. The girl must not be mentioned. He didn't imagine the Mexican Commander would be hard to persuade but he must put the best face on it for himself. No point in letting rumors start. Were the Texians to learn that his great victory came from the clever work of a female spy, God only knew how much his reputation, already battered to a bloody pulp, might suffer. She, not he, would be hero.

No, he could not let that happen. He had lost his political future in Tennessee because of a woman. He'd be damned if he let it happen again. He needed this victory, this glory, all to himself this time.

He let nearly an hour go by before he motioned to Deaf, who was standing nearby, to help him rise. It took two to help him back, to his shame, but he couldn't touch foot to the ground and was too much gone in trembling pain to hop it. Santa Anna was still in the tent, sitting rigidly before the pen and paper on the table. The letter, finely crafted, was finished. A guard stood on either side of him; four more were just outside the door.

Houston dropped heavily onto his pallet. "You can all go except Mr. Smith," he said. "Mr. Smith can translate for me."

The guards left but slowly, stopping a few paces outside. Houston smiled. They were not going to find out much either way.

"I have one more condition for you," he mouthed quietly to Santa Anna whose eyes widened. "You will not mention the woman in your tent. You will not accuse her. You will not name her. Because if I hear of her among my men for so long as you are my prisoner you may consider your life immediately forfeit."

And Smith translated.

Hidden deeply in a thick patch of brush, a bare hundred feet away, Rose had dozed through the morning and watched through the long afternoon, feeling almost as if her own life depended on the proceedings. She had not expected Santa Anna would be captured. The speed of his reactions, dead-asleep as he had been when the opening volley was fired, rendered him almost untouchable in her eyes. Seeing his bareback escape on the horse, she could have imagined him leaping rivers on his free way back to Mexico. But for all his craft with horses he could not make them fly and the General had outsmarted the Generalissimo once and for all by having Deaf Smith knock out Vince's Bridge. When Rose saw the scouts returning with him she vacillated for an instant between sorrow and joy.

And yet, the capture felt like a gift of God. She wondered why she should find it so, sitting alone in a bloody and bedraggled gown, all her earthly possessions gone, all her dreams of glory—even the humble glory of running the hotel, let alone consorting with a president—all gone.

What destiny awaited Houston now? Would she be part of it? She doubted it. If her treatment thus far were any shade of what was yet to come, there would be no glory in it for her. Houston, it seemed, had put her from his mind though Deaf Smith was kind. He had come back for her long before dawn, waking her, urging her up. She could not remain there, he explained. The area would be too well explored the next day. He had pulled her forward, half-carrying her for the long mile across the plain to Houston's camp. He had made a hiding place for her there at the edge of camp. He would bring her food, he told her, but she must not show herself.

But he turned his deaf ears to her questions. When would she see the General? Was he pleased? What were his plans for her? None. None that Deaf Smith knew of. Beyond Captain Moreland. The Captain would see her off the battlefield and "situated." Meanwhile, Smith showed her the nest he made in the brush, padded with a blanket. He left her with a jug of water, a couple of rags, a loaf of hardtack bread, an orange and cheese, He was not sure when he could be back, he breathed in her ear. But she was to keep silent and still.

She had used the morning to wipe most of the blood from her skin. She understood that her life was now in danger from the Texians. And she understood that Houston would not claim her.

Yet she watched, fascinated by the exchange between the two men, by Santa Anna's ability to rise, however unsteadily, to any occasion, and by Houston's transformation from the mouse to the cat. But Houston was not going to kill his quarry. She knew that long before the men around him seemed to grasp it, let alone Santa Anna. She hoped the Generalissimo was grateful, being granted a reprisal he would never, himself, have bestowed. She would like to believe the man understood gratitude though he had no inkling of compassion. If Houston were surrendering instead, no question he would be dead.

So there the choice had hinged. If she were doomed by Texas from the start—given that all the destruction would have happened, with or without her—it felt better to lose it all in service to a good man than to a bad one. Her definitions of good and bad had simplified greatly. Good had a heart.

She watched as Houston painfully dragged himself back to the tent where he had sent Santa Anna, Deaf Smith right behind him. The General looked almost broken, hanging from the necks of the stalwarts on either side of him. But she noted how he paused at the door, straightening himself, assuming authority. She saw the guards come out after he went in, leaving him alone with Deaf Smith and Santa Anna. She wondered what they spoke of and whether her name was mentioned.

Not too long afterwards Santa Anna was marched away to the jail. A tiny separate stockade had been built that morning. Houston did not reappear.

Smith did not come back to her until the last campfire had died down and the last man laid down to rest. His hand in the dark roused her. He laid clothes in her hands—pants, a shirt and a jacket—then turned his back while she got out of her dress, wiping at her skin with a wet rag before putting on the clean things. Pushing the blood-soaked gown aside, she remembered Luke's letter still in the pocket and pulled it out as Deaf laid a hand on her arm and drew her outside.

The slender moon was surrounded by stars in the clear dark skies and a small breeze was blowing from over the bayou, bringing the smell of salt and sea things. A sense of great freedom came over her, her pain seemed to fall away, and the memories, for a moment, disappeared. Striding along in pants, trying to match the long legs of her guide, she felt as new and easy as if she had been born yesterday. Her hair was tucked under a hat, her chest concealed by the jacket. Anyone seeing them on the faintly moonlit night would have supposed her a man. It was something she had never experienced before.

The freedom stayed with her as they crossed the plain to the other side where the stench of rotting bodies was already beginning to rise. Handing her a kerchief to cover her nose, Smith led her past the black shades of corpses, grotesque as when they had fallen, and on to the end of the camp. A man waited there with two horses.

Deaf Smith handed her over.

"God be with you, Miss," he said awkwardly. "God bless you." And before she could answer, he was gone.

Captain Isaac Moreland laughed softly, flicking the reins. "So I'm to have charge of you," he said. "The hotel hostess."

She drew herself up. "The hotel is burned down, Sir, and no one has charge of me now."

"Is that so?" Strong hands seized her arms and drew her to him for a rough kiss. Pulling back hard, she slapped him with all her strength.

"Hellcat, are you?" He chuckled, rubbing his cheek. "Very well then, Miss. You shall walk and I will ride until your temper has cooled." He seized her hands and bound them with a twist of reins about her wrists. "Don't want to lose you in the dark," he said, mounting his horse. "Now shall we go?"

But the second time she stumbled, less than a slow-walking mile down the road, he got off his horse and lifted her onto the second animal. "Reckon you're tired enough to be tame by now," he said, holding her only a moment longer than necessary. "If you can keep up riding as well as you do walking, I don't believe we'll have any trouble at all."

She said nothing, rubbing her unbound wrists.

Faint moonlight silvered the face looking up at her. "Like it or not, Miss, you need somebody just now and there ain't nobody else. Colonel Morgan's going to be tied up in Galveston for a while and Morgan's Point is pretty much burned to the ground. I understand that General Houston is interested in you but he has many other things on his mind and I don't expect he'll get back to you any time soon. So unless you want to wander around in the brush you'd better get used to me."

He handed her the reins and then mounted. The horses moved off at a faster clip. Ignoring her silence, he continued. "I've got a little house in Richmond if it hasn't been burned yet. Reckon I'll put you up there for a while. I've been ordered to Fort Travis so I can't use it much as I'd like to share it with you. Give you a place to be alone and get your life sorted out, maybe."

Still she had nothing to say. The horse hooves struck a rhythm like heartbeats, stirring dust on the empty road.

"Look Miss," he finally went on. "I'm not going to disturb you that way. Reckon you've had more than enough of that and you don't look like the kind, pretty as you are when you're dressed like a girl. But I promised the General I'd look out for you and I intend to keep my promise. He said you did a great thing for the country though he wouldn't say what it was."

So she was to be kept alone. Emily had provided not even the promise of refuge. Morgan had dropped her without a thought. And Houston, for whom she had given up such honor as she had left, was passing her off like a badly used piece of furniture. A smile twisted her lips. It was hardly fair to say she'd given up her honor for the General. She would have lost what little she had to the soldiers in the field on either side had she not been in Houston's plan and protection.

A sigh escaped her, sliding off her chest like a weight. For all she might dream and scheme or plan and ponder, it appeared that the great majority of circumstances remained outside of her control. It was not, altogether, a bad thing. Insofar as one was willing to give up being praised, one might also cease to be blamed.

"You all right?" Moreland grunted, half-turning in the saddle. "I'm going to pick up the pace. We got a ways to go before breakfast."

"Fine," she answered, loud and clear. "Just fine."

The horses broke into a canter and she felt the flutter of Luke's letter rising and falling against her hip. Her spirits lifted as the wind cooled her face. She was not without friends, however distant. She studied the broad back in front of her, leading the way. Life, she reflected, could be much worse. She could, for example, be entirely alone. Or dead.

21

It was Deaf Smith who brought the word. Lorenzo de Zavala had died. The pain Rose felt for Emily was abated by a twinge of relief. However tragic the circumstances, her own time of exile might be coming to an end. For almost seven months she had remained secluded in Moreland's small house in Richmond. It was a "dog run" house, as they called them, the most common building in Texas: two large rooms with an open porch between them; a double square, plus, built to catch the breeze from any side in either room. Her life had narrowed to that house and the yard and a walk to market once a week. She sought no friendships, spoke with no one. Refusing the amenities of Moreland's room, she had made a pallet for herself on the kitchen side of the porch and, except for necessary household services, remained out of his sight as well. It had not been difficult since he was rarely there, as he had promised. Promoted to major during his brief stint at Fort Travis, he had been called to command the garrison in Galveston. On his occasional weekends home she served his meals and otherwise avoided him. There was nothing she wanted to either hear or say. The screams of the dying which still echoed through her dreams were more than enough.

Respecting her silence still, Moreland stood quietly in the shadows behind the scout who delivered the message of Emily's loss. "We will need to leave immediately, Miss," Deaf said, handing her a paper-wrapped bundle as she stood by their horses in the yard. "The funeral is tomorrow." He indicated the package. "We got you a dress in case you got nothing to wear."

She almost cried at the unexpected consideration. Indeed, she had nothing at all except the calico cotton in which she stood and the soldier's pants and tunic she had worn for her escape from San Jacinto. Moreland had bought her the dress and regularly provided a little coin for food. She had asked for nothing else, unwilling to pay the price.

"You'd best put on your pants, Miss Emily." Moreland spoke for the first time. "It will be rough riding, and fast, if we are to make it by tomorrow afternoon." She noticed the third horse then and disappearing into the kitchen she took the man's clothes from the peg by the door and changed into them. She untied the string and wrapped her calico into the package with the rough black cotton. She re-tied it and was ready. There was nothing to leave behind.

De Zavala had succumbed to lung fever, they told her, as the three rode out of town in the early dusk. His rowboat had overturned on Buffalo Bayou, caught in the gale of an unexpected blue norther as he was crossing with his son. Though both were brought in alive, the father's chill deepened into death almost before the storm was over. Colonel Morgan had sent word of the situation though the funeral gathering would be small. The General was unlikely to come, still pained as he was by the wound in his ankle from which surgeons in New Orleans had removed some twenty fragments of bone. Besides, as the new president of the new republic of Texas, he was much too occupied with affairs of the state.

Rose listened and said little. Riding all night, by morning the little group reached the burned out ruins of Harrisburg where a few new buildings, including a shed of a restaurant, had risen among the ashes of the old. While the horses were fed, watered, and rubbed down, they sat on a rough hewn bench and drank strong coffee. A stout German woman stirred a large iron pot on the fire and ladled grits into bowls, apologizing for having neither eggs nor meat. "We could scarce afford it if you had it, Ma'am," said Moreland, laying thirty cents on the table as they took their leave. "We may have won our freedom but there is scarce enough money in all of Texas to pay for keeping it."

Deaf Smith changed horses and left them in Harrisburg, riding on faster and alone, bound to be there early, he said, to help with the coffin. Moreland and Rose rode on in silence, allowing their tired mounts to pick their own pace through the live oaks and scrub that lined the winding road.

It was close to midday, though the sun had disappeared into clouds, when they topped a rise and saw Vince's Bridge in the distance, re-built since that April day when Deaf Smith led a crew to destroy it and hold fast the two armies beyond it. But the sight brought back memories, crowding like unwelcome guests through a blown-open door. Their horses had swum the stream the last time she passed this way with Moreland. And she had wondered, she remembered, whether after surviving the carnage by the men, she was going to end up drowned by the river.

"You'll be glad to see Mrs. de Zavala again, I guess," said Moreland. He paused, awkward with sentiment. "It's been hard on you, I reckon, having no company to speak of. Reckon you were used to a lot back at Morgan's Point."

"I have not minded not seeing many people," said Rose, her face stiff with the effort to talk. "Sometimes I think I have seen enough already for a lifetime."

The wind coming in off the bay was cold and the sky was greying rapidly. She forced her mind past the bridge, past the battlefield and across the bayou into the cemetery. She hoped the rain held off. It would be too cruel for rain to fall on the funeral. The mourners should not have to be concerned with being cold and wet. They should be remembering Mr. de Zavala's goodness, holding up those thoughts like candles to honor him and lighten his widow's way. Of all the men she had met from Texas, he was, she thought, the most honorable and possibly the most intelligent. How Emily must be missing him! And with three small children. . . .

"You came from New York with Mrs. de Zavala, did you not?" Moreland's questions prodded, unwelcome, at her mind. "You were her servant there?"

"We lived together. I was her cousin." The words slipped out before Rose could call them back.

Moreland's eyebrow rose as he turned to stare at her for a moment. "Her cousin!" He offered a chuckle. "I reckon there's a lot of that going around back east. Plenty of half-brothers and sisters, too, I guess. Don't rightly know. My folks were too poor to have slaves."

"So you got your chance in Texas," said Rose.

"Why yes. And I intend to build on it." He looked round at her again. "But keep your hat on, Miss Emily. Whoever's slave you be, I know well that you are not mine."

He let his horse graze for a moment while he finished his thoughts. "I came to Texas for a chance I couldn't get in Georgia, Miss Emily. I always liked to read and such but we didn't have money for education. I could have done all right there with some kind of little business but back east, a person's position is pretty well fixed by their folks. It's not that way out here. I've got a chance to study law and maybe practice it when I get out of service. A man out here has got a chance to use his mind if he has one and move up if he can."

"As long as he's the right color," said Rose, under her breath.

If Moreland heard her, he did not respond.

Their horses' hooves thumped hollow on the bridge then measured off a few more miles at a slow walk, coming at last to the crossing that led east to Morgan's Point or forward onto the field of battle. Without a word Rose laid heels to her horse and galloped the tired creature across the little plain to the camp where so many of Santa Anna's men had fallen. Something cracked beneath the horse's hoof and she reined up sharp, seeing bones half overgrown with scrub, the rags of uniforms still fluttering from them here and there. Skulls stared back at her with weed-filled sockets from underneath the trees, still lying as she'd left them, but bare of skin and muscle. The tortured faces she remembered in her dreams had given way to vacant boney grins.

She felt like one waking from a nightmare only to discover that the dream had become her history. "They didn't bury them!" she gasped. "They're all still out there."

Moreland, following at a distance, rode up to her side. "I reckon the General didn't want the responsibility," he said. "Reckon he felt like Santa Anna brought them, he can take care of them. Like it or not." He shrugged. "They took a couple of them over to the de Zavala cemetery. Reckon they were relatives or something."

She did not realize until that moment how deeply she had denied the drama, how often she had imagined it not true. She had been grateful for her solitude; grateful to confirm with no one the slaughter she had witnessed. But there it was, still spread across the dying grass beneath the wind-beaten trees. Unburied. The silence was overwhelming. She wondered if the stench of decay had long since driven out the birds. Even with the armies camped there, she remembered that there had been birds.

"It's a sad sight, all right," said Moreland as he turned his horse. "Best not to look too long, Miss Emily. You need to change into your dress before we cross the bayou. The funeral may well be underway already."

Side by side they rode back through the tall brown buffalo grass across which he had, not so long ago, commanded the cannons that helped destroy the enemy. He was humming softly to himself and Rose recognized the song: "*Oh come to the bower I have shaded for you.*" Oh yes. The marching song for the Republic of Texas. She wondered if everyone had recognized the irony.

Not far back from where she had hidden to watch the Generalissimo surrender to the General she could see a little dock where two small rowboats were tied and a corral that held a score of horses. Moreland reined in his animal beside a broad and ancient oak and gestured."You can change behind there." Slipping down from the saddle, she stepped behind the tree and into the coarse black cotton gown. There was a veil in the package as well, thick and heavy, and she drew it over her head before returning to him. Dismounted, he led both horses to the corral and helped her into a boat.

He would be back for her on Sunday, he told her, moving the oars with firm strokes through the roughening waters. She could decide then whether to return with him or stay. "But if you want to travel, Miss Emily, you'll need to complete your papers in Columbia on the Brazos where the government has moved. If you need an escort, I'll have a few days free to attend you."

"Columbia?" She realized suddenly that she had no idea what was going on in Texas. Her world had stopped at San Jacinto and she found it hard to let it move again.

"I forget you've been out of touch though I reckon that of all people I should be most aware of it," he said as a smile flickered across his face. "Well then. Since April the government has moved from Galveston to Velasco to Columbia and will probably move again to San Felipe de Austin which most are calling Austin these days. The war with Mexico goes on though it affects us little here. The Mexican government invalidated Santa Anna's surrender but he has been true enough to his own word not to resume the conflict and those he commanded retreated and have remained to the south of the Rio Grande. But other Mexicans continue to harry us in the west, claiming that the Nueces, not the Rio Grande, is the Texas border, whether or not Texas be liberated.

"Our own soldiers are as independent a lot as ever. They took matters into their own hands to the extent they almost hauled President Burnet in for trial of some sort because he refused them leave to ride into Mexico and fight. It came to nothing except for a lot of changes in command though that wouldn't interest you. As for Santa Anna, they all wanted to kill him as soon as the General left for New Orleans to get his leg looked to. Burnet managed to prevent it by keeping him in jail until the General got back. Now I hear tell, Santa Anna has gone to Washington to attempt some sort of negotiation with President Andrew Jackson. But no one imagines his efforts will come to much."

He plied the oars while she took in the information. It was all very hard to absorb. Even the question was hard to ask in the vacuum her mind had become. "And General Houston," she managed at last. "What of him?"

"He was elected president of Texas the first of September along with General Mirabeau Lamar as vice-president. They assumed office on October 22. It was not supposed to happen until the second week of December but Mr. Burnet and Mr. de Zavala were very eager to resign." The raised eyebrow puzzled over her blank face. "You mean to say you did not know?"

She shook her head. "I have not wanted to know anything, Major Moreland. But now, I suppose I must."

"Mr. Austin was chosen secretary of state. He's the one who approves passports. But he's very ill. Some think he's dying." Moreland grew silent as the opposite shore drew near. A few hundred yards away a knot of people were gathered in a place already marked by grave mounds. A pile of fresh dirt stood almost as high as the mourners' heads. Rose did not see Emily.

"I have never met Mr. Austin," she said, "but I hope he does not die. There has been far too much dying already."

"Reckon we can't much help that," he said, tying the boat to the dock with a swift turn around the post, and turning to help her out. He glanced at her face then looked away. "We can only do our jobs and hope for the best."

They arrived at the cemetery just as the talking ceased, the mourners moved back, and the men with spades approached the grave. Deaf Smith was leading the widow away, carrying one of her children.

He stopped when he saw her and for perhaps a moment Rose stood quietly before them. Emily would not look up. She has come down to my station, Rose thought. She no longer sees reason to communicate. But the sight of her friend's bowed head brought a stirring in her, a will to reach out that had not touched her since the night Deaf Smith had led her, away from the dead and into the land of the living. The numbness in her mind seemed to tingle. To ache like feet awakening after a rest from a painful journey.

"Emily," she said softly. "Emily, it's me. Rose."

And they were together again.

Luther Collins arrived that night, stricken at having missed the funeral. His mule had broken a leg, he explained. And all the worse luck because he must move on by morning. The suffering everywhere was great and he had much to do. Comforted almost enough by one another, the women provided bed and breakfast and wished him Godspeed.

Letting the questions lie still, the women spoke only of feelings, seeking a new understanding. In the mornings and late afternoons while they minded the housekeeping or walked on the low dunes or rocked together on the porch, they listened to each other. By the third day Emily's face was not so swollen and Rose's eyes began to lose their haunted look.

"Major Moreland will be coming soon," said Emily as they rocked in the sunset on Saturday night. The breeze coming across the bay was warm and they didn't need the Indian blankets that lay on the backs of their chairs. A gift from Sam Houston, Emily had said.

Rose stopped her chair on Moreland's name. "Tomorrow, I suppose," she said at last. "I had best go with him, Emily. Columbia is a long way and not one I could well travel alone. And it seems I must go there for my passport. You will have to write me a letter saying you know me and all the necessary things." She sighed. "I do not want to leave you."

"Are you leaving Texas?"

"If I must. But part of me is rooted here with Lorenzo and I can never stay away." The tears flooded again. "I would rather be near his grave than near to any living person."

Rose looked at her friend, then shook her head. "I am deeply sorry for you, Emily, but I do not know what I could do to help short of giving up my own life for you which I am not prepared to do." She stopped in mid-speech, pained by the hurt in her cousin's face. "I didn't mean. . . ." she stammered.

Only the creak of rockers broke the long silence. "You are quite right to refuse," said Emily at last. "What is it, then, that you want for yourself?"

"That's the difficulty," said Rose and her laugh was bitter. "I still want it all."

"Not very likely, is it?"

"So what do you do?"

"You make choices," said Emily. "Hopefully, you choose on the basis of what's best for everyone. Not just yourself."

Rose said nothing. Emily went on. "It would be a great relief to me for you to be here, you know. And General Houston promised you land?"

"As to what the General will do, I cannot say. Nothing yet has turned out as I imagined. As to staying here, I cannot promise. Safe as I feel with you, there are other pulls on my heart."

"You mean your son? And Luke? But Rose, your son is quite safe now with his grandmother and Luke, it would seem, works best alone. Very dangerous work, I must add. I would think one rarely died of old age doing such work."

"I have not exactly been playing in parlors for the past year," said Rose.

"Forgive me, Dear, I did not mean to imply anything. I only mean that I need you right now and pray you will stay with me. But if you cannot, you are still my friend."

Rose laughed softly. "I cannot promise anyone anything right now. You will know I am here if you see me coming."

"You must do what you must do," said Emily, stiffly. "Just as I must." And then only the creak of rocking chairs broke the silence that descended between the two women, along with the dark.

Sunday services the next morning were held in the kitchen, overflowing into the yard. The help had grown as people, black, white and brown, came seeking shelter from the storms of war. The dozen servants now included several Mexican women left behind by Santa Anna along with several landless widows, all working for food and a place to live. Most of them came with children. Two of the old black servants had returned and a few young men from Mexico—survivors of the war from both sides—were working about the place, building cabins for the new arrivals and contemplating the planting of fields and an orchard. Lorenzo had befriended them, Emily insisted. They would all stay.

And she would stay to care for them. What help she needed, God would send her.

In firm English, that morning, she read the Scriptures to them. It was a well-known reading, The Twenty-third Psalm of David. "*The Lord is my Shepherd. I shall not want. . . though I walk through the valley of the shadow of death, I shall fear no evil.*" Afterwards, in Spanish, English, Southern dialect and Louisiana patois, the people said their prayers. And then, with tears in almost every eye, one after the other sang or said a few words of eulogy for Mr. Lorenzo. Emily closed with prayer. Rose managed an "Amen."

Luther Collins arrived as the congregation arose from their knees. He had not intended to return so soon, he explained, a bit flustered. But somehow he had been brought back. Almost as if he had forgotten something. "Perhaps I did," he said, turning his hat in his hands. If there were anything at all that I can do for thee, Mrs. de Zavala, thee must know I would gladly do it both for thy own and for thy dear husband's sake."

Rose feared Emily would not ask. "You can stay with her for a little, perhaps?" she said. "I must go and I fear to leave her alone though she insists there's no reason."

"Indeed! Indeed I should be quite obliged to remain for so long as the Father allows me. Though I should be happier, Miss Rose, if you were also here as her family and friend."

"I cannot." She did not want to explain, only pointed to where a man was stepping into the dory on the other side of the bayou. "Yonder comes my escort and I must be traveling soon."

Dinner was being served when Moreland arrived, resplendent in uniform with silver and turquoise studs in his shirt. He ate quickly, participating little in the conversation and obviously impatient to be gone. Leaving the table to the men, the two women hurried upstairs where Emily insisted Rose borrow a riding habit. "It's made for a taller person than myself," she said. Indeed the fit was perfect, but Rose refused any other clothes, packing only her calico and the black cotton into her small carpetbag along with the soldier's clothes. "There's no one I want to show off for," she explained to Emily. "I would rather be altogether invisible."

If either of the men's eyes brightened at the sight of her returning down the stairs, she did not notice though she did not resist when Collins took her hand in both of his and she stared him full in the face as he stumbled over saying good bye. Moreland watched them, impatient.

For the four days they took to reach Columbia, Rose barely spoke. By the time they rode into the courthouse square, Moreland had given up his attempts at conversation.

"I shall leave you here," he said abruptly, coming to a stop on the square in the center of town. "There's the courthouse," he said, pointing. "And there is an inn about midway down that street. It's called the Dove and quite respectable. I'll reserve a bed there for you along with dinner and a breakfast and collect you there tomorrow morning. I trust you'll be ready." He wheeled his horse and kicked up dust on the road past town.

Rose tethered her horse and climbed the wooden steps to the rough log courthouse. A red-haired young man standing by a tall mesquite on the square glanced at her, then stared, tipping his hat as he caught her attention. "Pardon me, Miss. I thought I seen you before." Rose said nothing, moving across the porch to the door. "Couldn't have been, though," the boy said, still staring. "That was in Santy Anny's tent there at San Jacinto." He grinned broadly. "That's where I killed that cannoneer. Some fancy officer. That wasn't you watching, was it, Miss?"

Rose did not bother to knock. She pushed the door open and stepped inside.

A startled young man looked up from a desk, then stood hastily, tipping a pot of ink on the paper in front of him. He righted it, swallowed his muffled curse, dropped his handkerchief over the mess and bowed all in the same moment. "Forgive me, Miss. I am Leonardo Black, clerk to Judge Sam Anderson and at your service." He adjusted his spectacles, peering at her face. "Do I have the honor to know you?"

She recognized him then, the young aide who had carried pen and paper for Santa Anna to sign after his meeting with Sam Houston that day after the battle. But he had not seen her, of that she was quite sure.

"Miss Emily Morgan," she said. "Miss Emily D. West Morgan. I would like to speak to the judge."

The eyes behind the spectacles widened. "Emily Morgan! You are the Emily Morgan!"

"I know no others, though they may well exist, and I cannot prove my own existence since I lost my passport. That is why I must see the judge."

"But you were the woman who managed Morgan's hotel and warehouses at Morgan's Point? The woman who was in Santa Anna's tent during the Battle of San Jacinto? You are she?" The eyes were very wide now and a light sweat had broken on the pale forehead.

"Enough of that nonsense," came a gruff voice from the door. "Mr. Black, if you will cease staring and introduce our visitor I shall be much obliged and we can get on to business."

Introductions were performed then, much to the young man's dismay, the judge led her into an inner chamber. From behind a mahogany desk he had surely imported from France, he surveyed her. With a barely concealed start she recognized the gold snuffbox in front of him. She had last seen it in the Generalissimo's tent.

Judge Anderson smiled as he deliberately dipped a pinch of snuff. "You do recognize it, then, Miss Emily? Do you know I have been waiting for you? Major Moreland said he would bring you, though as to when, he could not be precise. You lost your passport, is that correct? And where would you have lost it?"

Rose stumbled through the words though she had practiced them beforehand. "At the hotel in Morgan's Point," she said. "Where I worked for Colonel Morgan. It was burned by the Mexican soldiers."

"And you were carried off, ha ha," said the judge. "Well girl, I heard you provided fine entertainment for Santa Anna. Kept him occupied." A wink accompanied another dip of snuff. "And now you want your passport. You think to leave Texas? Now I'd say that's a pity."

Rose fought for control of her breath. Shame climbed her like a heat wave, reddening her skin and hardening her jaw. "So you will have my passport as General Houston promised?"

A meaty fist came down on the desk like a hammer. A broad red forefinger jabbed the air. "You will not claim promises from the President, Miss! You will follow *his* orders. I have two messages from Sam Houston to you. He gave me charge to deliver them as he spoke them though he would not write them down.

"The first is this. You are to receive a *sitio* of land for services rendered to the government of Texas. That's a square league, Miss Emily. About four thousand, four hundred and twenty-eight acres. An expensive service, I'd say." He leaned back in his chair. "This land is located just west of the Nueces River in unclaimed Texas territory and has been registered in the name of your son." He grinned. "You may have to fight for it, Miss, but it's yours for claiming."

"My son?"

"Why yes, Miss. Your son, Luke Sturn of New York City."

"But that is not my son's name."

"No? I understood, privately of course, that your father is Benjamin Sturn, Captain in the U.S. Navy. Is that not true?"

"It is, Sir. But that is not my son's father."

The judge's face reddened dangerously. "I have no time to dicker about names though I assure you Sturn's name was chosen for your protection. I merely wished to inform you of your reward. If you wish to change the name, that will be a matter to straighten out by and by. You will be returning to Texas, no doubt, to claim your son's inheritance. Meanwhile, there is a second part to President Houston's message."

Rose stood still in front of the big desk, feeling stripped. She had not been invited to sit. Fear tightened her throat. "And what would that be, Sir?"

The judge leaned forward, lowering his voice as he crossed his arms against his chest. "Should it ever come to the President's attention that you have mentioned or verified any rumors concerning any conversation between you and himself, particularly in regards to the Battle of San Jacinto, the claim to this land will be awarded to someone more worthy of the honor of being a Texan." He paused. "Do you understand that fully, Miss?"

Her throat was too dry to swallow. Dry as dust. "I understand," she managed.

"Very well, then." His voice resumed its former briskness. "Have you some document or letter proving who you are, Miss?"

She fumbled for the letter from Emily. He read it hastily, hitting the highlights out loud. "This is to certify and declare that the bearer of this letter is Emily D. West Morgan, known to me since birth, arriving with me in Texas on December 21, 1835, contracted for one year's service to Colonel James Morgan. Having completed her service, she wishes to return to New York and requires a passport which was lost in the war. Emily D. West de Zavala." He laid the letter down, looking at her quizzically for a moment. "You could hardly do better as a personal reference," he said, then raised his voice.

"Mr. Black!"

The door opened immediately. "You will prepare a certification that this is Miss Emily D. West Morgan who arrived December 21 from New York to Galveston and was indentured here for one year under Colonel James Morgan. Indenture being concluded, she is free to travel to and from the Republic of Texas. Document prepared on recognizance of Mrs. Emily de Zavala."

The whole process took no longer than an hour though Mr. Black had inordinate difficulty with his focus. Only repeated stern looks from the judge kept him moving forward with the business at hand. But Rose had no sooner stepped into the street than he burst out talking again. "It is said that General Houston paid her to lay with Santa Anna so he could surprise the Mexicans at play and take the battle. It is true, then?"

"Son," said the judge, gazing out of the window at Rose's retreating form, "if you ever say that again you had better be prepared for a duel with Sam Houston. I would not recommend it, myself. He is a reckless man when it comes to defending his honor. With hickory stick or pistols, he would kill a man for lack of respect."

"His honor?" said Black, persisting in spite of himself, half in love already with the beautiful young woman who had walked in and out of his life. "What about her honor? Has no one any respect for that?"

The judge fixed him with a steely gaze. "Her honor is none of our affair, Son. And should you make it so, I do not imagine we can work together anymore."

Rose was almost out of sight on the dusty street. "How very strange her name is the same as Mrs. de Zavala's," the judge mused softly. "There's a story there, I daresay, though I'll never live to learn it." He slapped his unhappy clerk on the shoulder. "Come now, Mr. Black, the world is full of beautiful women though it's true that many have not come yet to Texas. Shall we go down the street and drink to their imminent arrival?"

He kept his hand on the young man's shoulder as they stepped into the street. "You must understand, Mr. Black, difficult as that may be for a young romantic such as yourself, but political expediencies have their own requirements. President Houston has many enemies still in Texas. I am not among them. They would like nothing better than to sully his name by insinuating he won the war from behind a woman's skirts."

"But it would appear he did," the young man said, emboldened by the confidence.

The judge shook his head sorrowfully. "Son, I hate to do this, but you must consider it more temporary than a bullet." And drawing back a huge fist, he knocked Mr. Black to the ground. "I trust that improves both your memory and your manners," he said, giving him a hand up afterwards and lending him a handkerchief for his bloody nose.

"Now Isaac Moreland, there's a good man," the judge continued as they went into the saloon together. "A circumspect man. I don't believe the Comanches could get a thing out of him that he wasn't of a mind to tell." He laid a hand on the boy's shoulder again. "A mighty good man, Moreland. One of those Methodists. Poor but proud, with a good mind and heart. He's been reading law, I hear tell. Wouldn't be surprised if he becomes a judge someday. Circumspect. Mighty important quality in law."

Black said nothing as the judge found a seat and ordered ale for two. He was glad he still had a job. Jobs were mighty scarce in Texas.

In a tiny hotel room shared with two other women—widows also in need of passports—a few doors down from the tavern, Rose changed into her black cotton dress. In a corner of the restaurant downstairs, just outside the circles of lamplight, she ate her dinner alone and then returned to her room. Not bothering to undress, she muffled her face in the pillow and cried herself to sleep for the first time since she'd come to Texas. She wondered that she'd dared to hope for some small sign of recognition from the man she'd served so loyally. She felt again the desertion of her own father. The rejection as if she were of no account. Even her reward could not be claimed in her own name and her own son was not given the names of his parents. The small things crumbled her defenses, laid like stone against the pain she had already had to bear. Her tears went on and on into the night. But if the other women noticed, they gave no sign. In the crowded room, each lay still; each wrapped in her own cloak of need.

Rose awoke in the night feeling purged. Whatever had passed, she had her passport now. As to the claim in her son's name, that way, too, had straightened. She had denied him an identity for long enough. The child was registered nowhere; she had not known what name to offer him, having none she had ever claimed for herself, besides Emily's. So tomorrow she must visit the land office and clarify the name of her son. She would not deny him the inheritance that had cost her so dear.

Luke Cassal, Jr., she thought to herself. He must have his father's name, of course. How could it be otherwise? It was the only name he could want.

It did not occur to her, that midnight, that Negroes owned no lands in Texas. If she had known she would have been grateful the next morning that the land office had not yet opened when the hotel clerk interrupted her breakfast with the message she was wanted at the door.

Deaf Smith stood there, holding two horses. Moreland could not come, he said. Duties at the fort had recalled him unexpectedly. He stood, motionless in the bright morning sun, waiting for her direction. She realized suddenly that she had none.

"Mrs. de Zavala asked I deliver a message to you," he said tonelessly. "She decided she must return to New York for a short time to conclude business affairs. The Reverend Collins will be minding her home on the bayou and you will be most welcome there if you wish to stay with Mr. Collins," the scout permitted himself a shy smile. "She said that Mr. Collins would be very happy about the arrangement."

The thoughts rushed in, unbidden. Should Luther Collins choose to marry her, her place in the white world would be assured. Though poor, he was certainly a good man, one she loved already as a brother. Emily would be proud. The future would be neatly packaged. And in good time, she would claim her own land. For her son.

She could not help the question that rushed out. "To go or stay? Which would be better, Mr. Smith?"

He looked at her for a long time, taking the measure, it felt, of her soul.

"You keep quiet, you'd be pretty special in Texas, Miss Rose. But I reckon you have some people you have got to talk to back east. Reckon you have got things to settle before you settle down here." He paused. A tiny spasm twitched his face as he struggled to continue.

"It is all in God's hands, anyway. Why you do it—that's the heart of the thing. Whether you do it for yourself, or for something bigger." The shy smile returned. "The bigger thing, that's God. Goodness. Taking everybody into consideration."

She wavered, thinking of old and new securities, lost and gained. And then she thought again of her son. And his father. And the struggle to be free. And she thought of her friend's long, lonely journey to New York. She straightened, considering the things that only she could do. Whatever his personal desires, she knew Mr. Collins would approve. "I always wanted to be special," she said, her dimple and her blue eyes flashing. "Now I only want to be good."

"Mrs. de Zavala will be sailing for New York the day past tomorrow with Colonel Morgan," Deaf Smith said. "He sends the message you are welcome on his ship."

"If you will lead me to the port, Mr. Smith," said Rose. "I will gladly follow."

Epilogue

The Yellow Rose returned to Texas, not as Miss Emily but as Rose Cassals, bringing her very own family along. But that was much later, when her firstborn was nearly grown and ready to receive his inheritance. The years between were very full, though the sour was mixed with the sweet, as life's flavors might be judged. The return to Texas was—as Texas tends to be—an exaggeration of both extremes.

-i-

There's a yellow rose in Texas
That I'm a'going to see
No other darky knows her
Nobody, only me.
I cried so when she left me
It like to broke my heart
And if I ever find her
We nevermore will part.

Chorus:
She's the sweetest rose of color
This darky ever knew
Her eyes are bright as diamonds
They sparkle like the dew.
You may talk about your dearest May
And sing of Rosie Lee
But the yellow rose of Texas
Beats the belles of Tennessee.

-ii-

Where the Rio Grande is flowing
And the starry skies are bright
She walks along the river
In the quiet summer night.
She thinks if I remember
When we parted long ago,
I promised to come back again
And not to leave her go.

-iii-

Oh now I'm a'going to find her
For my heart is full of woe
And we'll sing the song together
We sung so long ago
We'll play the banjo gaily
And we'll sing the song of yore
And the yellow rose of Texas
Shall be mine forevermore.

–Anonymous

Glossary of Spanish Terms

El Presidente / The President

Generalissimo / Commander in Chief of all the armed forces of a certain country.

Querida / Dear, Lover

Descanza en paz / Rest in peace

Mi casa es su casa / My house is your house.

Empresario / Business leader, industrialist

Tejas / Texas

Indiginos / natives of the area

Deguello / throat cutting, massacre

Mas tarde / See you later

Senorita / Miss

Yo, no? / you mean me, yes?

El comandante / the commander

Y de mas / and there's more.

Senorita, ya llega El Generalisimo / Miss, the General has arrived.

Senorita, abre la puerta! Pronto! / Miss, open the door! Quick!

Y entonces / and then

Entonces soy El Presidente, El Generalisimo / and them I am the President, the general.

Si Senor / yes, sir.

como no / why not

A la victoria! / to the victory!

Adelante! / Let's go!

Por alla / Over there

Le terminamos / Let's get rid of them

Y tambien / and also

Ah no, Querida / Oh no, darling

El Cobarde / The coward

La Rosa / the rose

Esta bien / That's fine.

Como no, Querida / why not, Dear?

La Rosa Amarilla / the yellow rose

Ven, Querida / come over here, my dear

Soldados. Tres cientos. Nada mas. / The soldiers. Three hundred. Nothing more.

Cobarde / coward

manana por la manana / tomorrow morning

Tarde / later

Buenas noches / good night

Eres muy especial, mi amor. / You are very special, my dear.

Mi Rosa / my rose

Aqui nos quedemos hasta el adieux / This is where we will stay, see you later.

Antes del medio dia, quisas / Before noon, maybe

Estan cansados / They are tired

digame / Tell me

Porque / why?

El Presidente and los generales / The president and the generals

Muy bien / very good

Rosa! Donde esta? / Rose, where are you?

Que haces? / what are you doing?

Para la Rosa Amarilla / for the yellow rose

Nos retiremos / we will retire (go to bed) now.

Una siesta, y por la tarde, ya! / I will take a nap during mid day, okay?

O *quisas manana.* O *pasado. No hay apuro. No hay apuro.* / Or maybe tomorrow or the day after. There is no hurry.

Muchas gracias, mi general / Thank you, my general.

Appreciamos el descanso / We appreciate the rest

Te gusta, mi querida? / Do you like it, my dear?

Recuerden el Alamo! Recuerden Goliad! / Remember the Alamo! Remember Goliad!

Mi no Goliad! Mi no Alamo! / It's not my Goliad, its not my Alamo

sitio / piece, a certain amount